The Morning After

Fattaneh Haj Seyed Javadi

F
×
M

Firouz Media Limited
www.firouzmedia.com
IG: @firouzmedia

Kindle ASIN B09Z746SN9
Digital ISBN 9781739660345
Paperback ISBN 9781739660314
Hardcover ISBN 9781739660352

Author: Fattaneh Haj Seyed Javadi
Translator: Niloufar Madjlessi
Cover designer: Sina Rouh

Prologue

O heart, did you see anew what the pain of love did

What the parting of a lover to the faithful one did

Ah! The frolics of those bewitching eyes

Woe betide what the merry to the sober did

My tears turned the colour of twilight for my uncaring lover

Witness what the workings of the cruel faith in this plight did

O what the thunderous glow of a light from Leili's dwelling at dawn

To the wild lover's fragile ego did

O bearer, give me a cup of wine for it is unsung

What the hand of Divinity in the mysterious canvas of creation did

The one who created this colourful celestial sphere

Secretly compassed the heavenly skies

Love's sorrow burnt the heart of Hafez like lightening

See what the eternal beloved to the faithful one did

Hafez

O**VER MY DEAD BODY!**

-Don't say that, mum. This pettiness doesn't suit you. It's ridiculous, not like you at all. You already know I've made up my mind and I'm going to marry him.

-Your father is very worried about this marriage, Soudabeh. He's very upset with you.

-But why? I don't get it. It's unjust! An educated girl at my age, not allowed to decide her own fate? She can't even choose the man in her life?

-Of course she can. A modern girl can make her own choices, of course she must. But what she must not do is marry a guy who drops out of university to go into his Dad's business.

-She can't marry a man who has so much potential, who goes to the best university, but who's father expects him to drop everything and work with plaster and cement. You can't marry a man whose father can't even sign his own name. Looks aren't everything, Saboudeh. Your father needs to read for at least a couple of hours every night before he can sleep. Imagine living with this family? The son of a mother whose only talent is to gossip. The only thing this nosey woman enjoys is to pry into other people's private lives. You won't be able to stand them. You've been brought up differently, you….

Soudabeh got to her feet, "What have his parents got to do with it?"

-You're not thinking. You have to think about them. She's brought him up, He's fed him. And we've got nothing in common with them.

Soudabeh gripped the back of the chair and leaned in.

-So, we're the only well-bred people around? The only ones who deserve respect? It's only us who are cultured and have integrity, not them? Do we have blue blood?

-No, you've got it wrong. They're good people in their own right. It's notsimply them being bad while we're good. We're just different. Our beliefs, our way of life, upbringing and principles are different. I'm not being judgmental. I'm just saying never the twain shall meet. Our families are like two parallel lines, they'll snap if they meet each other head on.

-So I can't fall in love, then. I've got no choice and that's it. I have to wait for the aristocratic son of an *al-Dowleh*[1] or the grandson of an *al-Saltaneh*[2], carrying a title of nobility, to court me and become my suitor. I have to…

-Stop this nonsense Soudabeh. We are not saying you can't choose. We are only saying choose with open eyes. Don't be deceived by appearances; you can't judge a book by its cover. Choose, but give it thought. Don't make hasty rash decisions. Hold. your horses – look before you leap. You could ruin your life by being so stubborn. We'd love you to marry, and if it's someone you love, all the better. But we can't stand by and watch you make a huge mistake. We'll never agree to this marriage.

Soudabeh turned away from the window.

-Listen to me mum, stop talking like this. Leave the old bones alone. I've told you I'm an educated modern girl. Thank God you got to travel the world, you must see that the days when girls were beaten and coerced into marriage are long gone. I'm not one of those 'her indoors' types, from a hundred years ago, secretly forced to say I do at their wedding. Those days are gone. I'm glad Dad claims to be open minded too.

In a distressed voice, her mother said: "Not so, miss Soudabeh, those days will never be gone. For as long as girls and boys fall in love with the wrong people, this problem will be right there between parents and their children. For as long as parents can see the traps in the road, but can't make their kids see sense, they'll be jumping up and down like wheat in a hot pan…

Soudabeh stopped her short.

-And they want to force them into marrying a Quasimodo with means, or get them stuck with an old maid who is the daughter of a titled such and such? Yeah? Not so mum! I, for one, will never give in to force. Why can't you understand, this is my life. I want to make it for myself. These are not the days of antiquity!

A thought flashed through the mind of the young girl and lit up her face. She continued with glittering eyes: "Even in the days of antiquity, many girls showed willpower. They wouldn't give in to force. They built their own lives. Look at auntie! It's so close to home. Did she not marry the man of her dreams? Didn't she? Didn't she?

In a split second, her mother's eyes opened up wide with fear and pain. She gazed at her daughter. The young, headstrong girl stared back into her mother's eyes defiantly with her large hazel eyes, a full head of wavy hair, Greek nose, shapely lips, and olive skin. Her beauty brought even more pain to her mother's heart. Her daughter, an educated, intellectual artist of a good lineage and reputable family background, or as Soudabeh herself put it culture and backbone, had fallen in love with the only son of a so-cial climbing, unlettered family, who had made their money at an arriviste moment. Her unfortunate parents did not even venture to make enquiries about their background. They knew only too well that there was no accom-plished past and that it would be better to let sleeping dogs lie. She wished he was from a family of poor means, yet open minds; a small honourable family with a good name. Now, that would have been another story. Sadly, circumstances were different. Alas, these words did not sink into the beautiful head of this young, inexperienced girl; this greatest joy of her life; this young woman who had not suffered any hardships; a diamond about to wallow in dirt. How akin she was to her aunt; not only in appearance from head to toe, but in all her idiosyncrasies. As if she was the impersonation of her aunt as a young girl.

Mother broke the silence with her gentle, sorrow-stricken voice. She was fraught and tormented. She asked softly: "You mean our very own aunt!?"

The stubborn girl mimicked her.

-Yes, I mean our very own aunt.

-So, she's happy and prosperous now, with a good fortune?

-Yes, Yes. She is happy, came the angry, feverish answer. She would have been even happier if my grandfather, her noble and honourable father, hadn't made life hell for them; if he hadn't turned his back on them and disowned them…

Mother paused for a moment with a bitter grin.

-Listen to me Soudabeh, let's make a pact. Your father has asked me to tell you to get this boy out of your head, to forget him; to never mention him again. But, I will make another deal with you. You say your aunt fell in love in the days of antiquity, right? That she broke all the rules and inhibitions? That she behaved as she pleased? You think it was worth it? You believe she was right to persevere and get her own way?

-Yes, and I stand by my word.

-Fine. Let's make a deal to accept whatever your aunt says. If she tells you to marry him, then marry him. If not, you must accept her word and decline. Agreed?

Soudabeh paused for a moment in deep thought. She looked up and glanced at her mother with wariness and contemplation: "Provided you don't cajole her into doing anything."

-What do you mean? I don't understand?

-I mean don't influence her to act despite herself and make me repent.

Mother laughed out loud.

-It is a good thing that you know your own aunt. You're her spitting image. Even if I do cajole her, she will still do her own thing. She will do whatever she sees fit at her own discretion. Still, I promise. Provided you too, listen to her and accept her judgement. You will be free then. As you pointed out, this is your life. If you want to jump into the fire, go ahead.

She got up to leave the room. In a tone of voice archetypal of a beloved daughter, the hurt, angry girl said: "You're sulking again mum! Do you have to sulk every time we try to discuss the subject like two well bred, civil people?"

-I am not sulking Soudabeh. I am going to get auntie.

Soudabeh pressed her lips together, sat on a chair and prepared to confront her aunt.

The afternoon sun of a winter's day shined on the colourful Persian carpets through the lace curtains. Father's poetry book of *Hafez* was open on the inlaid table placed at the centre of the room. The paintings adorning the walls were all originals. Apart from the books he kept in the bedroom, father's wall-to-wall library covered an entire side of the living room. The gardener had arrived in the early morning to prune and spray the trees. Unlike the summer, the swimming pool was quiet and desolate. Not a single bud was to be seen on the celebrated Persian rose bushes, which were pruned and in waiting for the caress of the spring breeze. Mercifully, the winter had been mild this year. The sycamore trees encircled the entire six-hundred-metre garden like a fort, and the early winter sun glimmered pleasantly on their red and yellow leaves. The door leading to the garden was ajar, letting in the cool air through the screen and into the living room where Soudabeh waited. The young girl gulped in the air eagerly to sooth the heart burning inside her. The parquetted floors of the room and corridor were fittingly covered with colourful silk and wool rugs. Without a doubt, her beautiful mother also had refined taste. This stunning, graceful and elegant woman, so loved and spoiled by her husband, a woman who had never faced grief – other than when her husband was in a car accident on the road to the Caspian Sea and she was given a new lease of life after the incident had passed without serious consequences – now walked with a heavy heart, as if her long shapely legs could no longer support her weight.

Mother was wearing a white blouse and a black pleated skirt and carried a white cashmere cardigan on her shoulders. Her short, natural olive hair was well coiffed. Father did not like dyed hair and mother had respected his wish. As she left the room slowly, the sound of her orthopaedic shoes gradually faded away in the corridor leading to auntie's accommodation. Her mild fragrance lingered in the room. Apart from the parlour, dining room and living room, the ground floor only housed one other room - that of auntie. It was a room with a small window opening to the garden. The rest of the rooms were upstairs - bedrooms, father's study, and the children's study and playroom. The house was an indication of the owner's suave flair and gentle spirit. Father was an art lover and wrote poetry. He was also an avid reader. Mother painted. Perhaps not a practiced artist, but with good taste; the more reason for her condemnation in Soudabeh's eyes. How could they be so oblivious to the magic of love and ignore her feelings with their claim to good taste and art appreciation? How could they forbid her from marrying the man she loved?

Soudabeh's anger increased every second as time passed. Mother is teaching her a lesson. They think I'm a baby. Let them say what they want. I... I...

She heard the clatter of a walking stick. Auntie was coming with mother who was helping her along. She was wearing a brown woollen jumper and skirt and thick socks. A small beige and brown scarf covered her hair and a delicate agate ring adorned her white, wrinkled finger. Her hazel eyes, said to have been large, smiled caringly from behind her glasses. She moved forward with great pain despite her comfy cloth shoes. Her back was bent in two. She was around eighty; no one really knew her age. Even so, her senses were sharp, her hearing good, and her perception strong. Like all old people, the memories of long ago shined brighter in her mind and excited her more than the events of a day or an hour ago. What did she look like? What did she look like in her youth? Beautiful? Tall and good looking? Her present appearance did not reveal much. Everyone believed that Soudabeh resembled her aunt in her younger days which, of course, offended Soud-abeh; but she never said anything because she loved her so dearly - this handful of harmless skin and bones who only appeared when her presence was essential. As children, despite the presence of nanny and the maid in the house, and despite the television and many books and movies for enter-tainment, whenever mum and dad were out visiting friends or when they were entertaining, Soudabeh together with her brother and sister went to their aunt's room and sat at the foot of the bed next to her lanky legs to listen to her stories or fiddle around with her odds and ends. If mum noticed, she scolded them – come on children, you mustn't touch aunt's things; don't nose around.

Auntie would laugh and say: "Leave it my dear Nahid. They have my permission."

Only a small chest in her wardrobe had been spared from the children's scrutiny. Not because they had not noticed it or seized it on many occasions to use as a footstool to reach the higher shelves; but because it was always locked and it never crossed their little minds to ask their aunt about its contents. Apart from this small chest, a *tar*[3] also hung on the wall of auntie's room. It had been there for as long as Soudabeh could remember - an old, antique tar. It seemed to have such reverence that even the children would not reach for it. Only once had Payman, Soudabeh's younger brother, overstepped his limit. Soudabeh was fifteen at the time and Payman was eight.

Payman suddenly ran towards the tar and reached for it, saying: "Auntie, I want to play for you." His hand had touched the long neck of the instrument, abruptly detaching it from the wall.

For the first and last time in her life, Soudabeh heard her aunt scream: "Oh my! It broke." Soudabeh had jumped with the sound of the scream and caught the tar in mid-air. Her aunt's eyes were popping out of her head. She had leaned forward and stretched out her hands towards the tar, as if it would decide to change course during the fall in the direction of the bed and land beside her. Payman was scared and looked pale. No, he was not scared of dear auntie, but of breaking something which, he now knew, would be irreplaceable. It seemed to be her fragile bottle of life[4]. Meticulously, Soudabeh had put the tar back in its place and turned towards Payman to fulfill a threat she had made many times before – she hit him so hard on the back of the neck that he barked like a dog! From that day onwards, the tar stayed safe from the children.

Dear auntie would come, and with her came the aroma of mixed, roasted wheat and hemp nuts. She never failed to have a bagful of the roasted nuts in her cupboard, ready to serve. It was not for a lack of chocolates, cakes, and sweets though. It was as if she had a sweet shop in her room; nothing but the best. She always said: "Take this chocolate Payman, but eat it after dinner; otherwise mum will scold you." Or "Soudabeh, do you prefer chewing gum or sweets?" Or she would turn to Soudabeh's younger sister and ask: "Sepideh darling, do you prefer chocolate or sweets?" "I want wheat and hemp nuts auntie." All three would finish the entire bag in one go, and tomorrow would be a new day. The children sometimes marvelled at what was in auntie's chest. What other goodies did it hold? But they could never figure it out and went about their own business.

And now, mum was carrying the box under one arm as she helped auntie along with the other. Soudabeh's heart sank. It was as if that gloriously carved, old boxwood chest held more proof for her conviction.

Her aunt sat down with the chest placed in front of her on the table. Mum called Jamileh to bring the tea. A small crystal dish full of biscuits was on the table. Auntie turned to her sister-in-law and asked: "My brother's not home?"

What a futile question. His parking space, next to Nahid's car, was empty at the bottom of the garden.

-He's gone out.

-Where?

-He's gone skiing. He has taken Payman and Sepideh.

But, Soudabeh knew only too well that dad had gone out so he would not have to interfere and impose if mother and daughter yelled at one another. Jamileh brought the tea and left. As mum followed her out, she said while closing the door: "Advise her. For God's sake guide her."

Silence fell on the room. Soudabeh was weary of auntie feigning ignorance. She was angry: "Advise me then, auntie." Her aunt was still silent.

-Mum says if you approve, they will also agree. If not, neither will they.

She was looking at her aunt. Just say the word and set me free. Yes or no? But auntie continued to look out of the window in her solemn silence. At last, in a grave voice, as if talking to herself, she said: "The time has finally come."

-What?

Auntie turned around and gazed at her: "Who am I to say yes or no *dokhtar jan*[5]? I can only tell you my own tale and then, you are the one who must decide."

Soudabeh was impatient: "Auntie, you have told me a thousand tales. Stories of your mischiefs as a child, but…"

-No my dear, the real story remains to be told. I was keeping it for a day such as this one. Had I told it once, I would have told it a thousand times without being able to stop myself. This is the lack of companionship in old age you know! And then, it would not have borne the same weight…

She fell into another silence. Suddenly, she asked: "Do you really love him?" -Oh, yes auntie, a whole lot. But nobody understands…

There was a twinkle in auntie's eyes, as if they were young once again for a brief moment. those young, big, bright hazel eyes. Was this really her aunt's look or had Soudabeh seen her own reflection in her eyes? Now she understood why she was said to resemble her.

"I understand" and she was silent again.

Soudabeh breathed a sigh, or sighed as if taking a breath; it made auntie smile.

-Be careful my dear Soudabeh, be very careful. Don't do anything to end up like me, to live in someone else's home and become a burden to others, alone and childless. No, I'm not ungrateful. I'm not disloyal to your father. He has given me a home and supervised my properties. I'm not saying he has let me down. He has taken the trouble to look after me. Everything I have is yours; the children of my brother and sisters. Enjoy it. I have no other heirs. Even so, I'm ashamed. I know I'm a burden to your mother.

-Oh, auntie…

-No darling, listen to me. Your mother has also been kind to me. She's like my own daughter. But, still, every woman wants an independent and private married life, without intruders. I know what I'm talking about. It's very difficult to be tolerated out of respect. Oh, my dear, as kind as those around you may be, it's still not the same as being with your own flesh and blood. Even a bad child of your own is good. Even if he belittles you, it's still sweet...

-What about us auntie, we're not like your own?

-Of course you are my darling; especially you. You are one with me. I thank God a thousand times a day for your company in this house. Every time you come home and get out of your mother's car, I say my *van ya-kad*[6] prayer for your protection. I pray for your prosperity and happiness in marriage - for all three of you. May you never be the cause of your own unhappiness. May you be the bride that the sun shines on, a marriage made in heaven. I wish I never had to open this chest in your presence. Did you know any of this?

Soudabeh knew nothing.

Auntie leaned forward, took hold of an old key hanging on a gold chain around her neck and opened the chest. Soudabeh was amazed: "Oh auntie! So this is where you kept the key?"

Her aunt laughed: "Yes, you mischievous little things. All three of you have been after this key ever since you were little, haven't you?"

The chest only contained some odds and ends, papers turned yellow, a photograph or two, and divorce papers. This was auntie's precious chest. There were no dolls, no chocolates, no slingshots for birds, and no fabric and sequins to make dolls' clothes. There were no signs of the objects Soudabeh and her brother and sister considered to be treasures as children. Not even any dried sour cherries, cranberries, or fruit bars. So why did she keep such a worthless chest locked

Auntie drank her tea, lay back, and sank into the armchair while holding on to the handle of her walking stick. She stretched out her legs and crossed her left ankle over the right one. For the very first time, she was not complaining about the pain in her leg. She looked into Soudabeh's eyes caringly, and asked:

-Will you be bored if I start from the beginning?

-No auntie, no. I won't be bored, she answered enthusiastically.

CHAPTER ONE

It was spring time my dear Soudabeh, spring time indeed. Damn the spring I still love so much. It was the beginning of Reza Shah's reign. I know this much – a few years had passed since his coronation. How many exactly? Four? Five? Three? I don't know. Don't ask me when the Qajar Dynasty was overthrown and when Reza Shah took over. The winds of change were blowing. There was a lot of noise and hullabaloo. There was talk of the Qajar King leaving. Talk of *Sardar-e Sepah*[7], of Reza Khan's coronation. But, it was as if I was not in this world; I don't know, as if I was in a different world. I only remember what I desired.

She stopped talking, rested her chin on her cane and gazed into the frozen garden.

It's as if it was yesterday… Oh my dear Soudabeh, time flies by… By God, He has given us such a short life, most of which is spent in childhood and old age. The time for pleasure is so brief. Our elders were so wise to say 'life is short like the life of a flower.' You too, will not understand this until you are as old as I am. You won't understand the meaning of 'life is like snow under the mid-summer sun.' May you grow old dokhtar jan…[8]

She went quiet once more and gazed into the garden. Did she forget? Or had she fallen asleep again?

-Auntie!

Silence.

-Auntie!

Auntie was crying.

I don't know. I don't know anything about the Qajars, nor about Reza Khan. I was in a world of my own my dear Soudabeh, because I was in love. Let them come and let them go if they so pleased. Let the world turn upside down, or let it not. Of what importance was it? Only let him stay, right?

She looked into Soudabeh's eyes with her own tearful eyes and a melancholy smile, just like a young girl in love. Soudabeh's eyes were also full of tears.

-You said you really love him, Auntie asked again.

-Yes auntie, Soudabeh answered amorously.

-May God help you dokhtar jan. May God help you.

Yes, it was spring time and our house was abounding with flowers. The flower pots in the *andarouni*[9] and *birouni* courtyards were full of blooms. The garden of my paternal home was not just a garden, it was paradise. At noontime, the appetising smell of food from the kitchen at the bottom of the garden behind the tall trees filled the air and mingled with the scent of flowers. The fish pond had clean, clear water, because water from the *qanat*[10] aqueduct ran under our house. Even so, we still had a separate *ab-anbar*[11] and *pashir*[12] at the bottom of the garden, close to the kitchen. Our dayeh khanoum would not walk past the pond, because she was afraid of being spattered with water she deemed ritually impure and unclean. Firouz khan, father's coachman, was from the south[13] and loved water. Every time he came into the interior courtyard for a reason, he always asked: "*Dayeh khanoum*[14], is the splatter of water more unclean than the children's urine?"

And dayeh khanoum would say: "Horse dung, God damn you."

Firouz khan would laugh nonstop. Now I think to myself perhaps this was a kind of flirting.

There were so many servants, maids, and gardeners in our house, and so many comings and goings, both in the birouni and andarouni, that I cannot recall them all. There were no less than seven or eight people eating at *agha jan's*[15] table every day. My father's title was *Basir ol-Molk*. He owned three or four villages and was a well-educated, cultured man. He had spent a year or two studying in Russia and was an intellectual poet. He loved the opera, which he had visited in Russia. He was a kind father and a gentleman. He treated his children well. Not that he was like my brother who sits down and discusses politics and the arts and sciences with his children! Yet, he was very modern for his time so to speak. Even so, he commanded respect and we looked up to him. My mother, dear Soudabeh, was gentle and lovely liker her name, *Nazanin*[16]. My father loved her - again, as per their own traditions in those days. She was fifteen years younger than him, and the daughter of a well-known, reputable merchant. She bore three daughters for my father, of which I was the second born. She called him agha in so many different loving ways. My eldest sister was married and had a son named Mahmoud. My aunt was hoping to betroth my younger sister, Khojasteh, to her own son. She was five or six years younger than me. But for now, it was my turn as her older sister.

My mother yearned for a son. She was only thirty-two years old at the time and she had been off her food for a couple of weeks. Yes, my mother was pregnant again and suffered from morning sickness. My father kept saying: "Don't tire yourself Nazanin," or "Eat nourishing foods Nazanin," "Do this Nazanin, don't do that Nazanin." In the midst of all this fuss, a suitor was supposed to come to our house with his family to ask for my hand. We had a home tutor whose wife, Khanoum Baji, was our seamstress at home. The poor woman died suddenly of a stomach ache overnight. My mother fluttered about in her condition, saying Mahboubeh has nothing to wear. Dayeh khanoum would repeatedly say: *"Khanoum jan*[17], Mahboubeh has a trunk full of clothes. Why do you do this to yourself?" And mother complained: "Oh, don't rub salt into my wound dayeh khanoum; she has worn each one a hundred times." At last, dayeh khanoum had an idea. She threw her *chador*[18] over her head and ran to my aunt's place. They had an agile seamstress, but had kept her a secret from my mother for years. Women have these rivalries between them you know. But, I don't know what our sweet-spoken nanny said to convince my aunt who, according to dayeh khanoum, had frowned and said: "I know Nazanin khanoum has always been after this seamstress and this is just an excuse, but I will send her to your house tomorrow afternoon for the sake of my brother's daughter.

Tell Nazanin khanoum we will always do what we can; but she mustn't be so aloof."

Father was indoors when dayeh khanoum gave this message to mother for him to hear. My mother's eyes sparkled with the joy of having found a good seamstress, but apparently surprised at my aunt's message and fuming inside, she turned to father and said: "Oh dear, what a strange comment! Did you hear that? May she live long of course. It's very kind and ladylike of her to send her tailor to us. But, I don't know how I have let Keshvar khanoum down, or in what way have I been insolent towards her to deserve such remarks under every pretext. Why does she cause such unpleasantness, as if she enjoys tormenting me?"

Father turned to mother calmly and said: "So lady, be ladylike again and keep a low profile to truly avoid unpleasantness. The more this is prolonged, the more tedious it becomes."

-But, agha…
-No buts. He that loves the tree loves the branch. You already know how dear you are to me, forgive my sister's sins for my sake.

Mother's embarrassed answer came: "God forbid agha. Such comments! You're the jewel in my crown. Fine, I'll do it just for your sake."

My father turned to the nursemaid and said: "By the way dayeh khanoum, one mustn't repeat everything one hears." The resentful answer came: "By God agha, I was instructed to say so, and I did."

-From now on, sift through your instructions. Carry out the good ones, and leave out the bad.

At once, I sensed mother's heart sink. If dayeh left in anger, especially now that mother was in the family way, finding another spick-and-span nanny with her experience, who had been one with our household for years now, would be quite a task in itself. She mediated at once: "Of course, I'm not completely blameless either. I shouldn't have lost my temper. An expecting mum becomes weak and impatient you know"; and the crisis was settled. This is as far as my parents' quarrels went. It was as if they were reciting poetry, or as if there was a poetmachia going on between them. They both knew only too well where one must lower one's note and treated one another as gently as they would a flower. They turned a blind eye to each other's faults. These sacrifices stretched as far as all of us knowing that, once every fortnight, when my father stayed out on Tuesday nights, he was with Esmat khanoum, his second wife. What we did not know was whether mother also knew and turned a blind eye, or whether she was truly unaware of it.

Five years earlier, when I was ten and mother gave birth to my sister Khojasteh, father made no upsetting remarks at all. He even bought mother a gold bib necklace like always. But, we often saw him pacing up and down in the courtyard or inside the room, deep in thought. Until one night, he told my mother he was going to visit Mirza Hassan Khan. Mirza Hassan Khan was a respected man from an honourable family, but without means. We would hear dayeh khanoum say: *"Khanoum khanouma*[19] – this is how the maids addressed my mother – says he's a literary man and a lover of poetry; he plays the tar well, but she doesn't like him because he's a free, pleasure seeking man. Every time agha returns from his home, he smells of spirits."

Apparently, my father had too much to drink that night and had a heart-to-heart with Mirza Hassan Khan about how much he wanted a son and how his wife only gave birth to girls. In turn, Mirza Hassan Khan had played it foul and made his widowed sister - who was as thin as a matchstick - my father's concubine that same night, telling him that she has a two or three year old son from her first husband and that she might give him a son too. All you have to do is take her under your wing so she can live under your protection. This will be enough. When my father woke up the next morning, he was bitterly remorseful, but it was too late and he had to keep his word. Esmat khanoum conceived that same night and gave birth to twins nine months later, both girls and both dying at birth. After that, my father swore he would never drink again, lest he lost his mind. Of course, he went to visit Esmat khanoum once a fortnight as he had promised Hassan Khan; but she never became pregnant again.

As I was saying, my father loved my mother. She was a beautiful woman for her time - of medium height and somewhat plump, with ivory skin, a little colour in her cheeks, light hair, and big hazel eyes. I had heard my father say her shoulders were as beautiful as those of Russian gentlewomen in their low-cut dresses. My mother laughed out loud with happiness every time she quoted my father on this for the ladies of the family or her friends.

Anyway, as I was saying, it was spring and my aunt's seamstress was coming to our house the following afternoon. It was Imam Reza's (SA) birthday in three weeks and *Shahzadeh[20]* Khanoum, Ata al-Dowleh's wife, was supposed to come to our house to ask for my hand for his son.

Soudabeh asked with excitement: "Really auntie? The same one who was a famous statesman in Iran for years? Wow, I don't believe this! Did he really ask for your hand?"

-Believe it my dear, believe it. But I turned him down.

-Oh auntie, what a stup…

Soudabeh bit her tongue.

-What? Auntie smiled.

Yes, I was saying; don't interrupt me, I'll forget. He was about fifteen years my senior and they said he had just returned from Europe. The daughters of respectable families fell head over heels for him. His first wife had died in childbirth. A lot of women lost their lives in this way those days… There were no *hakims[21]* and medicines on every street corner like there are today. Anyhow, I was fifteen then and had no idea about anything. I was fifteen and on a merry-go-round. I was happy and peppy. I had no idea what having a husband meant. All I knew was that I would be an old maid in a couple of years…

Soudabeh laughed heartily. Auntie was also laughing.

Yes, other times other manners. Eighteen and nineteen year olds were old maids in those days.

Mother ordered Firouz khan to get the coach ready. She left to buy me some fabric for a new dress and took dayeh khanoum with her. Upon her return, she went to the *sandoghkhane[22]* as per habit to take off her chador. I followed her and dayeh khanoum, who was carrying the fabric, to see what she had bought and inspect the damage and poor taste. As my mother was taking off her chador, she told dayeh khanoum: "Everyone's getting older as time goes by dayeh khanoum; but this old carpenter in the passageway is getting younger day by day!" and she laughed. She was teasing dayeh khanoum.

Dayeh said: "What are you saying? This is not the same old man. That poor thing can't even walk. He just lies down in one corner. He can't afford to eat, but he spends money on smoking opium. He had gone to sleep and entrusted the shop to this nipper. He's supposed to be the shop boy."

Mother said: "He's a cute boy." And that was it. We all forgot about it. Sometimes, I think to myself perhaps this one sentence from my mother lit the fire. Maybe this one word made me curious and caught my interest. Maybe it was fate.

The seamstress came. She was a plump, sweet and good-humoured woman with a lit face. May she rest in peace. She flattered my mother and praised me as much as she could. I had just woken up. The breakfast tray was piled up with traditional sweet flatbread and butter brought from the country, and churned panir and jam. Dayeh khanoum kept pouring tea for me, my mother, and my younger sister. My sister and I drank and mother was sick. Dayeh khanoum and the seamstress encouraged and begged her in unison to eat and make up for it. At last, we were full and mother was exhausted. Another tray was brought for Anis khanoum, the seamstress. We left the room so she could eat her breakfast in peace. We knew she had had breakfast at home, but there was a world of difference between this one and that. It was worth eating again!

Mother had guests for lunch – her sisters, my paternal and maternal uncles' wives, and auntie. We were all ravenous with the aroma of the chicken and best rice from Rasht[23] cooking in Kermanshahi[24] oil in the kitchen at the bottom of the garden. My mother was sitting on the stool in front of her powder and paint. I remember we had upholstered, red velvet sofas all around our andarouni parlour, which we called *panjdari*[25]. There was a fairly small walnut table placed in front of every other sofa. The summers were spent in the sitting room, which was surrounded by embroidered floor cushions and pearl-embroidered backrests. In the winters, we had a *korsi*[26]. My father liked to sit by the fireplace in the panjdari and listen to the crackle of burning wood while I read him the poems of Hafez or love stories from *Nezami's 'Leili and Majnoun'*[27]. Everything was so serene.

The wife of Firouz khan the coachman, whom we called *dadeh*[28] due to her dark tan, brought in mother's makeup box and stood beside her with her fan. She fanned my mother constantly, lest she would sweat and her powder and paint turn into mud on her face. I was captivated. But, mother browbeat: "Don't you have anything to do girl? What're you staring at? There's nothing to watch here for a girl." She told me to go to Anis khanoum as she was putting on her eye *sormeh*[29]. "Let's hope your dress will be finished by tonight."

My dress was not finished by nightfall. It does not work as fast as a dyer's jar, Anis khanoum would say. Apart from the two dresses, she also had to make a white damask chador for me, all of which would take at least two or three days. Mother asked Anis khanoum to spend those few nights at our house. She was, of course, more than willing. The feast was on for her in our home, but someone had to take news of her to her son and daughter-in-law. My mother asked Firouz khan to go in the coach. It was a long way away into the weaving alleys. By nightfall, when the guests were leaving, my youngest aunt insisted on taking me to her place. Mother agreed only on the condition that I returned in the early morning for the trial of my clothes.

As we were getting on my aunt's coach, a thought crossed Anis khanoum's mind: "If it's not too much trouble, there's a carpenter's at the turn of the third lane from your house, near the *saghakhaneh*[30.] The shop boy knows our house. He lives a couple of lanes further up from us. The coachman can stop by the shop for a minute and tell him to let my son know I'll be staying here for the night. This way, Firouz khan won't have to go all the way to our place."

My cousin and I, who were almost the same age, sat cheerily in the back of the coach with my aunt. I was the last one to get on, and sat on the right hand side. A while into the drive, Anis message completely slipped our minds, except for the dutiful coachman who remembered. The carriage stopped at a small, sooty shop. It was nearly sundown. The inside of the shop was chockfull of wood, planks, and wood chippings and shavings. Someone wearing a pair of black percaline slacks and a white cloth caftan hanging over them down to his knees was bent over an old worktop in the middle of the shop planing a piece of wood. He had rolled up his sleeves and his long hair was scattered over his forehead, waving around with every move of his head bent over his work. He looked more like a dervish than a carpenter. Men's hair was oiled and slick in those days, like the hair of all the men I saw in my family; like the entire aristocracy. But this hair was wild and untamed.

He looked up as he heard the coach stop. His eyes wandered from the coachman over to the three passengers veiled from head to toe with their chador, *chaghchour*[31] and *roubandeh*[32], and back to the coachman again. He was surprised. What could these three ladies in this luxurious carriage want with him? The driver shouted: "Hallo chap." He approached indifferently, wiping the sweat off his forehead with the back of his hand: "Yes?" The stroke of his hand on his forehead appeared sweet to me. He was pleasant; that's all. He took the message and said: "Sure."

He did not speak to us, and we did not speak to him, and I forgot all about him.

-What kind of welt is this that you've bought me dayeh khanoum! Am I a clown?"

Dayeh khanoum protested: "How should I know my darling Mahboubeh. There was no pink as you said love, so I got red."

My mother lifted the welt up into the air unhappily: "Oh, dear dayeh khanoum, I had given you a sample."

-But they didn't have any!

-I will get it myself, I said irritated. Where did you buy it from?"

- At the bazaar entrance.

-Take the carriage and come back quickly, said my mother impatiently.

-It's not that far khanoum jan, said dayeh khanoum. I'll walk her there and back.

I was surprised at dayeh khanoum's words. How come such a lethargic woman had suddenly become so agile? How could I have guessed that she had vowed to light a candle to cure her headache? The poor woman had migraines. Who knew what migraines were in those days?

Anis khanoum pleaded: "God bless you dayeh khanoum. Please see if the carpenter boy has given my message to my son and daughter-in-law. My stomach's churning. That boy's a bit lightheaded. Also, tell him to go to our house and tell them not to worry if I'm delayed. I might have to stay one more day."

It was around noontime. The carpentry was still closed. We went shopping and bought the welt. On our way back, I could hear the rattle of the saw from a distance. Dayeh khanoum said: "Good, thank God he has opened up at last. The lazy boy! Will you wait a second for me to light these two candles Mahboubeh darling?"

I stamped my foot down impatiently.

Dayeh khanoum pleaded: "God bless you love, just one second; it's right here."

-Hurry then; don't take too long.

-Why don't you give Anis khanoum's message to the shop boy while I'm doing this? But, don't tell your khanoum jan I was lighting candles. Tell her dayeh herself spoke to the carpenter boy, alright? She'll ruin me otherwise." I said impatiently: "Alright then; light them quickly and come after me. I'll walk slowly until you catch up."

It was a sunny day, but it had poured down the night before and the path was muddy. When I arrived at the shop, the young boy was busy planing wood like the previous day, oblivious to his surroundings. I stood outside the shop while examining the muddy edge of my chador. I lifted it up a little, and instinctively said: "Ugh."

The sound of the plane stopped and I heard someone with a grasping, harmonious voice say: "Ugh to me young lady?"

I looked up and saw his eyes. He had a long neck with bulging muscles and veins under his dark skin, rolled-up sleeves and strong hands; his hair was scattered on his forehead; he had a grin on his face and an aquiline nose. Handsome? I don't know. Ugly? I don't know. But he was a real man. He was manly. Those arms could be a refuge.

Customarily, I would not even return his hello. It was shameful for me to engage in conversation with individuals of his class. But, it was springtime now. What was wrong with me? I don't know. I said: "Why ugh to you? Are you ugh?"

-I must be and not know it!

The scent of planed wood filled my nose. What an agreeable smell. The smell of hard work. It was as if a new fragrance had been added to the scents of spring; the outcome of muscle work. I looked at him in silence.

How could he tell I was young from behind the *picheh*[33]? Perhaps it was the tone of my voice. I said: "I have a message for you."

He looked at me in astonishment - the young woman who addressed him politely and formally and had a message for him.

He asked: "For me?"

-Yes.

-You do know that I am *Rahim*[34] the carpenter boy!!

What a lovely name. I liked it. "I know."

-Who are you?

-I am the daughter of Basir ol-Molk.

He put the plane down slowly and stood politely. "Hello Miss. I'm sorry I didn't recognize you. The message must be for Anis khanoum's son?"

-Yes. If it's not too much trouble, tell him her work might take longer than expected at our place. He's not to worry.

-Certainly.

-You won't forget?

-Not if I live.

I should have been struck dumb for having said: "God forbid that anything should happen to you; may you live long."

He stood aghast for a moment, looking at me with that grin appearing on his face again. He said: "Just to deliver your message?"

Hastily, I said goodbye.

He was getting too forward. I turned around and began walking. Dayeh was just leaving the saghakhaneh, dragging her feet. I was angry with her. The silly, lazy woman; she could barely walk in the agony of death. I was angry with myself. You brainless girl! I mimicked myself under my picheh: 'God forbid that anything should happen to you; may you live long'. You silly, mindless, long-eared girl! I was angry with him. You ragamuffin of a shop boy! These riffraff become so impudent just as soon as you indulge a little. The scoundrel of a tramp!

My heart sank at the sound of the plane starting again. What was the meaning of this?

Everything was ready. They were baking sweets. But I, who loved baklava, felt sick. Even the chickpea sweets made me sick. I hated flowers. I wanted to tear my new clothes to pieces. What was the matter with me? I was clueless. I simply wanted to die. Either I should die or…? Or what…? I had no idea.

I went past the carpentry shop twice in one week in the carriage. Planing and planing and planing; one look, and then planing and planing and planing again. The impertinent little fellow had recognised our carriage. I had not had the courage to leave the house all week. I must tell dayeh. No, I will tell Firouz khan. No, leave it. He will kill him. I would have the dog's blood on my hands. I will tell my father. No, that is even worse. My mother then… What shall I say? That he looks at the carriage every time we drive past the carpentry? Is this exclusively forbidden?! Alright, why do I look towards the shop then? I must not pay attention. Maybe this is how it has always been. Perhaps the butcher, baker, and sheep-head cooker also looked at us out of curiosity. After all, we are well-known, credible people in this community. The only difference is that I don't pay attention to them. It isn't important. Let him look until he drops dead. But I was being coquette too. *The worm is within the tree itself*[35]. I do not know why I wanted to pull back the carriage hood so he could watch me from over the chador!

The message came that my brother-in-law intended to travel to the village he owned to oversee his affairs. "Mahboubeh khanoum can come to her sister's house as a guest for a couple of nights so Nezhat won't be by herself." By herself? With all her domestics and retinues? I went. My sister continuously praised my future suitor. This goose had been cooked for me by her husband. He was the groom's friend and childhood playmate. He had brought me to the attention of Ata al-Dowleh's son. Nezhat also applauded the groom's mother and her lineage, and kept saying she is a grand shazdeh of noble birth.

I said: "But, dear Nezhat, they say her sister, the groom's aunt…"

-What about her sister?

-She's a woman with a past.

Nezhat clutched her face: "Woe, may God strike me dead, which sister?!"

-How should I know? The one called Tahereh.

-Who has said such a thing?

-Auntie Keshvar.

Nezhat shook her hand furiously: "Have you ever seen our dear aunt praise anyone? These people are of noble birth. They are upstanding people. Everyone talks behind their backs, because everyone's jealous of them. Have you ever seen anyone talk behind the backs of servants, nursemaids, or dadeh? People only backbite because these are upstanding people.

- So, why not backbite us?

-How do you know? Maybe they do and we're not even aware of it!

Nezhat showed me how to serve sweets, how to offer the hookah, how to sit… But, why did I feel so tired? I never wanted to leave my sister's house before. Why am I so bored? Why do I want to go home? I don't want her to be so chatty. I was head over heels when it was time to go home at last. I grew wings.

My sister asked: "Do you want *naneh*[36] to accompany you?"

-No, I'm going in the carriage. I'm not alone!

As my sister's coach driver was a feeble old man, it was alright to be alone with him. He lowered the carriage hood. I got on. I wanted the horses to grow wings. When we reached the top of the alley, I called out: "*Mashhadi*[37], I'll get off here."

-There are still a couple of alleys left little miss.

-That's alright. I'll get off here. I want to do some shopping.

-Then tell her ladyship that I accompanied you to the door.

-Fine, fine. Don't fret. Go.

I wasn't sure what I was doing. What shopping did I have to do? So, why am I not buying anything then? Why am I trembling? I wanted to glance into the carpentry shop, perhaps out of curiosity. So why do I keep telling myself I hope he drops dead? Who has to die? Aha, now I know! I am praying for my suitor to die!

There was still an hour left till noon and it was crowded inside the bazaar. He was moving the wood around. It was as if the entire population had come to a standstill to stare at me. Are they pointing at me? No, I must be imagining things.

May I be struck dumb to have said: "May God give you more strength." He turned around and froze on the spot. Did he recognise me from my voice? Or from the black taffeta chador and the expensive hand-sewn picheh? I was anxious. I stuttered in a loud voice for any suspicious passersby to hear: "Do you also make wooden frames?"

He was still standing there, quiet and aghast, holding a piece of lumber in his hand, taller than himself. His hair hung loose over his forehead. That same grin appeared on the corner of his mouth again.

-Depends on the frame khanoum.

-A picture frame.

-What size?

-Do you make small frames?

-Only for you.

The smell of wood filled my nose. The scent of wood. All of a sudden, I turned around and started running home. My heart was pounding as I hurled abuse at myself. Have you gone mad girl? What are you doing? Why did you have to run? Why are you shaming yourself like this? May God strike you dead. What did I just do? I will never come this way again, either on foot or by carriage. I'll go from the alley on the left. I will go the long way round… But, I went by there again. And now, every time the carriage drove past the shop, he stopped and followed it with his eyes. That impudent, shameless little man…

Little by little, the day approached for my suitor and his family to come and ask for my hand. The panjdari was ready. There were flowers, tulip lamp shades and sweets everywhere. The birouni and andarouni had been swept and washed. Mother was dressed to the teeth and wearing full make-up and heels. She was submerged in jewellery and gold. All perfumed and ready. What comings and goings! Everyone smiled at me and praised me. They called me *Khanoum kouchik*[38], khanoum kouchik. When my father sat next to my mother to drink his tea after lunch, he said to me: "Mahboub jan, can I have some of your baklava?" and smiled.

My father always called me Mahboubeh or *Mahboub*[39]. He seldom used the word jan. The plate of baklava was a little further up on the floor. 'Your baklava' meant the baklava of your wedding. This was a sign that father was happy and pleased with the groom. I offered him the plate with both hands. He took a baklava and gently tapped me on the shoulder a few times. He was a good-tempered, gentle man.

They arrived in the groom's carriage an hour before dusk to show it off, and knocked on the door. A Russian coach with two windproof, mirrored candle burning crystal lanterns, a glossy black carriage with red wheels and a seat pad with smooth springs covered with chevreau[40] skin, pulled by two horses of the same height and colour, both young. Even though it was springtime and the weather was getting warmer, the coachman, with a moustache curved upward and as clean and sparkling as the carriage itself, was still wearing a sheepskin hat. As if to reveal the grandeur of the scene even more, he sat upright in his seat and looked straight ahead.

My sister and I were hiding in the *goushvareh*[41] room. Khojasteh was giggling and I was muttering abuse in her ear. I kept telling her to shut her mouth, not to bring shame on us. But, I was at my wit's end with her. The guests took off their chadors in the side room and entered the panjdari. I was watching from the hole on the side of the coloured glass panel which was slightly chipped. The bridegroom's mother was a fat, old, haughty woman covered in jewellery, and yet one of those princesses with decorum and etiquette. Following her like ducklings following their mother were her daughter – the bridegroom's sister – and her daughter-in-law who was married to the groom's eldest brother. Next came the groom's tall, black dayeh, self-reliant, shapely and good looking, prouder than the mother herself [42] - as if the groom was truly her own son. She carried on saying my son, my son. She was also wearing a gold bracelet and the large kerchief covering her head was fastened with a gold pin under her chin. They exchanged greetings with my mother and sat down. The customary compliments were paid - you are most welcome, you bring us joy, we are honoured to be here, we are obliged, he is your humble servant, she is your obedient servant.

Then, the groom's mother asked: "Well, where's the bride? Will you allow us to meet her?"

My mother answered: "Of course, as you wish; we are entirely at your service. With your permission, she will be in attendance straight away."

My mother came out of the room and said: "Mahboub dear, come and pay your respects to shazdeh khanoum" in a relatively loud and formal voice for those who were in the room to also hear. Then, she quietly hurried into the room where we were, and said in a hushed voice: "You're in luck Mahboubeh; quick, bring the tea[43]. Don't spill it on the tray! Make sure it's piping hot!"

She went back into the room. I followed her into the room a couple of minutes later, carrying the silver tea tray that my dear dayeh had prepared for me with shaky hands. As soon as I entered the panjdari room in its entire splendour, I immediately realised that the thought of the carpenter boy was but a futile, vain illusion. It was as if I could see the distance between him and me with my own eyes. I? I who belonged to this life and these rituals and these types of husbands! There was a world of difference between us! It was as if a colossal wave separated me from my dream and brought me back to reality. I said: "*Salam[44].*"

The princess said: "Oh my, Salam to your pretty face. You have such an appealing daughter khanoum. *Masha 'Allah[45]*, a thousand times Masha 'Allah."

Mother answered: "She welcomes you and kisses[46] your hand." I did not want to kiss her hand in the least bit.

But I served the tea with the utmost meticulousness, in order of importance. First, I served the groom's mother who was sitting at the top of the room with her airs and graces. Then, it was the groom's sister who was either older than their daughter-in-law, or else her excessive unattractiveness made her seem so. Next was the first daughter-in-law who was very beautiful, serene and demure; and finally the black dayeh for whom I felt immediate love. As she was taking her tea from the tray with a smile, she said: "Masha 'Allah, may you grow old my daughter. Did you *COOK* the tea yourself darling?!!"

I was supposed to smile at this joke so they could see that my teeth were straight and orderly.

"My, what pearly teeth!"

My own dayeh stood to attention by the door, with crossed arms. I turned around to leave with the tea tray, when the groom's mother said in a loud voice: "Where to Mahboubeh khanoum? Stay a few more minutes and honour us with your presence."

I gave the tray to dear dayeh, who took it away. I turned around docilely. The black dayeh opened up her arms: "Come love, let me kiss you. I have always wished for this day for my son."

She took me by both armpits and gave me two generous kisses on both cheeks, leaving the moisture of her mouth lingering on them. I knew it was because she wanted to see if I was perspiring or whether I had bad breath. All the examinations had yielded good, positive results, because my mother had sprayed me with so much perfume that, like me, that poor woman must have had a headache for the rest of the day. I sat down with my hands resting on my skirt and lowered my head while answering the questions with a simple yes or no in a soft spoken voice. What an obedient girl I was!

Mother said: "Please have some baklava. Mahboubeh jan has made it herself."

All my talent in making the baklava had been limited to taking dayeh to the storage room, unlocking the padlock on the sugar tin, handing over the pistachio and almonds to her, cutting the baklava in the tray after it had been baked, and pouring the sugar syrup over it.

The eyes of the groom's sister swept over me from head to toe: "My, what a fine baklava! It melts in the mouth."

Lest she would be called jealous, my future sister-in-law said: "It is evident Mahboubeh khanoum is a girl of many talents. She's both pretty and resourceful."

I lifted my head up and looked at her. She was truly beautiful with her languishing black eyes, broad joined eyebrows, a slender nose, thick lips, and very delicate white skin. Nezhat, who was sitting next to my mother, said discerningly: "Well, of course, khanoum *bozorg*[47] has good taste. She hand-picks her brides." And the pretty bride smiled sweetly and blushed.

I eyed my suitor's family from the corner of my eye. I kept asking myself whether these respectable honourable ladies, with all their pomp and circumstances, could even imagine that I dream of becoming the wife of the local carpenter's shop boy? That I desire to turn my back on this life with all its domestics, retinues and pageantry? That I want to push these reverent, decorous ladies engulfed in perfume and jewellery to one side and run to the doorstep of that dark, small and unassuming carpentry black from the sooth of its lamp, and sleep on its threshold like a guard dog? Just lay there and watch him saw the wood with his waving hair hanging freely on his forehead? To simply breathe in the fragrance of wood? God only knows what a palace that small shop seemed to me; the fragrance of wood seemed like such perfume and the entire shop such a heavenly lodge.

As Khanoum bozorg – shazdeh khanoum – began praising his son, my mother said: "Mahboub jan, bring some more tea," meaning it is enough; leave the room lest they say the girl was frivolous, eager for a husband, and that she sat there listening obstinately to every word making her mouth water.

As I was walking past the chair the bridegroom's mother sat on, she took me by the hand: "No dear; where to? Sit here right next to me. Wouldn't it be a shame for these soft hands to work? There, sit on this chair. Well done. Your dayeh khanoum will take the trouble of bringing more tea."

You don't say - they really found me very acceptable. My mother, who was in seventh heaven, said: "Oh, khanoum jan, bringing tea is not work. Hands will not be damaged by bringing tea! Don't say these things in front of her; it will spoil her and she will have to be put on a pedestal from now on." And she laughed.

My mother had a charismatic and attractive mannerism. I don't know how she managed to win the hearts of all those she spoke to. She did not pretend. It was her natural disposition. She always said: "By God, I have managed to win everyone's heart except that of Keshvar khanoum," talking about my aunt.

Shahzadeh khanoum said: "It's only right that you put her on a pedestal. All my daughters-in-law belong way up there."

Nezhat turned to the pretty young woman with laughter and said: "You are lucky then."

The pretty daughter-in-law gave her head and neck a twist and smiled bitterly. She did not say yea or nay, implying *read your own detailed hadith*[48] *into this compendium of gestures*, indicating that shazdeh khanoum is one of those mothers-in-law!

Like someone who wanted to raise an argument, shazdeh khanoum emphasised: "Yes khanoum, may she rest in peace, she was also very dear to me. And as God is my witness, her daughter is now my chosen one. She has become my friend and companion, this tiny child. Not that Mahboubeh jan should worry! I will bring Ra'na up myself. She will be with me; she's the apple of my eye."

I knew the groom had a child by his first wife. His match had been made in heaven with his paternal cousin. She had died in childbirth a year or two ago and the child had survived. Of course, these things were not so important in those days; especially when one's suitor was a young man with so much hustle and bustle, and when the ring on his mother's small finger was the size of a pigeon's egg all by itself. The groom who was a prince, had travelled abroad and was perfect in every way.

His mother said: "Oh khanoum, this child is so sweet. I, for one, cannot even bear to see her upset, never mind in tears." She was filling my ear.

Dadeh khanoum brought the hookah, served another round of beverages and sweets, and khanoum bozorg talked about herself, praised her son and how modern he was, how well-spoken he was – not very surprising if he took after his mother. She talked about his appearance and his looks – which I hoped did not look like his sister's! And yet, she didn't wish to praise him, as she put it herself. It was finally time to go and I breathed a sigh of relief. We saw them to the door with the utmost respect. Shazdeh khanoum, her daughter and her daughter-in-law kept repeating: "We know the way. Please don't bother, don't come all the way, you put us to shame." At that moment, khanoum bozorg turned around, kissed me on the cheek and told my mother once more: "You have a fine daughter. Her eyes are captivating and beautiful. A good womb gives birth to jewels; your children are truly as good as gold."[49] My mother laughed: "Beauty is in the eye of the beholder. Thank you for your kindness. You bring us serenity. Thank you very much."

Nezhat pulled my dress from behind, meaning I had to return inside the building.

There was quite a celebration in the corner goushvareh room. Mother was overwhelmed with joy. Dayeh jan was snapping her fingers. Nezhat kept repeating: "Did you see her rings khanoum jan? Did you see what a bib necklace her daughter-in-law was wearing?"

Dayeh jan was saying: "My dear, their lineage is deeply rooted in aristocracy after all; they are highborn. The groom's dayeh was a lady in her own right."

In order to win her heart and share more of her happiness with her, mother said: "The bride's dayeh was no less herself."

A big smile appeared on dayeh khanoum's face: "Oh khanoum jan, you will charm the snakes out of their hole with this tongue of yours! Still, you didn't see their carriage! Thanks be to the power of God, there was not a speck of dust on it… But, Mahboubeh jan! Sweetheart, why're you sitting there in such a huff?"

-Because I don't want to marry shazdeh khanoum's carriage.

Mother said: "Well darling, there's nothing to cry about. If you don't want to marry her carriage, marry her son."

Mother, Nezhat and dayeh fell into a fit of laughter. I got up in a fury, went to the window, crossed my arms and stared at the clean, tidy spring garden. Mother stopped laughing and asked: "Well, what's the meaning of this girl? What's the problem? Did they say something to upset you?"

I answered angrily: "No, they didn't say anything bad. Khanoum bozorg just carried on about her dearly departed bride and her miss goldilocks of a granddaughter." I waved my right hand in the air and gave my head and neck a twist: "My grandchild this, my daughter-in-law that. They had come to ask for my hand you know. But, she only talked about her dearly departed daughter-in-law."

Nezhat said: "Don't be so unfair! Didn't she compliment and praise you enough?"

Mother, who had somewhat softened, said: "Well, to be honest, Mah boubeh is right. I wasn't too pleased about that. It was as if she wanted *to kill the cat outside the bridal chamber*[50] and secure a good footing for the child. It's true that the girl lives with her grandmother, but she's still her father's daughter."

I asked angrily: "And it makes you happy that this dime a dozen son of shazdeh khanoum wants to marry me? Carrying a *pistillum*[51] on top of everything else, which…"

Dayeh khanoum interrupted me: "Well, well, Mahboubeh khanoum now calls Ata al-Dowleh's son a dime a dozen…! You wouldn't be talking like this if you had seen him. Don't say this anywhere else or people will laugh at you…"

I was too shy to address or reproach my mother, so I turned to my elder sister and said: "Don't dream up such things for me! I will not marry this pop." And I said it with such confidence that I even surprised myself.

My sister pouted her lips and said: "What? It's really none of my business! It's *no crown on my head*[52] whether you marry him or not!"

Dayeh left the room to tidy up the parlour with a grumble.

My mother gently asked me: "Why? Are you being difficult Mahboub jan?"

-No khanoum jan. Why should I be difficult? But I haven't even seen him yet. I can't even imagine what he looks like. Should I marry him without getting to know him? And with a child too?"

-Knowing him is not your business. Your father has to know him, which he does. What if he has a child? She has nothing to do with you. She's being brought up in her grandmother's house. Poor Shazdeh khanoum kept stressing on this. Thank goodness they don't want for anything; they're not a financial burden to you; they won't let you down in any way. There's just the question of meeting him.

Mother pondered for a moment and carried on: "Well, why see him at all? He's just a man. All men are the same."

Nezhat laughed wholeheartedly: "Oh! Khanoum jan, listen to yourself talk! All men are the same? So if Mahboubeh has seen Haj Ali, she has seen

Shazdeh's son?"

Her remark made me laugh too. Haj Ali, our old cook with partially impaired hearing, a bent back, forever bloodshot eyes from blowing on the logs underneath the cauldrons, greying stubble, thick fat lips, large ears, and thin coarse hair looking like nails standing on his head was truly a fine example of a complete man!

Nezhat asked: "So, her ladyship would like a glimpse of him?"

-Yes, why not? Should I not see who I'm marrying?

Nezhat asked: "If you see him, will it be the end of the story?"

My mother clutched her face: "Oh Nezhat, may God strike me down, what are you saying?"

Nezhat continued without paying attention to her: "I said, will this be over if you see him? Case dismissed?"

-Yes, no more arguments if I like him. If I don't, I guess it's just the beginning of quarrels and squabbles with you and agha jan."

Nezhat said in a sulk: "If you don't want him, then you don't. Why squabble? You're not chained down. It's your life. I'll think of something and let you know."

A couple of days later, I woke up at midday. I had my breakfast. The carpenter boy at the top of the passageway was far from my mind. It was as if I had lost interest in him. My mother called me: "Come Mahboub jan, let's set the table."

My father had guests that night.

Setting the table, arranging the flowers and decorating the parlour were a few of my negligible responsibilities which I had learned very well from my mother. She had learned these skills under the instructions of a European lady. Our house was one of a few where these rules were observed with the utmost immaculateness and elegance. Mother, who was well-known for her good taste and housekeeping, was setting the stylishly patterned china plates on the table and I was holding the silver cutlery when, unexpectedly she said: "You have to go to Nezhat's Thursday night."

-What for?

-Wake up! What for? Because poor Nasir khan has arranged a gathering for the men and invited Mr Ata al-Dowleh's son so her ladyship can see the groom!"

Nasir khan was my sister Nezhat's husband. I stared at my mother and said: "You must first make sure whether his mother and sister like me or not, then make arrangements. There's a song and dance at the bride's quarters, but the groom's house is silent."

-Yes, they like you. They've sent a message wanting an answer. Your father has asked for some time to think. He has said we have to talk to our daughter first. Those poor things have accepted. They're very pleased with your father's liberal ways.

Aghast, I asked: "Will I have to go into the room too on Thursday?"

-No my dear. Don't be childish. You and Nezhat will watch from behind the door. There's no need to go in. It's not a gathering for women.

I carried on setting the table without a word. A few minutes passed. My mother said: "Mahboub jan, do you not want to pay a visit to your sister Nezhat's house?"

-Why? Was there anything else?

-No my dear, there's nothing else. But I think she feels hurt by you. Go make it up to her."

-Hurt by me? Why?

-You were rather abrupt with her the other day. She said Mahboubeh has no sense of youngest and eldest as she was leaving.

I laughed ashamedly and said: "Oh, how tender-hearted! Well, khanoum jan, I'll make it up to her when I go to their house on Thursday."

-No, you have to go today. If you go on Thursday, she'll say you've come for your suitor, not for me."

I said impatiently: "Fine. I'll go today, after lunch."

It was an hour or two past midday when I put on my chador and picheh, stood outside my mother's room and asked: "Should I go now khanoum jan?"

-At this hour? Everyone's napping right now. Take a nap before you go.

-No khanoum jan. I want to go now, so I can return today. Otherwise, they'll keep me overnight. I've a million things to do.

-But, your agha jan has gone out in the carriage. He won't be back for another couple of hours.

-Why do I need a carriage? It's very nice outside! It's not far, I'll walk.

-Then, don't go alone. Take dayeh with you.

-Oh dear… khanoum jan, dear dayeh has led in her feet. We won't get there until the afternoon. There's no one on the streets right now. I'll go alone.

Sleepy and drained of energy by the pregnancy, mother said in a carefree manner: "How will you return? It might get dark."

-I'll return in my sister's carriage. If there's no carriage, I'll walk back with one of her people.

Mother was lackadaisical: "I really don't know. Do as you wish. But I hope to God your agha jan doesn't find out." She lied down and fell asleep.

I left the house. The spring sun was pleasantly warm. The passage was quiet. Not a soul to be seen anywhere. I knew all the shops in the bazaar were closed, and would remain closed for another hour or two. I was only ten steps away from the carpenter's shop. All I had to do was take a turn and I would see the shop – the first door in the bazaar. But the sound of the plane was silent. Suddenly, all the joy I had felt for seeing my sister subsided. I only wanted to see him, bent over the wood, working. But everywhere was quiet. I went round the turn. I was shocked as I took another two steps

-Hello little Miss.

He jumped down from the top of a load of lumber which had been stacked high at the back of the shop, wearing the same pair of black per caline slacks, with the white caftan hanging down to his knees.

His sleeves were rolled up to his elbows and his tunic button was open. I immediately remembered this verse: "Not one seamed a shirt, which did not end as a shroud."

He took three long steps and reached the middle of the shop. There he stood, leaning on the wooden table where he kept his tools. The same spot where he planed the wood and sawed the lumber. The same spot where he did work I knew nothing about. I only knew it was called carpentry.

His hair, which was hanging in locks on his forehead, reached below his ears at the back. As if he was a dervish. His arms were bare up to his elbows. His blue veins protruded from under his dark skin, running along his long, strong muscles. He repeated: "We said hello!"

I looked at both sides involuntarily. There was no one around. "Hello to you. You don't close at noon?"

-Not when I'm waiting.

-You were waiting?

-Yes.

-Who for?

-For you.

My heart sank again. It struggled again inside my chest. Thank God I had my picheh on and he could not see my scarlet face. I told myself is this what you wanted? You knew the answer to your question from the start and you still asked? Don't you understand how he has overstepped his mark? How long before you slap him in the mouth? Despite everything, I asked in a soft voice: "Did you want something?"

-Didn't you want a frame? Well, I made one for you.

He took a small frame from the table and held it at me. Thank God. So his intentions were good. He had just said hello because he was looking after his business.

My heart settled down somewhat. Even so, I will change my chador from tomorrow. He seems to have marked it. That is how he recognises me; from my black taffeta chador and its drownwork. I said: "But I didn't give you any measurements."

-Well, you asked for something, so I made you something. If it's not to your taste, throw it on the floor and smash it under your feet. I'll make you another one. I've been sitting here and waiting for over a week now."

He took two more steps and held the frame at me. I did not want my hand to come into contact with his, but it did. His thumb and index finger brushed on the back of my hand as he was giving me the frame. It was coarse and rough, and manly to my mind. The fragrance of wood spread around with his movements; how little I knew about the agreeable smell of wood until then. The chippings creaked under his feet like autumn leaves. Oh, how could the fragrance of wood be so exhilarating?! There was no one in the passageway. And what if there was? I was buying a frame for my sister, to make up with her. I didn't hide the frame under my chador. Let passersby see it. It was no larger than ten by twenty centimetres. I had no control over what I said next: "Doesn't your wife mind that you don't go home at noon?"

-I don't have a wife.

-And you have no one in mind?

-Yes, I do.

My heart sank again. Are you happy now girl? This man is getting married and then you, Basir ol-Molk's daughter, have reduced yourself to a ha'penny in front of him. Nevertheless, my incoercible tongue carried on:

-Well, felicitations; who is it?

I told myself, what business is it of yours girl? You daughter of nobility, what business is it of yours who the fiancée of the local carpenter's shop boy is?

He said: "My mother's maternal aunt's granddaughter."

I felt sorry for him at that moment. He uttered these words in such a downtrodden, humble way, as if he had surrendered to his own boundaries, to what had been destined for him. I said: "Congratulations, *inshallah*[53]. So, we'll be eating your wedding cake soon."

He dropped his head. His wild hair was hanging over his forehead again. He looked up: "My mother is the one to be congratulated. I don't want this marriage. I pray to God that you'll be eating my *halva*[54] soon."

I laughed: "Heaven forbid."

I went quiet. Enough is enough. How much longer can I hang around here? I asked: "How much do I owe you?"

-For what?

-For the frame.

With a hurt pride that left no room for discussion, he said: "I'm not such a cad."

-But…

- No buts, we're the local shopkeepers here for goodness sake[55].

He took two small pieces of wood from the worktop and said: "How much are two pieces of wood this size worth that you should mention money. Let it be a keepsake from me. Please accept it."

I said: "With pleasure. It's the owner that's worthy. Thank you."

Unwittingly, I lifted my picheh and gazed into his eyes. He stood there aghast and speechless like a statue, blushing to his ears, and murmured: "Oh! What a masterpiece painting of nature!"

Not that he wanted to murmur intentionally; no, a louder voice would not leave his throat. I turned around without saying goodbye, but did not run this time. I walked away slowly, with demure, decorous steps. The spring air was at its wildest. I knew he was looking at me. I could feel the beam of his eyes on my back. I was walking slowly, walking and rambling to myself. I was delirious; may God strike you dead girl. Damn your foolish head and silliness… Oh, how sweet was the smell of planed wood and I never knew it… May everyone mourn you in your prime, girl. See how you are disgracing yourself!! What on earth has turned out to be so desirable about this shop boy? His robust built? Or that rough forearm showing underneath his calico sleeve? If only you'd die. If only I would die and rest in peace… Who must die? Who must die for me to be free? For my deliverance? If I did not know until last night, I knew only too well now. I hoped Ata al-Dowleh's son would die so I could be free.

"Yes, I was so naïve; so juvenile and love-stricken beyond words. What you see here is that same frame."

Auntie took out the frame from among the other tidbits in the chest and handed it to Soudabeh. It was old and blackened by auntie's kisses, her tears, the passing of time. But, it seemed the love spell it had held could still burn Soudabeh's fingers; as if she could see the young carpenter's enamoured face and his wild, nomadic hair in its nooks and crannies if she glared at it long enough."

Thursday was a busy day at Nezhat's house. Nasir khan had invited some of his friends over for the afternoon; a gathering for men, and Nezhat wanted to do her best; as if she wanted to show off the present groom's splendour to the future groom. We had to hide behind the door and watch him from the gap.

I had drawn my sword to find fault with him and turn the whole thing into an *Uthman's shirt*[56] situation.

Oftentimes, a girl's suitor would turn out to be old. With my luck, this one was not! I knew he would be twenty-eight or nine at the most. Then, he must be fat or bold. I hope he is bold, self-centred, or spoiled senseless. The likelihood of the latter was the strongest. aybe he is bad-mannered and uncouth. Perhaps, because he is the son of Ata al-Dowleh with a princess as his mother, he had not bothered to study or acquire a special art. I prayed to God that nine out of his ten words would be nonsense. I knew my father would accept any of these excuses from me straight away, especially as he was a widower with a child. After all, my father was an understanding man. To him, a daughter was not junk to be gotten rid of.

I was shaking like a leaf. Nezhat was laughing: "What's the matter with you girl? It's not as if you're going in the room. If you shake like this, you'll hit the door and plummet into the middle of the room!"

-Oh, please don't scare me sister.

I could not stay still. I do not believe any bride in the world would have wished her groom to be an unsuitable misfit as much as I did. Perhaps, even God himself was surprised to see his rich, spoiled, ungrateful fifteen-year old servant pray to him every single minute there was no one around: "Dear God, please let him have a squint", "Dear God, I hope he's bold", "Dear God, please let him stutter." "I vow to light ten candles if he has a limp."

But, as the guests arrived at sunset and went into the parlour, all my vows were wasted. Not only did I sigh with grief as I slumped trembling behind the door, looking inside the room with a watchful eye, but Nezhat was also compelled to admire him. As my luck would have it, my suitor was a well-groomed, accomplished young man, well-dressed and looking very hand-some and genteel in those elegant European clothes. I ran into the back courtyard, turned my face to the sky and protested: "Thank you God!"

Had there been any other girl in my place, or even if I was the same girl as a month ago, if only I had a few brain cells left, I would not have hesitat-ed. I would have said yes straight away and prayed that he would not change his mind. But what could I do? He had arrived a month too late. I could sense my own downfall, that I was being lost. That I had been lost, that there was no escape. I could no longer avoid it.

Nezhat called me quietly: "Where did you go? Come and watch then!"

Nasir khan placed a chair at the top of the room, opposite the entrance door behind which we were standing, and forced the poor groom to sit there. He kept repeating: "Please sit here. No, no, it's more comfortable here. It makes no difference; there's no higher or lower place in the room for sitting…"

Nezhat clutched her face quietly and said: "God help us, that chair's un-steady. The groom's going to fall." And her large figure shook with a stifled laughter which had taken over her.

Quietly, I was laughing too. "For God's sake Nezhat, stop laughing. They'll see us."

In the midst of her fit of laughter, Nezhat's broken voice could be heard: "You just watch… Leave me alone!"

I began inspecting him from his new, shiny foreign shoes with gaiters, up to his knees. He was sitting sideways on the chair. His left elbow was resting on the arm of the chair and he had placed his left ankle on his right knee. His right arm was on his left ankle. He had, no doubt guessed the reason for tonight's gathering. But, he did not look abashed or embarrassed. Was he in love too? Had he also been dragged here by force? My eyes roamed up to his chest, vest, white shirt and gold pocket chain, to rest on his hands, powerless to rise up any further. I yearned to see them, to see what they looked like. Were they similar to the hands of Rahim the carpenter at the top of our alley, or not? Of course not. These hands were soft and white; they had not been worked. Not a great deal whiter though. His wrists and the back of his hands were covered with dark scant hair, working their way up to the joints and tip of his fingers. A pair of beautiful hands, fit to be sculpted; I did not find them masculine at all. These were young, pampered, self-assured hands belonging to the sort of people who were accustomed to winning. Hands that told me: "Hey look at me, look at my owner, hey you! You've already seen my mother and sister, dayeh, the servants, and that carriage. Don't you wish I would find you desirable? Are you not afraid of losing me?"

But I was no less than him. I would not give in to force. I had already found what I sought, so why be afraid? Why not look at his face? I moved my eyes up to gaze at his face as much as the gap in the door would permit. He was truly handsome. His eyes and eyebrows were flawless. Undoubtedly, he resembled his mother's clan. His lips were full, small and red; he had an aquiline nose and a pencil moustache; he spoke in a firm, commanding voice… But, but I kept telling myself, do you know what the hell is the matter with you then? What more could you wish for? No. He is wearing cologne. No, he didn't grab me. He is not pleasing at all. That's it; he is only good for his cousin… Nezhat's body rubbed against the door, moving it a little. Those dark eyes immediately turned towards us. He paused for a moment, as if staring straight into my eyes. Then, he smiled and turned to my sister's husband: "Is it windy outside?"

-No, why?

-Nothing, I just saw the door move…

My sister's husband turned to the door, giving it such a stern look that Nezhat and I took a step back impulsively, as he was saying: "No, it must be a cat."

Lightheartedly, the shazdeh's son said: "It seems to be a frisky cat."

Nezhat said: "Oh, he's so witty!"

The more his virtues became apparent, the more restless I became. I thought to myself he is being a songbird. He thinks I have found him suitable from behind the door and fallen in love with him head over heels. I mocked him in my heart and came away from the door with Nezhat. She carried on: "He's really cute, isn't he? Quite a charmer." I was indignant: He has leering eyes. He's such a flirt that he wants to devour you even from behind the door. The gentleman is also very pleased with himself!"

Nezhat said: "By God, you seem to be looking for excuses. What's wrong with him? It gives one great pleasure to look at him."

It was best to cut myself short for now.

The real spectacle only began after their departure. Once home, my mother sent dayeh jan to me: "Well, Mahboub jan, love, you know that your agha jan won't make the wrong choice for you. What shall I say now? Shall I say that you approve?"

-No

What else could I say to dayeh jan? She said laughingly: "Alright then, I'll put this down to your bashfulness. Don't be silly now. Tell me what to say to your khanoum jan?"

-Oh dayeh, how many times do I have to tell you? I said to say no."

Dayeh struck herself on the head with both hands: "Oh, God forbid girl, what do you mean to say no! Are you out of your mind? Your khanoum jan will have a breakdown."

-Is khanoum jan getting married?

Dayeh was taken aback; she looked at me wide-eyed, and said: "You've become so impertinent girl! I don't have the courage. Tell her yourself. What on earth is wrong with this young man?"

-Nothing, there's nothing wrong with him. May God keep him safe for his mother.

Dayeh kept going on: "Is he young or isn't he … Is he acceptable or isn't he. Masha 'Allah, he's as dazzling as the sun… Is he rich or isn't he."

-What? What is it dayeh khanoum? You're giving a speech?

-What's the matter Mahboubeh? My mother walked into the room cheerful and carefree.

-Nothing

Mother turned to dayeh jan: "Well, what does she say? What answer should we give them?"

Instead of dayeh, I spoke in a sedate tone: "Say Mahboubeh said no."

Mother's eyes enlarged as she was looking at dayeh; slowly, she turned towards me and said: "What? To say… What did you say…?"

-Tell them I said no.

-Have you lost your mind girl?

-No, I haven't lost my mind. I don't want this man.

With a motherly, advising tone of voice she said: "Don't turn your back on your future Mahboubeh. Why are you doing this?"

-I will not marry a man who has a child.

It was as if another person uttered those words in my place. I even surprised myself when I heard them coming out of my mouth. In those days, the presence of a small child – or as shazdeh khanoum put it - this elfin of a child - in the home of a grandmother like shazdeh khanoum and a grandfather such as Ata al-Dowleh was not challenging enough to stop a young girl from marrying such a charming suitor. But, I put my foot down and said no and no and no. As there was more commotion and more advice, I became more resolute to reject him. Finally, my father interfered with his usual equanimity: "Tell Mahboub it would be regrettable. She must think hard. But, if she does not agree, do not insist. She's right in all her immaturity. Living with the child of another woman is not easy, whether it is under the same roof or not. She has to decide. She will know. She mustn't say it was your fault and I told you so later on."

And the dust settled. I felt calm and breathed a sigh of relief.

It was spring time. There was a spring breeze in the air. There was the fragrance of Night Jasmines in the flowerpots. It was the season of bold, black-eyed yellow violets. The time for sycamore tree leaves brushing against one another in the breeze, and the time of *Ghamar*[57] singing. Ghamar's songs. Every night that agha jan was high-spirited, he played Ghamar's records on the gramophone; and thank goodness that Ghamar's records played on the gramophone nearly every night that spring for the joy of my mother's pregnancy, in the hope that the new baby might be a boy. I could not put down the book of Hafez. My father summoned me whenever he was happy: "Mahboub, read Hafez to me", "Mahboub, read Leili and Majnoun". And every time he came home feeling melancholic and discouraged, every time he was angry and furious, my mother said: "Mahboub jan, run quickly, read Hafez to your father. He's troubled. Do your best! He is very angry."

In the days when my father had not yet repented from drinking alcohol, only my mother was allowed to take him his tray, with her own two hands. The tray had to be silver, the glass crystal, cut crystal no less, accompanied by a side dish of savoury minty yoghurt and cucumber eaten with dry bread, plus salt and pepper in their elliptical holders. All orderly and prissy. We had to leave the room; only mother could sit by my father.

-Don't you leave Nazanin jan. Don't go anywhere. Sit right here, next to me. Be mine just for one night in the year.

Later, when father was cheerful, when mother had cleared up the dishes and taken them away, we were allowed into the room. Then, my father would either read the newspaper, or ask me to read the poems of Nezami or Hafez.

-Mahboub jan, will you read to me?

A month earlier, I was not even aware which page I had opened or what I was reading. But, now I knew. I used a piece of paper to mark the page I wanted. Then I opened the book and read. My father would say: "Well, well, are you listening Nazanin? Well done." There would be laughter in my mother's eyes.

O heart, never be free of passion and spiritedness

Thus, thou shalt break free of being and nothingness

Should you see your beloved, be taken with her

Any idol you worship is nobler than selfishness

And then, he would say: "Now read the *shāhed*[58]. The shāhed is the main part."

Do not speak of love and ecstasy to the one with prudishness

Let him die unaware, in the pain of selfishness

Fall in love, for the world will end some day

The purpose of being remaining faceless

How well spoke that lover in the council of the magi

Why be with nonbelievers, if you do not worship their goddess

What elaborate preparations had been made for the baby! What garments! Everyone was waiting for the big day. My father kept saying: "Nazanin jan, don't go up and down the stairs too much." My aunt – the same one who wanted Khojasteh for her son - would say: "Nazanin jan, don't you do any lifting now!"

Dayeh jan would say: "Khanoum jan, don't bend up and down so much."

Nezhat, who was highly respected by both my father and mother for being the first born, would say: "Khanoum jan, will you send for me as soon as you go into labour?"

-What if it's in the middle of the night?

-That's alright. You have to send for me whatever time it is.

My mother would say: "May God strike me dead, I will die of shame in front of Nasir khan, at my age…"

When my sister insisted, mother would say: "Fine, fine, I'll send for you", and Nezhat knew she wouldn't, because she was embarrassed in front of her son-in-law.

It was an hour or two past noon when my mother went into labour. The carriage was immediately sent for the midwife. My younger sister Khojasteh and I, who were worried and flustered by my mother's cries, ran into the courtyard to greet the midwife. She was a pretty, clean, petite woman. She went into mother's room, while Khojasteh shouted every five minutes: "Has khanoum jan delivered yet?"

After a while, the midwife put her head outside the door: "It's of no use standing around here. It'll be a long while yet."

They brought hot water and delicate cloths; the carriage was sent for my mother's sister. Limping, Haj Ali went to fetch my paternal aunt. Mother did not want the presence of the latter at all. She did not want her to be there in case the fourth child was also a girl, but it was agha jan's orders. Agha jan who walked impatiently, sat in the goushvareh room momentarily, then got up from there and went into the panjdari. He paced up and down, asked for the hookah and did not smoke it when it was brought to him, and the whole thing was an extraordinary pandemonium orchestrated by my mother's cries.

No one thought of me. No one thought of Khojasteh. It was every man for himself. We were left to our own devices. I felt anxious for my mother's pain and agony for myself. I felt restless between two loves. What should I do? I am guilty. My mother is in pain and I am looking for a pretext to leave the house. To see him… for one moment, for an instant, just one hello.

Slowly, I made my way to the kitchen at the end of the garden. In that spot, the *Mahboubeh of the Night*[59] was in full bloom. I picked a stem heavy with flowers and returned to the room. I took my chador and called out: Dayeh jan, dayeh jan."

There was no sign of dayeh jan. I ran around looking for her: "Dayeh jan, dayeh jan." She came out of the sandoghkhaneh: "Don't worry love, it's still too early."

-I know it's still early. I'm going to the saghakhaneh.

She noticed that I was wearing my chador.

-Where are you going all by yourself love?

She was too flustered to be insistent or suspicious.

-I will return quickly. I'm going to light candles for my khanoum jan.

-Yes love, come back quick. It's almost sundown. It's not right for a girl to be out on the streets by herself.

-I'll be back this instant.

I waited for Khojasteh to go and wait outside my mother's room again. If she saw me, she would insist on stringing along. Gently, I came out of the sandoghkhaneh and ran into the room; I picked up the stem and hid it under my chador. I was fearful the scent of the flowers would give me away. Mercifully, everyone was too busy and preoccupied to pay any attention to me. I ran into the alley. Once outside, I slowed my pace. The slower I walked, the faster my heart beat. By the time I reached the turn of the passage, there was no air left to breathe. Or there was, but it was too thick to sink into my lungs. It was as if the whole of Tehran could smell the flowers hidden underneath my chador; as if the entire bazaar was watching me. First alley, second alley, I turned into the third alley. The rustle of the saw. He was sawing a piece of lumber in half. e was not aware of my presence at all. I stood by the shop door. I lifted my left foot a little and bent down, as if I was adjusting my shoe. I was holding the flowers in my right hand and resting my hand on the shop doorframe, as if holding on to stop myself from falling. The flowers could not be seen from the outside. Only he could see them from inside the shop. At last, he looked up to see who was blocking the shop entrance, or perhaps he knew only too well who it was.

He said: "Salam."

I turned towards him as I was fidgeting with the heel of my shoe and said: "Salam."

I cannot be sure how I still managed to breathe. He saw the flowers in my hand. I waited for a man who was passing by to go away and disappear at the top of the passage. I let go of the flowers and began walking. Two min

Gheymeh[65] stew was cooked in the kitchen at the end of the garden. My father had made a solemn vow to make a charitable offering of gheymeh and saffron rice once a year as an oblation in honour of his departed parents. That year, in the jubilation of his son's birth, he was offering it again. Rows of crowds lined up for two days behind a small door opening into the alley at the bottom of our garden. They brought their bowls and gave them to Haj Ali, who would hand them to dadeh khanoum to fill up with rice and a ladle of gheymeh stew full of oil and spices. She would hand it back to Haj Ali with half a *sangak*[66] flatbread to return to its owner. There were masses of people outside the door. They would fight and outwit one another to get a second serving. Don't ask - it was like Judgement Day. My sister Khojasteh stood and watched.

-Mahboub, let's go and watch.

-I don't want to come; you go.

-Why not? It's worth watching.

-I don't feel like it. I want to go light some candles.

-Again! How many more times do you want to go light candles? This is the third time you're doing it for khanoum jan.

-It's none of your business. It's not for khanoum jan's health, it's for our brother… Anyway, this is only the second time.

-It has nothing to do with me. You can go if you want, or you can stay.

She ran to the end of the garden, and I wanted to go, so I went. It was nearly noontime and I had to return quickly. I had no justification for stopping by the shop again. My racing heart shook my entire body as I turned into the alley. He was standing outside the shop. I paused for a second. What if he stopped me? It would bring shame on me in front of the locals. But he did not. He turned around and went back into the shop as soon as he saw me. In the blink of an eye I saw him drop something. It happened so quickly that only I saw it. But, I felt the entire bazaar was eyes and staring at it - a piece of white paper. I approached slowly and placed my right foot on it as I was walking. A fire reached my heart from the sole of my foot. I had a coin in my hand. I dropped it to the floor and bent down to pick it up. I picked it up together with the piece of paper. I could barely see. I saw nothing except those imaginary eyes that were staring at me and screaming what did you pick up? What did you pick up? When I returned home, I did not have the courage to look into anyone's eyes. Our life was so busy in those days. At home, my mother had brought a son into the world; outside the house, Iran had thrown herself into the arms of Reza Khan, and I dreamt of a carpenter's shop boy. Iran had been more successful than I, much sooner and much easier. It was as if the whole world was turning upside down.

All the hither and thither of the various ceremonies, the sixth night, the circumcision day, taking a bath, was a tale in itself, an eyeful to be watched. The night the *azan*[67] was to be read into the baby's ear, the mullah came. Following the serving of sweets and sherbet, my father handed him the baby in his swaddling-clothes by observing all the customs and covenants. The mullah read the azan in his right ear and the *eghameh*[68] in his left ear. His religious name was *Mehdi*[69], because my father had waited for him for so long; but we called him Manouchehr. His name and date of birth were inscribed inside the cover of the Koran[70] that same night.

But, I was oblivious to all of this. I was dizzy, mad. I was only too happy that no one was aware of me. May God bless you Manouchehr jan. The garden pond was covered with a low wooden bed for the hired musicians[71], dancers, and singers to perform on, and there was traditional music too. The whole family, all our uncles, aunts, their children and sons and daughters-in-law had been invited to dinner. It was a celebration of Manouchehr's birth and circumcision. My father had truly arranged for seven days and seven nights of festivities. Where should I go? Where could I read the letter? It had not crossed my mind until then whether he was literate or not! So he can read and write. Thank God for that. He has been to the *maktab*[72]. My entire body was shaking with fear, excitement, curiosity; where should I go? Dayeh stopped me and began complaining about Haj Ali's laziness; that he had nothing to do most days of the year, but just because he had served lunch that day and had to take care of mother's gathering that night, he had complained long enough to frustrate everyone, even though dadeh khanoum and another help had been assisting him since that morning. The routine of our lives had been completely upset. My father's happiness knew no bounds.

I breathed a sigh of relief when dayeh left. My entire body was shaking. Very slowly, I went into the sandoghkhaneh and closed the door. I put down my chador. If anyone comes, I will tell them that I am changing. But, no one came and I read that piece of paper. It was not addressed to anyone. On a square piece of paper, it was written with a very elegant handwriting:

I am losing my heart O lovers, O God

Alas, my secret I can no longer hide

Auntie took the paper from the chest and gave it to Soudabeh. It was truly a fine piece of handwriting. But, the passing of time had turned the paper old and yellowish; it smelled of sorrow. Suddenly, the contents of this old chest, which had seemed like a load of worthless odds and ends to Soudabeh when auntie had first opened it, took on meaning. They became important and displayed their true value. It seemed that a bleeding heart was still beating in this chest, despite the passage of time.

Auntie continued:

I am losing my heart O lovers, O God

Alas, my secret I can no longer hide

So, he is at the end of his tether too? He will not do anything to shame us, will he? So, he knows that I also… what shall I do? What have I done? What handwriting! So he is also a calligrapher. I can now tell my father that he is a calligrapher. But, what shall I do about the carpentry shop? And he is only a shop boy there… I will go and throw the piece of paper in his face and tell him you ought to be ashamed of yourself… you don't have the right to bother me anymore… you don't have the right to look at me from head to toe with such envy and desire anymore… you don't have the right to write love letters to me anymore… But, what if he says this letter was not meant for you? There is no name on it. It is not addressed to anyone. Perhaps it was not meant for me at all! Could he have someone else in mind? Why didn't I look around? Maybe another girl, another woman was walking behind me? Why did I belittle myself…? I will take the letter and throw it in his face.

Instead, I brought that worthless piece of crumpled paper to my lips and kissed it - I, the daughter of Basir ol-Molk. Shame on me! I wish I had broken a leg and not set foot in his shop. I will not go there anymore. Enough is enough.

I did not leave the house for a fortnight, and when I did, I went by coach. When we drove past his shop, I imagined his eyes devouring the sides of the coach, searching for me. He could not tell who was in the coach. Whether it was me, my sister, or dayeh khanoum carrying a message? Or perhaps, it was my father. In those days, my father was in such high spirits and carrying happiness to such extremes that every time he went out he ordered the hood of the coach to be closed. If I was in the coach, I opened my eyes wide from behind the picheh and looked through the coach window the best I could to see that long, wild, dishevelled hair hanging on his forehead, and those large, penetrating, disappointed eyes staring at the coach. As soon as I made the effort, the coach had already driven past that modest shop and taken me away from the bastion of my dreams.

Gradually, there was talk of a wedding date for my younger sister, Khojasteh, with my aunt insisting on her getting engaged to her son soonest. Mother wanted a couple of months of grace. Our cousin was restless. He wanted to marry Khojasteh and take her to Guilan[73], where they had many properties. My sister was not inclined to leave mother. She was still a child of only eleven, whereas our cousin enjoyed the calmness of Guilan, especially as his father had also been born in that green countryside and he had spent his childhood there. All his aunts, uncles and cousins also lived in that province.

My aunt kept asking: "When then? When will this son of mine know where he stands?"

Mother would answer: "But, *Abji*[74] jan, have patience, Mahboub is still at home."

-Well, suppose Mahboub doesn't want to get married. She may not like anyone. *Kings may come accompanied by their troops to ask for her hand, and she may say yes or she may say no*[75]. So, Khojasteh has to lose her chances and suffer because of Mahboubeh?"

Mother always calmed her down with poise and patience: "No abji, it's not like that. It might take time, but sooner or later, it will happen for sure. Everything will go according to plan in a few months inshallah. Let me recuperate first."

My brother was the centre of all attention. Mother began to gradually leave the house and take me with her. I welcomed the chance to accompany her. I wanted to get away from our house, our community, and that little shop; then, perhaps, the spell would break and I would be free. Maybe I would slowly get this longing out of my heart; the longing for him, his open collar and rolled up sleeves; that untidy hair full of locks and twists. Although going past that depleted, sooty shop was not without its pain, attractions and trials, the wound was healing. Little by little, I was able to turn my head away from it, control my heartbeat, turn to my mother unexpectedly and start talking nonsense. I was always amazed at how my irrational performance did not capture my mother's attention, nor did it lead to any reservations. Having betrayed my parents' trust made me feel guilt-ridden and even more determined to free my captive heart from its bond. But, it was not only my heart that yearned for him. It was every drop of my blood, every piece of me, every little cell. The only objector in my entire body was my destitute brain, unable to achieve its intentions hard as it tried. Nothing obeyed it. Even so, I still fought against myself, and no battle is more formidable than this one. I wanted to triumph. Nonetheless, another fate was in store for me. One day, while returning from my aunt's house, just as we approached Rahim's shop, just as I could not breathe and my heart was in my throat, mother turned to me laughingly, and said: "Your agha jan gave me some good news last night." As I was looking at her, bemused, she added: "You have a good suitor. Your uncle has asked for your hand for Mansour. He has told your agha jan let us sweeten our mouths too, now that all is sweetness and light for you."

Sitting on the coach seat, facing us with Manouchehr in her arms, dayeh giggled and said: "Well, well, congratulations love. Mansour is a very nice young man."

My mother said: Dayeh khanoum, be careful with the baby. Hold him tight; don't drop him."

-Oh, khanoum jan, it's not the first time I've held a baby. Did I drop the other three that I should drop this one…? As if I am butterfingered", and she sat there moping. Mother laughed. I was also brooding. Mother put it down to shyness. There were no excuses left for this one. As my dayeh jan said, he was my cousin, good looking, educated and rich – not as rich as Ata al-Dowleh's son, but not too far from it either – and he was unassuming. Although he was some ten years older than me, he was still only twenty-five. He had told his father that ever since Mahboubeh was born, I told myself she is going to be my wife. I have waited this long for her, and I will keep on waiting. She is the only one for me. I have wanted her ever since we were children. And yet, although I had seen him on numerous occasions with no inhibitions as cousins - and as the old saying goes the cousins' match is made in heaven - he had not once behaved in a manner whereby I would sense his feelings for me, at least partly. Perhaps, his family honour and integrity had helped him along the way. Maybe due to his exaggerated self-restraint and abnegation, or perhaps because he believed one-hundred percent that I was his, he saw no reason to be rash, or as our elders would say, undignified. In any case, my mother and dayeh jan believed this was due to his poise and honour. The more I delved into his past and his demeanour, the less I found fault. I had no more justifications. Any girl would have been envious of my blissful life and desirous of this marriage. Any girl but me; I was trapped.

When we reached home, I ran to the sandoghkhaneh again and took out that piece of paper from the bottom seam of the curtain hanging behind the bed clothes wrapper, where I had hidden it with great pain. The light green taffeta curtain was adorned entirely with patterns of flowers and birds, all hand-sewn with sequins. But now, hanging in the sandoghkhaneh, old and unused, half obscured behind the bedding, it was a safe hiding place that dayeh, my sister and mother would never discover.

I am losing my heart O lovers, O God
Alas, my secret I can no longer hide

I put that piece of paper to my lips again. An old wound which was healing had opened up once more with Mansour's proposal of marriage. As hard as I searched my soul, this one had no disadvantages. What pretext could I find? Dear God, this too was my misfortune! Outside the sandoghkhaneh, my father was sitting in the adjoining room, reading Nezami's 'Leili and Majnoun'. Little by little, the sun was working its way towards the summer heat and spring was coming to an end. Manouchehr was already two or three months old. The sun had so many different hues. In our house, it was content, bright and ceremonial, lighting up a room full of carpets, tulip lamps and vases from behind the windows adorned by richly coloured lavish curtains, pulled to the sides with tiebacks. It paraded the beauty of those heavy, red sofas and the shapely side tables. The pages of agha jan's book of poems took on a placid and romantic tone in its light and depicted a sense of happiness. But, when you turned at the end of the lane towards the carpentry at the top of the bazaar, the sun - hardly reaching that place - was rebellious and spirited. It was no more than a wild, passionate *Majnoun*[76], shining on the shop door of another Majnoun; a rebellious sun, inducing the shop boy to raise his head every single moment, glance at this ethereal glow, draw in the fragrance of the climbers hanging drunkenly over the wall of an esquire's garden to reach him, heave a sigh and return to the chores of sawing and planing, and hammer and nail.

I took out a piece of paper - a blank piece of paper - and scented it with a small drop of perfume. I cannot recall what perfume it was. Something foreign my mother had given me. It was expensive, saved only for the days of marriage proposals. I drew flowers on the edges of the paper and coloured them. I drew a ribbon, bow, and a nightingale. It must have taken a week or two. I carried on drawing and thinking about what I must do. Reason demanded that I stop. But, the wretched thing knew it had lost even before it had begun. It was aware of my helplessness. I wanted to listen to reason. I had a thousand logical arguments for myself. I vowed that I would not go back. But, it was like hammering a nail into a stone. I knew that I would go; that I would go to my peril headlong.

You cannot imagine what it was like for a fifteen-year old girl in those days; to fall in love was a sin in itself which could cause a blood bath; never mind writing letters; never mind turning down suitors. Falling in love? Falling in love with the carpenter's shop boy at the top of the passage? Woe betide! The daughter of Basir ol-Molk! Just the thought of it made the heart stop and the blood run cold. It was like water flowing uphill, as if blood poured down instead of rain. It was taking the bull by the horns, and I took it and I wrote. At last, I put down in writing the desire which weighed so heavily on my heart; it was the answer which had come to my mind the minute I had read his note, and I wanted to read it to him aloud:

'Tis to open my soul to you that I yearn for
'Tis to hear word of thy heart that I yearn for
'Tis but a raw desire for this open tale
To be kept from my rivals that I yearn for

I no longer recall what justifications I had for leaving the house. Dayeh's time was now taken up with Manouchehr. At times, I would go out with dadeh khanoum and send her back home under the pretext of having forgotten something; I knew it would take her quite a while to come back grumbling. At times, I went alone, using a thousand excuses. I left the house any which way I could. That evening, my father had a gentlemen's gathering close to sundown again; the entire household's time was taken up by him and also Manouchehr's colic. I left the house.

He had his back to the shop door, wearing his caftan and wraparound, ready to leave. The back of the wraparound had two or three pleats. I told myself if dayeh jan saw him she would say he is one of those beaus. This attire which was going out of style suited him so well. He was resting both hands on his waist, with thumbs tucked into the wraparound and slightly leaning backwards, as if to appease his back pain and fatigue. I stood there silently and watched him. I had come to complete my task. So, I was no longer worried about being shamed. I no longer looked left and right. Let the drum for our disgrace be beaten. I had made up my mind.

Perhaps his back felt pierced by my gaze, because he stood still in that posture, straightened his waist up slowly, and suddenly turned around. He forgot to say hello, as if he was mesmerised. He said slowly: "You came at last!"

I lifted my picheh and looked at him smiling.

-Do you know how long it's been?

At times he would say 'you', and at times he would be more formal. He was still shy with me. I felt I held the advantage over him. I said playfully: "I know."

-Do you want to drive me mad?

I said: "Why shouldn't you go mad when I have?" He looked at me in stupor. He could not believe that I was so forthright. He was speechless. said: "I didn't know you can read and write."

I had gained courage from his bewilderment, coyness and bashfulness. In my superiority, I revelled in addressing him informally. He said in a quiet voice: "I can."

-Where did you learn to write in such elegant handwriting?

-In *Tabriz*[77]. I lived there till I was twelve. My father was from that area. My mother is from the Caspian Sea area. We had a room in a mullah's house. He taught me to read and write in this good handwriting. I studied with him around six or seven years. We came to Tehran when my father passed away. I still practice my calligraphy when I find the time.

-Do you also read Hafez?

-No, but my mullah always gave me calligraphy samples from the poems of Hafez.

-You don't study anymore?

-I want to. I wanted to go to the *dar al-phonoun*[78].

I asked: "Why didn't you go?"

-As I said, when my father died, I had to earn a living and take care of my mother. In the meantime, I want to work and save money to go to military school.

I said: "Aha, that's very good. Although, it would be a pity to have your locks cut short." We went quiet again. I was happy. So he wanted to have a post. I wanted him even more as I imagined him in military uniform. I waited for the few people lingering close by to walk past. Then, I held out my hand and said: "This is for you."

Once again, he had that playful grin on his face. He looked at me with such dominant, laughing eyes, as if he could read all my thoughts.

-For me?

-Yes

He laughed and I could see his teeth.

-What is it?

-Take it; you'll see.

He moved forward swiftly and stood in front of me. We both gazed at one another. He had a penetrating look. Had it been any other time, I would have screamed. But now, I wanted it to last till the end of time. Yet, it last ed but a fleeting moment. He took the piece of paper from my hand and I started back home. This was the point of no return. I had burned all my bridges. I was restless until that evening, and sleepless until the break of day.

-Mahboub jan, your uncle and Mansour have been to see your agha jan to ask for your hand. What do you say?

I asked: "What did agha jan say?"

-He has said her mother and I would be very happy. What could be better. But, please allow me to ask my daughter's opinion as well.

-How strange that you should ask the daughter's opinion at last! The daughter says no.

My mother stood up: "Alright, alright, don't be silly; enough of the song and dance! Who do you propose to marry then? Do you know who Ata al-Dowleh's son, that you snubbed, married? The daughter of Abdol Ali Khan Sharif al-Tojjar. She has the beauty of the sun, and is very young, graceful and accomplished. Her father is in the money. Even so, despite all these virtues, her father was so excited when it came to setting the dowr, that he almost wanted to give money away and set a dowr for the groom instead of the bride in his haste…"

-Well, good for Ata al-Dowleh's son.

My mother replied begrudgingly: "And then, look at how you acted?! He has a child; the mother talked too much about her deceased daughter-in-law; I have to see the lad. Then you dragged the fellow to Nezhat's house and disregarded him by saying no. What is the meaning of this? I don't understand this behaviour!" And then, totally disregarding my rejection, mother continued as if relishing a sweet dream: "If only we could have your wedding and Khojasteh's on the same night."

I protested: "Khanoum jan!"

-Yes, it's better that way. We'll do the shopping for both of you at the same time, both alike. Two of everything for the dowry; similar rings, equal dowers. Yes, your uncle was correct; three joys in one year. A son and two grooms."

It was to no avail. I had to think of something else. My parents had made their decision. It was a serious matter this time. I had to tell them. But how? I did not have the courage. There would be pandemonium. But, perhaps later, when my father saw Rahim, his writing, and his congruity, to know that he wanted to become an officer, to see his looks – as I saw it – perhaps it would touch his heart. Maybe Agha jan will take pity on me. Perhaps he will marry me to him, bring him home and give him support until he enters the military; until he can stand on his own two feet and make ends meet. We can then buy a house for ourselves…

I was truly naïve. I was a dreamer. I did not know that my father's blue blood! would mix with the common blood of Rahim the carpenter boy, only if paper could be crossbred with fabric. Even thinking about it was sinful. Even the thought of it was madness.

I spent the next days and nights thinking. What shall I do? How can I bring the subject into the light of day? Who should I talk to? I could not find a solution. I could not find a confidant. The problem was bigger than my young mind could handle. I repented a thousand times a day and changed my mind again. But, a yearning filled my foolish heart as soon as I heard Mansour's name again. As if his name was directly connected to the young face sawing wood in the carpentry at the top of the passage.

At dinner time, my father chirpily filled his plate with saffron rice, *ghormeh-sabzi*[79] and *tah-dig*[80]. As he was drinking his glass of *douq*[81], he said: "My brother has invited us over".

My heart was in my mouth; I was red in the face. I lowered my head. My mother was also grinning from ear to ear. She discretely signalled towards me and asked: "Where?"

-The *Shemiran*[82] gardens. It augurs well. You can get some fresh air; my brother and Mansour and I can shoot partridges…"

Mother said laughingly: "Agha, you hunted your prey years ago[83]… Mahboubeh, why won't you have some rice?"

I was not hungry. I was weary of food. I was weary of life. I wanted to get up and run away. But where to? The thought of running away shook me to the core. Better face a danger once than be always in danger; die once, mourn once. I will tell them and get it over and done with.

I had been thinking all night. I stayed up so long that I saw the light of day shine through the coloured glass, leaving quaint patterns on the wall and carpet. I finally went to sleep and woke up later than usual in the morning. The aroma of fresh double hot sangak bread, cheese and butter, the samovar boiling, the clacking of *estekans*[84] and saucers being carried to the room facing the garden, dadeh khanoum's footsteps and her carefree conversation with my mother, and the sound of Manouchehr's cries woke me up.

My mother, dayeh jan, and dadeh khanoum were all sweetness and light preparing for the trip. My sister, Khojasteh, was very happy about spending a week in Shemiran; it was a world of its own up there. Especially when the gardens were the large, dense, woody gardens of our uncle and not agha jan's plot of land in *Qolhak*[85], resembling more an open farmland enclosing the fields in its green skirt for as far as the eye could see under the hot sun, sending us yields of tomatoes, cucumbers and aubergines. My father had recently planted half the land with fruit trees and intended to wall it in and start construction in it.

Our uncle's garden was an established orchard, with winding paths and a narrow brook running past the building. At the end of the garden, where the brook flowed in, it was like a roaring river. The serene gardens were full of fruit trees. The smell of walnut trees filled the air. When in bloom, the endless rows of almond trees and the buzzing of honey bees were truly otherworldly. And then, outside the gardens, further out in the valleys of the Alborz Mountains, there was partridge shooting.

I washed up. The pond water was clear and clean thanks to the qanat which flowed under our house. The weather was warm now and the windows were left open in the mornings. Sitting by the breakfast spread, listening to the boiling samovar and watching the pond and plants and flowers had a world of its own. After breakfast, I wanted to leave the house under the pretext of visiting my aunt; but, she turned up on our doorstep. After exchanging greetings, she proceeded to sit next to my mother and cuddle Manouchehr, uttering terms of endearment. Then, it was Khojasteh's turn as she walked into the room. When she finished her cuddling, she turned to my mother and said: "Nazanin jan, what's the fate of my poor son then? How much longer can he wait! I have come here today to make a final decision."

My mother answered with composure: "Abji, there's no decision to be made. As I said from the start, agha says Khojasteh cannot marry while

Mahboubeh is still at home[86]."

-I'm not saying to marry them; let's just have a small betrothal to be sure that the girl is ours.

Khojasteh left the room shyly. My mother said: "But abji, why are you rushing? Are we marrying a widow that we should have a small gathering? We said from the start, the girl's yours. But she's still only eleven. She's still wet behind the ears."

-This is one of those talks Nazanin. I myself was nine when I married. Now you're saying that Khojasteh is a child? No my dear, you're making excuses."

My mother said: "Oh abji, what are you saying? What excuses? I swear on your head that I'm also very happy about this union. Hamid is like my own son. Thank God, he has no faults that we should want to make excuses. If this is how you feel, alright then, I will talk to her father again and let you know."

My aunt had asked for Khojasteh's betrothal a number of times now, and my parents postponed a decision because I had not married yet, because Hamid wanted to take his wife to Guilan and live there, and because my mother did not have the heart to be away from her children.

When my aunt left, I made my decision. I got up and put on my chador and chaghchour to go to my sister's. Mother was busy with Manouchehr and her daily housework. She asked: "Are you going alone?"

-Who should I go with then! Dayeh is busy with Manouchehr and dadeh khanoum's foot aches. The weather's nice. I want to walk today.

-Will you come home tonight?

-Yes, I'll be back. Abji Nezhat will surely send someone with me. She won't leave me stranded!

My mother said: "You're constantly at Nezhat's house. Are you tailing your-sister?"

I reached the top of the third lane in the blink of an eye. Now that I had made my decision, I was no longer worried about my reputation. But that day, his master - a feeble old man - was in the shop, talking to Rahim. Rahim recognised me as I hesitated outside the shop. He became distracted and troubled. I kept on walking, but could hear his voice trying to get rid of the master carpenter politely.

-Fine. Why don't you go now? I'll have it ready in a day or two and take it to their home myself...

Apparently, the old man was adamant and would not leave. He spoke in a low voice and I could not hear him. Rahim repeated: "Yes haji, you said. Fine. You go and I'll work faster. I'll take it to their home tomorrow afternoon, before the evening call to prayers..."

I walked past the saghakhaneh aimlessly. I took slow steps. I was too embarrassed to light more candles; to ask God for help; to pray that my parents would accept and seal our fate soonest. I dilly-dallied. The old man with a foot in the grave was still in the shop. I moved on, bought some borage from the herbalist and distracted myself by watching the fabrics in the drapery next door. At last, from the corner of my eye, I saw the old man leave the carpentry slowly, as if he had led in his feet. Calmly, he emptied his chibouk and hung it from his wraparound with great tranquillity. He pulled up the back of his cotton shoes and began dragging his feet along. I went towards the shop.

-He finally left?

With the same playful smile and crossed arms, he leaned on the table in the middle of the shop and said: "Salam."

-Salam.

Without a word, he went to the back of the shop. There, he picked up something from the side of a smoky lantern placed on a small niche carved in the heart of the cob wall and came towards me.

-This is for you.

-What is it?

I held out my hand. He put a lock of hair tied together with a piece of string in it. I lifted my picheh and smiled at him... He smiled back and displayed his beautiful white teeth again.

-It's a green leaf from a dervish[87].

I looked at him spellbound. I dragged my heels. I wanted to talk, but could not think of anything to say. As if realising it, he said unexpectedly: "I want to come and ask for your hand."

My heart sank: "It's not possible."

-Why?

-They want to marry me to my cousin.

The smile froze on his lips. "Oh!" He was silent. His head hung down as if in a painful sulk. His hair was hanging on his forehead. He was spreading the wood shavings around with the tip of his foot. He lifted his head and stared at the wall in front of him. I could only see his profile, so handsome with that long neck. The vein on his neck throbbed. In an aggressive tone he asked: "Do you want him too?"

-No

Silence fell. We were both staring at the floor, deep in thought. At last I said: "I'm going to my sister's house to let her know that I don't want my cousin."

-Well, she'll surely ask who it is that you do want.

-I'll say our local carpenter.

He laughed out loud, and such a sweet laughter it was too. He looked at me. I didn't avoid his look, although I blushed and my face felt the heat of shyness. He asked: "Really?"

-Yes

-So let me come and ask for your hand in marriage.

-No, you have to wait. This is not a good time. Wait. First, my sister has to talk to my parents. Then I'll let you know.

Surprised, he asked again: "Will you really marry me? Me, with just the shirt on my back?"

He looked at himself, and back at me again, as if he wanted to stress on having just the shirt on his back. Every one of his movements were desirable. He had placed his right hand on the table. My gaze lingered on his long, hard muscles. I said: "Yes."

There was laughter in his eyes. He shook his head as a sign of regret and sorrow: "Wouldn't it be a waste? You're too good for me."

I asked: "Why? What's the matter with you?"

-The matter is that I have fallen in love empty-handed.

I laughed and said: "That's the only good thing about it." And I started walking towards my sister's house. On my way there, I kept my eyes on the lock of his hair in my hand; with a lovely colour and a beautiful wave, it was the same hair which hung on his face.

Again, auntie took an envelope out of the chest and gave it to Soudabeh. It held a lock of hair stuck on to a white piece of paper. It was nothing unusual or exceptional in Soudabeh's eyes. Thick, coarse strands of hair were pressed on paper, with a soft wave worn out by the passage of time. Some of the strands had been broken in two and were falling apart. Auntie was looking at the strands of hair as if she had returned to the past. It seemed as if it had just been given to her. Soudabeh was also deeply moved like auntie, for auntie. Auntie continued:

I told my sister I had come to stay for lunch. Although she was a little surprised by my behaviour, she was glad. She asked after everyone as I played with her son, but my mind was elsewhere. At times, my answers were meaningless. For instance, if she asked how is Manouchehr, I would say he is with dayeh jan. Her son began crying in my arms and, staring at the carpet in front of me, I gently tapped him on the back without really trying to calm him down. As my sister lacked milk to breastfeed him, a young dayeh breastfed her child. He was a year and a half old and still on breast milk. My sister took the child from me, pondering, and gave him to the dayeh to take away and feed. Then, she came and sat beside me, asking:

-So, what's new?

-We're going to uncle's Shemiran gardens for a week.

My sister asked: "Agha jan wants to shoot partridges again?"

-No, they want to talk about me and Mansour this time.

My sister was all smiles: "You wicked little thing, I knew you were preoccupied with something. So, all this distraction's not for nothing. Well, well, congratulations."

She sat closer to me, excited, and said: "Tell me everything. Has Mansour asked you to marry him? What did he say? Mansour's a lovely young man you know…"

I got up, went to the window and leaned on it: "May God protect him for his mother."

-Never mind Eftekhar ol-Molouk. Mansour's not like her at all. He's nothing like that. You can't tell he's the son of that mother. Don't worry; uncle knows how to deal with her. Now tell me, what did Mansour say?

Eftekhar ol-Molouk, my uncle's wife, was an unmannerly, jealous mischief-maker. Fortunately, none of her children had inherited her traits.

Apart from his governance and complete authority over the upbringing of his children, my uncle's calm demeanour, his correct upbringing and wisdom had had their effects on his children, among whom Mansour was the most composed and sincere one, and at the same time the most serious one, commanding utmost respect and kindness in the family. My father, who did not have a son until recently, especially loved him like his own son. Mansour also felt a special affection and respect for my father.

I said: "I'm not interested, but they won't leave me alone. According to uncle, Mansour says from the time I was an infant and he played games with me when he was ten years old, he wanted to marry me when I grew up. And now, he says I'm a grown up, rational person…"

My sister laughed out loud: "What about you Mahboubeh…? How long have you been interested in him?"

With hurt feelings, I replied coldly: "Me? It has nothing to do with me. It's a done deal as far as they're concerned. First, it was Ata al-Dowleh's son, and now agha Mansour. I have never wanted Mansour."

Naughtily, she lifted an eyebrow in amazement, and asked with a smile: "So, who do you want?" And began smoking the hookah brought in by her servant at that moment. I stared at her chubby hand holding on tight to the silver mouthpiece. She looked so carefree sitting on the cushion, smoking. I waited for the servant to leave the room, go down the courtyard steps, and disappear into the kitchen on the lefthand side of the andarouni courtyard.

Slowly, I walked away from the window. I looked towards the door and the curtain hanging on its frame, covered in hand-sewn sequins and pulled back to the sides with two wide fringed holdbacks; I looked around me at the stucco niches carved in the wall and decorated with *termeh*[88], and the bright tulip shades and oil lamps with clear or coloured glass shades waiting to light up the night. The round table in a corner of the room was surrounded by four walnut chairs. All around the room was decorated with carpet floor cushions and pearl-embroidered backrests. Two large Persian carpets with red backgrounds covered the entire floor. These were all part of my sister's dowry. Without a doubt, Nezhat was a happy woman, like my mother. I knew her husband loved her; he was in love with this young, plump, perky, jovial woman; an adroit leader with a sense of humour. I also knew that he spoiled Nezhat. She always got her own way. If she said 'die', Nasir khan would die. On the other hand, Nezhat was also shrewd and wise. She, too, loved her husband and knew when to be coquettish and how far to go. She knew everything had its limits. I often asked myself what kind of love is this? Is it like my love? If so, Nezhat was a lucky one. She has fallen in love with the right person. She had found a suitable man. I moved forward slowly. I was wearing one of the dresses my aunt's seamstress had made for me. I remember it was a pink taffeta dress. I had white socks on. The same ones that came from Russia and khanoum jan always bought for me and Khojasteh. I had glued a lock of my hair on my forehead with the help of tragacanth gel, just like the tail of a scorpion. My sister looked up at me full of admiration. But I was too sad to smile. I was going to sting, like a scorpion. I kneeled down next to my sister. I was playing with the belt of my dress; a wide belt also made from taffeta fabric, but in white. She smiled with kindness and asked: "Mahboub jan, why won't you drink your sherbet?"

-I don't want any abji.

-Whyever not? You are such a low-budget bride!

-Please don't talk like this abji. I don't like it.

She laughed and asked: "Why not? Are you shy? I knew you didn't turn down Ata al-Dowleh's son for nothing!! You had fallen for someone else. You were distracted."

I was silent. I had fallen for someone. My whole body was shaking. I was frozen. I was glad that my brother-in law was looking after his business with his farmers in the birouni area. I kept looking right and left, in case one of the servants came in. I leaned over and took the glass of sherbet placed next to my sister who was leaning back on the cushions. My mouth was dry. I tasted some of the sherbet, but it was pointless. The glass fell and the sherbet spilled as I was putting it down. My sister said: "Oh my, oh my, everything is sticky now. Zinat… Zinat…" She was calling her servant to clean the carpet. Hurriedly, I put my hand on her knee: "For goodness' sake, don't call anyone abji. I'll clean it myself."

I looked around for an old piece of cloth. Finally, having forgotten the spilled sherbet on the carpet, my sister looked at me with her mouth wide open, and said: "What's the matter with you Mahboubeh! You don't seem to be yourself. You're so distracted and scared. Is something bothering you?"

I was breathless. The words were stuck in my throat, suffocating me. I put my icy cold hand on her warm hand: "Abji, promise you won't kick up a fuss if I tell you something! Swear on agha jan's head you won't make a scene!" My sister took my icy hand and said: "Why're you so cold Mahboubeh? What's the matter?" Gradually, she became alarmed. She continued in a startled tone: "Tell me, tell me what has happened. Don't be afraid. Talk. Have you fallen in love?"

Her astuteness amased me. Even so, it was as if she herself could not believe what she had just said. She had only used that sentence to accentuate my disorientation and confusion. I lowered my head and said: "Yes abji, I'm in love." And without wanting to, my chin suddenly quivered and tears filled my eyes.

My sister looked at me, agape. She blinked a few times. Perhaps she was trying to wake up. Then, slowly, like someone speaking in a semiconscious state, she asked: "In love with Mansour?"

-No

It took her a moment to grasp the meaning of what I had just said. It was her turn to glance at the door in a state of terror. She lowered her voice even more. Her right hand was still clutching the hose of the hookah. She hit herself on the head with her left hand, leaned towards me and said: "May God strike me dead Mahboubeh, really?" I kept silent. A teardrop fell from my eye. "Tell me what on earth has just struck me, who are you in love with?" And, as she searched in her mind for all the young men I may have encountered in my enclosed life, she named them one by one: "Maybe you're in love with Shazdeh khanoum's son, the same Ata al-Dowleh's son you turned down. The same one whose aunt, Tahereh khanoum, you said…"

-No abji

"Who then, who?" She was staring at the floor, deep in thought, shaking her head from side to side. The coal on the hookah had gone cold and turned to ash, but she was still pressing the mouthpiece in her hand. "Our dear cousin, auntie's son? Oh, maybe you're interested in our maternal cousin? The one asking for Khojasteh's hand!

I was restless: "No abji, it's none of these."

-Who then? May God strike me dead! Who is it then, Mahboub? I hope he's not a family man. Is he allowed into the andarouni? Is he a relative? Where have you seen him?

"No, he's not family abji…", and I began to sob.

-No? Who is it then? Does he want you too? Have you made any promises, any plans?

I could not hold back my tears: "Yes dear Nezhat, he wants me too." Once again, she hit herself on the head and stared at me. I said: "Please don't get upset Nezhat, because… because… he's not of a very good lineage."

"He's not? Who is it then?" Now, it was her hand that was shaking. She let go of the hookah and clutched her head with both hands: "Is it Kazem khan, the son of Haj Nasrollah, eh? The same chubby, funny one?"

Kazem was the seventeen or eighteen year old son of Haj Nasrollah, my father's childhood friend. Every now and then, he came into the andarouni with his father to visit my father. He had a charismatic, appealing look; his father had told mine that, despite being too overweight, women still died for him. They say he is cute. He had said maybe the rascal has snake charms[89]. We would often laugh at the compliments the father paid to his son. Haj Nasrollah did not possess many riches, but he was a hard-working, honest man who had a shop in the bazaar where he conducted his business. As the elders would say, *he earned his daily bread like a sparrow[90]*. A pale, painful smile came to my sister's lips. I said sobbing: "No abji. If only it was him. Haj Nasrollah is a respectable man."

I uttered these words unwillingly. My sister half sat up, half knelt: "So, are you saying this man's father is unrespectable...? Oh, may God strike me dead. You're killing me girl. Come on, tell me and get it over and done with!"

It was too late now. There was no going back. The words had left my mouth; the bow had left the arrow and could not return. I wished I had turned mute. I wished I had not said it. This woman was about to collapse. "It's nothing abji. Drop it."

As I was getting up, she grabbed my wrist firmly: "What do you mean drop it? Where're you going? Sit down here and tell me, have you thrown caution to the wind? Tell me who this person is?"

I sat down. Tears rolled down my face silently: "I can't tell you."

-Mahboubeh, you're killing me. My heart is going to stop beating any minute now. Stop the waterworks! Tell me who it is? Has he told you himself that he wants you?"

-Yes Abji.

My sister clutched her face: "So you've already talked together? You've made your plans?" I remained silent and stared at her: "Come on girl, tell me where you found him? ell me what has just struck me? Will you tell me or not?"

I will tell. *Die once, cry once[91]*. So I said: "Fine, I will tell…" I stopped, and then continued slowly: "You know that carpentry at the top of our alley?"

My sister was holding and squeezing my wrist, half kneeling, half-sitting cross-legged, looking at me. She was all eyes and ears. The only movement

I saw in her entire body was the widening of her questioning eyes from fear. She could hardly make a sound: "Yes!!?"

-The shop boy who works there; his name is Rahim.

My heart quieted as I uttered his name. At last, I had shared this secret, this overburden, with another person. I had put the weight on someone else's shoulders. It was as if I was free; how I wanted Rahim.

My sister spoke as if in her sleep: "Who?" I looked into her eyes without further explanation. Little by little, the meaning of my words was sinking in. Desperately, she gasped for air. Her mouth opened and shut a few times, like the goldfish in the pond. Then, she said: "Oh, may God strike me dead. Have you lost your mind girl?"

-No dear Nezhat; I have not lost my mind. For pity's sake, tell my agha jan. Tell khanoum jan. I don't want anyone else…"

-Never in a million years! Do you want agha jan to collapse? Khanoum jan will surely die of grief. Her milk will dry up on the spot.

The task at hand no longer seemed difficult. I had overcome my fear. My sister clutched her face again. Her plumb, fleshy figure leaned forward as she struck her knee firmly with her left hand; she remained in that position for a moment. Then, she lifted her head, confused and mystified, as if she had not heard a word I had said; or as if she had misheard everything. It was as if she was in a different world. She asked: "Which carpentry are you talking about? You mean the one resembling a shoe mender's shop full of goblins? The one resembling a sooty hole at the turn of the alley? The same one which is dark inside and you can only hear a scraping noise coming from it?"

-Yes, the same one.

Puzzled, she carried on: "What were you doing there girl? How did you come to be in that place? How did you find this… this… character in that hole?"

She would not even say his name; or call him this young man, boy, or even person.

- I don't know what happened. This must be my fate.

-Come on, come on; shame on you. Even dayeh khanoum's son has a better job than him. At least, he has bought a shop in the bazaar. Are you not ashamed girl? Do you want to make yourself miserable? Make yourself the talk of the town? To tarnish agha jan's reputation? Tarnish everyone's reputation? You want to be the wife of a carpenter's shop boy?

I understood straight away that she was more worried about her own reputation in front of her husband and his family, rather than agha jan's reputation. She had every right; and yet, an intense rage suddenly shook my body. I was no longer afraid of this chubby sister who was only a couple of years older than me. Before she was married, we used to have fights once or twice a week and pull one another's hair. If it was not for dayeh or my khanoum jan, we would have torn each other to pieces. Of course, we always made up as quickly as we got into the fight. We were truly fond of one other. I always opened up to her, and she tried to help me in her childish world, as far as her wisdom allowed.

-Look Nezhat, one cannot help falling in love. There's nothing you can tell me that I don't already know. I've been thinking about this. He has told me he wants to join the army. This is good. With agha jan's help, he can find a position. For the love of God, tell my khanoum jan and agha jan to let me marry him. Otherwise, I'll take opium and kill myself.

I sounded so serious that she believed me straight away. I was sure that I would do it. Slowly, she said: "If agha jan finds out, he'll be the one to kill you first, even if you don't."

-Let him kill me. What the hell! I'll be free. I don't want Mansour. I don't want anyone else. I'd rather die. If you don't tell them, I will.

I started to get up. She took hold of my hand again. Her hand was the cold one now, like a piece of ice, and my hand was on fire.

-Sit down and let me concentrate girl. Stop this at once. Come off your high horse.

The more advice she gave me, the more obstinate I became. I was as stubborn as a mule. I only wanted him, only him. There was only one God, and only this one man. I said belligerently: "I came here to ask for your mediation, to intervene on my behalf. If you don't want to talk, then don't. What're you afraid of? They won't do anything to you! They're going to kill me? Never mind, let them. Don't worry! Nothing's come of it yet! It's not to your liking, I know. What's more, I'm not here for a sermon. I'll think of something else."

At last, my sister accepted with great reluctance. Lunch was served and my sister's husband came into the andarouni. I put on my white, flower-patterned chador[92] and sat there with my head down. The lunch spread was adorned with *albalou polo*[93], *kashk-e bademjan*[94], pickle, yoghurt, and douq. But I was not hungry. I had no appetire and just played around with my food. I thought to myself, how would this pleasant brother-in-law, who is joking and teasing with me now, react if he knew I had fallen in love with Rahim the carpenter boy? I was shaking. Although my sister did not feel any better, she was still trying to keep up appearances.

Her husband asked jokingly: "Mahboubeh khanoum, why aren't you eating anything? Are you trying to make a *haji*[95] out of your agha jan? You don't seem well!" He then turned to his wife: "Nezhat jan, you're not in good spirits either. What's the matter?"

My sister smiled pleasantly at his thirty-five year old husband and, sweet as honey, she said sadly: "It's nothing. Apparently, khanoum jan's feeling a little under the weather."

My brother-in law, who was passionately captivated by Nezhat's plumpness, pretended to be worried and blissfully told his seventeen-year old wife: "God forbid. What's the matter with her?"

-She has caught a little cold. It's nothing important. But I'm worried about Manouchehr jan. With your permission, we'll go there with Mahboubeh this afternoon. We'll also take Mahmoud's dayeh and the child. She might have to stay there for a day or two and breastfeed Manouchehr. Khanoum jan must not feed him when she's sick. If need be, I'll leave Mahmoud and his dayeh there for a few days, or bring Manouchehr back here with me."

-Of course, it's best if you bring your brother over.

I was amazed at my sister's ability to fabricate such lies on the spot. Her mind was ticking like a clock as she made excuses for me. Nezhat knew well that if mother became fretful, she must no longer breastfeed Manouchehr. Therefore, they had to find a dayeh who could feed him instead. This, in it self, would arouse suspicion; so, the best excuse was an illness and the use of her child's dayeh. My sister said: "You're right. We won't take dayeh and the child. They might catch khanoum jan's cold. I'll tell my own dayeh jan to bring Manouchehr over here. They can stay here together for a few nights."

I immediately understood that she saw fit to keep the house empty in case of possible arguments and escaping sounds. Nezhat had quickly and skillfully made and executed her plans.

Mother was surprised: "Nezhat jan, what's the matter? Why have you accompanied Mahboubeh?"

She was afraid there may have been an argument between Nezhat and her husband.

My sister laughed and said: "Khanoum jan, I'll go back if you're unhappy. You don't seem to want a guest!"

-Not at all love, you're most welcome. But why come now? Why did you leave straight after lunch? Why didn't you bring the baby?"

My sister gave mother a serious wink without dayeh noticing, and said: "Because I got worried when Mahboub jan said you had caught a cold. I came to see how you were. I didn't want the baby to catch it from you. Agha said not to bring the baby. You can send Manouchehr to our place with dayeh khanoum. Our coach is waiting outside. They can stay there for a day or two and come back when you're feeling better."

She winked at mother one more time. I saw my mother's hands were shaking. She had sensed this was a private matter, not for the ears of the help. Not having a private life was such a headache for the elite classes. Perhaps dayeh jan had her suspicions when she was swaddling Manouchehr, who was saturated with mother's milk and taking his afternoon nap, before taking him to my sister's coach, but did not really know what the matter was.

***

As soon as dayeh jan left, my mother and sister, who were forcing them selves to have tea and sweets, put down their tea glasses and stared at one another. My mother's bemused gaze was filled with questions. My sister had lent an ear to the sound of footsteps and coach wheels in the distance like a skilled Passion play director, to make sure the house was empty and quiet for the next stage of her plan. With a slightly angry tone of voice, mother asked sharply: "What's the matter Nezhat? What's all this nonsense? You well know there's nothing wrong with me."

My sister cut her short and told me: "Run along and find dadeh kha- noum." Dadeh khanoum appeared in less than two minutes.

-Dadeh khanoum, I have made a vow and want to light ten candles in *Shah Abdol Azim*[96]. I'm busy with the child. You go with Firouz khan and light these ten candles and put this gift of money in the mausoleum.

She put the money in dadeh khanoum's hand. "Use the rest to travel on the steam locomotive."

Dadeh khanoum looked at the money with avarice and said with flattery: "May your wish come true khanoum kouchik. May God bless you. May you always be in good health and humour." She paused for a moment, and then continued: "But, is agha not going anywhere tonight? Doesn't he need the coach?"

-No, agha's staying home tonight. I'll just say Firouz Khan's running an errand for me.

Dadeh khanoum was being crafty now: "I'm afraid it might get late by the time we get there and back. We might not be able to catch the steam lo- comotive... I must also visit my sister now that I'm going all the way there."

-That's alright. Spend the night at her place. But you must be back here first thing in the morning!..." As dadeh khanoum was about to leave cheer- fully, I caught up with her in my sad, shameful condition: "Take this dadeh khanoum. Light two candles for me and keep the rest."

I stuffed more money in her hand. She began her smooth talk: "No Mah- boub khanoum. Abji khanoum gave us enough money. We're going to Shah Abdol Azim anyway. We'll also light a couple of candles for you. It's no trouble!"

-Take it dadeh khanoum. I'll get upset if you don't.

-Thank you. May your wish come true.

Inside the room, my mother was clutching my sister's arm with both hands and waiting for dadeh khanoum and her husband to leave the andarouni courtyard. She was saying in a low, worried voice: "Oh, why won't they leave? They're dragging their feet. Oh, come on woman; she has lead in her feet! What's the matter Nezhat? I don't know which way to turn! Have you argued with your husband? Are you not talking to each other? Why did you send Manouchehr to your place? You're driving me mad…!"

Mother had tears in her eyes with worry, and my sister was consoling her: "Hold up khanoum jan. I swear to God there have been no arguments."

-What then? Why are you sending everyone away?"

Dadeh khanoum and her husband, Firouz, left. My sister watched them leave from the window, and said: "Sit down khanoum jan. You too Mahboubeh, you must also be present."

Mother turned towards me in astonishment and stared at me with a gaping mouth. I sat down slowly, crossed my legs and put my hands on my skirt, holding my head down. My heart was racing against my chest again and I felt white as a sheet.

My sister took my mother's arm: "Sit down khanoum jan. Sit down and let me tell you what's happened."

Abruptly, my mother pulled her arm out of her grip. With her habitual domination and authority, revealing her unbridled determination as a powerful mother once more, she said as she stood there: "Will you tell me what has happened or not? I'm talking to you Nezhat! Why're you so quiet? Talk!"

Nezhat was facing my mother. For a moment, she looked down at her fingers which were placed on the folds of her dress. Then, she looked up and gazed straight into my mother's eyes: "Khanoum jan, Mahboubeh doesn't want to wed Mansour."

I noticed her trembling voice.

Perplexed, khanoum jan looked at me and then glanced at Nezhat. She carried on in the same tense tone: "So? It was not necessary to empty the house for this. What's the matter with Mansour? The more I try, the less I find fault with him. Has he behaved in an untoward manner? Has he said something? Has anything happened? Why on earth doesn't she want to wed him?"

-She doesn't want him.

Little by little, mother seemed to be grasping the situation. But she still did not want to believe it: "She doesn't want Mansour? Alright, so she doesn't want Mansour; she doesn't want Ata al-Dowleh's son; so, who does she want then?"

-Khanoum jan, don't get upset now! The truth… the truth is, Mahboubeh has fallen in love…"

The room was as silent as the grave for a moment. Increasingly, my mother's eyes enlarged in anger and disbelief. She lifted one arm and put it on her hip in a slow movement. With a pale face the colour of milk, she turned towards me as I sat there with my head down: "Well, well! Congratulations. Fancy that! How dare she?!"

My sister took hold of her arm: "For the love of God khanoum jan, don't start shouting, don't cause any embarrassment to us."

-Cause any embarrassment to us? Me? Embarrass us? Embarrassment has already been brought on us. The young lady is in love now…? Who is this scoundrel that she wants…?"

She, too, began searching for a familiar young man in her mind; the son of a prince, a minister, or a lawyer; the son of a Khan ruler, an al-Dowleh or al-Molk title carrier…

The room was momentarily silent again. Then, at once, mother shrieked at my sister: "I'm talking to you girl! I asked who is this scoundrel she has fallen in love with?" She shouted at Nezhat as if she was the one to blame. As if she was the guilty one.

-Please don't get upset khanoum jan. You don't know him. I don't know him either…

This time my mother only asked: "Who?"

-That boy… That boy in the shop… That carpentry shop… He's the carpenter's shop boy at the top of the passage. She says his name is Rahim; Rahim the carpenter.

My mother's hand fell from her hip as she stood there looking at my sister. Even if her throat had been squeezed, her eyes would not have bulged in this startling manner. Suddenly, she plummeted on both knees without a word. The sound of her knees coming into contact with the carpet resounded in the room like a camel falling to its knees[97]. She hid her face in her hands. The blow was so hard that it had stripped her of her willpower. I was shaking; my sister was glaring at me and biting her lip. She asked softly: "Khanoum jan!! Khanoum jan, are you alright?!"

My mother lifted her head in utter desperation. It was as if the blood had been drained from her body. A painful, meek smile appeared on the corner of her lips and she looked tenderly at my sister: "Were you joking Nezhat jan?" But when she saw my sister's silence, she hid her face in her hands again, saying: "Ooh…!"

I felt sorry for my mother. My sister yelled: "Mahboubeh, run quickly to the cellar and bring some vinegar."

Mother said: "Vinegar? I hope it poisons me!"

I ran into the cellar and brought back a bowl of vinegar. My sister was talking to my mother. She was comforting her in a persuasive tone: "Well khanoum jan, she wants to marry him."

-How dare she? Over my dead body! Oh God, I'm ruined. How will I answer to agha? He'll say it's what you deserve for bringing her up like this!"

I held the vinegar under her nose. She hit it with the back of her hand. The bowl of vinegar flew and splattered in the middle of the room. My sister intervened: "What's this khanoum jan? Are you a child! Why don't you speak to agha jan first. No, on the other hand, I'll stay and talk to agha jan myself tonight."

Mother hit the back of one hand with the other: "May God strike me dead Nezhat. Have you no shame? Have you lost your mind to this wretched soul?" Then, she turned to me: "What I'm going to do to you will even make the birds in the sky feel sorry for you. You've gone and fallen in love now? In love with the carpenter's shop boy at the top of the passage no less! May you be struck down, you daughter of Basir ol-Molk. This is what I deserve for bringing you up like this!"

The sound of mother's cries filled the room.

My sister said: "Don't do this khanoum jan, don't do this. Your milk will dry up you know!" She put her arms around mother and kissed her.

-Let it dry up. It's best that my child doesn't have this bad, stressed milk. Thank you girl!! You've served us right… What shall I tell your father? Shall I tell him your daughter has become another *Leili*[98]? That she has fallen in love with the good for nothing local carpenter's shop boy? Am I to tell him you have to become the father-in-law of the carpenter's shop boy at the top of the passage? A starving pauper of a shop boy with just the shirt on his back!?"

Her voice gradually rose in anger. I am not sure how the rage in me suddenly boiled over and how I dared raise my voice at her. Perhaps, the emptiness of the house or the absence of my father gave me courage. I said: "So what if he's starving? Does everyone have to be filthy rich? He has a job. He's not a thief! Nezhat didn't tell you, so I'll tell you myself. He wants to join the military; he'll become an officer." I took a deep breath and continued: "To work is not shameful! Father himself reads Leili and Majnoun every night, and then you tell me…"

My mother threw her entire weight at me: "Lower those flagrant eyes, you disgraceful girl. Have you no shame? Are you not embarrassed?"

She took hold of my skirt. I pulled it out of her grip with all my might and ran. I heard her voice, yelling: "Pray that your agha jan doesn't come home tonight; otherwise, your remains will be carried out of this house."

I stood by the door and said crying: "So much the better; I'll be free."

-I spit in your shameless face!

Nezhat shouted at me: "That's enough Mahboubeh. Shut up and leave."

I ran out of the room and squatted in a corner of the porch. My unfortu nate sister was toing and froing between me and my mother all evening. On the one hand, she tried to convince me to hold my horses, and on the other, she lectured my mother.

-But Khanoum jan, is it only Mahboubeh who has fallen in love? A lot of people are attracted to one another; they marry and live happily ever after.

-Yes, they do fall in love, but not with the carpenter's shop boy at the top of the passage. Over my dead body!

My youngest sister, Khojasteh, had been watching us in total bewilderment the whole time.

Mother was yelling: "Did she not think about her father's reputation? Did she not think about her mother and sister's reputations? Did she not think about the reputation of this innocent child!..." And she pointed at Khojasteh.

Nezhat said: "Khanoum jan, Mahboubeh is right. He'll join the military in no time at all, to become somebody in his own right and hold his head high…"

My mother screamed: "Never in a million years. Mahboubeh will spit on her father's grave. She'll repent together with you. Do you suppose this idler is going to join the military? Before you know it, your own husband will either scorn you and throw you out or bring you a *havou*[99]. Every time you try to say something, he'll reproach you for what your sister has done. And what about this girl - this innocent Khojasteh- who will come for her then? Won't people say she's just like her sister? Their mother deserves to keep them both forever? Do you suppose anyone will ask after us ever again? That anyone will knock on our door again? People won't even allow their daughters to walk with Khojasteh, or hold a conversation with her. They won't even allow their children to associate with us, never mind ask for her hand in marriage for their sons. And they'll have every justification too. I wouldn't allow my daughter to come and go with such a shameless, barefaced girl either. Oh God, who can I turn to now?"

Gradually, mother tired out. She wrapped a chador around herself and squatted by the wall silently. I do not know if she was waiting for father's return in the evening, or whether she no longer had the strength to get up.

By now, Khojasteh who had been keeping me informed, was also squatting next to me. My eldest sister was by my mother's side.

Night was falling and the time was getting close for my father's return. My heart was in my throat. My mouth was dry. No amount of water Khojasteh brought for me did any good. My entire body was shaking. It was as if I was waiting for the executioner. My sisters helped each other in lighting the oil lamps. On Khojasteh's instructions, Haj Ali came out of the kitchen and swept and washed the paved courtyard area.

I could hear the sound of my mother's voice, lamenting to Khojasteh: "Dear girl, close the door and windows, I feel cold."

Khojasteh answered placidly, but with fear and caution: "In the middle of the summer khanoum jan? It is very hot!"

-I said to shut that door, so obey. I'm not well.

I heard the closing sound of the door and windows facing the porch. Behind the windows, inside the room, curtains[100] with white lace borders tied in the middle had been fitted to constrain the look of a *naamahram*[101] into the room. It was probable that my mother did not want the sound of my father's voice to go beyond the room and, perhaps, fall on the half-deaf ears of Haj Ali sitting in a corner of the kitchen at the end of the garden.

Now that dayeh jan and dadeh khanoum were gone, my sisters laid the dinner spread[102]. Again, there was douq and morello cherry sherbet, which my father liked so much and my mother did not like at all; again aubergine and walnut pickles, which my mother had prepared for the first time in the spring of that year, and which were not quite set and ready yet.

I heard my mother whimper helplessly to Nezhat: "People kept telling me not to make walnut pickle, that it could bring bad luck. I didn't listen. I laughed at them. I never believed such a thing would happen to me."

Nezhat gave a forced laugh in a hoarse voice: "Oh, what nonsense! You're repeating old wives' tales khanoum jan. Nothing has happened. You're just marrying off your daughter. I must say, she was getting past it too."

-Nezhat, have some shame. I won't allow this idle rogue to even carry Mahboubeh's coffin on his shoulders. She has made a faux pas with her head in the clouds and you're following up on it? I'll sort things out once and for all with her and your father tonight."

-For goodness' sake Khanoum jan, don't start as soon as agha jan gets in! Let him have a rest first, eat a bite, and then… Don't pour too much oil over the flames."

Mother sighed: "You don't need to lecture me."

At first, I heard my father's footsteps from the birouni. After a while, I heard his amazed tone of voice from the andarouni courtyard: "Where is khanoum? Where is everyone?"

Khojasteh came to me on the porch and began talking in a hushed, terrified voice: "Mahboubeh, come into the room for now so agha jan doesn't suspect anything. You can leave after dinner."

I sat glumly in a corner of the dinner spread. Father took off his shoes and walked into the room with his ebony cane which he used for style. Lights flashed in front of my eyes at the sight of the cane.

-How come Haj Ali opened the door? Where's Firouz? Oh, Nezhat, you are here too!

Hurriedly, Khojasteh said hello and ran to the bottom of the garden to bring the food that Haj Ali had dished out on my father's orders as soon as he had arrived.

Nezhat forced a smile and said: "Aren't you glad that I'm here agha jan?"

-Of course my dear, of course! You're most welcome. But at this time of night… Without your husband…?

Then, he looked around in amazement and asked my mother: "Aren't you well khanoum? You look very pale." As he was sitting down by the spread, he took off his coat and put it on a cushion. Mother answered: "Yes, I'm fine. I just have a slight headache. I may have caught a cold. Won't you have some pickle?"

My father helped himself to some *adas polo*[103]. He had barely eaten a couple of spoonfuls when he asked my mother: "Where's Manouchehr? I can't hear him."

Mother changed the subject: "Nezhat jan, why don't you help yourself to some sherbet?"

Father, who had suddenly found the setting unusual, turned to me: "Mahboubeh, what's the matter with you? Why are you sulking?" Then, worried, he asked in a relatively loud voice: "Khanoum, where's Manouchehr? What's the matter with everyone? Where's dayeh? Where are Firouz and his wife?" As he sensed our silence, his worries escalated. Perhaps, he was afraid to have lost Manouchehr in some way; a calamity which was likely to happen repeatedly in those days to newborns. This time, he asked with authority and concern: "Khanoum, I asked you where is Manouchehr?"

In a muted voice, as if coming from the bottom of a well, my mother answered: "At Nezhat's."

As per habit, I slowly shook the skirt of my dress; not that there were any crumbs on it, as I had hardly eaten anything. Just by force of habit. I got up quietly and left the room. Four pairs of eyes followed me with their own feelings and thoughts. My mother, who tried not to look at me, turned away with abhorrence. Straight away, my father's voice was heard: "What's going on in this house tonight?"

I ran to the corner room, but decided that staying there was of no use. I was too close to danger. Father would come looking for me in this room first, and then into the sandoghkhaneh, which had been my favourite hiding place since childhood. I held on to my chador with one hand and picked up my slippers with the other. I tiptoed back to the door and looked in from the gap. Father was standing over my mother's head, with his hands crossed behind his back. Mother pleaded: "For God's sake agha, please sit down so I can talk to you. I'm at a loss for words with you standing over my head."

Silently, my father took a couple of long steps to the end of the room and picked up the chair by the side table. He returned and put it down close to my mother, exactly facing her, and sat down. He crossed his arms on his chest. By now, he had opened up his sleeve buttons and rolled them up. A couple of his top shirt buttons were also open. The soles of his feet were almost touching as they rested on the floor with his socks on and his knees were kept apart, as if he wished to make space for my mother's figure.

"Alright, I'm sitting down. Go ahead now." His voice was authoritative.

Mother turned to Khojasteh: "Khojasteh, go to bed."

My father lifted one eyebrow in silent disbelief and looked at Khojasteh.

Khojasteh, whose head was hanging so low that only the parting of her hair could be seen, looked up and said: "Don't you want me to clear up the dishes?"

-It's not necessary. Nezhat and I will do it ourselves.

I stepped back as Khojasteh came out of the room. She closed the door behind her and looked at me with eyes wide open from fear; she bit her lip and said quietly: "Don't stay here. Go hide somewhere. Agha jan will tear you to pieces. Go hide."

As a sign of silence, I put my finger on my lips and gestured for her to go and sleep. My body was shaking and I could hardly see inside the room.

Father told my mother: "Well?!"

-I sent dayeh and Manouchehr to Nezhat's house so that…

Father interrupted her: "Doesn't this child need to be fed?"

-Yes, that's why I sent her to Nezhat's house. Mahmoud's dayeh can also feed Manouchehr. Firouz and dadeh khanoum were sent to Shah Abdol Azim by Nezhat as an excuse to light prayer candles. We wanted a quiet house."

-A quiet house? What for? To do what?

Mother kneeled down and put both hands on her knees: "I want to speak to you." Her voice was trembling.

-Regarding what matter?

-Mahboubeh

Mother lowered her head and continued: "She has told Nezhat she's not interested in her cousin."

-What does this mean? What is this? *She's making the cat sing and dance*[104]! First she said I have to see Ata al-Dowleh's son. When she saw him, she said she didn't want him because he was a widower with a child. Didn't she already know he had a wife and a child? And now, she doesn't want Mansour?"

-By God agha, this is exactly what I told her.

-What does she want then? How much longer is she going to sit at home? She's no longer a child! She's fifteen, sixteen years of age. She's still not sure what she wants?"

-Yes agha, she knows who she wants!

Father froze on the spot, as if a statue. A moment passed; he managed: "What did you say?"

-Agha, I beg you, on your ancestor's grave, don't kick up a fuss…

My father was a *seyyed*[105]. After a pause, mother continued with a voice that could hardly be heard: "She says… She says… To tell you the truth, she has someone in mind."

-She has someone in mind…? Who?

My father seemed like an executioner watching someone sentenced to death with great composure, whose head he was momentarily going to severe at his leisure. Thus, he gives her time. He was chewing the side of his moustache. Mother looked down.

-Well, what can I say agha…!

-I said who?

My father's voice became louder. My mother had been clever enough to close the door and windows.

-Agha, I'm afraid to say it. He's not from a well-known family.

My mother's voice faded into a whimper. It was so quiet you could hear a pin drop.

-Where has she seen him?

Nezhat was behind my father with her round figure and white skin, fiddling with her fingers. As she held her head down and drew circles around the flower patterns of the carpet with her fingers, in a voice that could hard ly be heard, mother said: "At the top of the passage." In a calm tone of voice, a calm before the storm and a voice that implicated the imminent firing of a cannonball, my father said: "Nazanin, I'm asking you nicely whom has she in mind?" He was so clearly reluctant to use my name.

-You won't get upset if I tell you? For the love of God…

-I asked who this person is.

-A carpenter's shop boy. The carpentry at the top of the passage. His name is Rahim.

Father continued to sit there like a motionless statue. Until that night, I had never seen the red colour of a person's lips suddenly turn to white. My father's lips were white. He kept staring at the opposite wall over my mother's head. There was a moment of stillness.

Puzzled and fearful, mother looked up to contemplate my father. His silence was more frightening than any yelling, screaming or quarreling. She said quietly: "Agha?!" As my father remained silent, she continued in a promising tone: "Agha, he wants to join the military. He won't remain a shop boy forever."

Still staring at the wall, my father began to speak in a deep, composed voice which was subdued, somber, and calm. It hardly left his throat, as if someone was squeezing it: "Where is she? Where is that girl?"

Mother took hold of his knees with both hands: "Agha, in the name of your ancestors, what do you want with her?"

-She's walking around the streets now? She's been let loose on the town and in the bazaars and doing as she pleases? Where is she? I said where is she?

My sister pleaded: "Agha jan, for God's sake, please forgive her. It was wrong of her. It was my fault; I should never have said anything to you. She's done something out of naivety …"

Father jumped up like a banger: "Out of naivety? Your mother had a two-year old child at her age. I have let her reins too loose. I will beat her black and blue under the lash until she perishes and forgets all about love."

My sister was whimpering: "Agha jan, what love? What're you saying?"

My mother said: "Agha, don't disgrace us. Our voices can be heard outside. *It is like spitting up in the air[106].*"

Father was screaming, as if he had lost control: "Disgrace? What could be more disgraceful than this? Do you mean to tell me that the servants, dayeh, wet-nurse, and all the rest don't already know? Do you suppose they're stupid? Even if they haven't found out by now, there's still time. Don't rejoice. *Our washtub will fall from the rooftop[107].* My sister was right to say don't give your daughters so much flying space. I said tell her to come over here right this instance! Where is this barefaced girl? She has to have her tresses cut[108]!"

My mother pressed her lips together when she heard what my aunt had said. My father was pacing up and down the room angrily. He held his hands behind his back as he paced up and down and my mother and sister followed him around the room petrified and pleading, getting in each other's way. Father was quietly and angrily waiting for me to be summoned. Mother said: "Agha, it's your own fault for continuously listening to Ghamar sing and reading the poems of Hafez and Leili and Majnoun. I could see that she was either listening to Ghamar's records lately or reading poetry. Well, this is the result... Is she the only girl who has ever fallen in love?"

My father stood facing my mother and pointing his finger at her: "No khanoum, one does not fall in love by reading poetry from Leili and Majnoun and Hafez, or listening to Ghamar. One falls in love first and then remembers these things, then gets Leili and Majnoun in the head and becomes sentimental. She's not the first girl who has fallen in love. But she's the first one to have found a drifter, with only the sky as his blanket[109]... He will become an officer! Ha, ha, ha!! I'll bet. I'm not a child khanoum. Tell her to come right now... Alright then, if you won't call her I'll go myself."

Father rushed to the door. I jumped back. I could hear my mother say: "What're you going to do agha? You're angry now. You might do something you'll regret!"

-Move back khanoum. Get out of my way!

-For Manouchehr's sake agha, don't upset yourself. On Manouchehr's life, have pity.

-On Manouchehr's life? Did this girl let me taste the sweetness of Manouchehr's existence? Did she let me be happy just for a spell after all these years? She has pumped the venom of snakes in my veins. A tramp with just the shirt on his back; a gigolot. She has brought disgrace on me…"

My sister pleaded: "Agha jan, your dinner is getting cold. Please eat first. It's all my fault. What have I done?!

I heard a terrifying noise. I knew father had kicked the rice dish, which in turn had hit the wall. My mother and sister screamed simultaneously. Terrified, I ran towards the door leading to the courtyard, rushed down the stairs into the courtyard and ran to the bottom of the garden. I was holding my shoes in my hands so father wouldn't hear my footsteps. I heard the sound of the doublet doors slamming and the screams of my father who sounded like a roaring lion foaming at the mouth: "I said where the hell are you girl?" One by one, he went through the rooms, sandoghkhaneh, and *hozekhaneh*[110] searching for me.

I dashed to the end of the garden and stopped by the kitchen door to put on my chador and shoes; I went up the couple of broken brick steps with sangfroid and stepped into the black, sooty kitchen. A lantern hung on the kitchen wall. Three large hearths had been built in the wall opposite. The floor bricks on both sides of each one of the hearths had been raised to form a base for the cauldrons – all black from the fire and smoke. An arched space in one corner, resembling a catacomb, was stacked with firewood and extended into the kitchen without a door. As children, we were terrified to set foot in the kitchen for fear of jinns. Every crackling sound from the stack of wood was a sign that jinns existed, and a confirmation of my dayeh jan's tales told under the korsi. The balls of charcoal had been left on the roof of the kitchen to dry for the winter korsi. A low, wooden door in the wall to the left side opened straight ahead into a corridor three or four metres long and led to the opening of the ab-anbar which reached down to the pashir by going down a few steps. After every meal, poor Haj Ali had to take the dishes down to this place and wash them with a mixture of Soaproot, ash and brick dust, bring them back to the kitchen and store them in a special clean storage space kept for this purpose. The storeroom had one stone workbench. Smaller utensils, trays, skewers, bowls and pots were placed on top of the workbench. Underneath it, there was room for the larger copper cauldrons, braziers, copper strainers and the like. I preferred to go into the kitchen, because there was a light burning in there. Haj Ali, who had just finished eating his meal with his greasy hands, looked up at me surprised, and stood up with great pain: "Was there anything you wanted khanoum kouchik?"

Once again, I heard my father yelling. The mansion lights at the other end of the garden were dimly visible from inside the kitchen. I was just becoming aware of the beauty of the courtyard area, the garden, the flowerbeds, the stained glass windows, and the glow of the light on the lace door curtains; and especially where the light reflected on the pond which stood at the centre of the garden. The outstanding rouge of the geraniums was magnificent. Never before had I admired the work of the old gardener and his son, who also had the task of changing the pond water, in such great and marvellous detail, and never before had I wished so hard to get away from this environment and take refuge in that sooty carpentry.

Slowly, I turned towards Haj Ali. I was hoping his bad hearing and obliviousness would prevent him from hearing my father's yelling. In a loud voice, I said: "I… I… Khanoum jan wants the hookah. Do you have lit charcoal ready?"

I hoped my voice would not carry to the other end of the garden. He looked at me surprised: "Where's the hookah bowl then?"

-I will fetch it right now.

Wearily and lazily, Haj Ali said: "But, I wanted to take the dishes to the pashir and wash them. I'll take them and come back while you are fetching the bowl."

-You don't need to come back. Take the dishes. I'll get the charcoal myself.

He looked at me and pushed his lower lip forward in surprise. Puzzled, he picked up the dishes. He was not sure whether to take the lantern or not! If he did, I would be left in the dark. He was going to leave without it. I said: "No, no, I don't need light. Take the lantern."

Surprised, the old man picked up the lantern and staggered towards the pashir. I knew he would not be back for another two hours. I wrapped the chador around myself and sat on the edge of the kitchen step in a darkness that I welcomed. Some time passed as I carried on looking at the building.

The minor activities happening inside, and only significant to me, reached a crescendo and subsided. I was oblivious as to how long it took. An hour? Two hours? I only know that my back was hurting from crouching on the step. I dared not move. It was as if I was dreaming. It was a nightmare. I died a thousand deaths until the lights went out one by one. I heard Haj Ali's footsteps staggering up the ab-anbar steps with the lantern. I stood up tired. My whole body ached, as if I had been beaten up. Haj Ali saw me. He saw me and glanced at me with a surprised and suspicious look in his eyes. Then, he looked towards the building and limped into the kitchen.

I tiptoed back to the main building, as if I was going to the slaughter-house, to the abattoir. I had resigned my life. Fortunately, everyone was seemingly asleep, or pretended to be in order to quench their anger and find a reason to evade killing this defiant and insubordinate girl.

Gently, I opened the door of the room where I knew Nezhat was sleeping and went in quietly. My sister sat up straight away as I closed the door behind me. The moonlight embraced the room and played on its colourful and lavish objects. I lied down beside her with a drained body and the chador still wrapped around me; she lay on her back, staring at the ceiling. I rested my head on my arm at a right angle, close to her ear.

-What happened?

She had pulled the sheet up to and over her chin and placed her arm on her forehead, so that I could only see her sleeve and her two large eyes.

-What did you expect to happen? See the evil you've done? Agha jan has forbidden that you leave the house. If it's absolutely necessary, you can only go by coach and only with khanoum jan or dadeh, and only with khanoum jan's permission.

Helplessly, I muttered: "Oh…"

-Agha jan said he'll send a message to uncle that you'll be going to his Shemiran gardens in a few days. They're taking you there to make arrangements for your marriage to Mansour.

Again, I said: "Oh!" and lay on my back on the carpet, next to my sister. I was submerged in my own thoughts. I could not see anyone or anything next to me; I could not see anything around me. I just prayed to God for death to come to me. I felt an indescribable anger and hatred towards Mansour.

My sister continued: "He has even forbidden everyone in this household to come and go by the bazaar. You all have to go the long way around. You must go from the left-hand side and bypass three or four houses. You must go from the other side…"

I was silent. It was as if I was dead. All I could see was his curly hair waving around on his forehead. And then, I could see Mansour - his oiled hair glued to his scalp - rigid and serious. A man with no feelings. I did not want him; it could not be forced! I did not want Mansour.

Now, my sister was resting her head on her left forearm and hovering over me like a tent: "Why don't you give it up Mahboubeh. Think a little. See what you've done to everyone? How can you marry a carpenter's shop boy with this grandiose lifestyle of yours, this life and all its splurging? Can you live with an idle rogue? What does this boy possess apart from the stench of wood…?"

I cut her off and turned my back on her: "Leave me alone. Go to sleep."

My sister asked: "At least tell me what you're thinking Mahboubeh?"

-I'm thinking about him.

I dreamt of the scent of wood.

All the doors closed on me. I was like a trapped cat − angry, stubborn and wild. I did not have the courage to face my father. Dayeh, having returned after two days, gave me suspicious looks in silence as she brought me my lunch and dinner. Mother avoided seeing me as much as possible. Every time I encountered her when I left the room out of necessity, I would drop my head and say a shy, embarrassed hello. There was no answer. Khojasteh was our go-between. It was as if even Manouchehr had become irritable. He was restless and would not feed. He slept very little. During the day, when he became agitated and cried, my mother also raised her voice over his.

-May God strike me dead! This girl makes me shake in anger so much that even this child has totally changed after having had my bad milk. May God strike me dead and get it over and done with. What a snake in the grass I have given birth to!

And despite everything, she still kept breastfeeding Manouchehr and complaining. Five days, ten days, twenty days passed by and I was still a prisoner in the house. I felt stifled and moody. I was besotted. I was crazy. I could think of nothing but him. Closing the doors on me had fuelled the fire burning within me. Now, I only thought of him. I wanted to distract myself, but was unable to. This drove me insane. It drove me to desperation. Every time I went near the front door, dadeh khanoum followed me under some pretext, mother called me, or dayeh khanoum came after me.

-Don't you go anywhere Mahboub jan. Your agha jan has forbidden it.

-Don't worry. have nowhere to go! I'm just going to pick some flowers at the end of the garden. I want to embroider from them.

I was truly a skillful embroiderer. My tablecloths left everyone speechless. I picked violets, roses and narcissi and draw their patterns on the fabric. hen, I looked at the flowers and embroidered according to their colours. I wanted to make a small handkerchief for someone whose name I was even too scared to think of in my own mind. But, no, I have heard that handkerchiefs bring distance. I will make a mantelpiece cover that he can put in the niche over the heater. He can put a mirror on it, look at himself every morning and comb that wild hair.

My father had removed the gramophone. Ghamar's records had disappeared. There was no sign of Leili and Majnoun or Hafez poetry books. Dear Lord, why have these things been taken away? Why have they invoked my father's wrath? I drowned my sorrows in them. What shall I do in this house all day long now, lonely and idle? Shall I just run around like a headless chicken and flap my wings? I wished Mansour away with all my heart!

It was nearly the end of August. My parents were in the hozekhaneh. It was just after lunch. Water poured down with a murmur into the tiled pond from the open fountain. Father was smoking his hookah. Mother was drinking tea. I had tiptoed down the stairs to eavesdrop. Nothing was mentioned about me in their talks. It was as if I did not exist. On the whole, my father had become taciturn and reserved ever since that night. He was often frowning. My mother would look at him anxiously, and I would stand listening behind the door where my parents sat. But, there was never any talk of me and my affair of the heart. This was even worse than the yelling, chastising, and punishing. If only they would say something. If only my father would threaten me and beat me to death. If he mentioned Rahim's name and talked about the carpentry at the top of the passage, it meant that Rahim was on his mind and his bother, that it was a problem in need of a solution. In that case, I could say there was no other solution but my union with him. But, what was the meaning of this silence? It meant there was no problem at all; that everything I had said was worthless, lost in the wind. It meant that my crazy heart had to beat against my tired chest until it was worn-out, still and docile; if only it would. But, with every breeze, I remembered his wild locks, passionate look, and mystic Sufi ways. Are those locks blowing in the breeze right now? How I longed for that small shop, and the sound of the saw and plane.

My mother climbed up the hozekhaneh stairs and called dadeh khanoum. Dadeh khanoum turned up dragging her feet. I heard mother say: "Tell Firouz khan to have the coach ready first thing tomorrow morning. Agha has been invited to his brother's gardens in Shemiran."

My heart sank. So, why wasn't agha jan going to the Gholhak gardens? To his own gardens, which was just growing into a real garden? Why was he going to Shemiran? To uncle's huge, bottomless gardens? Alone? At a time when we were all in the city, and there was no talk of going to the country this year because of mother's childbirth and the pursuing events? Uncle's entire household moved to the Shemiran gardens in the summers. His wife often invited mother, who made her excuses in turn. My mother did not like her and her sharp tongue. So, how come father was leaving for Shemiran this year without warning? I asked Khojasteh to keep an eye open. She was very good at pretending to be innocent and getting the answers to my questions from my mother.

Khojasteh said: "Khanoum jan says uncle has invited agha jan. He has said please join us in Shemiran in order to seal the fate of our children. Agha jan's going to make arrangements for you and Mansour as soon as possible." Khojasteh paused and continued: "Agha jan has said that it's no longer right for you to stay in this house. They must send you on your way. He has said a girl who has her head in the clouds has to be married off quickly, otherwise she'll cause an even bigger disgrace." Khojasteh blushed: "It has also been decided for khanoum jan to send a message to her sister as soon as possible, to come and finalise the plans for me and Hamid…" She laughed and added: "For fear of this affair with you, they're also marrying me off in a rush."

I said: "Congratulations Khojasteh. But, I don't want Mansour. I can't bear to see him, nor his loudmouth afrit of a mother. Would it be right to give in?! Seeing Mansour is like seeing the angel of death."

-Khanoum jan says: "Whether she likes it or not, I'll give her a wallop on the back of her head and sit her down at the wedding ceremony."

-I will kill myself. I'll take opium and kill myself. You'll see. I will never marry Mansour.

-Poor Mansour; he's not a bad boy. I feel sorry for him. You have gone mad Mahboub!

-Yes by God! You're right Khojasteh. I've gone mad. I know this better than anyone.

Agha jan left by coach in the early morning. I was still lying down when I heard the comings and goings and felt relieved. Once the sun had spread out, my mother changed and called Khojasteh: "Come Khojasteh, come get ready quickly and let's go to your aunt's house."

-No khanoum jan. Do I have to come? I'm too embarrassed.

I heard my mother laugh: "May the face of shyness be darkened by God. Get up, get up! We're only going to your aunt's place! Have you not been there a hundred times already? No one wants anything with you." How come my mother is laughing again? Why is she on such top form and joking again?

My mother and sister were ready to leave; to my surprise, dayeh followed them with the baby. Mother ordered Haj Ali to go ahead and get them a coach. As they were ready to leave, dadeh khanoum looked at my mother hesitantly and said: "Mahboubeh khanoum is not coming with you?"

Mother was abrupt again: "What business is it of yours?"

-Well, if Mahboubeh khanoum is coming with you, with your permission I could go visit my sister.

Much to dadeh khanoum, dayeh jan and my own amazement, mother said coolly: "You go then; what do you want with Mahboubeh khanoum?"

On impulse, dadeh khanoum and I looked at one other in surprise. Was there not supposed to be someone watching me at all times? How could mother give dadeh khanoum permission to leave so easily? Usually, the servants did not get leave to visit their families so readily. Especially when mother wanted to leave me at home and, naturally, dadeh khanoum would be responsible for keeping an eye on me.

Dadeh khanoum took a look at me and muttered: "Well… then… then… shall I really go?"

My mother answered impatiently: "Go on then, why all the chinwag! But, you must return before sundown. We have a million things to do. There's some food left over from last night. Mahboubeh khanoum will give you some in a pot to take for your sister."

Mother had mentioned me by my name. Did it mean she had reconciled with me? Was this a truce? I was unable to figure it out before she left the house. As for dadeh khanoum, how slow was this woman! Just imagine, she was going to visit her sister for a day after such a long time! I went to the kitchen and supervised Haj Ali while he was packing food in a pot for her sister. There would still be enough food left over for me and Haj Ali, so he would not have to cook again. And yet, he was not happy about filling the pot to the rim and I had to wrangle with him.

-Haj Ali, there's more than enough food here. hy're you reluctant to fill it up?

-Everything has its boundaries. Dadeh khanoum will become too cheeky.

Had it been any other time, I would have laughed. But I was stamping my foot down impatiently that day: "Hurry then! Will you fill it up or should I do it myself?"

Haj Ali filled up the pot begrudgingly: "Here you go, it's not as if any of it belongs to my father! I'll fill it up as much as you want. Let them eat themselves to death."

Haj Ali's room was in the birouni, close to the courtyard door. He limped back to his room. His eyes were always red and watery from blowing on the firewood under the cauldrons day and night. He always placed a hand on his hip and stooped while walking. He limped. No one knew whether it was from joint pains or a physical disability. Although he had the opportunity to eat as much as he wished in the kitchen, he would also wipe clean all the left-overs on top of his own share, but he was still thin and boney. Even though he was old and frail now, my parents always held him in high esteem; not only for his excellent cooking, but also for his blind loyalty.

I knew he would use this opportunity to sleep. So, how come my mother was leaving me alone at home? Did she feel sorry for me? Were my confine-ment days over? Did they believe that, over the course of these past three weeks, I had realised I was up a blind alley and had come to my senses? Or had the laws of detention been relaxed now that agha jan was out of town! Whatever! I will seek out that wild hair, those strong muscular hands, that jugular vein along that long neck protruding from underneath the tanned skin. I will seek out the scent of wood, the sound of the saw, and that sooty paradise…

I put on my chador and picheh and got ready to leave. Haj Ali was asleep in his room. I opened the bolt on the door and freed myself. In all that time, I had left the house only once, and that was to go to my sister's house in my father's coach, accompanied by dadeh khanoum - and even then, only travelling on the route to the lefthand side of the house. And now, it seemed as if I had been away from that alley, the passage and that small shop for an entire century. I could see that everything was still as bright, happy and lively as ever. People came and went as before. Nothing had changed except for me; I was walking on air and felt light. I wanted to laugh out loud. I lift-ed my picheh to see him better; for him to see me. If only I could sit by his shop like a pauper and watch him come and go every day; watch him work; watch him breathe.

I was at the turn of the third street. A fistful of hot blood suddenly rushed to my heart, making it leap into my throat. My hands and feet went weak. I did not have the courage to turn the corner and see him. I stopped. And yet, I did not even have the strength to stand.

I took a deep breath and turned the corner. All of a sudden, I went cold. I froze on the spot and stood still. The shop door was closed. I felt like a wave crashing on a cliff. How is this possible? At this time of day?! Two large planks of wood had been nailed crosswise to the closed door. So, the shop was not shut; it was closed down for a long time, forever. I stood there, dazed and stunned. I looked around persistently and suppliantly. Was there no one who could tell me what had happened? Who could I ask? Where could

I go? I stared back at the door. It was like looking at the corpse of a loved one. I turned around and started walking back home. My head was hanging down as if there were no bones in my neck. So, this is why my mother had taken the chains off my feet. This is why she called me Mahboubeh. This is why she was laughing. She wanted me to come and see it with my own eyes. Whatever had happened, it was my father's doing. Has he been locked up? Killed? What had happened? What have they done to him? Because, whatever it was, they had done the same to my heart. I disliked my father, and my mother's laughter. The more unyielding they were, the more stones they threw in my path, the more restless I became. Leave me alone. Leave me by myself.

Dear God, how will I ever see him again? Where can I find him? They had forced him away. I was returning home, but my feet were lagging behind. It was as if stones had been tied to my legs. I felt lifeless and impatient. I was tired and the way home seemed so far. I dragged my feet on the ground. I leaned my hand against the wall. I could hardly breathe. I had aged. Why was the air so dry, so scorching hot? Why did everything look so different? Why did the sunshine turn dark and dim? People became grim and somber. Life became serious, bitter. Why did the passersby hurry along so glumly? Why were the shadows on the wall awash with sorrow? I got home. The sycamore trees were lined up around the garden, row by row. The pond water was still and motionless. I went to the hozekhaneh. It was hot there too. I threw myself on the cushions. There was not even a tear in my eye; only rage and rebellion towards my father, towards my mother's deception who had bared the truth to me so tacitly; towards Mansour. Let them sit and wait for me to marry Mansour. If this is how it is going to be, I will also throw caution to the wind.

Haj Ali came by the building, saying *Ya Allah*[111], placed my food tray on the steps, and limped away. I did not touch it. It was a couple of hours past midday. I rose peevishly and threw my chador over my head. Perhaps he was back at work now. I must go and see if he is there or not. Although I already knew what I was meant to find out from that boarded-up door, I was still going despite everything. I was going to see his empty place; to see the closed door and imagine him standing behind it. I started lethargically and walked through two alleys, to reach the turn of the third one. The door was in the same state as it had been that morning. I drifted through the bazaar. I found it difficult to keep the chador on my head. I walked in a daze and did not know where I was going. What did I want? I stopped by the saghakhaneh, but did not light any candles. My heart was not in it. I felt suffocated. My mother was right, my father was right; I had become Leili and was wandering around like Majnoun. I was lovesick. I had to go back home. Why should I wander around here? The bird has flown the nest. I have to return to my own cage and die of my own chagrin.

-Khanoum, please help me for God's sake. I am an orphan…

That was all I needed. A ten or twelve-year old beggar boy was running after me barefooted in an old, dirty shirt with an open collar. If the shop had been open and I had been cheerful, I would have surely given this ragged pauper a good sum of money for the good omen of seeing him. But, at that moment, I found his persistence annoying. I felt hatred towards heaven and earth. He took hold of my chador, pleading: "I'm an orphan, khanoum, for the love of your children, help a poor boy."

My chador was getting dirty. I pushed him away angrily: "Get lost." He stood still for a bit and then ran after me again. As I was walking, I told him without looking back: "I said get lost."

He lowered his voice and said: "He has sent you a letter."

It nailed me to the ground. The little boy walked towards me quickly and stretched out his hand.

-Who's "He"?

-He said to say the carpenter.

Under the pretext of giving him money, I hurriedly grabbed the piece of paper from him and started on my way. I opened the letter in the *hashti*[112] of the house. Seeing the same beautiful handwriting made my heart race and the blood began to circulate again in my frozen body. The sun began to shine again, and life began to flow.

> *Auntie gave Soudabeh another piece of paper. The passage of time had left its trace on this one too and turned it yellow. In a beautiful writing, it read: "I will wait for you behind your garden wall."*

*The sensation of eagerness and affection carried into Soud-
abeh's heart from between the words in the letter, from underneath
the dust of time. Auntie had saved all the keepsakes. She continued as she took the note back and put it in its place in the chest.*

I was already in deep water and no longer concerned with being disgraced. I knew my parents were no longer concerned about me. They felt
reassured regarding the local carpenter boy. Thus, my mother would probably return late and I still had a few hours left until sundown. Haj Ali did not
matter. The old man kept himself to himself. I turned around carefree and
started walking towards the left hand side of the alley with measured steps. I
went right to the end of our garden wall. In this part, the walls were mostly
built close to one another. Even the coach – which my father had ordered to
use this side for a while - could only pass through with difficulty due to the
narrowness of the alleyways. When I reached the end of the garden wall, I
turned left again. Here, there was a narrow back-garden path where the sycamore trees from our garden and the neighbour's garden had merged from
both sides to cast their shadow on the ground. The rugged, dusty path was
covered with brushwood. Human and dog faeces could be seen in places.
This was almost a deserted spot. The back-garden path led to a vast plot of
land covered with brushwood and thorns, where a few half-dead lone trees
stood. I had never even half-glanced at this path or the land it led to. On that
day, this deserted spot became my paradise.

I stopped halfway. It was two hours past midday. There was not a soul
around in the scorching heat of the summer; even if there was, they would
not have recognised me underneath that old chador and picheh I was wearing. I had my back to the main alley when I heard his footsteps entering the
confined, narrow path from behind me. I could hear the sound of the brushwood getting crushed and felt humiliated by the lowliness of the place; as
if I was responsible for its unclean, untidy state. A moment later, he walked
past and stood in front of me. He was wearing a timid smile on his face. His
locks could be seen from underneath his egg-shaped hat, which he wore
slightly to the front of his head. His hair was also showing in the back of
his neck, just below the hat. Once again, the collar of his calico shirt was
open under the caftan, revealing his neck and dark skin. He was wearing a
wraparound, and I wondered how much longer these clothes were going to
last? What would he look like if he had to put them aside with the force of

time and wear a suit?

He put the palms of his hands together, in front of him, and said: "Salam."

-Salam.

The shadow of the sycamore leaves played on his face in the sunlight.

He asked: "Where have you been over the past twenty-three days?"

"I was imprisoned." His left eyebrow rose in astonishment. "I told my father. So, he banned me from leaving the house. Why is your shop closed?"

That playful grin appeared on his face. His eyes became mischievous: "You don't know?"

-No.

-Ask your father.

So, I had guessed right. It was my father's doing. But how?

-Your father has bought the shop. It's been almost ten days now. When I came to work one morning, I saw the shop was closed and boarded up. I knew straight away; I knew where this was coming from. I went to see my master; I asked him why he had closed the shop? He said Basir ol-Molk sent his man around with a message to name my price. I said I was not selling. He said Basir ol-Molk is only asking you the price of the shop. Answer his question. I gave a higher price. His messenger left and came back saying Basir ol-Molk has said he will pay you double the amount, provided the deal is done no later than tomorrow. So, I accepted. That's all.

I lifted my picheh in astonishment and said: "Then, my father has put you out of work? He has cut off your bread and butter? He has finally spread his poison?"

He blushed when he saw my face, and said: "Instead, this antidote has cured me now."

I repeated: "He cut off your bread and butter?"

-He probably knew I won't be able to swallow a bite away from you...!

And he laughed. His teeth showed again – white and lined up – as if a painting. He took his hat off and freed those wild locks to hang wild and untamed on his forehead, thick and slinky. He looked like a whirling dervish preparing for Sama. He kept twisting and squeezing the hat in his hands. He wanted to say something, but was too shy. He looked up to the the tree tops with a somber face and large, melancholy eyes. He grinned bitterly: "I knew from the start they wouldn't give your hand to me in marriage."

-Come and ask for my hand. Come and tell my father that you want to join the military, that you'll become an officer. Won't you? Eh?"

-Yes, I will. But it's no use. He won't even let me talk."

-Yes, yes, when he sees you…

He interrupted me: "Your father has seen me."

-What, when, where?

Eyes downcast, he kept fidgeting with his hat: "When your father bought the shop and boarded it up, I kept going back there for a day or two, standing guard by the door. I waited for you to come, and you never did. I didn't know what to do, how to see you! I was afraid they had forced you to marry that cousin of yours… what was his name?"

-Mansour

He looked at my face and smiled cynically: "Aha, Mansour khan. He's very rich, right?"

He had laughter and sarcasm in his reproachful eyes. He, too, had targeted my heart and soul.

Why was everyone at loggerheads with me? Why did everyone want me with a sore heart? I, who am already broken; my heart is already in a thousand pieces. I answered his look with a sad smile.

He dropped his head again, and said: "I waited and you never came. Until one day, I saw your father's coach going past the shop with the hood open and your agha jan reclining in it. When he arrived outside the shop, he caught sight of me as I stood there with my arms crossed. He pretended not to see me. I was beside myself. I told myself where is he hiding his daugh ter? What has he done to her? I jumped in front of the coach and grabbed the reins as it slowed down at the turn. I said: "Agha, may I make a humble remark? I have something to say."

I clutched my face instinctively: "Oh, may God strike me dead!"

The same playful grin appeared on his face again: "Why? God forbid should an angel with your splendor die. Regiments of young men will perish for you…" He went quiet and his glare pierced my heart.

To free myself from that feverish gaze, with a voice that hardly left my throat, I said: "Well? What happened next?"

-Agha looked at me with such anger that my knees went weak. If he had a gun, he would have fired it there and then. He leaned forward and in a deep, but enraged voice, said: "Talk." I went closer. I didn't want anyone to hear – neither the coachman, nor the locals. I muttered in his ear: "Why do you harass her? Leave her alone. I am the one she wants to marry. I am the one you have to face." It was as if your father had been bitten by a snake; he went blue in the face. God forbid, I thought he was going to fall down in front of me and breathe his last. He looked me over spitefully. He tried to breathe and say something a couple of times, but he could not make a sound. Then, all of a sudden, he jumped up like a spring. Before the poor coachman could react, he grabbed him from behind with his left hand and pulled him back so hard that his leg went up in the air and he almost fell to the ground. The poor man's right arm, which was holding the whip, flung up into the air. Your father roared like a lion: "Give this to me!" He snatched the whip from the coachman and before I could get myself together he brought it down on my body with such force that it wrapped around me from the top of my knee to the top of my shoulder and stuck there. He wanted to lift the whip and hit me again, but it wouldn't budge and I was pulled forward with it. Blood gushed out from the wound where my shirt was torn to pieces. When your father saw that the whip would not separate from my body, he shouted through clenched teeth: "You gigolot bastard; if you mention her name one more time, I'll have your neck broken into pieces. If you show your face around here again, I'll make your mother mourn you."

The whip loosened up by itself and fell. Your father threw it in front of the coachman and said: "Go". And he left. Look what he has done to me!

He gave me a piece of bloodied white fabric and said: "Take it. Keep it as a souvenir. My blood was shed for you. No worries."

The sight of his blood overwhelmed me. I said: "Ah!", as if I was the one who had been whipped.

Auntie took out a piece of fabric with traces of blood remaining on it as a black line, took a chagrined look at it and continued.

He asked me: "What shall I do now? I want to come and ask for your hand. I'll not stop at anything, even if it means losing my head."

-Wait until I let you know.

-How?

-Give me your home address.

He was worried: "What good is that? It's rented. If your father finds out, he'll buy that place too."

I thought of something: "I'll come to the end of our garden and throw notes for you; right here. I'll wrap the note around a stone and throw it over the wall. Come here every now and then and look around!"

-Every now and then? I wander around here every day. What can I do? Your father has taken my job and you my peace of mind.

I knew I had to become his wife. I will become his wife no matter what. I will not exchange a single strand of hair from this shop boy's head for a thousand shazdehs and al-Dowlehs. I said: "I've to go now."

He said: "I've given you so many tokens of my love – my hair… my blood… What will you give me as a keepsake?"

I said: "I was the first one to give you a keepsake."

He was surprised: "What keepsake?"

-My hear

And I ran, stumbling all the way. I raced through the thorny, rugged ground and brushwood which clung to my chador, covered me in dust and grazed my hands and feet. I ran, wishing my legs would cease up and I would stay there for all eternity.

One night passed and there was no sign of my father's return. On the second day, my father's coach came home around noon, but my father was not in it. Firouz khan hurried into the andarouni courtyard and asked for my mother. Mother threw her chador on her head and went into the yard. Firouz stood in front of her with crossed arms. Dayeh jan was standing behind my mother, holding the baby in her arms.

Firouz khan said: "Agha has ordered me to bring the coach and said to tell your ladyship his brother has invited you to the Shemiran gardens as from tomorrow morning, to rest there for seven or eight days with the little master, dayeh khanoum, and khanoum kouchik."

I was too clever not to understand this had something to do with me and Mansour.

The comings and goings began at once. Khojasteh was happy about being able to play with our cousins, mother was happy to marry me off and put an end to the disturbances, and dayeh khanoum was happy to rest in the cool air of Shemiran. To each his own

We got on the coach in the early morning hours and left for the Shemiran gardens. The coach drove through the alley on the right. The curfew had been lifted. At the top of the third alley, I saw the barricaded door of the carpentry again. I showed no reaction, as if nothing had happened. Mother, who was keeping an eye on me, felt reassured when she saw I was calm and indifferent. Perhaps I had given up. But it was not so. I had become even more determined. I had spent the whole of the previous night thinking and planning.

We were welcomed into the gardens by my younger cousins' cries of jubilation. The cool air of Shemiran and uncle's bottomless gardens so full of refreshing waterways and trees even brought joy to me. Even though Manouchehr had stranger anxiety, he too, was good-tempered on that day. He screamed with the joy of seeing the children and threw himself forward and struggled to go into their arms from dayeh's. It was almost noon. My father had gone to shoot partridges with uncle and Mansour. My uncle's wife, who was well-known in the family for being no better than my aunt in using bitter language, making flippant remarks and gossiping, greeted me with open arms this time. She embraced me and kissed me, repeatedly calling me her daughter and beautiful bride. My mother laughed wholeheartedly. My two cousins, with an age difference of only a couple of years between us and with whom I had grown up and brawled throughout my childhood years, fell silent as soon as I walked in that day and got up to give me their place reverently, as if I was something made of china that they were seeing for the first time. They lowered their voice in my presence, spoke cordially, and were ready to serve me.

At lunchtime, there were endless comings and goings in the garden and its old building. Lunch was being served. The spread was laid on the floor, from one end of the big room to the other. Uncle's domestics were rushing around. After all, this get-together was a prelude to the wedding of their master's son. Fresh herbs were placed on the spread, together with douq and sherbet, fresh cucumbers, grapes and pears − all of which were the special produce of uncle's gardens. The spread was garnished with local bread and yoghurt. One help was barbecuing kebabs in the back of the building, and another was bringing the dishes of *baghali polo*[113] and lamb. Dayeh jan, who had handed Manouchehr over to mother, was spinning the *atashgardan*[114] to help light the samovar for tea after lunch. Just watching this scene shook my resolve and made my plan seem foolish. This was the life I belonged to, where Rahim's presence was ill-matched. Even the thought of him was a vain dream, it was absurd. Was I going to rebel single-handedly in the midst of all this luxury and splendor, all these family traditions and social restrictions? Even harbouring such a thought was infantile and impossible, an absurdity.

My father, uncle and Mansour arrived on horseback − all three happy and boisterous. A couple of bearers accompanied them. They were returning from the foothills of the Alborz Mountains, having shot a few partridges. Uncle said: "For Mahboub". What did I want with partridges? The poor birds had been slaughtered. They barely had any meat on them. I wished the shots had killed me instead! I was stuck between a rock and a hard place! Mansour's behaviour only made things worse. He was clumsy, shy. At times he called me "You" in a formal manner, and at times he called me informally, as he did when we were kids. He brought douq for me, put rice on my plate, and scolded his sisters to make more room for me. And those poor souls, who were sitting on either side of me, had left half a yard of space on both sides. When I was not looking at him, I knew he was staring at me; when I looked at him, he blushed and quickly turned the other way. I said to myself, I will ignore him until he gives up. But he did not; he did not understand. The poor thing could not even begin to imagine the turmoil in my heart. Nevertheless, I must admit, he was a good-looking, elegant young man. No objections could be made to his civility and conduct. Once uncle's plentiful wealth and titles were added to all of this, it was clear why all the young girls desired to marry him. All, except for me. To my eyes, he was like a snake. Seeing him repulsed me. Watching his innocent clumsiness and timidity, which were the cause of secret laughter and chatter among Khojasteh and my cousins, gave me goose bumps. It was my bad luck again, that he was so good; that I was so bad. That no matter how hard I tried to let him into my heart, it would not happen.

After lunch, he reclined on a cushion, folded his left leg into a right angle and rested his right elbow on it. He felt bolder now. Every now and then, when he was sure no one was looking, he glanced at me and smiled. He had a nice smile which lit up his eyes. He really wanted me. I had no idea how long he had harboured these feelings! He had never let on. I understood this only too well on that day and it hurt me. His admiring looks stabbed me like piercing arrows. I despised and shuddered at everything about him which appeared to be a virtue to others, from his soft hands, to his posh clothes, the boots he wore, his english moustache, his meticulously combed hair with every single strand in its place, and his polite, lofty tone of voice.

What angered me more than anything was the fact that he believed I reciprocated his feelings, and maybe even more so. He presumed that this is how it had to be. There was no room for questions and discussions, there was no other way. He naturally supposed that by asking for my hand, he had done me a favour and expected a positive answer. His egocentricity and self-confidence was more repugnant than anything else to me.

Close to sunset, a kilim was spread all along the porch which led to a large swimming pool and was separated from the surrounding garden with just a single step. Beyond that, witchgrass vanished into infinity between the rows of trees in the orchard. A bed[115] was put in place for my father and uncle to sit on and was also covered with a kilim. And of course, the spread of lettuce and oxymel, *halim*[116], fruits, tea, hookahs and mixed nuts completed the afternoon tea. The women were sitting on the floor. My uncle's wife was sit ting at the foot of the large coal samovar and poured the tea. Each estekan of chai was placed in a gold-trimmed saucer and served in a small brass tray, with a small brass or glass bowl on the side holding a few sugar cubes. Khojasteh and my uncle's children were running around and playing. Every now and then, one of them ran and picked at the spread, took some lettuce and oxymel or nuts and returned to the others with full hands, paying no attention to the screams of my uncle's wife and my mother or dayeh, who asked them to sit down like civilised people and eat first before going to play.

Manouchehr had been freed from his swaddle, but a wax-soaked cloth was placed underneath him as a changing mat, in turn covered with two or three cloth nappies to prevent accidents. He was lying on his back, his legs covered with a thin sheet which creased to one side as he twirled his hands and feet when watching the children and screaming with excitement. My father kept pulling the sheet back on his legs with great tenderness and saying: "Shame on you son." And uncle would laugh.

We were such a happy family! It was such a beautiful sight! If only God would have mercy on me and bring me back to my senses with my brain ruling over my body; how grateful and content I would have been for the happiness which was about to be bestowed upon me. But, a different fate was in store for me. I was present in body that day, but not in soul.

The pool water, also used for watering the lawn, flowers and gardens, was green and slimy. Two large turtles wiggling in it kept the children amused. A couple of rabbits were kept in a cage in a corner of the garden. A fawn, tied down to a tree by its leg with a very long cord, was browsing adrift in the garden.

Khojasteh came running with one of our cousins: "Come Mahboub, come see the fawn. It has such beautiful eyes! It's really lovely!"

My cousin said: "We also have two rabbits. They're really nice to watch. Come on, get up and come with us; don't be lazy! I want to show them to you."

My younger cousin pointed to his two sisters and said: "We also have two cows."

His sister hit him on the head and laughed. I said: "I don't feel like it right now. Maybe later."

My father glimpsed at me. Ever since we had had to face one another and keep up appearances in the gardens, no words had been exchanged between us apart from my hello and his answer. But, there were no bad tempers either. He did his utmost to overcome his anger towards me and make things look alright. But he was cold. Only I could sense how cold and distant he had become. I seemed to be a weight around his neck. He wanted to get rid of me.

It was getting dark and the domestics were lighting the lanterns. My uncle's wife said: "It's dark now. They'll go with Mansour jan tomorrow to watch…" Then, she laughed and added: "Of course, with the permission of her agha jan and Nazanin khanoum."

My father forced a smile and my mother laughed wholeheartedly, with the happiness of a woman whose daughter was going to be a bride. I could see in Mansour's eyes how much he desired a stroll in the dark. The poor thing did not know what went on in my heart. He did not know I did not want a stroll in the gardens; that I was not feeling like myself.

In the room I shared with my mother, dayeh, Khojasteh and Manouchehr, I spent that entire night making plans till dawn. The chance I had been asking God for had been thrown into my lap by my uncle's wife. I had to grasp the nettle. Perhaps, God was merciful towards me again. Perhaps, he had taken pity on my broken heart…"

However, what I had in mind was so very different from Mansour's vision! From her sleeping corner, dayeh jan said: "Mahboub jan, may God bestow good fortune on you. You're in luck love. You won't mind if I say your cousin's as tall as a box tree[117], Masha 'Allah."

I did mind, but I pretended not to. I turned my back on her and did not answer. Khojasteh was laughing and my mother was doing her baby talk with Manouchehr who was still awake and wanting to play. I could tell how happy she was from her tone of voice, her behaviour and peaceful manners. She agreed with dayeh.

Dayeh asked again: "Khanoum, don't set the *shirini khoran*[118] date too close! We have a million things to do; it can't be rushed."

As if she had forgotten my rebellion of the past few months, of putting my foot down and telling her day and night that I wanted the local carpenter boy, my mother said: "I'm not sure yet dayeh khanoum. I think it might co-incide with *Mab'as*[119]. Just baking the sweets will take an entire week. But, on the other hand, autumn is coming. I would like to get things moving so we can put chairs and tables outside in the garden. This morning, *zan amou*[120] se-cretly showed me the ring; the stone was as large as a thumb nail. She said I was keeping it for Mansour's wife, do you like it or not? She has many hopes and wants to give it her all for her son's wedding. She's worse than me and constantly worrying about the wedding preparations. She's right of course. I'm also beginning to worry…"

It made my blood boil. As the saying goes, my mother was *talking to the door so the wall would hear*[121]. This meant that I had to marry my cousin. Dead or alive, this was it; you are screwed if you do, screwed if you don't. I told myself if this is how the cookie crumbles, then let them believe it. It is true, as they say that *describing the pleasure is worth half the pleasure itself.*

In the morning, we all had breakfast together on the porch overlooking the swimming pool with the same enthusiasm and comings and goings. The sun had already spread out when my amou jan and agha jan, who had been for a walk in the gardens, returned to the building and went into one of the rooms to discuss their property affairs, as zan amou put it. Mansour, who had been lingering around until then, or sitting on the bed reading an old newspaper, put the paper down, walked straight towards me and addressed my mother: "Khanoum amou jan, I was supposed to show the fawn and the rabbits to Mahboubeh today. Will you give her permission to accompany me?"

As if he had already acquired my permission beforehand! As if I, too, was eager to accompany him. He did not ask or say a word to me as I sat there with my head down, staring at my hands.

My mother said: "What're you waiting for Mahboubeh? Get up, agha Mansour's waiting for you."

I went for my chador, when my uncle's wife said: "Oh, a chador's not necessary my dear girl. There are no naamahrams in the gardens and Man-sour's your cousin. Cousins are a match made in heaven."

I flushed, not from shyness, but from anger. This was going to be a forced marriage. Mansour threw a sharp glance at his mother, and said aggressive-ly: "Khanoum jan!" It made me feel good. But they were not going to give up. Both zan amou and khanoum jan were in stitches.

It seemed that a top secret order had warned the children not to follow us and stay away from the gardens - an enforceable command not to be taken lightly. It was quiet everywhere. Only the chirping of sparrows could be heard with the uproar of the brook flowing in through an opening in the wall at the bottom of the gardens. The weather in Shemiran was not hot like Tehran. It was pleasantly cool at this time of year and, hand in hand with the serenity of the large, luscious gardens and cool intertwining brooks, it gave everyone great pleasure. It was our Garden of Eden.

In my uncle's gardens of a few acres, all kinds of trees could be found. Grapevines were trained on trellises in one corner, and corn was growing in another smaller corner; as children, we always acted as corn pests. As we neared the end of the gardens, fruit trees grew in number and became more densely populated. Amou jan was especially proud of his apple orchards and pear trees, and then there was the scent of walnut trees which I loved so much.

Mansour began to talk calmly and slowly. I could not register what he was saying. I was shaking like a leaf from the fear of what I intended to do. I regretted the whole thing a thousand times, but changed my mind again.

Mansour asked softly: "Mahboubeh, has zan amou spoken to you?"

I pretended not to know: "What about?"

He laughed sedately: "You know what about."

I remained silent.

He continued placidly, as if fooling a child: "I'll do anything for you; anything you want. I don't want you to think everything's just to my liking, or that of my agha jan and khanoum jan. If you wish, I'll get a separate house for you. You won't have to touch anything black or white[122]. You must take piano lessons. I'll engage an instructor for you. I'd like you to learn French…"

-I have learned French with my agha jan.

-That's even better. You can complete it. You'll also do embroidery. I only want you to attend get-togethers and entertain fine ladies such as yourself, although not as beautiful as yourself."

All of a sudden, I felt sorry for him. He felt towards me as I felt towards Rahim the carpenter boy. What a silly game it all was. He smiled affectionately and his warm glance gazed over my face. He was a man who would truly strive to make his wife happy, if he loved her. He had inherited his father's respect for the sanctity of family life. In one word, Mansour was an honourable man. A real human being – a reality even I could not deny. This is where I felt helpless. I loved him. Without the shadow of a doubt, I loved him and did not wish him bad luck and misery; I wished him no harm; I loved him the same way I loved his sisters, my cousins; the same way I loved Manouchehr.

Mansour picked an apple as we walked alongside the brook. By now, we had reached the age-old walnut trees. Each one of us only looked straight ahead, aware of the other one's presence. A relentless shaking had taken over my body again. The same shaking which took over and brought me face to face with the fear of death every time I decided to lift the curtain on my terrifying, home-wrecking secret in the presence of others. I had escaped my father's male chauvinism once, and now I had to be prepared to be subjected to the same fanatic passion by my male cousin. I had to turn him down and face its harsh consequences. That day, we saw no rabbits and no fawn. We just strolled along – I, unwilling and reluctant, and he, enthusiastically with an innocent fervour. I stopped walking and sat down on the stump of a walnut tree by the brook.

He smiled and asked: "Are you tired?" Begrudgingly, I did not answer. "Why won't you talk? You weren't so shy when you were a child. Cat cut your tongue?" And he laughed and added: "Here, I picked this for you. Don't you like apples?"

-I don't want it.

I went quiet again. I was fiddling with my skirt. He felt bolder now and took a step forward. With a friendly, familiar gesture, he rested his right hand on the tree trunk bent over my head and put his left hand on his hip. He was still holding the apple as he loomed over me. In an extremely soft tone of voice, which would have sounded sweet to any other girl, he asked: "Do you want me as much as I want you?"

Undeniably, he did not even dream that my answer would be negative.

Suddenly, I could hear myself speak. I cannot tell what force made me open my mouth and say: "No."

I said it so bitterly that I even shocked myself. I am not exaggerating when I say he shook like a tree exposed to violent winds, then stood up straight and asked: "Why?"

-Because I don't.

He became anxious: "But why? Have I done something wrong? Has anyone said anything? Has my mother done something again?"

I looked up, pleading: "No, no. I swear to God Mansour, no."

-Then tell me what the matter is?

He glared at me persistently and questioningly. I continued: "I want to tell you, but I'm afraid. Will you swear not to get angry and kick up a fuss? Will you swear not to tell anyone? Will you give me your word? Swear on your father's life."

He was astounded, but gradually regained his composure and said: "Talk to me. I won't tell anyone."

-Will you promise? Will you swear?

-I told you to speak up. I swear on my mother's life that I won't say anything. What is it?

I was afraid that if I waited any longer his impatience would turn into anger. I said: "Mansour, I… I… It's not that I don't like you. You're like a brother to me. I swear to God, I love you as I love Manouchehr. But…"

He leaned back on the tree opposite. He crossed his arms and looked at me with a cold stare. His eyes looked like two pieces of lifeless glass. He said: "Like Manouchehr?" I lowered my head: "Well, yes."

-So that's it. Now you tell me?

He was angry with me, and angry with himself for having murmured sweet nothings into my ear from the top of the gardens to this place, reducing himself to a ha'pworth. His sense of pride had awakened, replacing all other feelings. Strangely enough, he looked more handsome to me this way. I asked: "When should I have told you then?"

-You should've said from the start that I don't want Mansour.

-I did say.

-Whom did you tell

He was surprised. He could not understand what I was talking about. He could not make head or tail of it.

-I told everyone. I told my khanoum jan and agha jan. But they won't listen. They're forever finding me suitors. No matter how much I swear to God and all our wise men that I don't want to marry, it's in one ear and out the other…

-Why don't you want to marry? Never mind me, but what about your other suitors? What's wrong with them? Are they old? Blind? Deaf? What's wrong with them?

His glare pierced my eyes like two cold, sharp blades.

-Nothing, there's nothing wrong with them. It's me…

-You?

-Yes… me. I want someone else.

I did not look into his eyes, but I felt his intense sense of male chauvinism, a combination of both jealousy and family pride.

-How dare you!!

The state he was in, I felt he was going to hit me; but he did not. He was too much of a gentleman to raise his hand on a woman. I said: "Shush. For the love of God, don't make any noise. My agha jan will kill me. You promised. You swore on your mother's life."

He fell silent. He pressed his teeth together with such force that his jaw could be seen sticking out from underneath his skin. He went red in the face, paced up and down, bit his lip and asked: Does amou jan know? And your mother?"

-Yes, I have told everyone. That's why they want to force me into marriage.

They think I'll forget.

He sneered.

-Huh! They want to force you into marriage so you'll forget? Am I the stupidest person they could find?

I pleaded again: "Mansour, please don't raise your voice."

He asked: "Who is it?"

-You won't believe me if I tell you.

-Yes I will. You're capable of anything. Tell me who it is?"

I was not sure whether telling him would be the right thing to do. But I threw caution to the wind come what may. I was not sure whether I wanted to take revenge on my parents, or whether I wanted to talk to someone and get it all off my chest, even if that someone was an interested party. In that moment, I looked upon Mansour as an older brother, and I was not afraid of his scorn.

-A carpenter's shop boy

He was nailed to the ground instantnly. Hearing the bitter truth froze him too, like all the others. Slowly, he turned towards me and began laughing out loud in anger and contempt: "A carpenter's shop boy!!" He paused for a moment and peered into my eyes, searching for signs of a joke or a tease. He thought perhaps I was making fun of him, but deep down, he knew it was not so. He said with hatred: "Ugh! It turns one's stomach. Aren't you ashamed of yourself?"

Quickly, I said: "He's a shop boy for now. He wants to join the military once he's saved some money."

He mocked: "Oh! So, he wants to join the military. When, inshallah?"

Why wouldn't anyone believe me? Why did everyone laugh every time the military was mentioned? What was wrong with it? Was it not possible? I

said sarcastically: "You'll see when he does. Is it only landowners who can be officers?"

He looked at me with such anger that I went quiet. He took a few steps and said: "So, that's how it is… I'm not even worth as much as a carpenter's shop boy?!"

I could not convince him. He kept repeating carpenter's shop boy. I tried to console him: "Of course you are; I swear to God. Why do you talk like this? You're worth much more. But, what can I do? I even surprise myself. I'm absolutely captivated by him."

I was as surprised as he was by my own impudence, boldness and straight-forwardness. He was abrupt with me: "Alright then, that's enough. Let's go back."

-No, we can't leave it like this. What're you going to tell them?

He asked: "What am I supposed to say? I'll say Mahboubeh doesn't want me; that she's been twisting me around her little finger all this time."

-No, for the love of God, don't say that. Agha jan will kill me.

-What do you suggest that I say then?

-Tell them I don't want Mahboubeh…

He interrupted me: "I will not make a fool of myself. Until yesterday, I kept saying I do, and now I don't? I suppose the next thing is, I have to put your hand in the hands of Mr carpenter boy. No my dear. I will not be handed a white feather."

-For God's sake Mansour, have mercy. I'll be disgraced.

-Have mercy? Do you have mercy on anyone? So be disgraced! You look me in the eye and tell me with great impudence that you're after someone else? If only it was a decent person at least. A shop boy!! Yeah! I can see how afraid you are of being disgraced!

I could feel the anger rise in me again. So now, I even had to look up to this youngster who was just sprouting a moustache? I had to let him raise his voice at me too? He, who had grown up with me; who was not superior to me in any way. He had no rights over me. Even he wants to impersonate a man for me now? He is ordering me around. I don't want him; it can't be forced.

I said abruptly: "Would I have been a good person had I wanted you? Now that I'm saying no, I have to be disgraced? It can't be forced. Go and disgrace me if it makes you happy. Go and cry it in public like a case of sour grapes. First and foremost, If I'm disgraced, it will also mean disgrace for you."

-Why will I be disgraced? What has it to do with me? I'm not the one who has fallen in love!

-No dear. I'm in love; your cousin. Go tell everyone Mahboubeh wants a carpenter's shop boy. Let everyone laugh at you, reproach you and, as you put it, let them say Mansour wasn't worth as much as a carpenter's shop boy! Let your sisters stay at home and turn into buttoned up spinsters until their hair turns the colour of their teeth. Spit upwards and let it drop on your own face. Let everyone say Mahboubeh's cousins are her own match. Didn't you swear to me? But, that's alright. Go tell, so my agha jan and amou jan can squash me under their feet and you can watch to your heart's content.

He listened in silence. He could see I was a blast furnace and could not believe this rebellion by a fifteen-year old girl. Then, pensively, he said: "Are you finished? What an animal you have turned out to be! Just go, but on one condition only. I never want to set eyes on you again." He threw the apple in the water with infinite hatred, and said frowning: "I didn't realise you had developed such rubbish taste. You've become so impertinent and headstrong. Just as well I found out sooner rather than later."

-So, what're you going to tell them?

-I'll think of something.

-Stop frowning. Don't take on this air.

-Would you like me to play the tambourine? Do you want me to dance for you?

-No, but everyone will find out like this.

-Don't worry. They have no idea what a rare gem you've turned out to be!

He was right.

He turned around slowly and began to walk away. He looked crushed. The burden buried in my chest had been shifted to his. I was no longer afraid of him. But I had a guilty conscience. I felt ashamed and embarrassed within myself.

There was a lot of whispering and murmuring. My uncle's wife went from one room into the next, running around like a headless chicken. Finally, she went to see my mother. They went into a room together and closed the door. Khojasteh and my cousins, who were laughing and whispering when we went for our walk at the end of the gardens were now quiet and watching the events in bewilderment, each from their own corner. The domestics tried to come and go quietly, and dayeh jan grumbled at Manouchehr for the first time.

-Oh, child; you're such a crybaby!

Mother came out of zan amou's room irritated and walked straight into our own room. She was short with dayeh: "Pack everything. We're leaving early tomorrow morning."

Dayeh slammed her hand on her knee: "Oh, khanoum jan! Why're we leaving? We were supposed to stay for the week. What about Mahboubeh and agha Mansour?"

-Nothing. What about them? It's off.

Like someone who had suffered an electric shock, dayeh said: "It's off?"

-The boy has told his mother he doesn't want her.

-Ooh, how come! He was begging for her hand up until yesterday!

Mother was restless: "Well, he isn't anymore."

-But why? What's happened?

-He's told his mother Mahboubeh is childish. She's spoilt, pampered. I want a wife. I don't want to play doll. I thought I was interested until today. But now, I can see that I'm not. It's never too late to mend. She's like a sister to me. And then, he's left on horseback. Even his poor mother doesn't know where he's gone - to the city or shooting!"

Dayeh, who kept rocking back and forth and hitting herself on the knee unhappily, finally turned to me and said: "I'll die for you girl, don't you get upset now…"

I could not stop smiling: "No dayeh jan, there's nothing to be upset about."

Mother threw a sharp look at me from behind dayeh who was busy packing.

We had just gotten off the coach outside our house and I had not yet reached the sandoghkhaneh to take off my chador, when I heard my mother yell impatiently: "Dadeh khanoum, tell Firouz to get the bath stoker to come early tomorrow morning and light the boiler. Also, run and inform *Agha Begum*[123] that we're lighting the bath tomorrow and she must come and wash the children. If she wants to play hard to get and make excuses that she has other customers, get someone else; it doesn't matter who. I don't have the patience to mollycoddle anyone."

Mother hated dust and dirt. This obsession bothered her especially more when we went to the gardens or the country. Perhaps, the small boiler in our house was lit more often than that of any other house and Agha Begum, the rubber and shampooer who was well-known for her skills, came to wash us in our home bath frequently.

Khojasteh grabbed my arm as we were taking off our chadors, dragged me into the sandoghkhaneh and closed the door. The sound of my mother's footsteps returning to the andarouni and climbing the stairs kept getting closer every second. Khojasteh asked in a hurry: "What happened Mahboubeh? What happened? Why did Mansour behave like a demon all of a sudden?"

As I was folding my chador calmly, I said: "Oh, you've picked out the right time! I can't talk right now. Khanoum jan will be here any minute now. Wait until bedtime, I'll…"

The door of the sandoghkhaneh flung wide open and slammed against the wall. Mother walked in irate and furious, followed by dayeh who was carrying the baby. Shocked and scared, Khojasteh withdrew to the back of the sandoghkhaneh. Mother came straight at me. I wanted to run away, but she stopped me on the spot by slamming her hand on my chest. I fell on the wooden trunk of uncut fabrics and sat there, helpless. With a face like thunder, she said: "Where to? Stay right where you are! What did you say to Mansour to change his mind?"

Dayeh khanoum was looking on dumbfounded, unable to make head or tail of my mother's words. Terrified, I said: "Nothing khanoum jan. I swear to God, nothing."

-How come all of a sudden he decided he didn't want a wife then?

-How should I know?

Mother bent down and pinched my left and right thighs with both hands from over my dress with all her might. "How should you know? *All the fires blaze out of your grave*[124]. Do you suppose I don't know? Are you kidding me? You don't know why? Eh, you don't know?"

She twisted my flesh with such force that I felt faint; I screamed: "Ouch, ouch! My flesh's coming off khanoum jan."

-Good! The less I say, the less I do, the more you…

She let go of my thighs and went for my forearms resting on my skirt. She pinched the flesh on both my forearms and twisted it: "Have you decided to disgrace us? Do you want to kill your father? How much of this bad milk do I have to breastfeed to this poor baby? You've disgraced us. You have beaten the drum of our shame."

My head sank in my shoulders from the pain. I curled up, screaming: "Ow, khanoum jan, I'm dying."

Khojasteh was pleading: "Khanoum jan, you're killing her. You're tearing off her flesh."

It was as if my mother had lost her mind. Dayeh kept repeating: "Oh khanoum, let go of her. You're killing her."

Dayeh ran around in circles. She wanted to stop my mother, but she was holding Manouchehr. Heedless of Manouchehr's cries of fear and dayeh's yelling, mother said: "Do you suppose I didn't understand? You want to pull the wool over my eyes? May God bless Mansour who bought back our honour; who didn't reveal anything. Shame on me. How will I hide my shame if your uncle's wife finds out? She'll tell the whole world. It's not too late. She'll find out eventually. May God strike me dead and free me from this life."

This time, she went for my arms, pinching both at the same time. She was pulling my flesh with such force that I was half-raised from the trunk. I nearly fainted. Finally, dayeh gave the baby to Khojasteh and said: "Take him"; then she grabbed my mother from behind and pulled her away from me. "You're killing my child khanoum. Let go of her, that's enough."

The chador had fallen off mother's head. She sat in a corner of the sandoghkhaneh and leaned on the bedding. She rested her elbows on her folded knees, held her head in her hands and started to cry. She cried out loud. I could only see the back of her small, delicate hands and her hair. I kept moaning and rubbing my arms. Mother had thrown a fit and Manouchehr was screaming at the top of his lungs with fear. Khojasteh cuddled him and took him out of the room.

Dayeh kept asking in consternation: "But what's the matter khanoum? Why're you doing this?"

-What is the matter? She's feeling amorous. She's fallen in love!

I am not sure whether this divulgence on the part of my mother was because she was no longer able to keep a secret she was even unable to reveal to her own sister, or whether it was due to diplomacy. Had the domestics sensed anything? Had they been able to link the whipping of Rahim the carpenter boy and the closure of the shop to my home detention? If there had been any rumours up until that moment, dayeh would have taken part in them with dadeh khanoum and Firouz. But, from this moment on, dayeh who had surely acquired the privilege of having my mother's trust now, was going to stand up to the other domestics and put an end to any tiffle taffle in order to display her superiority to them, and her faithfulness to mother.

My mother, the epitomy of good character, composure and strength, a woman who was the complete image of a collected and dignified lady, a woman who would only show her anger with a simple frown, the pressing of her lips, or a turn of her head and a stare, a woman whose cheerfulness we could only guess from her douce smile, was now sitting in a corner of the sandoghkhaneh sobbing, while dayeh was trying to console her. My mother said: "She just harps on one string and insists on this boy… *the chicken has only one leg!*[125]"

Then, she sprang up to her feet and came at me again. Dayeh stopped her and yelled at me: "Go on then, get out; get out of this room! Do you want her to kill you?"

It was as if I had borrowed an extra pair of legs. I jumped out of the sandoghkhaneh chador in hand. I have no idea why I did not think of it sooner myself! I could hear my mother and dayeh whispering. I had hidden a piece of ribbon in a corner of the room. I took it out. I found a piece of paper in a great hurry and wrote on it:

I turned down my cousin. I told him I don't want him. I said I only want you Rahim. Only you.

I was running to the garden when Khojasteh appeared, holding the baby: "Where to? Are you going out?"

-No. Khanoum jan's going to hit me again. I'm going to the end of the garden until she comes off her high horse.

In a condemning tone, Khojasteh said: "Really! You're so cheeky! You're the one who has to come off your high horse."

I threw my chador on and ran to the end of the andarouni garden, underneath the trees. I found a small pebble. I wrapped the piece of paper around it and fastened it with the ribbon. I looked back at the building. It was doubtful that they could see me. The garden wall was not very high. I forgot about the pain in my arms and legs and threw the pebble over to the other side and returned to the room quietly.

That night, dayeh khanoum came to the terraced roof where I slept[126] and spent a long time talking to me. Exhausted by the rough road trip from Shemiran to the city, and peeved by the pain in my arms and legs, I cried but would not give in. The chicken had only one leg.

My aunt would not give up either. She kept sending messages asking for Khojasteh's hand. Khojasteh would not say yea or nay. She was unhappy about moving to the north and living far away from her family. But, she was not a rebel like me. She had only just turned eleven. She was still a child, but a pretty one. She had beautiful hair and delicate skin. Her figure was not full yet. To my eyes, she was too good for our cousin Hamid. She was very talented. She studied French with my father and also had home tutoring. She wanted to go to a girls' school, but father would not allow it. He preferred to home tutor his daughters. In the end, my mother sent a message: "Wait for a while please. Mahboubeh's situation with her cousin is not clear yet. I will let you know."

My parents' ill humor and touchiness resumed from the day we got home from the gardens. The confinement and clampdown was on anew.

Early the next morning, the boiler was lit for our bath. It was ready first thing. Agha Begum the rubber arrived, had tea and sweets in dadeh khanoum's room and went down the couple of steps leading to the bathroom straight away. She went through the tiny *sarbineh*[127] and into the bathroom. Khojasteh was the first to be washed. Then, mother took Manouchehr who had just woken up into the bathroom with her. My clothes were ready when dayeh jan came. My eyes were puffy from the crying of the night before. Dayeh jan said: "Look what she's done to herself! Have you seen your face in the mirror?! Are your clothes ready? Do you have everything you need?"

-Yes dayeh jan.

Tragacanth and soap were kept in the bathroom. Dayeh said: "Wash your face, it's too puffy. This Agha Begum's one of those sneaks. If she sees your face, she'll spread the news through the grapevine. She'll add a hundred other stories to it too. And, praise be to God, she spends every day in a different house; she'll blow the whistle and spread the news like wildfire." She took me by the arms to help me up. I moaned from the pain in such a way that she pulled back her hands as if she had been bitten by a snake, and asked frightened: "What's the matter?"

- It hurts where khanoum jan pinched me.

-Pull up your sleeves, let me have a look!

I pulled up my sleeves; I myself was startled as soon as I set eyes on my forearms. The bruises on them were the size of the palm of a hand. My dayeh jan said: "Dear God, see what she's done to this girl! Let me see your arms."

They were even worse. It was as if a black and blue piece of fabric, the colour of aubergines with scattered red and purple spots, had been wrapped around them. My dayeh jan took a look at my thighs too. They were no better than my arms. Mother came out of the bath wearing a white flowery chador over her bath *lachak*[128], carrying a pink-cheeked Manouchehr also wearing a bath lachak and swaddled in white cloth. It was as if the head of a beautiful doll had been glued on to a pestle. She yelled angrily: "Dayeh jan, tell her to come; Agha Begum's waiting." And, as she heard no answer, she yelled again when she reached the stairs: "Mahboubeh, Mahboubeh, I'm talking to you!"

Dayeh khanoum pulled up the wooden *orsi*[129], stuck her head out, and purposefully shouted in a loud voice that Agha Begum could hear in the bathroom: "Khanoum, Mahboub khanoum can't take a bath today. She's indisposed."

As dayeh khanoum was still hanging out of the window, mother who was inside now, said from behind her: "Why're you hollering dayeh khanoum? It's shameful. Haj Ali's in the kitchen, he'll hear you." And then she pointed to me: "I know nothing's the matter with her. Stop putting on an act! Get up quickly and go take your bath!"

Dayeh took my arm and lifted my sleeve: "Is she supposed to go looking like this? See what you've done to this girl? All we need is for Agha Begum to see her bruises and set tongues wagging." Then, she turned to me: "I'll alweays sacrifice myself for you my child. I'll give you a bath myself when Agha Begum's gone."

As mother was leaving the room begrudgingly, she said: "That's just it. If it wasn't for all these tender loving sacrifices, she'd not be so spoiled and unruly now."

Dayeh followed her: "Of course, she's not my own flesh and blood, but I've brought her up. She's like my own child. When I saw her arms, I told myself may God break your hand khanoum jan. The girl's body is all bruised."

To my great surprise, mother remained silent and I did not hear another word from outside, except for dayeh khanoum's grumbling. Perhaps my mother had taken her old age into account. Perhaps she had respected her compassion and loyalty. Or perhaps, she had simply pitied me.

I wrote another letter. I told the story of my battering. When my father left the house for his luncheon and my mother was taking her afternoon nap next to Manouchehr, I quietly strolled down the garden. Haj Ali was washing up the lunch dishes at the pashir. It was two hours past noon. I was about to throw the stone over the wall when I heard the sound of footsteps. I hesitated. Who could possibly be out there in the sticks, in that narrow, out of the way path? I will wait until he leaves. The sound of the footsteps stopped, as if that person had stopped. Suddenly, I thought it might be Rahim. How could I find out? I turned my back to the wall and yelled in a fairly loud voice: "Where are you Haj Ali? How come there's no one at the bottom of the garden today? Immediately, I heard the sound of coughing, and then Rahim's voice: "This pathway is so dusty!"

In a low voice, I called: "Rahim?"

-Is that you Mahboub? Are you alone?

-Yes

And then I threw the stone over to him. A short time elapsed. He seemed to be reading the note.

-They beat you?

-It doesn't matter.

-It doesn't matter? It matters a whole lot. They're torturing you to death.

I said: "They don't believe you want to join the military. You are, aren't you?"

He paused: "The military? Yes, I am… I'll show them."

-When?

He paused again: "Well, I've been following up on it … It'll take a few months… But it won't be any later than next year. Will you run off with me?"

-Oh God, no! Do you want my blood to become *halal*[130]? Let's wait and see what'll come of all this.

-How much longer should I wait? It's driving me crazy.

I said: "If they don't give their consent, then we'll think of something."

He said: "Hurry up with your thinking. I'm wasting away."

Haj Ali turned up with his limp, and I said in a low voice: "Haj Ali's here. Good bye."

Two or three weeks passed since our trip to the village in Shemiran. It was towards the end of the summer. Even so, we were still sleeping on the terraced roof. In the summers, if my father's bed was placed in the andarouni courtyard, our place was on the roof. And if he fancied sleeping on the terraced roof, we had to move to the courtyard; in this case, we had to get up in the early morning so Haj Ali would not see us sleeping when he came to the andarouni courtyard for his daily chores. That year, for the occasion of Manouchehr's birth, and because my father did not want him to suffer from the heat, we were sent to sleep on the terraced roof. Mother always came up some time after us. Dayeh, Manouchehr, and Khojasteh would already be asleep. But, I could not sleep. How l wished Rahim would walk with a stiff military attitude in his uniform and sit next to Mansour with his head held high. Then, I could stare at my dear cousin's posh, toffee-nosed airs reproachfully and sneer.

The door knocker sounded. My parents' quick, indistinct chitchat could be heard; they sounded surprised at the knocking on the door at this time of night. Then, the door latch opened, followed by the sound of male footsteps, the greetings of my father, and my mother paying her civilities: "It's been a while! You've remembered us at this time of night!?"

So, it was a familiar guest; a relative. But who?

Hearing my uncle's voice froze me on the spot. He said sullenly: "I'm intruding. I've come to have a few words with you and my brother…" And the voices faded away, like they were walking down the hozekhaneh stairs. I heard nothing more. My heart sank. My sixth sense was telling me that this untimely presence was not unrelated to my situation.

Barefooted, I cautiously climbed down the rooftop staircase. There was no one in the building. They must be in the hozekhaneh. They do not want to be overheard. It is a private affair. It is about me.

Slowly, I went down the butlery stairs, which led to the courtyard at one end and connected to the back of the hozekhaneh at the other. I heard them speaking in soft, vigilant voices. I peeked in through the gap in the hozekhaneh's back door which was locked. My uncle was sitting on the wooden bed covered by a kilim next to the small pond. He sat there with his profile facing me.

My father had folded his legs into his chest, holding them tight with his arms wrapped around them, and my mother was sitting next to him on the edge of the bed. She had lowered her head and was quiet. She just looked up for a brief moment to say: "Oh dear! I'm just sitting here. Let me get some watermelon, tea, or a hookah or something."

Impatiently, my uncle gestured with his hand: "No khanoum. Please sit down. I've come to say a few words and take my leave. I haven't come to be entertained. Leave it for another time." Then, without further ado, he asked: "Well, what have you decided then?"

Father lifted an eyebrow in surprise: "About what *dadash*[131]?"

-About your daughter's indiscretion. I'm talking about Mahboubeh.

It was as if the sky had fallen on my head. God damn you Mansour. You could not hold your peace in the end!

Mother looked up at uncle's face in a pleading, worried manner. She was asking him with her eyes to keep our secret.

My father remained silent. Undoubtedly, amou jan knew a lot more than he let on. With a sad, reserved voice, my father finally asked: "How did you guess?"

-I knew that Mansour had always wanted Mahboubeh. So why would he suddenly make a turnaround after walking and talking with her in the garden for just an hour? I hounded Mansour. I didn't let up. At last, I sat down and had a good talk with him earlier this evening, when his mother and the children were out. I loosened his tongue. He said it's Mahboubeh who doesn't want me. She said leave me alone. Let me marry the one I want.

My mother clutched her face: "Oh, may God strike me dead."

Keeping his composure, my uncle said: "What's the meaning of this gesture khanoum? It's meaningless. The issue must be tackled with self-restraint."

My mother said: "But agha, this is not a problem that can be solved."

My father asked: "Did Mansour mention whom she wants to marry?" His voice was low and subdued.

My uncle answered: "Yes, he did. He said it's someone who wants to join the military later on."

Father asked again: "He didn't say what he's doing now?"

My uncle dropped his head. He did not want to shame my father: "Yes. He said he's a carpenter's shop boy for now."

-He's right. My daughter has fallen in love. She wants a carpenter's shop boy. She's put her foot down and wants to marry him." He paused, then added: "Heh! That monstrosity… He wants to join the military!! This is how he has stolen this silly girl's heart."

-Well, let her go.

Both my parents looked up in great disbelief. My own two eyes had also opened up wide and were doubtless glistening in that dark corner.

-Let her go? What are you saying dadash? I won't even give her dead body to this lout to carry. See what a kerfuffle this girl has kicked up! What dishonour! I'll set the record straight with her this very night. I'll throw her dead body out on the porch."

He was going to get up when my uncle grabbed his arm. Mother also sprang to her feet, stood in front of my father and told my uncle: "Agha, for the love of God, stop him."

My uncle, who was the elder brother, said in a curt tone: "What's the meaning of this? Why are you behaving so childishly? Imagine you've killed her; will it bring back your honour? You want to get the constabulary in-volved! Or will it be of any use if you beat her through and through? A radical decision has to be made. According to Mansour, this girl has thrown caution to the wind. He said she looked like a hypochondriac. He was wor-ried that if he argued with her too much and tried to talk her out of it, she might tear the clothes off her back and take to the desert. So, why don't you marry her to this young man. He'll join the military and you can also help him out…"

My father interrupted him: "He'll join the military? I didn't expect to hear this from you. This good for nothing wanton? If he was going to join the military, he would've by now. I'll change my name if he does, so help me God! Hell will freeze over first. I wouldn't be so concerned if he was at least capable of carrying his own weight…"

Calmly, my uncle said: "Try to be rational. There's a way for everything. How will this end? She says she wants this young man? Well then, ask the boy to come over with dignity and honour, put them hand in hand and send them on their way. She's not doing anything illegal. She wants to get married."

As if he carried the weight of the world on his shoulders, my father sat up and leaned on the back of the bed. He was white as a sheet. He said: "Yes *khan*[132] dadash; you're playing with fire, but from a distance. You're sitting on the sidelines and asking me to win the match. But, what can I say? It's my honour that's at stake here. She's not your daughter. She's mine. If she was your own daughter, then you'd know what I was talking about. Would you give her away so easily if she was your own?"

My uncle interrupted him: "Really! She's not my daughter? Yes, it's true, she's not my daughter; but she's my brother's daughter! In all her foolishness, she's said something good to Mansour. She's said that if I'm dishonoured, the entire family will be dishonoured; everyone will say her cousins are just like her. When I think about it, I see that she's right. Now, why don't you ask this young man over, see him and evaluate him. He might be a good person. You say he'll never be an officer? That he's a carpenter boy for now? It's fine to be a carpenter. Work is work. Does a job indicate anything in particular? You haven't seen him yet, have you? Maybe he's telling the truth and he's going to join the military."

-How could I not have seen him agha? I just can't understand what this senseless girl sees in him. He has no charm and no accomplishments; he's just an insolent, idler of a bloke with a rough voice. He speaks like a lout and leaves his collar open, showing up his hideously wide shoulders which are as broad as a barn door. His hair is scattered all around his head like a gigolot and he has flagrantly glaring eyes. Can such a person become a military man? This is just window dressing, dadash. I'll breathe my last and you'll live to see it all. Spit in my eye if things don't get even worse than this.

Wonders never cease! How could my father and I, two people with wide open eyes, see a single young man with such contrast? A manly voice, which was music to my ears, seemed harsh and loutish to my father. His wild, untamed hair which seemed mystical to me, seemed vulgar to my father. His large eyes and that ardent, passionate look were flagrantly glaring to him. How could he call that distinct, long, sunburned neck and shoulders, with veins bulging from underneath those manly muscles, as broad as a barn door.

My uncle asked: "What do you want to do now brother? What's done is done. The girl has not disgraced anyone...!"

My uncle went quiet straight away. Disgraced. This was exactly what I had done. Aggressively, my father said: "Not disgraced anyone? What's disgrace then? Does it have a tail or horns?"

Uncle said: "For heaven's sake, she wants to get married. Love's not a crime. Didn't Heydar khan's daughter fall in love and marry? Didn't Mortezagholi khan's son fall in love with that old, widowed woman with two children and marry her in the end? Mahboubeh is not superior to Mahd-e Olia[133] who fell in love with her own son-in-law who was the son of her cook...!"

Father waved his hand impatiently: "You speak such words dadash!! Are you reciting history? That cook's son was also the Shah's minister. But my daughter has fallen in love with a wanton; someone with no roots, a boneless man. It's beyond our dignity. As Nazanin said, he's not our cup of tea. He's not our type." As a last word, my uncle said: "You turn everything I spin back into cotton wool[134]. But, you must know that it's in your own interest to do this. You might end up with a worst infamy on your hands! What if she eats opium[135]? What if she elopes? She'll upset the applecart in the end, you know! According to what Mansour was saying, I don't see a happy ending to this affair. You must let her go soonest and bring this whole thing to an end."

Mother softly hit herself on the head: "Oh! May God strike me dead. What will people say?"

Father said: "Nothing khanoum, people will simply laugh in our face. They'll say that Basir ol-Molk's daughter, with all her grandiose airs and those hoity-toity manners, has married a carpenter's shop boy in the end…!"

Mother said: "Dear God, I don't know what sin I've committed to deserve this punishment. Why was I struck by this disaster? I, who have provided a dowry for every poor, deprived girl. I, who have always helped every helpless, destitute person…"

It was as if my father was talking to himself "As Nazanin put it, even dayeh khanoum's son displays greater dignity than him. Dadeh khanoum and Firouz the coachman's son-in-law is more respectable than this person. Still, we're lucky she didn't fall in love with the gardener's son – the same one who cleans out our pond. Now, dadash is saying to get the jingle and ding-dong of music going, and call everyone to come and watch me put my daughter's hand in that fellow's hand and let him laugh in my face."

Mother hit herself on the head again:"Oh, what am I going to tell people?"

My uncle said again:"Khanoum, you keep saying what am I going to tell people, what am I going to tell people. What do you mean by people? If we hold our heads high and slap their mouths shut, they'll never dare talk!"

Father sighed: "Everyman cries out because of strangers, *Sa'di*[136] is the cause of his own outcry."

It was quite apparent who my father was referring to! When family members wanted a topic to be exposed without spreading the word themselves, there were only two women among all the relatives they disclosed it to. Of these, one was auntie Keshvar and the other was my uncle's own wife. These were two meddlesome, green-eyed, telltale mischief-makers who were unable to put a lid on their mouths. This was a way of life and entertainment for auntie Keshvar whose husband, according to my mother, had died a long time ago of all the grief this woman had caused him. This aunt, who had inherited large fortunes from both her husband and father, made venomous remarks more potent than a viper's bite at her brothers' wives, while singing the praises of her brothers. Before my mother had a son, every time she saw her, she would say: "I love my brother; how I long to hold his son in my arms." When Manouchehr was born and my father gave my mother an emerald ring, she said: "You have to have luck on your side. I gave birth to three wonderful sons, and each time my husband stuck a gold coin on my forehead - plop plop, plop. You must truly appreciate my brother Nazanin khanoum."

My aunt's present to my mother, on the occasion of Manouchehr's birth, was a pair of lightweight, flimsy gold earrings. From that day onwards, she boasted about it everywhere she went, saying: "By God, although I'm a widow, I thought Nazanin khanoum would take offence if I didn't give her a gold present. She has given birth to a boy after all. She expects it. I told myself I have to give her something gold, even if it meant I had to beg and borrow."

Eventually, in order to be freed of her debt, and to prevent his wife from being reproached by people for expecting gold from her widowed sister-in-law, my father sent her a broad, gold bracelet under the pretext that his sister had brought them good fortune by cooking Nazanin 'ash[137] craved for by pregnant women, and so the baby had turned out to be a boy; and thus, he managed to keep her mouth shut.

My uncle's wife was also no better than auntie Keshvar, although not quite that zealous simply because, not only was she preoccupied with her husband and children, she also respected Mansour and my uncle who put the fear of God into her. Nevertheless, my uncle's wife also suffered by my aunt's sharp tongue and drew in her horns in front of her sister-in-law. And now, if these two cunning women were to find out what had happened, their joy would know no bounds. Their prying and their jealousy towards my mother's happiness would go hand in hand and lead them to beat the drum of our disgrace. My father knew this only too well, but did not have the courage to tell my uncle in the face.

My uncle was a gentle and honourable man but, in turn, suffered from the sarcasm displayed by his wife and sister. So, he said: "Why do you draw a veil over your words dadash? If you mean my wife…"

My mother scratched her cheek with her nail: "Oh, God forbid agha. What are you saying?"

My uncle pretended not to hear her, and continued: "If you mean my wife, leave her to me and Mansour. I simply have to tell her that Mah boubeh's bad name only means a bad name for her own daughters and that they'll stay home to become old maids; or if Mansour yells at her once, it'll keep her mouth shut. As far as abji Keshvar is concerned, I'll send her a message that people dishonour themselves in a thousand ways, but blood is thicker than water and their families cover up for them. Do we have to fear our own sister's tongue more than our ancestral blood foes? I'll send a message and swear on our father's grave that if she speaks one word of this matter, if she uses her sharp tongue, if she feigns ignorance in front of other people to make roundabout remarks and set tongues wagging to hurt the family honour, I swear to God never to mention her name again. It would be as if her brother's dead. She can read my elegy and forget about me. I'll see her on resurrection day. I swear on my father's grave that I'll do it."

Mother breathed a sigh of relief. Everyone knew that my uncle was a man of his word. Until that night, neither my father nor my uncle had spoken in that tone about auntie Keshvar or my uncle's wife. It was only on that night that my mother in the hozekhaneh, and I behind the door, came to realise that those two men had suffered in silence as much as the rest of us. But, what could they do? One was a sister, and the other a relative-in-law.

Mother turned to father: "Well, agha's right. The girl's not doing anything against the law. She wants to marry. What can we do? We have to give her away."

My father looked at her, vexed: "You're softening up too? Was it not you who said Mahboubeh has to walk over my dead body? How come you've turned around now?"

Mother had a lump in her throat: "What else can I do? I don't know which way to turn?" Then, she turned to my uncle: "Agha, I swear to God I've been sweating blood. If I take my daughter's side, I'm afraid my husband will succumb…" Tears ran down her face as she continued: "If I take his side, I'm afraid my child will die of grief. As you said, she might take something and kill herself. I beg God for death a hundred times a day. One day, I wanted to eat opium and kill myself. God only knows, I felt sorry for Manouchehr who would become an orphan."

My father was shaken. He took a sorrowful, tender look at my mother and said: "What did you say? Oh, thank you very much! All I need right now is for you to leave me alone in this unfortunate situation. As if I didn't have enough pain, you have to rub salt in the wound!"

Mother was trying in vain to wipe her face with a corner of her chador. Tears were also streaming down my face behind the door and I worried that they might catch its sparkle in my eyes from inside the room and notice me. Mother was crying her eyes out: "She's my child. She's my flesh and blood. I feel pity for her. My heart goes out to her. I know you feel the same agha." She stopped my father from speaking with a gesture of her hand: "No, don't say it's not so. I've been watching you. Because you know she's too scared of you to come into the courtyard for early morning *wudu*[138], you get up earlier and pray in the room. Then, I see you standing in a corner of the window waiting to see her." She turned to my uncle: "Ever since this affair, he has not even looked at Mahboubeh. He won't allow her to show her face in front of him. And she's scared stiff to break the rules. Yes agha, he looks from a corner of the window to see Mahboubeh who comes to the pond like a pigeon terrified of the cat. She wipes off her tears and performs her wudu. Halfway back to her room her face gets soaked in tears again and she returns to restart her wudu. She goes and comes back again. At times, she sits by the pond staring; and you agha, you stand sighing inside the room. You're not one of those fathers to raise a hand on her. You said a hundred times that you'll crush her under your feet. But what happened? Why didn't you? Why don't you get up and kill her! I'm not my father's daughter if I try to stop you…!"

My mother began to sob. In a soft voice, my uncle said: "Khanoum, stop talking like this! Bite your tongue!"

My father kept his head down. His left knee was folded and his right knee was at a right angle supporting his right hand; his left hand rested on the bed. As he sat there, he said in a soft, depressed voice: "Instead of reproaching and reprimanding her daughter, she feels sorry for her. She reproaches me. Alright khanoum, say what you want!"

In a slightly raised voice broken by her sobbing, my mother said: "Do you suppose I didn't reproach her? I didn't hit her? That I didn't pinch off her flesh? I beat her so black and blue that dayeh felt sorry and said I hope you break your arm. She was right. I liked what she said with all my heart. I hope I break my arm. When I pinched her, I noticed she was nothing but skin and bones. Her flesh was sagging. My heart goes out to her. My child looks pale. She has no strength to talk, no strength to walk. And we're all harassing her. You're right agha. By God, I feel sorry for her. At first, I was livid when she refused to take her meals. I thought she was being head-strong. I sent dayeh to talk to her. She came back and said may God bless you khanoum, I'll not interfere. I don't have anything to look forward to in this world; do you want me not to have any happiness in the next either? If you and agha are not afraid of God, I am. I asked her why? She's only her nanny and she still cried. How do you expect me not to cry?"

Her crying interrupted her words. I was also shaking and sobbing. I was afraid they might hear my voice. I kept biting my hand. My mother took a hold of herself and, as tears rolled down her face while she constantly wiped off her eyes and nose with a corner of her soaked chador, she continued: "Dayeh khanoum said do you know what Mahboubeh's saying? She says dayeh jan, what're you going to tell me that I haven't told myself a million times already? I tell myself to think about my father's honour. To think of the reproaches which will be targeted at my mother; think of Khojasteh who'll also lose face… I cry all night long. In my prayers, I beg God to kill me or free me of his love. But he won't; what can I do? Dayeh said I told her Mahboubeh jan, why're you being so stubborn and refusing to eat? She said dayeh jan, I swear to God, I'm not being stubborn. I can't swallow any food, no matter how hard I try. The more I try, the worse it gets. I keep seeing his face. Do you suppose I don't know that he's a carpenter's shop boy? That he's not our sort? Do you think I don't realise that one strand of Shazdeh or Mansour's hair is worth a hundred of him? Do you think I haven't told myself any of this a thousand times? But what can I do with this pain that's eating away at me! I swear to God dayeh jan, this is a disease. I wish I had measles; I wish I had cholera, smallpox. At least agha jan and my khanoum jan would come to my bedside and take care of me. They would bring a hakim to cure me. But now, with this incurable disease, they have left me to my own devices at a time when I can't distinguish right from wrong. They thirst for my blood. I want to kill myself so they will be free of me. But I'm afraid of God. Dayeh jan, please tell my agha jan – tell him he wants to join the military. Tell him he'll become an officer. Tell him to imagine that he's killed me, to allow me to marry him and leave. Tell him imagine you've bought a slave and freed her. Think of it as a sacrificed sheep for Manouchehr's health, that I've caught all the aches and pains of khanoum jan, Manouchehr, Khojasteh and Nezhat to make them healthy. Imagine I passed away that time I caught scarlet fever. I swear to God, it'll be a pious act. What am I supposed to do? Why won't anyone help me? Think of me as another Leili, you who spend so much time reading Nezami!"

Mother went quiet, and then continued: "She's melting away like a candle. I'm afraid my child might lose her mind."

Everyone was reduced to silence; a silence only broken by my mother's occasional sobbing. Finally, with a dull, somber voice, my uncle said: "By God, I've brought the essential message home and given you my best advice. You can take heed from my words, or you can take offense. Give her away if you ask me; there's no other way. The more you show aggression and deny her, the more it will fire her passion. This is how it has been from the days of creation. Do now what you'll have to do in the end."

My father turned the palm of his right hand upwards as a sign of hesitation, and said quietly: "Even I myself don't know what to do. I'm up a blind alley!"

My uncle said: "Nothing. Just declare them legitimate as a pious act. Marry them on the quiet and send them on their way."

My father lifted his head up towards my uncle. Then, he crossed the palm of his left hand with his right hand and said: "Bear this in mind dadash. Mahboubeh will go; but she'll be back. Take my word for it. She'll be back. I'll change my name if she doesn't."

As uncle was getting up, depressed and sad, he said: "There's no remedy. God willing, it'll have a happy ending."

My mother said: "Goodness, I didn't bring any refreshments."

-Please khanoum. I didn't come to be entertained. God bless, good night.

As my parents sat there wearily, they made an effort and said in unison: "Bless you. It was our pleasure. You've honoured us. You're most welcome."

They did not think to get up to see him off and uphold the ceremonious traditions, nor was uncle aware of their inadvertence in any way. All three were too distraught to pay attention to such things. Uncle opened the hoze-khaneh door facing the garden and went up the stairs to disappear in the dead of night. Father sighed and told my mother: "Tell Mahboubeh to send this chap a message to come here an hour before dusk Tuesday next week, to see what he has to say!"

Lethargically, mother asked: "You know the shop's closed; how's Mahboubeh supposed to find him?"

-You're so trusting khanoum. Mahboubeh knows very well where to find him.

Quietly, I climbed up the rooftop staircase and crawled under the sheets. I felt light, like a weight had been lifted off my shoulders. I could see the twinkle of the stars. A cool breeze blew from Shemiran. We slowly approached autumn. Everything was so calm and beautiful. Were these stars always there? Were Tehran nights always so peaceful and relaxing? Did this breeze always caress our faces so softly? So, where had I been all this time? Why had I not felt it? Why had I not seen?

The following morning, I was charged with the delivery of my father's message to Rahim. At the first opportunity, I threw a note tied around a little stone over the wall.

On Tuesday, I was restless from the early morning. I was a bundle of nerves. Khojasteh asked me once every hour: "What does he look like? What does he look like?"

-For goodness' sake Khojasteh, leave me alone. He'll be here soon. Then, you can take a good look from behind the window." I expected him to be entertained lavishly, the way Shazdeh and his mother had been entertained. But, there was no sign of it. Mother was like a feverish person. She even had no patience with Manouchehr. Dayeh lit the samovar and placed a plate of leftover sweets in a corner of the panjdari room. An uncomfortable silence reigned over the house; the silence of a king's palace in defeat. Tired and dispirited, my father sat on a chair immediately underneath the chandelier, facing the yard. The orsi windows were open and Haj Ali had swept and washed the paved courtyard area in front of the garden like every other day. Dayeh put a bowl of ripe, fresh, red watermelon next to the sweets on the table. That was all. A chair was placed opposite my father. He arrived an hour before sunset. Khojasteh was in the goushvareh room by my side. Mother had stayed in the butlery. I was sure she was standing there, behind the closed door so she could watch him from the glass pane without constraints. From a fair distance in the yard, dadeh and my dayeh jan observed him from head to toe with great interest.

He wore a *labadeh*[139] and a pair of new trousers. There were three pleats on the back of his wraparound. His *guiveh*[140] were also new and I noticed they were pulled up at the back for the first time. His wild hair showed from underneath his egg-shaped hat and covered his neck. I wished he would take it off sooner so his hair would fall freely on his forehead for Khojasteh to see and admire my taste. His shirt collar was slightly open again, as if it did not have a button; or as if he would suffocate if he buttoned it up. He was guided up the porch steps and into the panjdari by dayeh. My father shifted and crossed his legs as soon as he appeared. He stood there, at the door, and placed both hands in front of him, one over the other. My father had his back to us which meant that Rahim was facing us, so we could watch him from our hiding place. I noticed his firm, strong hands were trembling slightly. My heart sank. He said modestly: "Salam Sir".

Father answered aridly: "Salam. Come in. No, no, there's no need to take off your guiveh. Come in." It was as if a thorn jabbed at my heart.

He walked in, throwing a mystified, admiring look around the room. He took off his hat and held it in his hands. He was twisting it from sheer excitement. His hair was let loose. In a tone of voice clearly showing his reluctance and grief, my father said: "Sit down!" He was going to kneel on the floor. Father said with authority: "Not there; on that chair."

Khojasteh chuckled and said: "This is what you want?"

I said: "Shut up. He'll hear you."

But I felt dejected. Not only was I offended by my father's manorialism, I also did not expect Rahim to be so docile and intimidated. He sat on the edge of the chair with his feet together and his hands on his knees. I said to myself let me see if my father will still treat him like this when he is an officer? And I was overwhelmed as I imagined him in his military uniform, boots, hat, and sword.

My father asked: "How old are you?" He answered while still looking around the room. My father asked again: "Where's your father?"

-He died when I was young.

-I see. So your father has passed away. And your mother? Do you have one or not?

-Yes

-Anyone else?

-No one

As if my father was afraid of seeking more information, he said: "Do you want my daughter?"

He dropped his head and remained silent for a while. Then, he looked up and stared straight ahead at the goushvareh room where we waited. He was unable to look into my father's eyes. He could not see me, but it was as if I was looking straight into his eyes. He said: "Yes."

-Do you want to take her as your wife?

He turned towards my father, surprised: "I pray to God every day; there's nothing I want more."

Begrudgingly, my father said: "And God has answered your prayers.

He went quiet and looked down. My heart beat for him again. I did not want my father to give him a hard time. My father said: "Listen carefully. If I give you my daughter, will you make a life for her? A good, decent life?" He pointed around the room and added: "I don't necessarily mean this kind of life; but a suitable, well-off, respectable, comfortable and honourable life."

-I'll do everything in my power. I'll sacrifice my life for her.

-Keep your life for yourself. I don't know what ideas you've put in her head to make her lose her mind and build castles in the air. But, open up your ears and listen well. I'll buy a house in my daughter's name where you can live, and a carpentry shop for you to earn a living. Every month, dayeh khanoum will bring her 30 *tomans*[141] as an allowance. Her dowr must be 2500 tomans. Heaven help you if the slightest cloud of sorrow overshadows her life. I will uproot you altogether and destroy your lineage. I will ruin you. Do you understand?"

-Yes Sir.

-Go and give it some more thought; let me know.

-There's nothing more to think about. I have thought long enough. I love her. I won't let go of her even if it's the death of me.

My father waved his hand with hatred and impatience: "That's enough. Give it a rest. Come back here in ten days, on Friday eve. It's the Mab'as celebrations. You'll marry your wife and take her away with you. You'll bring everything that's necessary. Are you literate?"

Oh, why was my father talking in this manner! Is he employing a servant that he questions him like so? It was making my blood boil.

-Yes, I also do calligraphy.

My father took out a piece of paper from his pocket which, as I found out later, was Hassan khan's home address – his second wife's brother – and gave it to him. Respectfully, Rahim took the paper with both hands. "You'll go to this address tomorrow morning. I've asked this gentleman to take you and buy you a suit and a pair of leather shoes. You'll come dressed properly on Thursday, do you understand?"

-Yes Sir.

-Good. You may go now.

I felt sad. I could not tell whether it was due to my father's haughtiness, or the empty-handedness of my future spouse. My father knew we were busy looking from some corner, so he crushed him. He wanted to parade our superiority and his subservience in my face. I was outraged.

He got up, looking ill at ease in this grand house. He was not himself – that wild, passionate Rahim. He was a wild tiger who had been entrapped, who had been tamed. Despite everything, he found the courage to mutter: "Give my regards to Mahboubeh." In a harsh, irritated tone, my father said: "Go."

He ran his fingers through his hair and pulled it back to put his hat on. My heart went wild again.

Over the course of the following ten days, my father called dayeh khanoum and charged her and Hassan khan with the purchase of a small, traditional house, not too costly, in a middle-class area to put in my name. He also bought a suitable, decent shop in the same area in my name. Dayeh furnished the house to her own taste, with the basics of life and a few carpets which were of course *khersak[142]*. She only took two or three complete sets of bed clothes and satin quilts to that house out of the ten or twelve sets which had been previously prepared for my dowry. She went back and forth every day to take the necessary household items. Cauldrons, copper tray, sieve, some china, a silver tray and tea glass holders, a hookah and silver hookah mouthpiece, a set of cutlery, two tulip lamps, *a mardangui[143]*, two or three floor cushions, two oil lamps and a lantern. It was dayeh khanoum who took my dowry to my future home and decorated it single-handed; a home I had not yet seen.

How different it was from taking Nezhat's dowry to her house. For Nezhat's wedding, many *khancheh[144]* were brought from the groom's house, carrying sweets, mirror and candlestick holders[145], hand-woven termeh, henna, and confectionary; and, in turn, my mother sent the dowry on large trays for her son-in-law, Nasir khan. Satin and velvet bed clothes, silk rugs, coloured tulip lamps, a chandelier and a number of mardangui were put on a caravan of mules; absolutely everything under the sun, from pearl embroidered cushions, and toiletries and makeup to kitchen utensils; full sets of china, glassware and silverware; curtains with hand-sewn sequins, termeh, cashmere shawls and a complete set of bathroom toiletries. A small garden next to my father's Gholhak gardens was put in Nezhat's name, plus three shares out of six of a village. The other three shares were to be part of my dowry, which my father never acknowledged.

And what a wedding reception they held for Nezhat! Seven days and seven nights of celebrations in the andarouni and birouni. And the magnificent *sofreh-ye aghd[146]*! A termeh had been spread on the floor and decorated with a silver mirror and candlestick holders as tall as a man; the *kasseh nabat[147]* was truly spectacular. My mother had ordered it in different colours; the rue tray was silver; a decorated sangak bread with *Yar Mobarakbad[148]* calligraphed on it; my father entrusted gold coins to my mother for the shabash, to wish happiness for the bride and groom. It was wonderful to watch! People living as far as seven neighbourhoods away had heard of the wedding! The crowd stood outside the garden wall to watch. The bride's dress was a tale in itself. It had been made by an Armenian lady who had a shop in *Lalehzar[149]*. The day Nezhat had her eyebrows and face done for the first time was as grand a day as the wedding itself. My parents had grown wings. My father was being really talkative with Nasir Khan. He kept patting him on the back as they talked and laughed.

My wedding was a different story. It was quiet and dull. Nobody felt happy. I was the most listless of all. I wanted to run away from that house as soon as possible and be rid of all that mental pressure.

Come Thursday, my parents sat in a corner, brooding from the morning. Khojasteh helped my dayeh jan to setup the goushvareh room with sweets, sherbet, some fruits, and a tulip lamp. There was no sign of a mirror and candlesticks; there was no wedding spread. The difference between my wedding and that of my sister's was from earth to heaven. But I was not complaining. I was miles away and did not care about these ceremonies. If it was not for dayeh jan, even that bit of sweets would not have been placed in that small room. My sister Nezhat came to lunch. Her husband had found an excuse to go to his village for inspection. I knew he was ashamed of having such a brother-in-law. No one asked where Nasir Khan was! My sister was too ashamed to even bring her child, lest she also had to bring his dayeh to see the groom. Nasir Khan was as hurt as my parents, harbouring the same low morale.

The weather had been cooling down little by little. It was the beginning of autumn. The doors opening onto the courtyard area which led to the garden had been shut. About an hour before sunset, the mullah came to conduct the ceremony. Then, Rahim and his mother turned up. Rahim was wearing his new suit, a waistcoat and black leather shoes. He still had the same wild hair. He was truly handsome and attractive; although, I preferred him in that same labadeh and open-collared shirt. He came across as a little uneasy dressed in those clothes.

His mother was a small, slim woman named Zivar khanoum. She had dyed her white hair with henna and had a middle parting which showed from underneath her muslin head cover. She had small, black eyes darkened further with Kohl. Her slender nose and proportionate lips were not without similarity to Rahim's nose and lips, except for Rahim's large eyes which, evidently, must have taken after his father. Zivar khanoum had a brisk mannerism. She was wearing a new, inexpensive chintz dress. As soon as she entered the room, eagerly rejoicing and exulted, she put down the sugar loafs she was carrying and gave me two firm smacks on my made up cheeks. Joyfully, she said: "I had wished for this day for my son."

Her perfume was cheap rosewater. I sat there with my maquillage, as if in a dream, wearing the same pink satin dress which had been tailored for the time Shazdeh had come to ask for my hand for his son. I just wanted Rahim to come and take me away soonest. He was kept waiting in the yard prior to the ceremony instead of being entertained in the same room as the mullah. I just wanted to be free of these inquisitive, sad or disenchanted looks, from these insincere formalities that dayeh and dadeh khanoum had arranged, from this contemptible ceremony they had concocted for me.

The mullah went to the panjdari room, where my father sat unresponsive, disconsolate, and cold. He sat himself by the door of the goushvareh room, where I waited, and read the sermon. When he read out the amount of the dowr, which my father had set at 2500 tomans, Rahim's mother clutched her face and said: "Oh, may God strike me dead!"

The sermon was read three times[150]. I had to wait for a *zir-lafzi*[151] before saying 'Yes'. But I was worried. I was worried that they may not have anything to give as zir-lafzi. So, after the third time, I immediately said yes. Dadeh khanoum showered me with *noghle*[152] and money as shabash, which Khojasteh picked up joyfully, joined by Rahim's mother who was behaving like a child. The humility of the scene was bothersome. Khojasteh's innocent efforts, and the affectionate attempts of dadeh khanoum and my dayeh jan did not suffice. They were not enough to reverse the realities; to camouflage the reality that my parents did not want this son-in-law; to conceal his poverty. Rahim's mother laughed happily and put noghle in her mouth.

Then, Rahim came in with the same huge eyes, dark skin and playful smile and, once more, I had eyes for no one but him. I was wrong; he was even more desirable in a suit. Dayeh took his hand and brought him by my side. He sat down and put his hand in his pocket; he brought out a pair of gold earrings and put them in my hand. Then, his mother stepped forward, put a gold bangle around my wrist and kissed me again. There was no gemmed ring with a dazzling sparkle to catch the eye. Instead, I was glaring at the sparkle in his eyes. No bride in the world felt glummer and more fortunate than I at the same time. Especially when he took my small, soft hand in his strong, masculine hand, and said: "You're mine at last!" And the same playful smile appeared on his lips showing his string of white teeth.

My eldest sister, who was standing on the threshold looking at me despondently, came forward. She put on a pair of wide gold bangles around my wrist and kissed me. She did not say a word to Rahim. I doubt that she even threw half a glance at him. I could not be sure she would recognise him if she saw him on the street. The room went silent. To break that bitter stillness, Rahim's mother delivered a cry of exultation and applauded. Dayeh took a round tray and began playing a rhythm on the back of it. Rahim's mother, Khojasteh, and dadeh khanoum were clapping their hands to the rhythm when my father banged on the door with his fist in the adjoining room, as if he was banging on my heart. In a loud, harsh voice, he said: "What's this? You've raised the roof dayeh khanoum!"

Obviously displeased, dayeh answered from this side: "Well agha, our daughter's getting married. We're celebrating; it's auspicious."

Authoritatively, my father yelled: "Hand them the tambourine to take home and play until the break of dawn. Don't make any noise here."

Disappointed and displeased, dayeh put down the tray. We did not know what else to do. My eldest sister left the room and came back with this message: "Come Mahboub, agha jan wants to talk to you."

Just me. It was as if Rahim did not exist. I got up, went into the panjdari and closed the door behind me. My father was leaning back on a couch. He was resting his head on the back of the couch and stretching out his feet into the middle of the room. His right ankle was resting on his left one. Not only was his jacket unbuttoned, but his shirt collar and half the top buttons on his vest were also open. He seemed to be short of air. I had never seen him so troubled and untidy. His limp hands were hanging down from over the couch handles. His face was white as a sheet as he stared at the ceiling. He had been robbed of a jewel. My mother was sitting on the windowsill, leaning back on the coloured glass of the orsi. She, too, seemed to have no life in her. She was not even wearing her chador. She sat there in her flower patterned dress with her lifeless hands drooping on her knees. She got up and walked towards me when she saw me. She placed a relatively large diamond ring in my hand, without saying congratulations. She said: "Keep this as a souvenir from me", and she left the room in tears through the back door.

My father remained silent for a while. I was at a loss. I just stood there keeping my head down and clutching my hands together. My sister was by my side. Father turned his head towards the ceiling. In a low, listless voice, he said: "Did I tell you I'll send you an allowance of 30 tomans every month?"

I wanted to say when was the last time you spoke to me? But, I just said:

"No agha jan."

-I'll give it to dayeh khanoum to bring to you every month.

He lifted his right hand with great difficulty and dipped it in his vest pocket. He took out a glamorous bib necklace and held it out to me: "Come, take this; it's for you." I took a few steps forward with great respect and took the necklace. "Put it around your neck."

I put it on with my sister's help. My father took a look at the necklace and my young, made-up face. Like a patient in pain, he frowned and rested his head back on the couch again, letting his hands hang down by the wrists from its handles. There were no presents for Rahim. There was not even a mention of his name.

-Well, go now. Godspeed.

I plucked up the courage to talk in a voice hardly leaving my throat: "Agha jan, will you pray for me?"

In our family, it was customary for fathers to pray for their children on their wedding night, giving their blessings and wishing them good fortune. I had seen my father pray for Nezhat, bringing tears to everyone's eyes, even the bride and groom. They believed in prayers in those days. Prayers worked in those days.

A bitter grin appeared on the corner of his lips. Silence fell between us, as if he was thinking how to pray for me. As he sat there, my father lifted the first two fingers of his right hand lethargically. As he continued to lean his head back on the couch, he said: "I have two prayers for you. A good one and a bad one."

I waited anxiously. Worried and concerned, my sister held her hands out suppliantly: "Oh, agha jan…"

Without paying any attention to her, father paused for a long time before saying: "My good prayer is that God doesn't allow you to become captivated and tied down by this man", followed by another silence. His chest moved up and down with a sigh before he continued: "And now, for the bad prayer; I pray that you may live a hundred years." I was nailed to the ground where I stood. I exchanged a surprised look with my eldest sister. What kind of curse was this? This was a benediction in itself! My father knew what was going on in our minds. He said: "You're telling yourself this is not a bad wish; that it's very good indeed. But I wish that you may live a hundred years, to say 'what have I done to myself' every day and become an example to others. Go now."

I had almost reached the door when my father called me back. Not that he used my name, no. He just said: "Wait girl."

-Yes agha jan.

-Until the day you're this man's wife, my name will not cross your lips, nor will you set foot in this house.

I just said: "Goodbye."

-Godspeed

Khojasteh and Nezhat kissed me. Unlike the custom of the time when girls cried as they left their father's home, none of us cried. Crying belonged to weddings where there were no bleeding hearts.

We boarded my father's coach. The hood was up – perhaps due to my father's feelings of shame, or perhaps because of the cool autum air. Dayeh placed some sweets and sugar cubes, plus a large saucepan of food in the coach and joined us. As Rahim's mother was getting on, Rahim bent down and said: "No *naneh*[153], there's no room. Go home."

His mother said: "But it's your wedding night tonight."

Again, that same playful smile sat on Rahim's lips: "That' why I'm telling you to go home!"

A thorn jabbed at my heart once again. I did not like it.

We sat politely with our hands resting on our knees, facing dayeh like two statues. On her instructions, the coach drove through a few streets and alleys, coming to a halt outside a small house in a fairly crowded area.

Dayeh took a key out of her pocket and opened a small, green door. We entered a narrow corridor, where a lavatory could be seen on the right hand side. At the end of the corridor, a single step led down into the courtyard. On the left hand side of the courtyard, there was a room connecting to a shed by a door. A small amount of firewood had been stacked there. At the centre of the courtyard wall to the right, there stood the dark opening of a passage with a barrel-vaulted ceiling. A few steps led down this narrow opening into a blackened kitchen. Slimy green water filled a small pond in the middle of the yard. Opposite the entrance, a staircase in the corner of the yard went up to a small porch which led to two rooms. The larger room was the main room, or parlour, with a door opening onto the porch. It led into the smaller room through an interconnecting door, which became our bedroom and sandoghkhaneh. This room had a window facing the yard. But it could only be accessed from the main room, which I called the parlour. And what a parlour it was! Just four and a half metres by five metres.

Dayeh had carpeted the floors with my khersak rugs and arranged the floor cushions around the larger room. She had hung fairly pretty, but inexpensive, flower patterned curtains on the windows. A concave space had been incorporated into the wall of the small room next to the parlour; it looked like a space for a closet which had never been fitted. Dayeh had also hung a curtain there and stored my trunk and other items behind it. She had covered the mantelpiece with a cloth which she had stylishly folded up in the middle and held in place with a pretty pin, to look like a butterfly. Over the cloth, she had decorated the mantelpiece with a tulip lamp, a small mirror, and a comb. I was a bride who did not even have a mirror and candlestick holders. The other tulip lamp was in the larger room, or parlour as I came to call it enviously. This room had two windows opening onto the porch on both sides of the door. There was a small flowerbed next to the pond, two metres by one, as dry as the desert. The entire house did not even measure a hundred and fifty metres.

Dayeh was taking our belongings out of the coach and spreading them in the kitchen and sitting room. I stepped into the yard and stood there, staring around in bewilderment. The entire house was not even the size of the backyard of my paternal home. That humble ceremony, this modest house, and a difficult and painful day which had been my wedding day had brought me to my knees. A small ab-anbar was situated directly beneath the large room, and I was afraid the floor of the room, forming the ceiling of the ab-anbar, would cave in and swallow us up. Shattered, I stood at the foot of the wall, staring at the brick floor and walls of the yard looking dreary and alien in the last light and shades of the setting sun. I was a fawn in an arid, unfamiliar wilderness, alone and lost, with the hunter behind me and a mysterious, unknown land spreading ahead. I was alone and heartbroken;

disenchanted with my father, my mother, and the world. I wanted Rahim by my side. But, he was busy helping dayeh jan. Apparently, he saw the house, which was also new to him, in a different light. He came out of the room and noticed I had shrivelled up in a corner of the yard, with my back still to the wall. He came to me, rested his right hand on the wall over my head, and took me in the shadow of his being. I was seeing that wild hair and playful smile so close to me for the first time. He asked: "Why're you standing here? Please come into the room; spend the night." He smiled, showing his strong, white teeth, and I longed for him again. All things sad seemed to wash away from my heart with a gentle, limpid flow, like a vanishing fog in the glaring sunshine. He had gained such dominance over me and my soul that he could bring me to my knees with just a smile, one look, a single word. If need be, I would have fought for him all over again. Once again, I would have trampled over the grandeur and glamour of wedding feasts. I would take a hut as my home any time, if only this man would open his wings and hold me in their shadow. I was only just noticing that he was head and shoulders taller than me. Although dayeh had laid the dinner spread, I no longer felt hungry. I did not feel like eating. I did not even want dayeh's presence there anymore. I wanted seclusion and I wanted Rahim. I enjoyed his sense of humour. He no longer smelled of wood, but his hair was still as wild and his eyes exuded the same glow which had captured my entire being. Only his presence alongside me calmed my heart and alleviated my sorrow. He cheered me up, as if I had been given some good news and glad tidings.

Rahim asked again: "Would you oblige tonight?"

I rested my head against the wall, closed my eyes and said: "Tonight and every night.

He threw his head back and laughed out loud. I was entranced. Dayeh lit the tulip lamps, placed them in the niches in each room and called us to dinner. I was finally able to eat a full meal after such a long time. I cannot tell whether it was because the pressures placed on me by my parents had been lifted and I had been let out of my supervised cage to choose my own path in life, or whether because I had achieved what I wanted. I was like a free bird, with no fear or anxiety – full of joy.

Trepidation filled me with when dayeh got to her feet. She said: "Mahboub jan, I have to go now. You know how Manouchehr cries after me. Khanoum said to return quickly and take care of him. After all, your kha noum jan is very tired."

My mother was tired? She had worked really hard for her daughter's wedding? What had she done? What feather was it in my cap? And now, she had summoned dayeh on my nuptials[154]! A night when the bride's family stayed at her place until the morning and did not leave her by herself? But, in my parents' eyes, my husband Rahim was not worth this much. In their eyes, he had to accept me any which way I was and be glad with it. Even if I had squandered my innocence and had two illegitimate children, he still had to oblige and accept me. Me, this blue-blooded person, a cut above the rest. Therefore, dayeh's presence was also unnecessary.

Offended, I rose to my feet and said: "I'll go wash my hands."

Dayeh ran down the stairs and brought me water in a pitcher from the pashir. The pond water was filthy and slimy. She knew I would not touch it. Rahim also joined me. Dayeh poured the water and we washed our hands and faces and dried them. Rahim let the lantern and put it on the single corridor step leading to the street for dayeh to see where she was going. Poor Firouz khan was waiting for dayeh in the coach, hungry and thirsty. Despite my insistence, my dayeh jan had not seen fit to give him his dinner, and had said: "What's all the fuss? He doesn't have to eat first thing in the evening. He can eat at home. It's not as if it's late, is it! Don't worry, he won't die of hunger."

Dayeh took me up the stairs and into the parlour. Once there, she opened the door between that room and the smaller room which was to be my bridal chamber. She had spread the pink satin quilt over the mattress on the floor. She brought both tulip shades with candles burning inside them into the room and placed them on both sides of the niche. Bright, colourful tulip shades with the portrait of Nasser el-Din Shah and his handlebar moustache on them looking at me from inside the niche.

Dayeh took my hand and said: "Sit down."

I kneeled down on the quilt and placed my hands on my knees. I was like a headless chicken. I was shaking. I sat facing the door. It was as if I was surrounded by fog and smoke, waiting for an unknown that was both alluring and startling. I felt alone. I had no one. I had been disowned. Nevertheless, I put my faith in the only refuge I had left in life and was hopeful.

Dayeh put sixty tomans in the palm of my hand, and said: "Your agha jan gave me this to give to you. Spend it yourself…" She paused and added: "I cleared up the dinner spread, but I didn't have time to wash the dishes. Your khanoum jan is waiting for me. She told me to return quickly. Your husband's not a bad man. Masha'Allah, he's good-looking. But, you must learn the ropes and take charge of your life right from the start. Don't ever forget who you are! You mustn't give in. I wish I could stay here tonight; but your khanoum jan wouldn't allow it. Still, I'll come to visit you often."

I could not understand what she was saying. I felt dizzy. I was stunned. I was edgy. I stumbled like a drunkard. As if in a dream, I said: "Give this to Firouz khan", and placed a couple of tomans in her hand. She said: "It's too much." I said: "That's alright. And this is for you."

I gave her three or four tomans. She did not want to take it, but I insisted. She kissed me on the forehead, got up and went out of the door, closing it behind her. Then, I heard the door of the parlour closing, followed by the sound of her footsteps on the stairs. I heard her talking to Rahim, saying: "Guard Mahboubeh with your life." She said goodbye and left.

I heard the sound of dragging feet, the sound of the front door closing, and the sound of horse hooves and coach wheels, which were never heard in my father's big house. This house was so close to the street. Dayeh left, and with her my past and carefree childhood. I have to let go. I have to get these thoughts out of my mind. I am alone in this house. I don't know where Rahim is! I don't know why he won't come! I finally did it. What have I done? Is this small room that I am looking at in amazement my home? Oh, I want my mother and agha jan. I want Khojasteh to fight with, Manouchehr to play with. My dayeh jan, dadeh khanoum and Firouz khan and Haj Ali, so I won't know when it's morning and when it's night time! So I won't know when and how the food is cooked, when it is served and when it is cleared up! What am I going to do with all these dishes piled up in the kitchen now? No, I mustn't cry. I want to have dreamt it all; I want to be in our own house when I wake up in the morning… Ah, it's Rahim's footsteps coming up the stairs. I am so happy to be his wife. It's so good to be here. The door of the parlour opened and shut. Life in my father's house was so tedious and ordinary. The door of the room I sat in opened. My father's house became distant. My mind went blank.

Rahim was standing in the doorway, leaning on its frame. He lifted the lantern he had brought from the yard with his left hand. I sat there, but did not lower my head. The glow of the lantern lit more than half of his face. Half of his dishevelled hair hanging on his forehead was more lit than the other half. The light shone on him and lit his neck and chest which was visible from the open collar of his shirt; and I watched his dark skin and the veins protruding over his hard, masculine muscles. I was besotted, as if I was watching a sculpture, or a painting I had acquired at great expense and great pain. I was mesmerised by its amazingly desirable proportions. I had lost nothing. I had made a good choice.

With that attractive, playful smile, he said: "At last…" I looked down. He said: "No, let me watch you to my heart's content."

I lifted my head again and smiled.

He stood there and watched me carefully. In a low voice, he said: "Do you know what I went through all the nights you were sleeping peacefully?"

Surprised I said: "Sleeping peacefully?" Intuitively, I held out my hands to him, and continued: "My hands were stretched out towards the heavens every night. I pleaded with God. I pleaded dear God, give him to me; let him be mine."

He walked in gently and closed the door. He placed the lantern between the two antique tulip shades in the niche, and I turned towards him as I sat there. Like someone who was talking to himself, he said: "I don't know what I've done! What good deed I've done to deserve you? I'm still in a daze. I must be dreaming. I'm afraid I might wake up. How did you fall into my lap from the sky Mahboubeh? How did you appear outside my dark shop every day like the beautiful moon[155], to take my breath away girl?"

I closed my eyes and laughed with all my heart after so many long months.

Auntie went quiet. She was tired, both physically and men-tally. Soudabeh rose to her feet slowly. She went to the kitchen to warm up a glass of milk and honey to bring to her aunt. She took her time purposefully. She delayed her return on purpose to give the old woman time to rest. It was already five o'clock in the afternoon. When she returned, auntie had fallen asleep on the chair. Soudabeh put the glass of milk on the table and stared into the garden with a heavy heart.

Auntie suddenly woke up. Soudabeh handed her the glass of milk: "Drink this auntie. Leave the rest for tomorrow morning if you're tired."

"No my dear, I'm not tired. It's not the tale of a thousand and one nights to tell you every day. I only feel like telling it tonight. I only want to do this tonight."

She went quiet again. As she was sipping her milk she seemed to talk to herself softly and sorrowfully: "Although, it's no less than the thousand and one nights."

Auntie handed the glass back to Soudabeh and continued.

CHAPTER TWO

Where am I? Is it morning yet? The samovar's boiling. I'm tired. The sun's up. It's so bright. The smell of freshly baked bread. I'm still sleepy. It's too early. I'll wait for dayeh jan to come and wake me up… All of a sudden, I was awake. I'm here. In Rahim's house; my house. I'm Rahim's wife. So, who has lit the samovar? I turned around and stared at the sky through the window.

The door opened and Rahim walked in. "Won't you get up, lazy lady?"

I laughed: "Oh, you won't believe how hungry I am."

-I know. The samovar's lit. Breakfast is ready.

-Wow, I wanted to get up and do it myself…

-You don't need to get up fragile lady. I have lit the samovar and bought you fresh bread. I've also washed the dishes.

I said shamefully: "The dishes? May God strike me dead!"

-God forbid.

It was a couple of hours before noon when we left that small room to have breakfast. The samovar was going cold. I took a piece of sangak bread. It was fresh, but the cheese was not; it had a musty odour.

-Rahim, this is musty.

He laughed: "Let me see." He smelled the cheese: "This is good cheese! I bought it myself this morning. There's no musty odour! Eat it and don't be finicky."

I laughed too: "If only we had brought some cheese from my agha jan's house.

-Cheese is cheese. What difference does it make?

He skipped going to work for three, four days. Even so, he had been to see the new shop.

I would say: "Rahim jan, don't you want to go to work?"

And he would say: "Are you throwing me out?"

-No, of course not. But, what about your shop?

-I've to buy some equipment first. I've nothing to work with. But it'll sort itself out, inshallah.

I ran to our bedroom and came back: "Here, take these fifty-four tomans. My agha jan gave it to me. Will it be enough for what you need?"

-Of course it'll be enough. But you keep your money. Your agha jan has given it to you.

I said: "There's no difference. Inshallah, when your work's sorted out, you'll return double the amount."

He laughed and pushed the money towards me. I kept insisting and he kept refusing. In the end, I took the money and said: "If you don't take it, I'll toss it in the heather."

I had such a determined expression on my face that he said: "I've never seen anyone more stubborn than you girl." He took the money and squeezed my hand so hard that I screamed with joy and pain. He kissed my fingers.

I paused momentarily; then asked with hesitation: "Rahim, are you thinking about the military?"

Surprised, he said: "The military?"

-Yes, don't you want to join the military? Didn't you want to become an officer?

All of a sudden he remembered: "Yes, yes, of course…" He got thinking for a moment and added: "But, I have to sort out the shop first. When that's done, I'll hire someone as my replacement…" He smiled with the same playful look in his eyes: "Yes, I'll hire a boy; a carpenter's shop boy. Of course, only if he doesn't turn out to be an amorous adventurer! Then, I'll join the military."

We both laughed.

I did not know my way around housework. I did not know how to work. Worst of all, I did not know how to do the shopping. Going to the grocer's, butcher's and baker's embarrassed me. He would get up in the early morning, buy the bread and lit the samovar. Then, he did the washing up while I wrapped up the bedding. I did not like it. I did not want my husband to do the dishes. I wished we had a maid; I wished we had some help. But, it was not possible. Real life was showing its face. Life was not just a Ghamar song; it was not just Hafez, or Leili and Majnoun. It was not throwing notes over the wall. It was no longer loving, thievish glances and heart rendering sighs. There was also another side to it. There was also bread and meat and water; it was also blood, sweat, and tears, and earning your daily bread; hard work and household chores; washing, cooking, and cleaning. Nevertheless, life was sweet with him. It was simple, yet difficult.

Whenever he saw me in the kitchen - that dark entrenched kitchen – preparing lunch, he would say: "You look like a pearl lost in a coal shed, a diamond in the rough." Or: "Don't cook lunch Mahboubeh jan; we'll eat the leftovers. It would be a shame to ruin your beautiful hands.

I felt encouraged. I did not talk to him about the hardships of my daily work. He would not let me do the dishes under any circumstances. Every time he returned from work, he washed everything after we had eaten. He said you will ruin your hands; you'll grow a hump. Even so, I was only just beginning to discover what it was like to sweep the yard, cook a meal, and clean the house.

Every little chore seemed hard and repulsive to me. The noisy local children and the loud chatter of the neighbours tormented me. My father's house was so big that no noise ever penetrated into the garden and its grand buildings. It was not the size of a walnut shell, like this house. Why was it so crowded and noisy around here? The ear-piercing voices of *abehozi*[156], the seller of cooked beetroot, and other peddlers split the air; the rag-and-bone man buying clothes, shoes and coats; and then, there was the screeching of the children and the comings and goings and chitchat of the pedestrians and, at times, the sound of hooves, coach wheels and carts. I always listened to these sounds, to differentiate between them and compare them to our own area.

The worst times were when the pond had to be emptied and cleaned, and the nights when it was our turn for the water. The local *mirab*[157] came, and with it all the noise and, at times, the neighbours fighting over water. I stayed in bed. As it was cold by then, I would pull the quilt up to my chin and listen to the conversation between the local mirab and Rahim, their comings and goings, and the filling of the ab-anbar and pond. Then, Rahim would come inside. He would rub his hands together and say: "Oh, it's getting cold."

-There were so many comings and goings and so much noise. What were you doing?

-Hey, what noise khanoum jan! You're so not in the picture. This is such a good neighbourhood my dear. You should see our place!

I did not ask what went on in their place. I did not want to know. My mind was at ease that Rahim was clever enough to fill up both the pond and the ab-anbar. And now, he had come back to me, cold and frozen from the autumn air.

My other concern was taking a bath. We did not have a bathroom at home. I had to go out to the public baths. And there was no one around to carry my bundle of clothes and washing items. I had to pack it under my arm like dayeh jan and dadeh khanoum, and carry it myself. I mourned the days I went to the baths. I just packed a very small bundle so I could carry it under my chador. I went in quickly and ask for a rubber. I was not well-known here, like I was in our own neighbourhood. The rubbers did not make their regular customers wait for my sake. I had to wait for my turn or wash myself. No one praised me here. There were no signs of rubdowns and endearments. There was no pickle and leftover *gousht koubideh*[158]. I was still asleep in the mornings whenever Rahim went to the baths. He always returned before I woke up, which made me happy, because I did not want to see him coming home carrying a bundle under his arm. It reminded me of Haj Ali. The next dilemma was the laundry. I had no idea what to do with it. All our clothes were dirty and piled up in a corner of the sandoghkhaneh, next to the room on the other side of the courtyard, by the entrance.

The first month that dayeh came and brought my thirty tomans, I said: "Dayeh jan, tell our washerwoman to come to us once a fortnight."

Worried, she said: "No love. She won't come this far out. By the time she gets here, it'll be midday." I understood that she did not see fit for her to see how I lived.

-So, what shall I do?

-I'll find someone for you around here. I'll ask the shopkeepers.

Dayeh jan washed our clothes that day, and she was able to find a thin, tall, hard-working woman before the end of the month. Her name was Mohtaram, and she came to do our laundry once a fortnight. Rahim did not interfere in these affairs.

Thirty days passed before Rahim's mother finally came to visit us. She seemed like a funny, good-humoured woman. Although, she was nothing like my own khanoum jan, or even my mother's sister, my uncle's wife or auntie. She was alert and speedy though. She insisted on helping me. I said: "Khanoum, there's really nothing to do. I'll just pop out to do some shopping for lunch and I'll be back."

She insisted on taking the money from me and doing the shopping. I breathed a sigh of relief. Shopping embarrassed me more than anything. Dayeh had brought us rice and cooking fat from my father's house. But, shopping for meat and vegetables was torture to me.

She wrapped her chador around her waist and washed and prepared everything tidily. I did not mind at all, but I had to stand on ceremony and help. So, this would last for two or three days; and then what? I had to take my basket and go to the shops all over again.

Rahim came home and all three of us had lunch together. My mother-in-law was kind to me. I was extremely polite to her and behaved as my mother did; as I had been taught. After the afternoon tea, my mother-in-law put on her chador to leave. I wanted to escort her to the door with Rahim. But she said no; as I insisted, she made me swear on my father's life not to go to the door with her.

-No, Mahboubeh jan. On your father's life, there's no need to come. I'll get upset.

She walked to the middle of the yard with Rahim, but no further. She stood there, whispering to him, very quietly and calmly. Rahim was restless. He shook his hands angrily and walked back and forth. He pointed to the window of the room I was in. He even walked to the stairs at one point and went back again. Eventually, my mother-in-law waved her forefinger at him angrily, as if threatening him. Their sound of their voices rose gradually. I just heard Rahim say: "Lower your voice; she'll hear you."

They began whispering and quarrelling again. Suddenly, my mother-in-law turned around like lightening and walked angrily towards the door at the end of the corridor. She opened the door and left, slamming it behind her. Rahim seemed frozen in the middle of the yard. He stood there for a while, staring at the door. Then, he lowered his head, lost in thought. Slowly, he started walking back to the parlour, the same small, humble parlour, and walked up the stairs looking humiliated.

-What's the matter Rahim?

-Nothing. Is something supposed to be the matter?

-No, but you seemed to be arguing with your mother.

-No, we were saying goodbye.

I laughed and said: "This is how you say goodbye?"

-Leave me alone Mahboubeh; don't you start on me now.

He did not speak in anger. He seemed to be begging. He was restless. He could not remain in one place. I kept quiet. I did not want to annoy him. Whatever was wrong, he would either solve it himself, or come to me in the end for consolation. He was not himself until that evening.

-Will you eat dinner?

-No Mahboubeh. I'm not hungry. You eat.

Rahim went and sat on the window sill which measured only half a metre from the floor. He rested his elbows on his knees and dropped his head. What bothered him so much? What did his mother say? It must have had something to do with me, because Rahim said she'll hear you. He must have meant me. I was not supposed to hear what they were saying.

I went and sat at his feet, on the floor: "Rahim jan, I won't eat if you don't…Tell me what's wrong?"

-It's nothing important. I'll sort it out.

-Well, tell me so I know; have I done something wrong?

He looked up at me and smiled sadly, asking: "Is it possible for you to do anything wrong?"

-What then? What's the matter? Why won't you talk to me?"

-I'm afraid you might get upset. I'll find a way around it myself.

I was losing my mind. What is the meaning of this? What is this torment that I cannot bear to hear about? I asked impatiently: "Rahim, I'm going crazy. For God's sake, tell me what happened! I swear to God, I won't get upset! I'll suffer even more like this. Why won't you talk?"

He hesitated and stared at the palms of his hands. He seemed ashamed to tell me. Finally, in a voice which could hardly be heard, he said: "I've borrowed something from someone. Not me that is, my mother has borrowed it for me. Now, that person wants it back."

I calmed down somewhat: "Well, that's nothing. You scared me. Just return it. What did you borrow?"

He stared at the floor with his fingers entwined together: "The earrings I gave you at the wedding."

It was as if a bowl of ice water had been poured over my head. I went cold. I fell apart. I had to stop myself from sighing. There was a momentary silence. He continued, slowly and shyly: "I was going to put money aside and pay her. But my mother says that's not possible. She wants the actual earrings… Mahboub, I'll buy you a better pair."

My heart was bleeding. I had never even dreamt of a day such as this one. Nevertheless, I felt sorry for him. His pride seemed to melt away drop by drop like a candle and drip onto the floor. I put my hand on his knee: "Rahim jan, I want you, not the earrings. Why didn't you say anything sooner? I'll go get them right now."

I got up and ran into the bedroom which doubled as our sandoghkhaneh and returned with the earrings and bangle his mother had given me. He said: "Why the bangle? This is my mother's. I'll pay her in installments."

I wised up. So, his mother had also asked for the bangle - the very same woman who had endeared me from dawn to dusk that very same day. The same woman I had hoped to accept as a mother had turned out to be so deceitful. I said: "So, your mother has also asked for the bangle then?! You must return everything to her."

He got to his feet to face the window, and said: "Well, she says it's a souvenir from my husband. I gave it to you to keep up appearances. I had to give your wife something at the ceremony…" He paused again, and added: "If you like it, I'll give my mother the money. I'll pay in installments."

I developed an instant hatred for all gold and jewellery right there and then. I said: "No Rahim. Take them. I want nothing from you. I didn't marry you for gold and jewellery."

He sat down on the window sill again and took my hands: "Mahboubeh, you put me to shame…"

I put my hand on his lips. My whole world sat in the corner of that little room. I said: "No, don't talk like this Rahim. I'll sacrifice everything for you."

He kissed the palms of my hands one by one, and said: "I'll cover these small hands with gold bracelets. I'll put diamond earrings on these delicate ears, and put a bib necklace around this ivory neck; you'll see Mahboubeh, one day when I'm rich. I'll work day and night for you; I'll do it. You'll see! Let this year pass. Let this shop take foot… I'll join the military, Mahboub jan, I'll do anything you say."

My heart melted away. I put my arms around his neck with happiness. To hell with the bangle. To hell with the earrings…

It was as if the whole world was eyes and looking at me as I walked down the narrow alleyway with my picheh down. A few kids, some clean and some dirty, were loose in the alley. Life went on as usual with the comings and goings of the carts, coaches, vendors, and housewives doing their shopping; ordinary people going about their business and shopkeepers engaged in their daily routines of dealing with customers and shop boys. Some sat in the sun with nothing to do but collect louse from their collars. And I, Basir ol-Molk's daughter, was going to the grocer's, butcher's and green grocer's on foot, basket in hand, all alone. I did not want to tell Rahim of my agonising trips for fear of making him sad. I wanted to be a complete wife to him. I would say: "Hello sir, do you have fresh herbs for *sabzi polo*[159]?"

The green grocer would look at me puzzled, and say boorishly: "What are these then? Grass?!"

What a rude, vulgar man! Is this the way to talk? The devil is tempting me to turn around and walk away. But, we have nothing for lunch. f I don't shop here, where else can I go? He's our local green grocer. I will always have to deal with him. I would ask the butcher for two kilos of meat. He would ask: "Do you have guests abji?"

No, I did not have guests. There was just Rahim and I. But, as no less than two or three kilos of meat was ever bought in my father's house daily, and as my mother always ordered Haj Ali to cook food for an extra two or three people every day, I was embarrassed to ask for less. I was still ashamed of asking for a *charak*[160] or *seer*[161]. I wanted to say what's it to you that I have guests or not!? Do you know best or my mother? Are you more experienced or Haj Ali? But, perhaps the guy is right after all. There's only just the two of us! And I always ended up saying: "Fine, give me just the one kilo." Baffled, the man would look at me from head to toe and hand the meat over while grumbling to himself: "She hasn't a clue what she wants."

I would become angry again, and I would stop myself short again. Other women came and haggled for hours with the butcher and green grocer over two and a half seer of meat and a kilo of herbs and vegetables. They wanted good meat; the herbs had to be fresh and not covered in mud. My meat was always bad, fatty and hard to cook. The herbs were covered in mud. Whenever Rahim saw the meat, he took it back and changed it, or as I put it, bought good meat. Nevertheless, I was gradually getting used to this life. Yet, at times, the sorrow of having fallen from the heights of comfort in my father's house tore at my heart; but only sometimes; the times when Rahim was not there; the times when housework dragged me down; the times when I felt really lonely.

It was the first of the month again, and dayeh came. She brought my monthly allowance of thirty tomans and asked after my health. My parents had not sent their best wishes. She asked me if I was content, if I was happy. Of course I was. I waited for her to sit down, and said: "Dayeh jan, tell me everything. How's my khanoum jan? Is agha jan well? Manouchehr, Khojasteh, the family, and our relatives, are they all well?"

-Yes love; everyone's doing well, thanks be to God. Khojasteh says hello.

-How's Nezhat? Her husband, her son?

Dayeh laughed: "May she be saved from hell fire after what she's done!"

I was excited: "What has she done dayeh jan, what has she done?"

-Nothing; she's just been her usual self, making the same provoking remarks as always.

-To whom dayeh jan? Tell me; what's she done?

Happy and jolly, dayeh said: "Well, she'd gone to this gathering. As it happens, Ata al-Dowleh's daughter was also there; the same one whose brother came to ask for your hand. Do you remember?"

-Yes, yes; I remember. The same really ugly daughter?

-Yesss… The same snobish one who seemed to have fallen down from heaven. As they were busy chatting away, Ata al-Dowleh's daughter suddenly addresses Nezhat, who was sitting at the other end of the room, to say: "Well, Nezhat khanoum, I've heard that Mahboubeh khanoum has wed, with the grace of God. Congratulations." Nezhat says I knew straight away she was being sarcastic and cynical. So, she says: "Thank you. May we always live under your auspices", and then she begins talking to the lady sitting next to her. But, the woman wouldn't let go, and went on to say: "Apparently, she fell in love." And Nezhat answers with great cheekiness: Of course… and how so khanoum. She fell in love head over heels." Then, shazdeh's sister says: "We couldn't believe it when we first heard. Don't get upset you know… but wasn't Mahboubeh too good to marry a carpenter's shop boy? We were truly surprised." Nezhat says I was ready from the start to deal with this, so, I turned my backside around slightly – and Masha 'Allah with that backside resembling a vat…"

Dayeh laughed. I laughed too, and said: "Oh, dayeh jan. May God strike me dead! What're you saying?"

Yet inside, I was shaking with anger and grief. I did not show it. My dayeh jan said: "Isn't it true? She's a well rounded up dear don't you think…? So, she turns her body around as she sat there, and sits with her back to her, lop-sided. Unabashed, she tells her in front of everyone: "Oh! Why didn't you believe it khanoum? She hasn't done anything unusual. She's just married a young man. What if he's a carpenter? It's an honest job. You, who live among princesses[162], you must have your eyes and ears full of such things. However, what's surprising is Tahereh khanoum's behaviour, whose disre-pute is a book as thick as the book of *Masnavi*[163] all by itself!!"

I said: "Oh, dayeh jan, may God strike me dead. She said it just like that? In front of everyone? She said that about Ata al-Dowleh's sister-in-law? The woman's maternal aunt?! What did she say in return?"

-Her? What could she possibly say? She didn't make a sound. Then, she used a headache as an excuse to leave. Your khanoum jan scolded Nezhat and said she had said a very bad thing. But, my Nezhat jan told her: "Why? Other people have a thousand stigmas to hide, but they behave as if noth-ing's going on. And now, you think I should sit quietly and let that ugly chimpanzee make snide remarks at me in front of everyone? No khanoum jan. I can't worry about what people have to say the whole time the way you do, and grin and bear it. I won't take any nonsense from others like you do. I'll take the wind out of their sail and pay them back in their own coin. Let them say Nezhat has a big mouth. Let them be warned. These people who are blind to their own faults and find fault with others deserve this."

And we laughed and laughed with dayeh. How I loved Nezhat and how I laughed with dayeh that day. She had given that woman what she deserved. I said: "Dayeh jan, kiss Nezhat for me. Give those chubby cheeks a smack on my behalf. Tell her thank you. You gave her what she deserved. Tell her I miss her."

My chin quivered in anticipation of tears, but I managed to stop myself. I kissed dayeh as she was leaving. It was as if I was kissing my agha jan; as if I was kissing my mother, Nezhat, Khojasteh, and Manouchehr. As if I was kissing the ground of a friend's home.

When she left, I put the money in the niche. Rahim was happy when he came home at lunchtime. He had received an order for a job. I asked: "Who from?"

-From one of the carpenters who is really busy. He said he has a job to renovate all the doors and windows of a dignitary's house. But, he won't be able to finish on time. He saw my work and liked it; so, he gave me a part of the job."

He took five tomans from his pocket and put it next to my money on the niche. It was a deposit. I was happy that he had a job to do. I knew his work was flawless and that he would go far very quickly if he kept at it. But, the way he spoke made me sick at heart. I wished he would not say dignitary. When he used this word, it was as if he was looking from down upwards. Thus, as his wife, I was also dragged down to his level, shoulder to shoulder. I wanted him to say one of us… or, I don't know, something else, anything suitable. After all, the daughter of one of those dignitaries was living in his home. But, he seemed oblivious to the fact. Did he not wish to climb up the ladder? He had simply accepted his place in life and considered it normal? Did he not feel degraded? Had he no high hopes? Did he not want to grow wings and fly high? I don't know, I don't know how to put it, but I felt sombre. I was especially sad after hearing what Ata al-Dowleh's daughter had said. I had stepped into a strange world. I managed a smile to encourage him; but it was a wretched one. The poor thing could not understand my pain. He asked straight away: "Are you sad Mahboubeh?"

-What about?

-I don't know!

-No, I'm not sad. I just miss my khanoum jan. That's all.

He laughed and sat beside me. He put his hand under my chin and lifted my head up. He looked into my eyes with those wild eyes, and said: "I don't want to hear you talk like this anymore! You've to become a khanoum jan yourself now.

Whenever I saw his eyes from so close up, at such proximity to my own face, so reachable and without barriers, I felt overwhelmed. I forgot the noblesse, the poor and the oppressed. I lifted my head up to be closer to him. He smelled of wood. I do not know why I lost my enthusiasm! I did not like it.

After our evening meal, we always sat in the bigger room I called the parlour. I was truly hope-sick. That room was used as a parlour, sitting room, and dining room all in one. We had no other space. The entire house was the size of a roost. So, why did I feel unhappy about not entertaining and socialising? I had no room to entertain my family members anyway, those who stuck up their noses, counted the rooms, and made inventories of our belongings. I could not entertain them as I desired, in a way that would stop them from whispering and gossiping.

The weather had cooled down little by little. Rahim made me a small korsi, which we put in a corner of the parlour and arranged the quilts, mattresses and cushions I had brought as part of my dowry around it. I had nothing pretty to cover it with. I remembered the shawl dayeh had brought over with my dowry and left in my trunk, behind the curtain. I brought it and spread it over the korsi. At nights, we lit the oil lamp and placed it in the round, milled tray on the korsi. We had dinner sitting around it, drank tea and cuddled up together on one side as I read the love poems of Leili and Majnoun or Hafez to him.

Be a captive to love, for this is the thinking
For all the amorous, this is the calling

He would either fall asleep, or listen and laugh. He was not much of an enthusiast for such things.

I would ask: "Didn't you enjoy this Rahim? Didn't you like it? Indeed, you must befittingly become an officer."

One night, he brought a piece of blank paper, ink and a reed pen, and said: "I want to write you a verse, so you'll know that I, too, understand some things." Then, he sat next to me under the korsi, and with a truly elegant handwriting, he wrote:

I am losing my heart O lovers, O God
Alas, my secret I can no longer hide

Suddenly, past memories struck me like a rush of hot air in the face, making me blush. I insisted that he hang his beautiful calligraphy on the wall, over the niche.

It was one afternoon when his mother came to our house again. I sat her down at the top of the korsi with reverence. Rahim did not pay much attention to her, and I put it down to the fact that she had taken back the bangle and earrings. I insisted that she stay for dinner, and she stayed without needing much convincing and civilities. She kept chattering away and laughing, showing her strong, white teeth. If the passage of time could be wiped off her face, only Rahim's nose, lips and mouth would remain. But her eyes were small, penetrating and mysterious. I no longer believed her endearments. I no longer trusted her. She behaved as if she had never pulled the earrings off my ears. She would bravely stare into my eyes and talk about everything and anything under the sun. She told me how her first two children, born before Rahim, had died of illnesses; that they were both boys, and how Rahim was everything to her; that he was the strength in her knees and the light of her eyes, and how she had hoped to see him wed. Out of reverence for my mother-in-law, I was sitting opposite Rahim who had sunk under the korsi up to his neck.

Rahim grumbled: "Naneh, you talk too much! Have you rubbed a raw egg on your chin[164]?"

That night, all three of us slept under the korsi, and I felt miserable again. In the morning, Rahim woke up before me as usual, and laid the breakfast spread in a corner of the room. I wanted to get up and help him. But I was feeling tired and lazy.

When I sat by the samovar to pour the tea, his mother's eyes twinkled, and she turned to Rahim: "Rahim, is your hen laying her golden egg?"

I did not understand the meaning of her words, and asked: "What did you say khanoum?"

Indifferently, as he sat with his elbow resting on his knee, Rahim poured his tea in the saucer and blew on it to cool it down – a gesture I disliked – and said: "Nothing; she's asking if you're top heavy? No, she's not."

His mother rolled her eyes and said: "Well, when I saw that Mahboubeh jan didn't get up to make the tea, I told myself something must be up. Mah boubeh jan, Rahim wants you very much you know! He never bothered in our own place."

Anger raged through me. I did not expect to hear such words. No one ever said an unkind word to me in my father's house, never mind make any cutting remarks. Politely, I said: "Well khanoum, I never bothered in our own house either."

She laughed out loud, and said sarcastically: "Well then, this is why you're so spoiled my dear."

I felt a lump in my throat. I put my tea down slowly and sat up. I wanted to give her a harsh answer, but I did not know how. Respect for my elders, and modesty and timidity, prevented me from doing so. The respect I had for Rahim stopped me. This is how I was brought up. I was unable to shut my eyes and open my mouth - over nothing at that; over jealousy, like this woman who was my mother-in-law. I wished Rahim would support me; he had to. I could not, and would not, be disrespectful to his mother. But, he did not seem to notice how upset and hurt I was. His mother understood though, and said: "Oh, goodness love, why won't you eat anything? You want to give birth one day woman. A woman has to eat to have the strength." She had made her stinging remarks and wanted to wipe out the evidence now.

-I'm not hungry.

She ate her breakfast with a great appetite. Rahim followed suit. On the spur of the moment, I felt great anger and hatred towards them. I felt in a minority, trapped and alone. I wanted to say something, to object; to leave the room and slam the door. I wanted to tell Rahim to stop his mother. I wanted to tell her to shut up. But, discretion prevented me. I had always been told: ***You must remain a lady***. When his mother finally took off and left the house with Rahim who was going to work, tears rolled down my face; not out of helplessness, but rage; out of anger at my own shortfall, and Rahim's inattentiveness and distraction.

The New Year was around the corner. Once again, I longed for my paternal home. Dayeh had not come for forty days now. I had just washed away my tears when she arrived that morning. She was distracted and troubled. She took the breakfast dishes from me to wash. As she was doing the dishes by the pond, I sat next to her: "Dayeh jan, agha jan and khanoum jan sent no messages for me? Did they not say to say hello?"

-Well Mahboubeh jan, the house was so busy when I left. Baking… looking after the baby… This Firouz is getting lazier every day. And dadeh khanoum does nothing but eat and sleep.

-Dayeh khanoum, don't change the subject. Did they say to say hello or not?

Dayeh placed the estekans upside down in the basket and, without looking at me, said: "Truth be told, they didn't."

I said with irritation: "They want to give me grief like this."

Calmly, she said: "Their own hearts are so broken that they have forgotten your sorrow."I shuddered with a sinking feeling.

-Why dayeh jan, what's happened?

-The truth is, I wasn't going to tell you anything because I didn't want to upset you. But, I'll tell you now, so you won't think your khanoum jan and agha jan are dancing on air day and night without thinking about you.

She paused and stood up. She took the basket of washed dishes and put it next to the wall, in the pale end of the winter sun, and said: "After your wedding, khanoum jan sent messages to her sister and hinted a few times that they should come and talk about Khojasteh if they so wished. They kept putting it off. About ten or twenty days ago, your aunt came to visit your mother who had a cold. While they were talking, she said: "Inshallah, you'll get well soon and get back to your home and life." And I said: "Yes, in time for Khojasteh khanoum's wedding." Your aunt pretended not to understand and said: "Oh well, Khojasteh is still a child." I was irritated and said: "How a child, khanoum jan? Up until a few months ago, you were pressuring us to wed her to your son!" And, with the state she was in, your mother kept saying: "That's enough dayeh khanoum. What're you saying? Khojasteh's not without suitors! Let go, stop it! But, I didn't stop. So, in a rather straight forward manner, your aunt said: "Up until a few months ago, Mahboubeh had not married the local carpenter boy. I have no objections myself; I'm more than willing. But, my son says he won't become the brother-in-law of a carpenter's shop boy. God only knows, these are his words. As for me, I'm grief stricken."

I was fuming. Khojasteh was suffering because of me. She was suffering because of my whims and caprices. How could my aunt have broken my sick mother's heart so flagrantly? That evil woman! A headache roared in my head as dayeh carried on talking. She said: "Your mother answered: That's quite alright abji. Something bad always gets stuck with its owner. God forbid, why should you die of grief? May your enemy die of grief! I know that you're not to blame. Just tell your darling Hamid jan for me that if Khojasteh didn't have this disreputable relative, her family wouldn't have allowed an incompetent, useless person like you to ask for her hand and relentlessly give her such a hard time day and night!" After which your aunt was offended and left. Now, she's not on talking terms with your mother. You'll forgive me love! She's your aunt, but she's such a snob. It's true when they say if you give a debtor an inch, you'll end up owing them. Your mother has been crying her eyes out since that day. Your agha jan has been so upset that it was only today that he remembered he hadn't sent your allowance, even though seven or eight days have passed from the beginning of the month.

I asked: "What about Khojasteh? How's she doing?"

My heart ached for my sister. Dayeh said: "She pretends that it's not important. She says to hell with it; I never had eyes for him anyway. But, one night, she cried to me and said dayeh jan, don't you believe for a moment that *I chop chives for this cousin of mine[165]!* You know only too well that I didn't want to go and live up north, away from my family and everyone. But, it breaks my heart to know that, up until a while ago, they kept flattering us; and now, they've disgraced my agha jan and khanoum jan in this manner. So much for family. Curse all families; bless total strangers who may have more sympathy. Instead of sympathising with my mother under these circumstances, my own aunt's rubbing salt into her wound."

My tears were waiting for an excuse to pour down: "It's all my fault dayeh jan. I've brought disgrace on my parents… I've caused all of this. I've ruined Khojasteh's chances of getting married."

Dayeh took me in her arms, and said: "Why're you giving yourself so much grief love? This is your cousin's shortcoming; his lack of wits. He has lost such a wonderful girl. This is not the right way to do things. If every time a man didn't like his brother-in-law he took his wife to court, not a single married woman would be left in this town. Just let go. Haven't you got anything better to do? Are you crying for Hamid? Not to mention that figure of his to top it all! He's like a short-legged hen! What you really need to say is good for Khojasteh."

Dayeh made me laugh. My cousin's build and height truly deserved such a comment. Nevertheless, my headache worsened by the time Rahim returned. Dayeh was in the room when he knocked on the front door. He opened it and walked into the corridor. Although he wore a suit now, he still left his shirt collar unbuttoned and smelled of wood. Instantly, I felt ashamed for my dayeh to see him in this state. His appearance only confirmed my aunt and Hamid's comments. Hastily, I said: "Rahim, don't come in like this. Button up your shirt."

-Why?

-Because my dayeh jan's here.

-So? Is she seeing me for the first time?

Still feeling irritated from that morning's events, I said: "No, it's not the first time. But, why shouldn't she see you tidy? This isn't right; wait a second."

I saw the flames of anger in his eyes, but ignored it. I buttoned up his shirt. He stood in the corridor with no objections. But his silence and surrender germinated from anger and stubbornness. He was standing there like a statue; just like a scarecrow. The clothes seemed to hang on him. Bless the way he looked in the first place! He kept his arms away from his body on purpose and went into the yard, dragging his heels. I said quietly: "Rahim jan, bless you, wash up at the pond first."

He bent down by the pond in silence to wash up while turning towards me at the same time. He glared at me in anger mingled with sarcasm. Then, he turned around and went up the stairs. Dayeh came to greet him at the top of the stairs and said hello, to which he answered with obvious indifference. Dayeh gestured at me from behind him, to ask what the matter was. I bit my lip and threw my head back, meaning 'let go, it's nothing.' But, I suffered in silence. Why was he treating my poor, unaware dayeh in this manner? Why did I not react like this to his mother, with that bitter, stinging tongue of hers? It's my own fault. I have proved myself incompetent. I should not have walked his mother to the door and said you have honoured us, come again, feel at home. Why didn't Rahim realise these things? Why is he so unappreciative? I was more angry at myself than anyone else.

Dayeh left and my headache worsened. It was close to sundown. I ignored Rahim and crawled under the korsi to sleep. He came and sat by me. He was good-humoured again. He asked: "What's wrong Mahboubeh, are you upset?"

-No

-Yes, there's something wrong.

I said: "No, I've a headache", and burst into tears.

He laughed; the laughter of a grownup at a spoiled child: "Hey, hey hey, you can't cry over a headache! I'll cure it myself."

He went and fetched all the herbal remedies he knew about, and made me take them. He made tea. He warmed up the leftovers from lunch. Once again, I remembered my father's home - my father's home where I did not have to lift a finger. I remembered how dayeh kneaded and spread the dough to make sweets, and I cut them out with a mould and placed them on a tray. Then, she would take the tray away and bring back the baked sweets for me to put in a dish. Poor dadeh khanoum would grind the walnuts for me to make macaroons. Another help would bring the water to the boil for me to put the rice in, taste it, and tell them it was cooked enough to be drained and steamed; and poor Haj Ali poured it out onto the straw sieve. This is how I had been taught to cook. And now, I suffered single-handed in this house. I felt so sorry for myself that I began to cry again.

Rahim asked: "At least tell me what's wrong? Is it something I've done? Maybe your dayeh has said something."

-Goodness, no!

-What then? Tell me! Is it because I hadn't buttoned up my shirt?

I realised that he understood the reason only too well. He knew it was because of the open button; because of his uncouth way of walking in front of my dayeh jan; because of his contempt for that kind woman. Nevertheless, he still pleaded ignorance. I said: "No", and sobbed.

He said: "You know you're really amusing when you cry. I want to make you cry so I can watch you; watch you when your chin's quivering. But, you can't cry for nothing!"

I said: "Don't you know? Didn't you hear what your mother said this morning? I don't want you to make breakfast tomorrow morning. I am not useless; I can do it myself."

He laughed and said: "Aha, so that's what's bothering you? She meant no harm. Didn't you see how much she pampered you? Didn't you see how upset she was when you wouldn't eat breakfast?"

I became even angrier at his mother's cunning and his lack of common sense.

I said: "There's no appetite left after people treat you as they please!"

-Alright then, my mother did wrong. Are you happy now? Don't cry anymore. Do you want to break my heart?

Instantly, I was ashamed of my behaviour. I was ashamed that he had said my mother did wrong. I felt sorry for him. I said: "Oh, don't talk like this. She wasn't wrong at all. Maybe I took it the wrong way. Maybe I read more into it than there really was."

He laughed and said your mood changes every minute, like the spring air.

We made up.

-Oh, what a foul smell; it's that awful smell of freshly baked bread.

Rahim said: "I've never seen or heard such a thing! That awful smell of freshly baked bread?"

-Yes, why're the walls in this room green? Green makes me sick.

He said laughingly: "Alright, I'll get the painters to paint them red tomorrow."

I craved uncooked rice. I chewed on it by the handful. We were only three weeks away from *Nowruz*[166]. We had removed the korsi and slept in the small room again. Dayeh had brought Nowruz sweets and *sabzeh*[167] from my father's house; my father had sent an extra twenty tomans on top of my allowance for the New Year. All the smells made me feel sick; the smell of flowers, sweets, fresh bread. Only the tender breeze of spring pacified me, and only after I had spent a good few minutes throwing up and my intestines were completely empty of anything I could possibly bring up. It was only then that I felt the caress of the cool spring breeze on my face. I would wash up and feel better. Rahim would come and help me back into the room. I would say: "Don't come close; don't touch me; I feel sick."

-I make you sick?

-Yes, you smell. You smell of humans.

He would laugh and ask: "What do humans smell like?"

-I don't know. I just feel sick. You've got to sleep in the parlour tonight. I want to leave the window open all night.

-You'll catch pneumonia girl. It's still cold outside.

-I'll suffocate in a closed room. It smells of carpet; it smells of curtains. I feel sick.

And Rahim laughed, confused and mystified: "What kind of disease is this then?" And I remained mystified as to why he did not notice all those smells! How could he miss something so obvious! Has he no sense of smell?

Dayeh khanoum came over with a few pots of night jasmines from my father's house. I could not bring myself to tell her that she, too, smelled of humans. So, I just said: "Oh, dayeh jan, what're these fowl smelling flowers? Take them back; we don't need them."

Amazed, Rahim laughed: "See! Even night jasmines smell foul and we didn't even know it."

Dayeh diagnosed my disease: "Congratulations Mahboubeh jan; you're expecting."

I had set the *Haft Sin*[168] which, despite all my efforts, still looked modest to me. Rahim and I were sitting by the Haft Sin. It was a bitter sweet moment. Sweet, because I was with Rahim. He was the man of my house. He was sitting at the top of the Haft Sin spread, looking at me and saying: "I want to be looking at your face when the year changes[169]." Bitter, because it reminded me of the New Year in our own house. It reminded me of the last

Wednesday eve of the year, when we celebrated with the younger members of the family by jumping over the fire, eating nuts, and yelling and shrieking blissfully. It reminded me of the Haft Sin in our own home, which was so full, so complete. All of us gathered around it. Only my father sat on a chair and took his gold watch out of his waistcoat pocket. When it was near the time of *tahvil-e saa*[170], he read the Koran and the special prayer for the changing of the year. He would then look at his watch. The cannon ball was fired when the year changed, and we kissed our parents' hands and each other's faces joyfully and received our gifts of money. The doors were opened right away and the visiting began.

We went to visit my paternal uncle and aunt, and my mother's elder sister; then the family came to visit us. Nezhat and her husband, my paternal uncle and aunt, and my mother's elder sister, who came to return our visit; their children also came, and my maternal uncles who were younger than my father. My younger aunt, and my cousins, both on my father and mother's side… Those who were married and all the younger members of the family, and those who were single. Then, my parents' friends came, following which we returned Nezhat's visit and the younger people who had come to see us. We visited all our family members, friends and acquaintances. And, on the last day of the celebrations, we either went to my uncle's gardens in Shemiran, or my father's garden in Qolhak for *sizdah be dar*[171], with a whole squad of children, and dayeh and dadeh and other domestics. We all sat around the lunch spread, from one end to the other, which was adorned with bowls of *'Ash reshteh*[172], lettuce and oxymel, steamed broad beans, and dishes of sabzi polo with lamb. Then, it was time for tea and hookah, sweets and nuts, and then the return home in a totally exhausted state, to sleep it off until noon the following day.

I imagined all my family spending time together. The night before last was Chaharshanbeh Suri[173]. Rahim and I sat together, just the two of us, eating nuts and listening to the sound of children's firecrackers and *ghashoghzani*[174] while the town was immersed in the smell of blazing bonfires and smoke. What shall I do now? Whom do I have to go visit now? Who will come to visit me?

I had saved my money and secretly gone to the bazaar with dayeh, to buy Rahim a gold pocket watch and chain for Nowruz. I wanted his waistcoat to be adorned with a gold chain. He was excited when I gave him his present at tahvil-e saal. He laughed and gave me an engraved frame displaying his own elegant calligraphy inside it.

I took the frame from him cheerfully. It made me happy if he turned to poetry and calligraphy. I said he had to hang this one on the wall too; on the wall of the room we slept in; and he did. I was curious to know what present my father had given to Nezhat this year! And to Khojasteh, Manouchehr, and my mother! I, of course, had been totally forgotten. It was as if Rahim read my mind and said: "It's a green leaf from a dervish".

I felt sorry and looked into his eyes with compassion: "Rahim jan, shall we go visit your mother?"

-It's not necessary. She'll come here.

-But, it's not nice. She's your mother. It's disrespectful.

-No, it's not. She's happier like this.

I did not insist. I understood that he did not wish for me to see his mother's house.

His mother came. She brought me a cut of inexpensive fabric; the kind my mother gave to dayeh jan and dadeh. I was disheartened, but did not show it. Politely, I sat her at the top of the room.

-Aww khanoum. Thank you. You have such good taste! As it happens, I really needed some material."

She gave her head and neck a twist and sat down with mincing airs. My next guest was dayeh khanoum, who was obviously not liked by my mother-in-law. Even so, dayeh was a dear guest to me. I quietly gave Rahim three tomans when we were alone in the small room.

-Rahim jan, give this to dayeh for the New Year.

He lifted his eyebrows in surprise and said: "This much…?!"

-Yes, for my sake.

-But, why this much?

-Please lower your voice. She'll hear you. Give it to her for my sake.

I had already given dayeh her gift of money. Still, I wanted Rahim to secure his mastery and superiority. I wanted my dayeh to see Rahim as the master of the house.

Dayeh came again. And again, my parents sent no messages for me.

-Dayeh jan, how's Khojasteh?

-Your agha jan is teaching her French. He also wants to buy a piano for Khojasteh jan to learn to play. She has told your agha jan she wants to take the entrance exam for the *Namousse School*[175]. But, your agha jan has said he'll find the best home tutors for her.

A thorn jabbed at my heart; not out of jealousy, but out of regret. I asked: "Don't they want to marry her? Doesn't she have any suitors?"

I did not have the heart to hear her say Khojasteh has had to stay home owing to my unsuitable marriage. I prayed to God that it was not so - that she had not lost her chances to marry because of me. Dayeh said: "Of course she does! She has many. But, she won't accept them, nor will agha. Once, I heard with my own two ears that your father said Khojasteh is still truly a child. I want her to learn all the arts and etiquettes in the best possible manner before she marries. I want her to take a husband who will make up for the other one, that I may be freed of both chagrins at the same time.

I stopped being worried about Khojasteh. Dayeh put my mind at rest. But, sorrow set in my heart. I understood the bitterness of my father's remarks only too well, and it left a bitter taste in my mouth.

I still suffered from morning sickness. A combination of having no one and staying at home over the Nowruz holidays and sizdah be dar, together with my morning sickness all made me sensitive and restless. I threw up non-stop. Rahim would come into the yard, help me up by the side of the pond and walk me back into the room.

-No Rahim, you mustn't sleep here. Go into the parlour.

He caressed me, but his hands were rough and smelled of wood. I did not like it. I lost patience one night. On the spur of the moment, I took a container out of my makeup box and handed it to him.

-What's this then?

-Nothing. Put it on your hands. It'll soften your skin.

-I guess my skin makes you sick too. So now, I've to rub this stuff on it like a woman?

-God, no… This isn't just for women… It'll make your hands softer. You'll feel better. My agha jan also uses it. His hands were so soft. Young men also use it; everyone uses it. Mansour…

Quickly, I bit my tongue. But, he gave me a hard glare, threw the container to one side, and stood up. I thought he was going to sleep in the other room. He said: "Why do you make excuses Mahboubeh? I won't use these things. And if you don't like it, I won't touch you anymore."

He left the house and slammed the door behind him. What had I done? Why did I make excuses? But, I did not. Did he not know that I was pregnant? I did it for him. I wanted him to be a proper gentleman, clean and tidy. Why did he not want to better himself? Was it beneath him? Was he afraid of losing his masculinity? Was he afraid of being branded a loser? But, I should not have talked to him that way. He is right; I have been spoiled. I say anything to him under the pretext of pregnancy and morning sickness. Where did he go? What if he doesn't come back? It will be just me in this house! All alone! It's what I deserve. I did wrong. I treat everyone badly. Oh, how I miss him already. I remembered how he flung the container to one side. The movement of his hand; the movement of his hair; the anger in his eyes; I wanted him. I wanted him by my side right there and then.

It was already dark when he returned. I pretended to be asleep. He opened the door and came up the stairs, dragging his feet. He entered the parlour, opened the door separating the two rooms, and said: "I'm back."

I breathed without a sound. My eyes were shut, meaning I was asleep. He said: "Don't pretend to be asleep. I know you're awake."

He came and sat next to me. I sat up to be next to him. He had a strong smell of alcohol on his breath. I said: "I'm not well Rahim. Go away, let me sleep."

He went and slept in the parlour.

It was already towards the end of May, and I was gradually feeling better. One Friday morning, I woke up feeling a bit weary and sluggish.

-Rahim, I'm bored. I'm rotting in this house.

He asked grimly and sarcastically: "Where do you want me to take you? To the gardens of happiness?"

-Yes!

He looked at me and laughed: "Get up. I'll take you there."

-Not now. Let's go to Lalehzar in the afternoon, for a promenade.

Exhausted and listless, I dozed off after lunch. The dirty dishes were left by the pond. Neither one of us felt like washing them. In the afternoon, I put on my chador and picheh and we took a coach to Lalehzar Street. We went to see its interesting spots. The sun was setting. The crowd was fun to watch. He said: "Do you want to walk? Get something to eat? Are you well?"

-Yes, I'm fine.

We got off the coach and walked for a while. It was very refreshing. Rahim was even more desirable in his suit and waistcoat, with the gold chain of his watch hanging from its buttonhole. A street vendor was passing by, selling bites and pieces. I cannot remember what it was at all. Whatever it was, he had piled it up on his food cart. Rahim asked: "Do you want some of these?"

Excited as a child, I said: "Yes, buy me some."

Two young women and a man passed us by at that moment. Both women had lifted their picheh. Their lips and cheeks seemed too red with makeup. They had vile faces. Their brazen eyes were made up with Kohl. One of them was holding her hand over her mouth giggling and, in a voice ready to burst into laughter, the taller one said: "Shut up, it's not nice." The young man accompanying them was distracted. It seemed to me that the taller woman was looking into Rahim's eyes flirtatiously. Rahim turned around slightly as he stood there. On the spur of the moment, I believed I saw that playful look and that half-hidden smile on his lips, which I felt belonged only to me. In that fleeting moment, I stood there looking at him, while he chased those women with his eyes. He turned around and asked: "How much shall I buy?"

-None

He looked puzzled: "What do you mean? You were hungry just now!"

I started walking ahead angrily: "Well I'm not anymore. Get a coach. I want to go home."

-Why are you doing this Mahboub?

-Doing what? I'm tired. I want to go home.

And, as if I had just noticed his attire, I said: "You look very chic today! All clean and buttoned up, complete with leather shoes and all!"

-Have you just noticed? This is how you want it. Why're you being so difficult?

I turned away angrily and waited for a coach which was coming towards us. He took a step forward to call the coach. Inadvertently, I lifted my picheh. He wanted to help me get on, but I pulled my hand away. I sat in the coach. I felt hot. Jealousy, and what I believed to be his insulting behaviour towards me, burned me up from head to toe. A young gigolot passed by the coach and his shameless eyes rested on my face momentarily. He whistled and walked away. Rahim, who was now inside the coach, just noticed that I had lifted my picheh. He bit his lip and the vein on his neck swell up.

-Why've you lifted your picheh? Do you want to get me involved with strangers? Do you want me to start a bloodbath?

-Not at all. I want you to know that I, too, can lift my picheh.

He answered in a bitter, biting tone: "I already knew that."

The arrow had hit its target, it had hit my heart. But, I lay back casually against the old leather seat, and said: "Well, that's good; it's good that you married me knowingly, with open eyes." And seeing the vein on his neck swollen from anger soothed my heart.

He stared at me with those angry eyes all the way home, and I watched the town calmly with my picheh up. But, my heart was in turmoil. We arrived home. He opened the door and followed me inside. I took off my chador in the middle of the yard, went up the stairs and into the room. Furiously, he followed me in. At the same time, his foot caught on the sieve, which he kicked to one side: "Damn all sieves."

I wanted to laugh. As he came up the stairs, he took off his shoes outside the parlour, walked in calmly and coolly, and closed the door behind him. Carefully, he unbuttoned his jacket and took it off. I sat in a corner of the room and watched him as I rested my hands over my folded knees. He grabbed the collar of his jacket and threw it on a cushion angrily. Then, he turned towards me and said aggressively: "God help me if I go out with you again, I got my fingers burnt this time. Damn my parents if I wear that thing again. You've not taken a husband. You've just taken a servant to do your dishes."

I jumped to my feet: "I've not taken a servant; and washing the dishes is not going to kill me." Hurriedly, I ran down the yard steps. The early evening air still felt cool. But, I did not care. Irritated, I sat by the pond and began washing the dishes. I hit the bowl against the jug and slammed the pots and pans on the floor. I kept telling myself he will come out any minute now. He will come. He has to come and take these off my hands and pamper me. He will apologise to me. Some time passed, but there was no sign of him. Then, a light came on in the room. It was dark outside. He opened the door leading to the porch and stood there. He was leaning against the door frame again, with that same playful smile all over his face again.

-You're taking it out on the pots and pans.

I did not answer. I did not even look up. I just carried on with what I was doing.

-Come inside. You'll catch cold.

I was quiet. I had a lump in my throat. Then, he said: "Mahboub?!!" Uncontrollably, my head turned towards him. He was holding up the oil lamp in his left hand, next to his face, next to his curly locks. He held out his right hand to me with his sleeve rolled back up to his elbow. I saw the same muscles, the same veins, the same sculpture I wanted to watch for hours. Did he have any idea how he touched my heart?

He asked once more: "Mahboub, won't you come in?"

I stood up like a rabbit charmed by a snake. The dish I was holding sank to the bottom of the pond. I started to walk back without even looking. Submissively, I rubbed my hands against my skirt to dry them. I stood in front of him. My chin was quivering. He said: "Aha, this is how I like it – the way your chin quivers. I want to watch you till the end of time."

We went into the room and he closed the door. Tears began streaking down my face. I stood facing him and shivering as he took my hand. It was only then that I realised how cold I was. I was frozen. A shiver went down my spine from the warmth of his hand mingling with the cold of my own hand. I said: "I know what you'd been drinking that night you left the house."

-It was because of you, to drown my sorrows.

-Because of me?

-Because you wouldn't let me in your room.

From that night, he slept in my room again.

I resembled a roof roller in my last month of my pregnancy. Dayeh khanoum visited us more often. I sensed my parents' concerns from her regular visits. The weather was cold. My hands, feet and face were swollen. My nostrils were wide open and my lips had thickened. I hated the mirror. I was ugly.

-Why do I look like this dayeh jan?

Dayeh would answer impatiently: "You'll be alright love. You'll be alright. Rahim agha, this is the address of the midwife who delivered Manouchehr and also Nezhat khanoum's baby. She's very skilled. Take it. You'll need it."

Rahim laughed: "It's still too early dayeh khanoum."

-No, it's not early. She's in her last month. For goodness' sake, send for the midwife as soon as she's in labour. Don't dilly dally! Someone else might call her for another birth.

Rahim said: "Dayeh khanoum, there are lots of midwives around if nothing else. She doesn't have to come here and sit tight like a watchful astrologer from two days beforehand. They charge an arm and a leg; money doesn't grow on trees."

Dayeh pleaded: "Let them charge. Mahboubeh is worth it. Please, don't worry about the money. Ask her to come early. You're just a single-handed man. God forbid, something might happen."

This sort of talk pained my heart. I tried to convince myself that Rahim's refusal was not due to ignobility. That it was simply due to thriftiness. He said: "Don't worry dayeh khanoum. If you're so anxious, I'll go and get my mother tomorrow to come and stay with Mahboubeh until the birth.

The following morning, Rahim made up the room on the other side of the yard at the top of the entrance corridor and temporarily brought his mother over to our place. I was relieved. She took over the shopping. She also did the cleaning, cooking and washing, as if she enjoyed the work. I thanked her a thousand times a day for everything she did. She always said: "Oh, you really stand on ceremony, don't you? It's my son's house. I can't sit around like a guest doing nothing, to be waited on hand and foot."

Yes, she would say it is my son's house!

The washerwoman came and knocked on the door. Rahim's mother opened the door. She whispered to her for a while. The washerwoman stood by the pond, looking lost. Ever since Rahim's mother had come to stay with us, I could no longer leave the laundry in the store room, next to her room. I folded it and left it in an old, half-broken basket at the bottom of the ab-an-bar steps. Rahim's mother came up the parlour stairs. I wanted to call out of the window and tell the washerwoman to go pick up the clothes in the ab-anbar by the pashir. My mother-in-law came into the room and said: "Mahboubeh, why do you want a washerwoman for? Give your clothes to me to wash."

-No khanoum. What're you saying!? This one's not a job for you. She comes regularly once a fortnight. Besides, I'll have my hands tied once you're gone."

She white-eyed me: "Oh, oh, how you throw your money away! Two foolish youngsters throwing good money after bad."

I did not want her to touch our dirty clothes. She was Rahim's mother, and my mother-in-law; not the local washerwoman.

The washerwoman did the laundry and hung the clothes on the line in the yard before leaving. It was almost noon when Rahim came home. All of a sudden, I saw my mother-in-law fill up a small wash-tub with water and go towards her room, dragging her feet on the ground. She returned carrying a few pieces of her dirty laundry. She sat by the pond and began washing them. I was not sure what her plan was. Why did she not give her clothes to the washerwoman this morning? Instantly, I could feel the anger rise in me.

I was getting top heavy. I could no longer walk up and down the stairs as often as I used to. I shouted from the window: "Khanoum, why didn't you give your clothes to the washerwoman this morning?"

She gave her head and neck a twist: "I'll do it myself. Did my naneh have a washerwoman, or my father? One will not die by washing two pieces of clothing!"

I could feel her bad intentions in my bones, but was not sure how to react. I ignored her and laid the spread for lunch. When I heard Rahim's footsteps as he walked into the yard, I went to the window and watched. Rahim took a look at the clothes line, which hung from one end of the yard to the other, and then took a look at his mother.

-Wasn't the washerwoman here today?

-Yes, she was.

-So, why didn't you give her your clothes to wash?

-Well, Mahboubeh didn't say anything to me. She didn't say to bring my clothes and give them to the washerwoman. She didn't say a word. But, that's alright. It's only a couple of dresses."

My entire body was shaking. I was not accustomed to this kind of insidiousness. I felt that his mother was a makebate intending to cause trouble. Whether Rahim noticed or not, I do not know. I just heard him take the words out of my mouth: "You should've given them to her to wash. She doesn't work for free! She's being paid. And if you wanted to wash them yourself, you should've done so in the early morning; not at lunchtime. Are you trying to make me angry?" He kicked the wash-tub: "Take this away. If you're unhappy, go back to your own place."

-Oh, my dear child, I've come to help your wife. Where do you want me to go?

-Like I said; if this is how you're going to behave, my wife doesn't need any help.

I felt good; the commotion was over.

The layette was sent from my father's house, from changing mat and nappies, to umbilical cord care, winter and summer clothes, and hand-knitted cardigans and jumpers. My mother's taste was impeccable. The baby's mosquito net had been decorated with little butterflies. My mother-in-law noticed the layette from a distance, but ignored it. She did not even come near it. I wished I would give birth soon, so she would return to her own place.

The midwife was sitting next to me. She was asking for boiled water and clean cloths and telling me what to do. The pain was shattering my body from the inside. Every time a contraction came, I thought to myself it would not go away this time. I would not be able to bear it this time, that I would stop breathing. I was in an ocean surrounded by waves of pain from all sides. Wave after wave of pain. I was struggling to breathe a painless breath. I wished to go back in time, to the night before. Or fly ahead to tomorrow night. I wished for the time when it was over. Rahim was by my side. He looked at me with innocent, worried eyes. His hair was hanging over his face again. The muscles in his neck and its vein palpitated with worry and excitement. His rough, coarse hand held mine. I saw him, and did not see him at the same time. I recognised his voice, caresses and words in the midst of a cloud of pain. If I was to have some peace, if there was any hope of consolation, it was only thanks to his presence; feeling his presence by my side, suffering alongside me. He seemed to ask: "Mahboub, are you in a lot of pain?"

Amid the short breaths I managed to take between the pain of the contractions and the wonder of their immensity and strain, which was now unremitting, I kept saying: "No… no… It's an easy birth."

I was breathless, as if I had been running. I was sweating and my husband was wiping my forehead. Where was my mother? Why would she not come to me? When will they come to my side? When will they remember me? And if I died tonight, we would only meet again on resurrection day. And the pain started once again.

My mother-in-law was busy coming and going. The midwife left the room briefly.

-Rahim jan, come close.

-Tell me what you want?

-Give the midwife a good tip.

-Don't worry, I'll keep her happy.

He kissed my forehead. His hand was trembling in mine. My mother-in-law walked in at that moment and witnessed the scene. With a wicked laugh, she said: "Mahboubeh khanoum, you won't let go even now? Let the pain of this one be over before you lay the groundwork for the second one! You are a brave one, aren't you...!"

I gave her a harsh glance, and then looked at Rahim. Suddenly, my eyes became two vessels of tears. Rahim looked up and told her mother: "Mother, will you stop or not? Have you come to be her pleasure or her plague?"

I gave his mother a terrified look in that painful condition. I was shocked by Rahim's manner of speaking. I was sure his mother would leave feeling hurt. Did she feel insulted? Would she become a bigger enemy of mine? Would she hate me even more? I was wrong about the first part. His mother laughed casually, and said: "Yes sir, I'll shut up until your chicken has laid her golden egg."

My guess was also not so accurate about the second part. My mother-in-law did not become a bigger enemy of mine. She had been my biggest enemy from the word go. I asked: "Rahim, what does it mean? What does golden egg mean?

As my mother-in-law was leaving the room, she laughed and said: "It means once your baby's born and has captured your father's heart, then you'll see how he'll put the entire six parts of a village in your name! If not an entire village, then at least three parts of it without fail."

Rahim remained silent and I screamed in pain.

It was a boy - round and chubby with flushed cheeks. He was swaddled and wet from the water the midwife had washed him in. His hair was black and thin, but curly. My heart sank. It would grow to be just like his father's hair; wavy and wild. He was sucking his thumb noisily. His eyes were shut like a kitten's. I was lying comfortably on my clean mattress, where the midwife had changed the sheets and removed the wax cloth. Rahim kissed my forehead and gave me an *ashrafi*[176] gold coin. I knew his business was doing well. He had been putting the money he made in the niche every day; every day, until his mother came to stay with us. From that day onwards, he kept his money and mine in this very same chest and gave me the key. I was sur prised, but I did not say anything. Deep down, I knew he had bought the ashrafi coin with the same money, but I was not sure whether to be happy or not? Was this a borrowed ashrafi? I wanted to ask, but did not deem it wise. Now, God had given me a jewel, compared to which big jars of ashrafi[177] turned to dust. My son.

A week went by. I was not well. I knew that some women suffered from depression and melancholy following the birth. Unfortunately, I turned out to be one of them. Rahim sat up by my side for three or four nights and watched me. He watched the baby. He watched him feed. He watched my unwanted tears. Then, one night, when I was lovingly kissing and cuddling my baby, he said: "You're ignoring me now Mahboubeh khanoum! You leave me in the dust now that you've someone new?"

He was jealous of his own son and the place he held in my heart. I looked up and laughed: "You jealous thing!"

-At least let him sleep in my mother's room at night.

-But he has to be fed. Let him stay here for the first two or three months. Then, when he starts sleeping through the night, I'll give him to your mother."

Dejected, he said: "Bah! You might as well say until his wedding night. Goodbye sir, I'm off." And he really left. He was in a huff. When he returned late that night, his breath smelled of alcohol.

His mother took the baby during the day, as I was still bed-ridden. Almost everything was under her control now. Dayeh came. It had been snowing and it was cold. A brazier of hot coal had been left in my room. Dayeh was thrilled with the news of my delivery and, as soon as my mother-in-law left the room, she said quietly: "My dear girl, watch out for the coal fumes for yourself and your baby…" She paused, and then continued: "Also, breast-feed the baby for as long as you can. You won't get pregnant while you're breastfeeding."

I was really hurt. Did dayeh also look down on Rahim? Why did she not want me to have another baby with him? Could it have been my mother's advice? Was she communicating her orders? She gave me forty tomans, and said: "This is a gift from your agha jan." And she left.

It was already the sixth night of the birth[178] when I recalled my mother's delivery. What a jubilation it had been! All that feasting and all the comings and goings! And now, I had been left all alone in this little corner. Only my mother-in-law was home. Rahim had not yet returned. When he came, he was almost beyond control. I was angry with him. I had been crying. The baby had fallen asleep next to me. His mother was washing the dishes in the yard. I was ready for a big fight with him, but forgot all about it as soon as I set eyes on his flushed face and honey sweet eyes. It was amazing how all my dejection, sadness, grief and life's adversities vanished into thin air as soon as I heard the sound of his footsteps. I truly wanted him. He said: "Salam, lady of ladies!"

I knew he was being sarcastic, so I did not answer.

-You're still lying in bed!

-I'm in pain. I cannot sit.

-Yes, you're right. *Rostam's*[179] naneh also lay in bed for forty years.

He laughed and staggered drunkenly.

I also laughed.

-Don't act spoiled Rahim.

-You mustn't spoil me then.

I said: "You're so sweet that I can't stop spoiling you."

His eyes crossed mine and left me breathless.

-You'd lose your head one of these days if you couldn't sweet talk your way out of these situations girl!

He brought his head close. His breath revealed all: "You've been drinking again?"

-Yeah, you don't like it?

-Not one bit. Don't drink anymore.

As he brought his head closer to say something, his mother opened the door without warning and appeared in the doorway as if talking of the devil. She put one hand on her hip and, half joking half serious, she said: "Will you two never stop...! Enough is enough; as if you were still newlyweds!"

Rahim turned around. He put one hand on his knee and leaned on the other one; in a drawling voice, which seemed rather blatant, he said: "Do you mind saying what could be more important?"

-For goodness' sake, it's the sixth night of your baby's birth. You've to choose a name for him.

Rahim turned to me: "What name have you chosen Mahboub jan?"

The drinking had changed his mood and made him jolly. I said: "As God sent you to me, and as you are his father, I would like to name him *Enaya-tollah*[180].

He laughed out loud: "If God gave me to you, then my name should be Enayatollah…"

With disgust and abhorrence, his mother gave her neck and head a twist, and said: "That's enough. It's enough. What's the meaning of this behaviour? Don't be so childish. Your elders have to be respected. Usually, they're the ones who choose the baby's name. A grandfather, a grandmother or someone!"

I objected: "Khanoum, the grandparents have already made their choices in their own time, and chosen their children's names. It's our turn now. If we are his parents, we want to call him Enayatollah."

All of a sudden, tears began cascading down her face. She left the room with a long face and went out on the porch through the parlour. She sat down on the first step and began crying aloud: "I'm the wretched grandmother you know. Even a dadeh and slaves are better off than me. These two won't pay me even the slightest respect. It's my own child's fault. They only want to use me as a servant, to buy, cook, wash and babysit. I'm at their every beck and call and this is how they pay me back. To hell with me and my luck which was bad from the word go. Just take a look at how controlling this crafty little girl is...!"

Rahim and I looked at one another in astonishment: "Where are you going Rahim? For God's sake, don't start any arguments. I can't stand it."

He did not answer. I heard his voice from the porch: "Alright, why're you running riot for? Do you want to catch your death of cold and cause trouble for me?"

She answered, crying: "Don't worry; I won't cause any trouble for you. I'll make it easy for you. Are you feeling sorry for me? If I had been a mother to you, you would've had more respect for me."

-So, what're you saying now? Do you want to name the baby yourself?"

-God forbid, of course not; why would I be so nosey! I just have to wash his nappies."

-I asked you which name you had in mind?

-Which name? Your father's name, Almas khan."

-Alright then, name him Almas. ou don't have to bawl and howl over this!"

Things calmed down. My mother-in-law's tears dried up. My heart missed a beat. Almas khan's face, my grandmother's dark eunuch with his chubby, plump figure and sad eyes, came to my mind.

Rahim returned to the room, alone. He closed the door and said: "That grown woman! What a fuss she's kicked up over a baby's name! Well, all she had to do was to say from the start that she wanted to name him Almas and get it over and done with."

I pleaded: "But Rahim jan, Almas is the name of slaves! My grandmother's eunuch was called Almas. I don't like it."

He pretended to be hurt and angry: "Don't you start now! A name is a name. Aren't slaves human beings? If you don't name him Almas, my mother will leave and our hands will be tied then."

I said: "Don't get angry. I just…"

-You're the one who makes me angry over nothing. You're always looking for excuses. For once in her life, my mother has expressed an opinion and asked me for one little thing now. Look at the fuss you've kicked up!" He left the room in a huff and slept in the parlour that night.

My son was named Almas. Little by little, I got up and began to walk. I could now look after the baby and do the housework at a slow pace. One cold, snowy morning, when Rahim was leaving for work after breakfast, my mother-in-law said: "Well Rahim jan, I'll also say my goodbyes."

It tasted like honey in my mouth. Rahim asked: "Where to? Why're you leaving so soon?"

As my mother-in-law was taking the samovar out of the room, she said: "Well, Masha'Allah Mahboubeh's feeling better now. I've to go home too. Of course, only if you see fit."

Rahim went down the stairs, carefree. He was about to go out of the door and go to work when I noticed that my mother-in-law made a sign at him. The whispering began once more. Then Rahim returned to the room. My mother-in-law went into the kitchen. I knew their whispering would always land me in trouble. He said: "Mahboub jan, my mother has something to say, which I think is not a bad idea. She says, why should you have to pay for two households? Why should you have to pay my rent as well? She says she'll hang around here, in her own corner. Especially when there's enough room…"

I said: "But, Rahim…"

-What? Are you unhappy?

-No, but we won't have any privacy and independence. It's so restricting.

-Why? Do you have to carry her pick-a-back? What does she do? Does she do anything else besides serving you? Has she tied your hands and feet that you're not independent? Do you simply want me to pay an extra rent? Alright then, I'll go tell her right now to get her things; that Mahboubeh says you have to go.

-Oh, may God strike me dead! Don't tell her that! It's really bad. When did I say that?

Deep down in my heart, I was cursing his mother. I knew she was the troublemaker. But, I had to say: "Alright, let her stay. Do whatever you see fit." "Mahboub jan, why don't you talk to her too. After all, she's my mother."

This was too much for me. I knew I had the face of a curmudgeon; but I still said: "Alright."

He said: "Gods bless", and left.

It was as if I had lead in my feet. I went into the yard. My mother-in-law was not there. I found her in the kitchen. I went down the steps with great difficulty. I was still in pain. She was keeping herself busy with the stew pot. I said: "Khanoum, Rahim sees fit that you remain here and live with us."

I was unable to use common words. I really wanted to show my resentment in some way; but I could not, and I hated my own weakness.

She turned around. Her eyes were glistening. I could not say whether it was due to intense joy or extreme craftiness. She said: "Well, Mahboubeh jan, I really don't want to leave my home; but, Rahim tells me insistently stay and help Mahboubeh. She's young. She's not agile enough to do the housework and take care of the baby at the same time. So, I thought what should I do? If I say no, he'll get upset. I said, now that you insist, I'll stay if Mahboubeh jan is also happy. I don't have the heart to leave you in the dead of winter you know. It doesn't matter if it's hard for me. If you tell me to stay, I'll say very well. What can I do? He's my child. I can't see him unhappy."

I so wished that I could do what I longed to do; to take her hand and throw her out of the house. But, I could not. I was a powerless stick in the mud. I had not learned how. I had not learned to stand up for myself. I had always been told to let go. I remembered my mother's advice again: "You be a lady Mahboub jan, you be a lady." I would burst with anger, yet smile. I remained silent. She manoeuvred her way into my life and achieved her goal. She stayed and I even became obligated to her.

Dayeh jan came. She had brought my allowance. She said in a hushed voice: "How come she's still here!?"

-She'll be staying with us. She came under the pretext of helping me and never left. She's taken anchor and outstayed her welcome. But for goodness' sake, don't say a word to my agha jan! Don't tell my khanoum jan either!"

-Why would I tell them? To upset them even more?

I changed the subject: "How's Khojasteh?"

-You won't believe it. Masha'Allah, she's grown taller. She has a face as beautiful as the sun. She takes piano lessons. She has all sorts of home tutors. She draws beautifully…"

I heard no more. I could not distinguish the rest of her words. I was wrapped up in myself; in my own life. It was as if I was left out of that world; a world which was beautiful, alive, and splendid; a world I had left behind. I had turned my back on it. I had been abandoned. When dayeh left, my mother-in-law asked: "What was dayeh khanoum saying?"

-Nothing much. We talked about ourselves mostly.

She clenched her mouth as a sign of displeasure and grumbled in a loud voice as she walked around the house, doing her daily chores: "Did I say you were talking about me? So I'm an outsider now? Why don't you just say she had brought the allowance! Do I want to take it from you? I'm used to working like a donkey for free. You would've had to spend a fair sum if you'd taken on a servant…"

And I thought to myself so she wants money from me? No, I have an evil mind. Can anyone be so inferior and avaricious! Can anyone be so materialistic as to expect money when living with her son and daughter-in-law! Nevertheless, when dayeh brought my allowance the following month and left, I went to her and said: "Khanoum, here's two tomans for you. Buy a chador for yourself. I don't know your taste."

She rolled her eyes and said: "Oh, what's this; it's not as if I expect anything from you!" And she took the money and hid it inside the collar of her dress.

I remembered Shazdeh khanoum, who had come to ask for my hand for her son. I remembered her rings, her demeanour and mannerism. Just between us, she was a real lady. I said: "I know you have no expectations khanoum. I wish to give it to you."

When Rahim came, he said: "This money is short. Did you give any to dayeh again?" And he laughed with a laugh that seemed silly to me.

I said: "No, to your mother."

-What for?

-For God's sake Rahim, don't say anything. She works hard in our house. She looks after the baby, she cooks. Please don't say anything; it's not nice."

I remembered the smile of Ata al-Dowleh's son. I recalled him saying it seems to be a frisky cat. I heard Rahim say: "So what? It's her duty. Did she want to sit around for you and me to wait on her? She has a free house, free lunch and a free dinner; she has to fling her cap that she's no longer a millstone around anyone's neck in her old age."

My heart sank. I understood what I did not want to know. A millstone? Rahim was totally oblivious to what I was going through. He was the spitting image of his mother. He was not to blame; she had brought him up after all. I felt trapped in a swamp, sinking in deeper as the sands of time ran out. Rahim sat under the korsi, ate his lunch and lay back for a while. Then, he got up and left for the shop.

I was restless. Now, I understood the reason behind this unbecoming conduct, this inferior disposition, this itchy palm… I kept consoling myself. Stop it Mahboubeh; this is what you wanted. Why the preoccupation with his mother? Does your own egotistic aunt not greed for money although she is rolling in it? Does she not make your mother shake to the core? Is she not a sneaky one? But, I knew only too well that the difference between them was from the earth to the heavens above. As per the nature of some malignant old women, my auntie Keshvar was avaricious and miserly. Nonetheless, her mannerism and behaviour was composed, serene, weighty, and respectable. She was not shallow and insubstantial like my mother-in-law. Nevertheless, this woman was my mother-in-law and I had to bear with her. I had wanted it. As you make your bed, so you must lie in it. It will be all right. I will manage Rahim. I will open his eyes to the world little by little. I will show him right from wrong, good from evil. He will join the army. He will become an officer. He will mingle and learn. I just have to wait for this year to pass. He had promised. He had asked for a respite until the end of the year.

Gradually, my mother-in-law took the reins of my life in her own hands under the pretext that I was unripe, immature, inexperienced, and a thousand other flaws she attributed to me. I became a feeble being who could not even control her own child. In the second year, after yet another eventless Nowruz, she took the child, who was now a year old, into her own hands; she dragged him into the kitchen, into the yard, and everywhere else with her day in day out. In those days, there were no pacifiers. A piece of cloth and a sugar cube was used to make dummies for children. My mother-in-law would wrap up a piece of sugar cube or candy in cheesecloth, tie it up and give it to my son. But, she would wet it in her own mouth first to pacify my child more quickly and stop him from crying.

I would say: "Oh khanoum, this child is fragile. For goodness' sake, don't put it in your own mouth." Or I would say: "Khanoum, don't drag this child hither and thither in the yard. He'll catch cold. Let me wipe his nose, it's not nice. He wipes it with the back of his hand. It's ungainly."

She would lift her eyebrows and say: "Gee! As if I haven't brought up a child before. He'll get sick from my saliva? Why didn't his father get sick then? Masha'Allah, he's strongly built and sturdy! A child has to run and play. He has to fall down to grow up." Or she said: "His father wouldn't stay home for one minute when he was a child. He was always playing in the mud outside. And as you can see now, a thousand Masha'Allah, he's like Rostam. It makes me proud to look at his shape and build." Or she would say with resentment: "So what if he has a runny nose! I can't wipe it every minute of the day; I've a million things to do! Anyone would think a suitor's coming any minute now; we can throw off disguise with ourselves!"

I would say: "It's not a question of disguise. He has to be clean so he won't get sick, so we can look at his face. One can't bear to take a look at him. "

She would cut me off: "Don't worry my dear. He'll be looked at; and they'll say he's handsome into the bargain. I promise you they'll be after him despite his runny nose. His father hasn't turned out so bad, has he? I promise you rich, aristocratic girls won't let him out of their sight; they'll flatter him and chase after him."

I understood what she meant only too well. I understood the sharpness of her words. I wanted to give her a knockdown answer, but was at a loss for words. I was afraid of arguments. I was afraid it would displease Rahim. I was afraid of how it would end. I, who would not take orders from heaven or earth, now gave in to this old woman. I would squeeze my lips together and return to my room.

Gradually, my son began to talk and his first words were the swearwords and abusive language his grandmother used jokingly or seriously. The old woman took him to the green grocer's, the corner shop, or the butcher's despite my opposition. She petty quarrelled with the local shopkeepers and insulted them. My son learned those swearwords very quickly. To make matters worse, my mother-in-law's jokes were always laced with abusive words; she used words like rascal, lazybones and bastard time after time, as easy as eating pie, and my son did not hesitate to do the same if he was refused something he asked for. His father enjoyed his use of these words, which seemed sweet in his childish language, and said: "Say it Almas, say it so I'll give you what you want." And the child would repeat everything and get treats as rewards. Mother and son would burst out laughing.

Angrily, I would tell him: "Sweetheart, these are bad words; don't use them anymore! If you swear one more time, I'll hit you."

He would stick out his tongue, wiggle his hip and grimace. I would slap him in the mouth. His grandmother would hug him, wet the candy in her mouth and give it to him. I knew the mouth I had to slap was that of the old woman; but I had no options. My son's tears and dripping nose always ran together. I would clean him up once, twice, ten times. But, he always ran around barefooted to the pond, to the front door, to the kitchen, and around the yard. And it was back to square one again. His hands were cracked, his knees were always black, and his dirty face was always striped with tears. What could I do? I was in a minority. I could not win them over; neither Rahim nor his mother cared. I could see that they were totally oblivious towards the good and bad in my son's actions and behaviour. To them, everything about this child, the way he talked and behaved, was natural and commonplace. I tried to make him call me khanoum jan; but his grandmother kept repeating: "Stop Almas jan; your naneh will scold you!" It was as if she wanted to contradict me: "Almas jan, let me cook the rice. It's scorching hot; you'll burn yourself!... Go to your naneh."

And barefooted, he held on to the edges of the kitchen steps with his hands and climbed to the top to come to me, dirty and sooty. In the evenings, when we were together in the room, with Rahim doing his calligraphy and me my embroidery, he would come up and ask for something: "Give me naneh."

I would shout at him: "You said naneh again?! Speak properly and I'll give you what you want."

The poor child would start crying. My mother-in-law would roll her eyes, and say with displeasure: "Oh! What' this?! As soon as the child goes near her, she pesters him and makes him cry. Come naneh, come give me a hug."

My child would go to her in a huff. Apathetically, Rahim would tell his mother: "That's enough then. Don't go adding fuel to the fire." And then, he would address my son: "She wants you to call her khanoum jan. You call her khanoum jan and get it over and done with. Why do you keep saying naneh, naneh, you son of a …!"

It was an odd story and a bitter pill to swallow, so I kept quiet. Who was supposed to correct this child? Who was supposed to correct this mother and son? My efforts were fruitless. My protests surprised them as much as their behaviour shocked me. We did not understand one another. One night, Rahim told his mother: "Naneh, I feel like *kalleh paacheh*[181]. Shall we have some tomorrow?"

His mother was excited: "Yes love. Give me the money to get some for you."

I said: "Oh khanoum, what a difficult task! It's very difficult to clean. Leave it."

With a heathen expression, which grew stronger every day somehow, Rahim said: "Phooey! Do you suppose my naneh cooks it herself[182]? She'll buy it at the bazaar in the morning."

The following day was a day off. Rahim woke up at nine in the morning. My mother-in-law had already been to buy the kalleh paacheh, I do not know where from; she had kept it warm on the charcoal brazier in the kitchen. I got up and brought back two china serving dishes from the set which was part of my dowry. As I was walking towards the kitchen, I saw Rahim's mother carrying a copper tray, in which she had poured out the the shop-bought kalleh paacheh. Panting, she carried it up the steps and placed it on the spread, next to the pickle and sangak bread. I stood there aghast, with the dishes in my hand. I said: "Khanoum, I was just bringing the serving dishes; why did you use the tray? We have dishes!" Rahim was busy eating so eagerly that he could not even hear what I was saying. Her mother was no less enthusiastic. Laughing, she sat my son down next to her and said: "Almas jan, come and eat kalleh paacheh; it'll give you strength. See how tasty it is!"

She took a small piece and put it in his mouth. The child cried and pushed back her hand. My mother-in-law ate it herself, and said: "Don't eat it then; so much the better. I'll eat it myself."

I sat down calmly, and took my son in my arms. I wiped his hands and face. My husband said: "You're not eating Mahboub?"

-No, I'm not hungry.

He laughed: "So much the better. I'll eat it myself."

I was appalled by their mannerism. It was time for me to pour my heart out and say the things I had bottled up inside me for such a long time. It was no longer enough to speak allusively. The problem had to be resolved. I said: "Rahim jan, what have you decided then?"

As he was placing a bite in his mouth, he asked surprised: "Decided? What about?"

I asked: "Isn't your business going well? Aren't you happy with your shop?"

-Yes, why?

-Well, you were going to get a shop boy. You were going to join the army. Don't you want to follow it up and see what needs to be done?"

As he was chewing the food eagerly, he said: "Aha, I'll go. I'll go one of these days soon."

His mother grinned sarcastically. I insisted: "When will that day come Rahim? There's a time for everything. You have to go while you're still young. They say you have to study for it. So, why won't you get up and do something about it?"

Rahim said: "Will you let us eat a bite in peace, or do you want to make it all taste as bitter as the venom of a snake Mahboubeh?"

Satiated and full, his mother got up and sat by the tea set. She poured out a glass of tea with her oily hands and, to change the subject, she said: "Leave it Mahboubeh jan. You didn't have any kalleh paacheh; have some tea at least."

Irritated, I said: "I don't want any."

I got up and went to our room, slamming the door shut between the two. I heard my mother-in-law talking in a timid voice, but loud enough for me to hear: "Well, what's wrong with her? Why's she behaving like this?"

Rahim said: "Leave her alone naneh. Pour some tea. She's probably upset about something else." I could hear the sound of tea being slurped. My mother-in-law said: "She's upset about something else, and she takes it out on me?"

My mother-in-law began whispering. She was having a word in Rahim's ear again, putting ideas into his head. The door suddenly opened and slammed against the wall. I saw his mother sitting next to the samovar quietly with my son, the light of triumph glowing in her eyes. Rahim was wearing a white shirt, trousers and waistcoat. He intended to go out after breakfast. Where to? I had no idea. His jacket was hanging on a nail on the bedroom wall. At first, I thought he had come to take his jacket. His collar and sleeve buttons were open, as always. I took a look at the jacket and a look at him as I stood by the window. He asked in an angry voice: "What's the matter with you?"

I turned around calmly. I crossed my arms and looked at him - greasy hands, open collar, untidy, unkempt hair, and infuriated. I remained silent.

-Why didn't you eat anything?

-I didn't feel like it.

-You didn't feel like it, or was it beneath you? Why're you behaving this way? Is it not fit for us to know?

I said: "Don't you understand? Don't you understand that I'm tired? That this is no life for us? That life's not just about eating kalleh paacheh and sleeping? That life's passing you by, and you're being so lazy? Don't you want to get a decent job? Aren't you worried about this child? Who has to bring him up? You're satisfied with this lowly life?" I pointed out to the room and the yard.

He placed his right hand on the door frame. I thought to myself the door is going to get greasy now. He yelled: "Why won't you let me be happy in my own home? What do you want from me? Why do you keep making excuses?

A one year old child needs correction and upbringing? He needs tutors? I don't understand what you're saying. Talk so that I can understand what's going on deep inside you! I am what I am. What you see is what you get. Didn't you see me from the start? I didn't chase after you, did I? You came, you saw, you liked."

His yelling had scared my son and he was crying. Rahim hit his bare chest with his hand: "You married me, me, Rahim the carpenter. What do you want from me? At first, everything was alright with me; my open collar, my coarse hands, my unkempt hair, my labadeh, my ghaba, my guiveh. And, how come everything about me is ouch now? Am I not the same one as: 'Tis to open my soul to you that I yearn for?"

He was imitating me. His mother's vile laughter filled the other room. She laughed with great pleasure. I said: "Rahim, Rahim, do you know what you're saying. Stop it!"

He yelled again: "Now, you keep giving orders any which way I turn. Rahim jan, put this oil on your hands to make them soft. Rahim jan, button up your shirt, your chest is showing, it's not nice. Rahim jan, comb your hair and tuck it under your hat. Get a hair cut; eat from a plate; pull up the back of your shoes; button up your jacket. Do this, do that. All that's left for you to do now is give me a full makeup. Ten times a day you ask me Rahim won't you join the army? When will you go? What happened then? Was I a military man the day I met you? When did I tell you I'll join the army?

I said angrily: "Didn't you? Didn't you tell me outside the garden wall?"

-So? You kept asking me if I'd join the army behind the garden wall, and you wouldn't give it a rest! I said something to cheer you up, and now I've to pay for it…"

Infuriated, I shouted: "Didn't you say you'd join the army the day khanoum took my wedding bracelet and earrings off me? Didn't you say you'll buy me better ones?"

My mother-in-law shouted from the other room: "Aha, so khanoum feels like gold and jewellery. Why do you drag me into this? Didn't you find any walls lower than mine to climb over and bully? You're still eyeballing that pair of earrings…"

Rahim cut her off: "You blame me now? Do you want me to climb up people's walls like a thief to buy you gold? Do they give away gold and jewellery in the army? You've tired me out. I feel harassed. I won't put oil on my hands. That's for your dear cousin. I never eat anything I haven't worked for to have to grease my hands! Even if I do it today, it'll be the same story all over again tomorrow. Listen to me Mahboubeh, this is my last word. I will not join the army under any circumstances. It's not an easy task. I have to study, burn the midnight oil; there are expenses…"

I said: "My agha jan will pay the expenses."

-Don't keep throwing your agha jan's money in my face. I am what I am, and I'll not get any better. I've taken a wife, not a husband! Take it or leave it."

The vein in his neck was swollen again, like a broadsword fighter, and looked disagreeable under his dark skin. His hair was hanging on his face in a wild, chilling manner. His white teeth were fiercely pressed against one another. His hands were rough, like a primitive man. There was not an ounce of dignity in his entire body. He had mocked and ridiculed everything that I loved and held sacred. I said: "Enough is enough; go now. Don't yell. Don't lower yourself in my eyes any more than you already have."

Insidiously, his mother said: "Rahim dear, don't distress yourself so much. You couldn't even eat your food in peace. Mahboubeh just said something. Forgive her. She's sorry now." I stood in the room, facing the door, and said: "Do you think I couldn't hear how you were whispering spells into his ear? Are you happy now? All this is your doing."

All of a sudden, she raised her voice and hit herself on the head: "I'll be damned; I work like a maid in this house and take this nonsense without making a sound. Is it my doing? No dear, it's not my doing. You no longer see Rahim in the same way. You don't love him anymore. You're no longer head over heels in love with him. You're jaundiced. Don't let me open my mouth now!"

Authoritatively, Rahim said: "Naneh, be quiet now!"

-Yes, I'll shut up. This is what I deserve. Damn me if I stay here another minute."

I took the crying child into my arms. I was shaking like a leaf. My mother-in-law hurriedly packed her clothes into a bundle and put on her chador. The edge of her chador was dragging on the ground. She slammed the door as she wailed and left. Rahim turned to me: "Are you happy now? Is this what you wanted? There you have it!"

He went and sat by the breakfast spread with a frown. After a few minutes, he got up, kicked the sugar bowl which was in his way to one side, came into the room I was in, took his coat off the nail, grabbed the money from the niche, and left.

I burst into tears. I washed my son's hands and face as I was crying, and dressed him in the clothes that I wanted. I felt weak in the knees as I took away the damned tray of kalleh paacheh and emptied it. I cleaned the room, took my son in my arms and hugged and kissed him to sleep. I washed the dishes. The house was clean and shiny now. My son woke up in the afternoon. I played with him; we worked on his talking; I took him for a stroll outside and returned home. Rahim had not come back yet. I gave my son his dinner and he went to sleep. There was still no sign of Rahim. I had bought an alarm clock, which was in the niche over my head. He came at two in the morning. He could barely stand up straight. I closed the bedroom door. He stood behind the door: "Let's make up Mahboub."

I did not answer. He kicked the door. I said: "Don't make any noise. The child is sleeping."

-I don't care that he's sleeping.

-Stop it Rahim.

He fell to the floor behind the door. In a listless, stretchy voice, he said: "Mahboub jan, open the door." And he fell asleep where he was.

We did not talk for three or four days. I would not talk to him, but was happy that his mother was gone, and hoped that she would not come back. When Rahim came home on the fourth night, it was obvious that he had been drinking again. His drinking plagued me more than anything else. My child was sleeping and I was embroidering. He took his calligraphy set and sat beside me without a word. I was looking at him from the corner of my eye. All at once, he asked: "What shall I write?"

I did not answer.

-Don't be silly. Tell me what to write.

-How should I know? Anything you fancy.

-I fancy you.

And he wrote: "Mahboubeh, Mahboubeh, Mahboubeh."

I smiled involuntarily and felt my reproachful look soften. His piercing look in the light of the oil lamp took away all my willpower again. I was beyond myself looking at his playful smile. He held out his hand to me, and said: "Mahboub!" And I fell into his arms.

-Mahboub jan, I have to go and fetch my mother.

I was disheartened once again, and said: "Well, she left of her own free will."

-Left where? She has nowhere to go. She has probably gone to *Varamin*[183], to stay with her nephew. She can be a guest there for a day or two. But, she can't stay forever. I have to go get her." I kept quiet. He sat by my side and said: "Will it upset you?" Nothing could upset me when I was close to him, when he was kind.

-No, why should it upset me? Go and bring her back.

And that woman had a foot in the door again. I kept telling myself it was my own fault. I did not let them eat in peace. I was looking for excuses. Rahim was right. I threw my father's money in his face. He is right; a man is a man, and a woman is a woman. I humiliated him in front of his mother. Suddenly, I felt sorry for Rahim. I was ashamed of my own behaviour. That same night, when I was lying down next to him, I said: "Rahim jan, it was my fault. You must forgive me." He laughed and mesmerised me over and over again.

The first of the month came. Dayeh came. My mother-in-law was out shopping. As soon as dayeh saw me, she said: "My dear, you look so pale. What' the matter?"

-Nothing dayeh jan.

-You don't have to lie to me. I'm good for nothing and ought to be walled in alive if I don't know you any better. Have you argued with Rahim agha?

-No, I swear on father's life.

Now that I had sworn on my father's life, I had to tell the truth: "Well, yes, we did argue to tell you the truth. But, it happened a while back. For goodness' sake, don't tell my khanoum jan! Rahim has been very bad-tempered lately."

Dayeh mimicked me: "She tells me not to tell khanoum jan again! Have I lost my mind girl? But, you're also to blame. Why're you dressed like this? Do something with your hair. Buy some clothes. You're still wearing the same clothes you brought over from your father's house."

-But, I've nowhere to go dayeh jan.

-Do you have to go somewhere? Your husband's young. He's handsome. Wear it for him.

She preached me for a while, and then I changed the subject and asked: "So, what's new dayeh jan?"

-I have some good news.

-Quick, tell me what.

-Mansour agha has married.

I said: "Huh?"

She said: "Yes, Mansour agha. Ask who with?"

-Well, who with?

A thorn jabbed at my heart. Surely, I did not want Mansour. So, if this was not the thorn of jealousy, what could it be? Dayeh said: "With Mr Guity Ara's daughter."

I had heard Guity Ara's name before. I was aware of his good reputation and social standing. Such a correct, suitable choice by Mansour made me fall apart. I felt dejected. I don't know why, but I wanted his spouse to be unsuitable and inadequate. Making a great effort so dayeh would not notice how I felt, I said: "Oh yes, the same one whose garden is next door to my uncle's? The one who's a gifted literary man and a poet?"

-Yes, the same one. Your agha jan says half his house is filled with books. He says he's a pious man, an honest man. God only knows how much your father respects him.

I answered with defiance and pride: "Well, so much for her father's graces and accomplishments. Tell me something about the girl herself. These aren't her own virtues."

Jealousy would not let go of me. I wanted to put Guity Ara down to make myself feel better; but it was not possible. As much as I searched for a fault, I could not find one. Guity Ara was a respected scholar. There was no doubt about that. As his wife was also a shazdeh, and the shazdeh were classically pretty and appealing, then Mansour must have an attractive wife. I was convinced that I was jealous. Of course, I did not keep my eyes peeled for Mansour; but I do not know why, in a corner of my heart, I was hopeful that he would ultimately not be blissful and content in his life; that he would always keep an eye out for me, that he would always long for me, and never be any happier than I. My stomach churned. I kept telling myself what did you expect? Did you want Mansour to spend the rest of his life crying the blues for you? Yes, it seemed that this is what I really wanted from the bottom of my heart. Dayeh added: "Well, I don't really understand these things, but they say the girl is also very academic. Apparently, she also writes poetry."

I knew that Mansour was also very gifted. I had seen him play the tar. I said: "Then, Mansour must be over the moon!

-No dear, it's not quite what it looks like.

I asked: "Have you seen the bride? Is she pretty?"

-What can I say? She's not exactly pretty; but they say she's a great lady. They say her father has put his all into educating her. They say although she's a girl, she excels her brothers in art and culture. They say that her father has left his library to her in his will. He has said there's no difference between boys and girls; my daughter's no less dear to me than my sons. This one daughter is set to one side, and her sister and brothers to the other. I have only seen her once, on the day of her *patakhti*[184]. She had tucked herself inside her hijab; only her eyes could be seen.

I was excited: "What was she like?"

-She wasn't bad. She has the eyes and eyebrows of a princess, you know. They say her paternal grandmother was from Georgia. Of course, the Georgians are well-known for their beauty. Her eyes looked greenish."

I was bored again. I asked: "What's her name?"

-Nimtaj

Dayeh lowered her voice, as if she was speaking of something confidential. She added quietly: "But, they say she's two or three years older than Mansour agha. She was an old maid. She's almost thirty-four years old. She has set her conditions with Mansour agha from the start and has told him I'm not into comings and goings and get-togethers; but I won't stop you. You can go by yourself. She has said I'm free, and so are you. I like to spend my days praying and housekeeping. You can also go about your own business. You can do whatever you like."

In a half-joking, half-mocking tone of voice, I said: "Why? Maybe it's beneath her to go anywhere. Maybe she's too weighty."

Dayeh shook her hand as a sign of ridicule, and said smiling: "No dear; you believe that? *Faati won't go out only because she has nothing to wear*[185]. The girl is pockmarked. She doesn't want anyone to see her face."

To my surprise, I felt her words tasting sweeter than honey in my mouth. I had such a devious disposition! So, Mansour was not blessed after all. I rejoiced for no reason at all; as if someone kept telling me in my heart that this is what he deserved. But, I did not let on. Now that I knew the truth, now that I had gotten to the bottom of things, now that the world was at my feet, I felt sorry for Mansour. "Oh, the poor thing! So, why did Mansour marry a pockmarked old maid?"

-Your auntie says it's for her money. But I don't believe it. They live comfortably, but there's not enough there to blind a young man like Mansour. They say one of the less refined women in her family once told the girl sarcastically: "Every time I see the tah-dig of lentil rice, I think of you." And the father answered in her place: "In return, my daughter is so learned and has so much intelligence in lieu of attractiveness that her face is smoother than a faultless Chinese painting in the eyes of the erudite. *O brother, bring forth a good character.* And this is exactly how it is. You've to see the utmost respect Mansour has for her, calling her nothing but khanoum the whole time."

I asked: "What does my uncle think?"

-Your uncle loves Mansour agha so much that he accepts anything he has to say.

I said: "Good, I'm glad dayeh jan! I'd like to see what my uncle's wife, who found fault with everyone, has to say about her own daughter-in-law now?"

-Who has the courage to say the bride has any weaknesses? Your uncle's wife will extract everyone's insides! She spent the entire time during the patakhti calling the bride's mother and Nimtaj herself shazdeh khanoum, shazdeh khanoum, until everyone had had enough. In the end, the girl herself turned around and said: "Khanoum, my mother's a shazdeh, but I'm not! I'm Mansour agha's wife. You can call me by my name."

-So, she's not a bad woman.

-No, she's not. Like I said, everyone sings her praise. They say that she's a complete lady! That she has backbone. It's not only her relatives who sing her praise. Everyone, from strangers to domestics all like her. They say when she wanted to take a maid to her husband's house with her, they were fighting over her. Each and everyone wanted to go with khanoum, because she's so nice. Your uncle has put the Shemiran gardens in Mansour's name. This girl has told agha Mansour: "Build a house for me in these gardens, and I'll live there." Mansour agha has insisted: "But it's a long way away; it's cold in the winter." She has said: "No. I'm not into socialising. If you want me to be comfortable, let me live there." And Mansour agha has said: "As you wish."

Suddenly, I felt the urge to get up and look at myself in the mirror in the niche. Dayeh was right. What an awful appearance I had! I, who was so young and so pretty, did not have a single new thing to wear. Without hesitation, I said: "Dayeh jan, let's go shopping. I want to buy some fabric for you to give to khanoum jan's seamstress to make a dress for me."

We were looking for fabric around the streets. Crêpe de Chine. Dayeh said: "Why just the one? Have two made in one go, to have handy."

I asked: "But, whose size will she cut it in? Who will try it on?"

-Why, Khojasteh jan of course!

-Oh, has she grown that much?

-Masha'Allah, she's become quite a lady. She's just a little meatier than you. You're all skin and bones child.

Happy as a child, I asked: "When will you bring my dresse dayeh jan?"

-In seven or eight days.

When I returned, my mother-in-law was sitting on the corridor step, cracking pumpkinseeds with the woman next door. My son was playing with the water in the pond. The neighbour knew I did not like her. I hated this sort of slackness, laxity, cracking pumpkin seeds and gossiping. She said hello, to which I answered coldly; she got up and left. My mother-in-law gave me an irate look and asked with a sarcastic smile: "You look cheery today, where've you been?"

-We went to buy fabric with dayeh jan. She took it to the seamstress for me.

-Well, may you be in good health and wear it at weddings and gatherings.

I held my head high and said with pride: "As it happens, there's an upcoming wedding. Mansour agha's wedding."

-Congratulations; who with?

I said with importance: "With Mr Guity Ara's daughter. They say her father's a learned man." And as she showed no reaction, I knew I had to speak to her in her own language. I said: "Her mother's a shazdeh."

She sneered: "Oh yes, one of those spent shazdehs?!"

Her stinging tongue was hard to bear. Belligerently, I said: "Since when is Mrs Guity Ara a spent shazdeh? The whole of Tehran knows him. If you're not aware of it, that's a different story."

It was as if she had the answer tucked up her sleeve. I had underestimated her powers of aggressiveness and utter shamelessness. She gave a twist to her head and neck, and said: "Well then, there must have been something wrong with the girl", and left for the kitchen.

She had taken revenge for my coldness towards the woman next door. I stood there, astonished and angry. I was angry, mostly because she had guessed right.

Upon dayeh's insistence, I wore the dresses that had been tailored for me and brought over by her; I twirled around a couple of times for her to see. That kind old woman endeared me as if I was really her own child. She would comment on my figure and my beautiful hair. She would take my son into her arms and give him motherly kisses. Then, softly, very softly and calmly so I would get the least upset, she would say: "Masha'Allah, what a lovely son; he's sweet as honey… But, Mahboub jan, my dear, don't get pregnant again…" And as she saw my harsh look, she would immediately add: "It's still too early you know. This one's still too young."

I told myself these are not her words. They are my khanoum jan's recommendations; agha jan's orders. I decided to get pregnant as soon as possible. My mother-in-law came into the room to take away the samovar. As she saw me wearing the dress, she turned away with bitterness and left the room without a word. She did not say whether it was good or bad. My dayeh jan said: "She's jealous you know!"

-No dayeh jan; you say such things!

-Say what you want, but my hair didn't turn white in a flour mill[186].

My own bleeding heart suffered more than anyone else's. I now understood the meaning of my mother-in-law's glances and gestures only too well. I kept telling myself damn me if I get pregnant again. For as long as things are this way, this one child is more than enough for a lifetime. I had become a *Keshvar Zivar doll*[187]. My parents pulled me from one side, and my mother-in-law and husband from the other; and I was being torn apart.

My periods told me that I was not pregnant yet.

I had stopped breastfeeding my son for a couple of months now. My mother-in-law was angry and bad-tempered again. She constantly kept an eye out to hear the news of my pregnancy. She would say: "It's because you're so weak. You don't have the strength. You must take remedies." And I, who was not so keen on having another baby, calmly answered: "No khanoum, it's not due to weakness. It's because I've been breastfeeding all this time."

-I also remember the time you were not breastfeeding only too well; it was the same story. How can someone bursting with good health come from her father's home, and then not get pregnant for six months?

She would not leave me in peace. I knew I would not be able to cope with this woman's sharp tongue. Even so, I said again: "Maybe the weakness is on Rahim's part."

She put her hands on her hips: "Oh! Really! Anything else? So, where did this one come from? The son of Almas khan is weak? When he drew his broadsword he took over an entire neighbourhood. And I was always either pregnant or breastfeeding. Now, if all my children died, that's another story.

From the words of this woman, I gradually learned more about the characteristics of the family I had married into. I understood, but did not want to know. With each passing second, a new heartache was added to the old ones. Little by little, I grasped the concept of gentility and the meaning of crudeness. I kept telling myself Rahim is different. He is good. He will be better. It will be all right.

I had just returned from the baths. I put on my Crêpe de Chine dress, which I had kept hidden from Rahim. I let my hair loose around my shoulders. I put on my maquillage and perfume. My mother-in-law, who was waiting by the dinner spread for Rahim to come home, peeked at me with intense jealousy.

-Good day to you. Where to? It's good news I hope!

-Nowhere. I'm staying right here, at home.

I felt cheerful and bubbly. I looked pretty. I was taller and thinner than before. I had ripened and I knew it. The thought of Rahim's reaction made my heart melt away. I could tell from his mother's jealous tone how pretty I looked, and I wallowed in it.

She asked: "All this done-up face is for staying home?

I laughed: "Well yes, does one have to look smart only for the outdoors? All this done-up face is for my husband."

She squeezed her lips together with jealousy and hatred, and said sarcasti cally: "God only knows, if I combed my hair, or reddened my cheeks with some Four O'clock petals, the mother-in-law cursed me a thousand times. She'd say you have your eye on someone else. She'd not let go until my husband had beaten me black and blue."

Casually, I said: "Your mother-in-law was wrong." And I continued doing myself up in front of the mirror.

She gave her head and neck a twist and added: "I don't know… Maybe I was too green. Maybe I was not this clever."

Quickly, she went as quiet as a mouse when Rahim got home. I do not know if it was out of fear or diplomacy.

Rahim's mischievous smile and his eager look indicated that I had been triumphant. He sat by my side after dinner. His mother picked up my son, who was asleep, and took him to her room. Ever since I had stopped breast-feeding him, she had insisted on separating him from us and kept him sleeping by her side at night. Not that it upset me. I was accustomed to having a dayeh. In a family like mine, hardly any child slept next to his mother at night. The dayeh were like second mothers. But, the problem was that my mother-in-law incited my son against me. She wanted to make him so dependent on her that he would never be able to live without his grandmother; so that I would have to give in to living with her. When she left the room, Rahim pushed his calligraphy set to one side, sat next to me, and asked: "What has happened to make your eyes aim at my heart again?" I laughed. He said again: "Mahboub, what do you do to look prettier every day?

He was resting on his left hand and leaning towards me. I said: "Nothing. I just have a good husband."

-Is that it?

His look, his playful laughter, and his magnetism all drew me to him. It was pouring down outside. I shut my eyes. Someone was knocking at the front door. At this time of night?! Rahim got up reluctantly as I turned away from him reluctantly. He picked up the lantern and went to open the door. I heard the sound of talking, my mother-in-laws footsteps, and then her greetings.

-Well, well, you have honoured us. You're most welcome. What brings you here? You've gone out of your way to come and see us!

I heard the harsh, coarse voice of a man, and a mixture of greetings being exchanged. Rahim rushed into the room: "Get up Mahboub, get up. We have guests. It's my cousin, with his son and daughter."

He was as nervous as if the prime minister himself had turned up unannounced. He tidied the room quickly and put the calligraphy set back in its place. I put on my chador and prepared to face my husband's family. The door opened. My mother-in-law said: "No, please come in. No, no, you first."

Two large men, similar to those who worked in Shemiran or Gholhak, in my uncle and father's gardens, were standing on the porch. Wearing old, inexpensive suits, they were taking off their timeworn shoes weighing down with mud and sludge. They came into the room, bringing in the smell of rain, sweaty feet, burned wood and chibouk, and the odour of dirty clothes dampened by rain. They were big, dirty and coarse. Their appearance and odour sickened me. A petite, young woman followed them into the room. She was not pretty, but it could not be said that she was ugly. She had tanned skin, small eyes, and narrow lips. Her nose was upturned. Altogether, she was cute and appealing. The state of her chador and appearance did not surpass that of her companions. She took off her shoes and entered the room. I noticed her socks had been mended. I felt sorry for her. The front of the cotton dress she was wearing had been stained with grease and the wiping of wet hands. It had a stale whiff of tea towels about it. Nevertheless, they were members of my husband's family. Politeness dictated that I respect them, and I did.

In an elastic, coarse voice, the larger man said: "*Sam Aleikom*[188]".

I said: "Please come in. You are welcome. We're delighted. You bring pleasantness with you."

His son and daughter accompanied him inside. His daughter said hello with a sweet smile. I remembered the day Ata al-Dowleh's family had come to ask for my hand for their son. I remembered his mother, his sister, and their pretty daughter-in-law with her dainty look and timid, respectful smile. So what? I did not want the boy; it couldn't be forced.

The men knew their limits. They were impressed straight away. They were awed by me. They kept their hands crossed in front of them like waiting servants and sat down by the door. The little woman was impertinent. She went and sat at the top of the room and, in answer to my mother-in-law's question, she said: "No auntie, really, we've eaten; I'm not just saying that!"

Even so, I went to the kitchen with my mother-in-law and helped her prepare a tray of food from what was left over from our dinner. My mother-in-law turned to me and said: "No, this is not nice Mahboubeh jan. Go get one of your china serving dishes. I've to keep up appearances in front of them."

I brought the china, but my blood was boiling. Not because I had to bring the china, but because she was trying to make this coarse, common man seem like an upstanding, reputable person to me. She wanted to force me to bow down to them.

-Mahboub jan, you take in the dinner tray tonight. You're the lady of the house you know; they expect you to do it. You've to keep complimenting my nephew; he's very sensitive."

And thus, she appeased her inferiority complex by breaking my spirit.

I asked: "khanoum, what does your nephew do?"

She said with vanity: "He has one of those beefy jobs, you know. He has a shop in the ready-to-wear clothing bazaar. He sells second-hand clothes. It's true that he lives in Varamin, but he also has a house in town. He has three concubines. At first, he had a small farm in rural Varamin. But now, you have to see what an income he has from selling clothes! He keeps all three of his concubines in his house in the city. He pays for their living. He pays for their bread, meat, sugar and tea. And they repair clothes for him, one better than the other. His business is finely tuned."

I asked: "His wife's not unhappy? She's not upset? She doesn't complain?"

She roared at me: "Why should she be upset? She has her bread and butter, and she's his first and last wife. He had these two children with her. What more does she want? *Go to Guilan if you want death*[189]. The concubines run the business, and she reaps the benefits. They say he has not yet spent a single night in the house of his concubines. His home is in Varamin; the concubines run things for him, and take care of his affairs."

I realised why he had taken concubines. In the ready-to-wear clothing bazaar, where old clothes made out of cheap fabrics were on sale or second-hand clothing was repaired, sorted, and then sold, having cheap or free labour was a luxury to be taken advantage of. This coarse man was clever enough to take needy women as concubines and make them work. The likes of him were everywhere. In order to win their husband's favour the women competed with one another and slaved away day and night, putting the fruits of their labour at his disposal to sell and, in return, they were happy with some meat, bread and a roof over their heads. Their hearts simply rejoiced in adopting a husband's name. I prepared the dinner tray with abhorrence.

In a mature, mellow and collected tone of voice, my mother-in-law said: "Because, you know what? When I left here in a sulk last time, I went and stayed with them. Of course, I didn't tell them the truth; I just said I've come to visit you. Now, they've thought that, if they don't return my visit, I'll be very offended. Of course, they're right. My nephew stands on ceremony. The poor things have gone to all this trouble. They're true human beings. Look, they've brought us eggs, bread and yoghurt." The yoghurt was too sour to eat. The bread was stale. I cannot say why, but I felt sorry for his concubines. In my opinion, this man was a parasite. But, my mother-in-law kept singing his praise non-stop while putting pieces of the bread in her mouth. She seemed to really enjoy it. She said: "I'll give Almas eggs tomorrow. It'll make him strong."

We sat in the room. My mother-in-law poured tea and the cousin, who was an older man, puffed away at the hookah. The odour of their sweaty feet and dirty clothes suffocated me. I took trips into the bedroom quietly, closed the door linking the two rooms, opened the window ajar and took breaths of fresh air before returning to the next room. I saw the nephew, this lay-about man, leaning on the wall, smoking the hookah and chatting with my mother-in-law. I saw that his son, who seemed to have come from behind the mountains[190], had stretched his feet out into the middle of the room and was dozing off like a drunken person. I saw that my husband was totally engrossed by Kokab. The girl was being coquettish. I pretended not to notice. I kept telling myself I was wrong. I kept thinking to myself she's not worth it, and I would say to her: "Please, have some tea khanoum."

-Thank you, I already had some.

In a significant tone of voice, Rahim told me: "Her name's Kokab. Call her Kokab honey."

It was as if he was the one calling her Kokab honey. He was talking to the door so the wall would hear; and the poor door was breaking under the weight of its own sense of honour. Its heart broke. Its blood boiled, yet it kept saying you are imagining things. Kokab was holding the corner of her chador in a way that Rahim and I could see her face, while she had her back to her brother and father. It was as if she had veiled herself from them. She gazed into Rahim's eyes and said in a hushed voice: "Agha Rahim, Masha'Allah everything about you is good. You also have good taste. You've taken a lovely wife!"

-Not more so than yourself

I felt a burning sensation. It is true when they say you see red. I must have been seeing red, because I did not see anything else; it was as if I was looking through a blazing screen. They were flirting right under my nose. They used me as an excuse to flirt, and her father, brother, and my mother-in-law did not seem to notice at all. They were deep in conversation about a world I knew nothing about. A conversation not worth a penny. They were assessing the bazaar, the bad back of Kokab's mother, the high price of fabric, that one of the concubines had pinched pieces of fabric for a patchwork she had made; that if the women were better workers, if they worked harder, the nephew's business would be even more prosperous. They talked about Karam, his son, working on Allahyar khan's farm.

Bedtime came at last. My mother-in-law said: "Mahboub jan, I'll bring the child to sleep in your room tonight. I'll sleep in the storeroom. Cousin, you sleep in my room with Karam. Goodness Kokab jan, not at all, it's no trouble! Make yourself at home. We'll prepare a place for Kokab khanoum here in the parlour."

The nephew stood up in all his gigantic height. He seemed to occupy half the room. With the same coarse voice and demanding tone, he said: "Well then, which one's your room? Where should Karam and I go?"

They did not stand on ceremony. They did not know how. He had pulled up his loose-fitting trouser legs above his knees with his right hand and was walking with his legs wide apart. He looked like a woman holding up her skirt to prevent it from wrapping around her legs.

Karam, who was thirteen or fourteen, had not even said hello to anyone since his arrival. He followed his father like a calf. Rahim and his mother overtook one another in making them feel at home. They kept complimenting them. I could not grasp what it was about this man that appeared so respectful and grand to them. I found no justification, except to say they were all birds of a feather. This was a manifestation of the world in which my husband had grown up. It was in his blood; he enjoyed living in that world and felt comfortable in it. These were the people my mother had said were not of us. They were the ones Nezhat had said were not for us. They were the same ones my father said had no backbone; this was the other side of the coin. This was Rahim's quintessence. This was the mud my husband had been moulded in. And I had wanted him, and still did.

I remained behind with Kokab and Rahim. As Rahim went towards the smaller room, our bedroom, he said: "I'll go get a mattress for you."

It was as if he could not see me. As if I was not present. With total indifference towards me, Kokab stirred a little: "Oh, don't go hurting your back."

Rahim turned around. With that unkempt hair, piercing, enamoured eyes and open collar, the same playful smile appeared on his lips again. He took a look at her and said: "You must be really worried about my lower back[191]!" She laughed and answered: "Really." I followed Rahim into the bedroom and closed the door. In an aggressive tone, I said: "What do you mean Rahim? We have no mattresses!"

He pointed to our own mattresses. The look in his enamoured eyes, which had turned bitter and morose as soon as he had walked into the room, crossed mine: "What are these then?"

-But, they're ours!

-So what if they're ours! They don't want to take it with them.

-Where will we sleep then?

-On the rug. One night won't turn into a thousand nights. They're guests in my home. They're my relatives after all. I didn't sprout under a bush you know!

-But…

-No buts. Are you upset? I'll go tell them to go home, that my wife won't give the bedding.

He started towards the door. I ran after him and grabbed his arm. "Rahim!"

Abruptly, he pulled his arm away. "Leave me alone. Can't I have a couple of guests in my own home?"

-Don't do this Rahim jan, don't do it. It's not becoming. Lower your voice. Don't embarrass us. The guests will be offended. Come, come, take the mattresses and linens.

In a foul temper, he turned around slowly and took away all three mattresses one by one. My satin quilts; those embroidered sheets. He took them to the room at the end of the yard for that big, coarse cousin and his son who were covered in manure and muck from head to toe. I was sure my bedding would be riddled with lice the following day. I was not even sure whether they knew how to sleep in them!

He took the third mattress into the parlour and pulled my pink satin quilt over it. "There you go Kokab khanoum. You must forgive us if you're short of anything."

-Thank you.

I lay down on the bare floor on the khersak carpet with Rahim and my son and pulled my chador and cashmere shawl – which I had taken out of the trunk – over ourselves.

Rahim said: "Keep the shawl for the boy. I don't want it."

-But, you'll catch cold Rahim; it's still cold.

-I'm not cold. Go to sleep. Why does this child cry so much? I'll slap him in the mouth!

-Oh, don't do this Rahim. My baby's teething.

He turned his back on me and slept on the floor in a temper.

I was just about to fall asleep when Rahim got up silently. The door made a sound, there was a pause, and then another sound, and it was shut quietly. Boiling blood rushed into my heart. I went rigid. Maybe I was dreaming! But no, I was wide awake. Why had I become so skeptical! Maybe Rahim had gone to the lavatory. Absolutely, absolutely. Didn't he go out on other nights? Except, I was not so suspicious at that time. I would sleep soundly and not give it a second thought. And yet, how come I did not hear the opening sound of the parlour door leading to the porch? Did he not have to open and close that door too?

I heard a short laugh - the laughter of a woman and nothing more. I sat up. My world had collapsed. I was not crying, no; there was no more room for crying. I was well past it. I felt suffocated. Was it from jealousy? No; it was my sense of honour. It was his insulting behaviour and the indignity of it all. Because, Rahim died in my heart the minute I heard the clicking sound of the door. Should I open the window? No, my son will catch cold. How could he? And with that woman? So dirty from head to toe, soiled, common and lowly. How could he prefer her to me? How could he? In my own home, in my own bed; right next door to my bedroom. How impertinently bold, how audacious. How he belittles me... But no! It is my imagination. He will come up the stairs any minute now and I will be ashamed of my own thoughts... But where is he? It has been a quarter of an hour. Half an hour... I take a look around the room. It is as if I see it for the first time; as if I see the house for the first time; I saw myself and where I had ended up. I looked at my son who was lying on the floor beside me, innocent and pure, in his filthy clothes and that disgraceful look his grandmother had conjured up for him. I felt sorry for him more than anything else. Where could I go? What could I do with him? Shall I leave him in this hellhole or take him with me? How could my own husband prefer this girl to Basir ol-Molk's daughter? Basir ol-Molk's daughter with her beauty, perfume and powder! Ah! I wished I was dead. The servant of my mother's house was cleaner and more respectable than this woman. What if my father found out? No, why should my father find out? It was just enough for dayeh to smell something fishy... How kind I had been to this man, and now...! What will I see if I open the door? Dear God, are you punishing me? You ungrateful man. I used to say I will put it right, but it was not meant to be. I did not know a man's nature could not be changed. I did not grasp that if he was good, he would always remain good, and if he was bad, *teaching manners to an unworthy person was like placing a walnut on a dome*[192]. He tells me with great insolence that he cannot bring guests into his own house! This is your house? You insolent man... He is just like his mother. Insolent and impertinent. He cannot distinguish good from evil. He feels no shame, no gratitude. I have brought it upon myself. My father was so right to say that this boy has no backbone. He told me so many times! Everyone tried talking sense into me! It was my own fault. I brought it onto myself and now I have to bear the consequences. Oh dear God, what have I done? I repent...! Suddenly, I was taken aback. I broke out in a cold sweat. Was this not my father's curse for me? That same bad prayer? How quickly it had come true. Oh agha jan, ***I repent! I repent!*** May God damn you Mahboubeh, did you have to fall in love?! An hour passed. I held my head between my hands. Morning would not come, neither would Rahim. I lay down next to my son. There, in the middle of that room, with eyes wide open, I stared at the sky from a corner of the window not covered by the door curtain, until it turned grey. The door made a sound... a creak. I closed my eyes. Rahim came in and lay quietly beside me on the floor.

I was not myself in the morning. I had a headache. I went into the kitchen and busied myself by helping my mother-in-law. I did not wish to lay eyes on the face of that filthy, worthless woman. I did not want to lay eyes on Rahim and his breeding.

Rahim, who had not gone to work, was not unhappy about my absence from the room. He came and went bright-eyed and bushy-tailed, chirpy as a nightingale. I could hear him talking and laughing with that woman, her father and her brother. They had breakfast, and did not leave. Why won't they leave? I already had a stomach full; I had a bleeding heart. Lunchtime came. My mother-in-law told me: "Go back to the room; it's not nice. They'll be offended. I'll serve lunch."

-No khanoum. You go. I'll stay here.

All of a sudden, she put down the skimmer, placed her hands on her hips, and said: "What's the matter Mahboubeh? You look like a pain in the neck again! Is it because my poor nephew's stayed here for a night?

I said: "Leave me alone khanoum. I really don't feel like it! Don't you go arguing with me too. My heart's bleeding enough as it is..."

She opened her mouth and said: "Oh yeah! Your heart's bleeding? Why's your heart..."

I turned my back on her and went up the kitchen stairs, slamming my feet on the steps as I went. At the top of the stairs, in the yard, I came face to face with Rahim. Talking under his breath like greased lightning, he said:

"Look here Mahboubeh, don't let them leave tonight! Insist that they stay. They won't stay unless you ask them to."

This man was so immodest. How could he not feel any shame? I wanted to say to hell if they don't stay. *Let them go where the Arab threw his spear[193]*. But, if I said that, I had to explain why I did not want them to stay. Then, Rahim would become even more forward and the veil of modesty would be torn between us. And maybe I was wrong after all… maybe… maybe. I pressed my lips together in great anger, threw a sharp look at him, and walked away.

There was no need for me to insist. They stayed without being asked after all.

That night, Kokab was even more insolent. She told my mother-in-law: "It's my turn tonight. You did the cooking; I'll clean up and do the dishes."

My mother-in-law turned to me and said: "See how well she manages a home! Masha'Allah, she's quick like a bunny."

The tone of her voice was venomous. Rahim said: "I'll help you then."

They took the stack of dishes outside and stayed behind longer than was necessary. When they returned, Rahim looked flushed and Kokab was quiet. I wanted to get up and say I will do it myself, but I did not have the strength. The soles of my feet were frozen - as if two pieces of solid rock. My mother-in-law either did not notice, or pretended not to. The cousin smoked the hookah, drank tea, and complained about the avarice and overeating of his concubines and the illness of the one who worked harder than the others. His talentless, footloose, and fancy-free son had stretched out his feet in his disgusting socks again and was submerged in the great pleasure of a cat nap. It was time to go to bed again. Again, I pretended to be asleep. Again, he pretended to be asleep. I felt as if he was not all that worried about me being awake tonight, because he got up quietly, far sooner than it was necessary for me to fall asleep, at a time when I could have still been awake. He paused briefly. The squeaking of the door again; the sound of the closing door again, and my torment again, which was more petrifying than the torment of death. It cannot be put into words. My head felt hot again. I was breathless and gasping for air. I sat up again, held my head with both hands and squeezed it. Everything looked dim anew. I took a deep breath. Help me dear God. What have I done? ***Oh, I repent! I repent!***

Once again, I did not have the strength to get up the following morning. I would not look at Rahim's face. I felt like a corpse. I was startled by the colour of my own skin when I looked in the mirror. I was taken aback. Any child could see how devastated I was. And yet, it was incredible that these people who squirmed together like worms, who were worlds apart from any ethics and morals, did not seem to notice me at all, to understand how I felt, or notice my silence and disregard. *They had their heads in the manger[194]*. I was the chicken who had to lay the golden egg. This was enough for them.

On the third day, I was in the kitchen, passing the time aimlessly and keeping myself busy. Rahim came down the stairs. He wanted to talk to me. I did not want to see him. Instantly, his mother's footsteps echoed in the yard.

She stood at the top of the stairs leading down to the kitchen, placed her hands over the low lunette above the stairs and stood listening. Rahim was pleading: "Mahboubeh jan, ask them to stay tonight too."

-Ask them yourself. I'm neither here nor there!

-They won't stay unless you ask them.

I turned my back on him and said: "They stayed last night alright, without being asked."

-But, my cousin wants to leave now.

I sniggered: "Now? Just before lunch? Is this the time to leave for Varamin? Don't worry, they're being civil. They won't leave, even if you tell them to.

His mother put her weight on one leg and came down the stairs noisily. She said in an angry voice: "What do you mean, ask them to stay? I'm bushed from lifting all the heavy cauldrons. They have anchored here."

For the very first time, I wanted to take her in my arms and kiss her wrinkled face. She was like an angel of mercy sent from heaven. Rahim raised his voice as he turned towards his mother: "What business is it of yours? There's no need for you to lift the cauldrons anymore!"

When it was in his own best interest, he would even shut his eyes on his own mother and all respect for her. He knew very well how to put his mother in her place. The mother and child passion woke in him only where I was concerned. I did not speak. I no longer said be quiet, don't shout. I did not say it is not nice, the guests will hear.   was not to blame for this uproar. I had been completely hospitable in every possible way!

As she was twitching her back and neck, his mother asked: "And how come you're giving your cousin a leg up all of a sudden? You've turned out to be quite a gentleman, haven't you!"

Rahim perceived the sarcasm in her words, and said: "Close your mouth shut."

I had busied myself by blowing on the firewood underneath the cauldron.

-I will not close it shut. I'm bushed. Take a look at what the ticks have done to me in that store room!

She pulled up one of her sleeves to her elbow. In all fairness, the bugs had really given her a hard time. There were swollen red patches all over her arm. She continued: "They've bitten me to pieces. I have to walk all night long, until the break of dawn. I keep scratching my head, chest, and back. I'm telling you Rahim, don't you go asking them to stay now…! And if they stay anyway, I'll come and sleep in the parlour with Kokab.

I felt good. The cousin and his household left, and Rahim went to see them off.

It was already noon. We were sitting in the room with my mother-in-law when, unexpectedly, she asked: "Mahboub, why're you so pale? You've withered away!"

Since the ticks had bitten her to pieces, and imagining she would be upset with the cousin and sympathise with me, I began confiding in her. I started crying, and said: "It's because of Rahim."

-Rahim? hat's he done?

Sobbing, I continued: "What's he done? He went to Kokab every night."

I said it, and regretted it. My mother-in-law looked at me with devouring eyes: "Oh, what's this again! You're painting us in a bad light now?"

-I'm not painting anyone khanoum, what paint? It's a disgrace.

Casually, she said: "No dear. You imagined it. Rahim's not like that, neither's Kokab."

-I saw it with my own two eyes khanoum. I'm not a child. I was wide awake every night.

-Well, if you're telling the truth, why didn't you go and catch him red-handed and drag him out of her arms? Why didn't you show them up? You should've disgraced them both."

She was right. Why did I not go? Because it was not possible. Even thinking about it was hard to swallow for me. I could never do it. It was not in me to do such a thing.

-I was afraid Kokab's father would come and start a blood bath.

-No my dear. You were afraid he might have to marry her.

-Marry her? This trash? Over my dead body!

I kept objecting and hating myself for it. I was fighting for something which was no longer of any value to me. Nevertheless, I still wanted to be triumphant.

-Why shouldn't he marry her? Why do you get upset? Did she mind that you came and took her fiancé away from her? Didn't you snatch Rahim up?

-I didn't snatch him. He didn't want her. Now that he's gratified with me, he's running after this cheap, easy woman.

I was astonished at the words coming out of my mouth, which were beneath me. I was amazed at myself for arguing with this woman. I could see myself sinking a little deeper into the swamp, and I still could not control my tongue. She laughed: "What's good for the goose is good for the gander. How come flirting was good for you, but it's bad for Kokab? Well, everybody wants a good thing. My son's handsome. He's good looking. Girls and women won't leave him alone. Is it his fault? How come he was good for you, but he's ooh for Kokab? Anyone who doesn't have money doesn't have a heart?"

I got up: "This will teach me not to confide in you again. I'll sort things out with Rahim this very same day."

I was pacing up and down the room like a roaring lion in a cage. His mother walked around the yard and grumbled. My son was loose around the place. He would either run after his grandmother, or come to me. He could not understand our behaviour. The door opened and Rahim came in. He turned to his mother: "They're gone. Are you happy now?"

His mother replied: "Why should I be happy? Your wife's happy now. Come and see what a fuss she's kicked up since this morning!"

Rahim said: "The hell she has." Angrily, he raced up the stairs two in one. It was spring time and the air was fresh. Spring was in the air. He flung the door open and walked in. He stood facing me, and said: "Tell me, what is it that you want?"

I asked: "You really don't know? Aren't you ashamed?"

-What have I done to be ashamed of? Have I committed murder?

-Do you think I'm stupid? That I don't know where you went every night?

I could not even bear to utter her name. I expected Rahim to deny everything; to prove me wrong. But, coldly, he said: "So what if you know? I'm glad I went; good for me. What're you going to do about it?"

I looked at him with my eyes nearly popping out, and I screamed: "So what if you went? Have you no shame? You left your wife and went to that woman? And now you're being a bully? Didn't she tell you to get lost?"

-Of course she didn't. She wants me.

I turned my back on him and mimicked him: "She wants me! Stop it Rahim. Have you no shame? Didn't that woman have any reservations? Any modesty?"

-Were you ashamed? You were like her too!

-What did I do? Did I come to your room?

-*There was no water, otherwise you were a skilled swimmer*[195].

The arrow hit the bull's eye. I heaved a sigh. Damn me. I only had myself to blame. Every person is the architect of his own fortune. I said: "You're right. A lowlife like me deserves a husband like you."

He raised his voice and yelled: "You've found your tongue these days! Have you turned into a madwoman? What is it? What do you want from me?"

His glaring eyes were those of a male beast separated from his female. Oh, how I hated every part of his body and those coarse, unshapely hands. Was this the same Rahim? I said: "Nothing. I want nothing from you. Go do as you please. I don't want to see you anymore."

His mother appeared: "So, you don't want to see him anymore? You're hung up on someone else?" She turned to Rahim: "If you'd made a couple of more babies for her, she wouldn't be babbling away like this. If a woman's not tied down by kids, she'll start getting ideas in her head and get out of control. If she has to change nappies every day and wash filth, she won't have time to be abusive and accuse her husband's family of all sorts of things and roll-call her husband."

She went to the courtyard in an irate state to calm down my son. Through the window, I said: "Khanoum, you mustn't interfere. Keep your self-respect."

The spring breeze played around with the hem of her skirt and the corners of her kerchief. But, I could not feel the spring air. I could not sense the sweet smell of honeysuckle, or the freshness and splendor of this season and the glory of nature. She turned towards the window and said: "Have you left any respect? I know what's bothering you. I know why you're picking a quarrel. You want Rahim to join the military. He's not the one you're worried about. You just want to see him wear a military uniform, put on his boots, carry a sword and become an officer, so that you can wear your Crêpe de Chine dress and show off to everyone. Don't worry; you've already made your Crêpe de Chine dress. You'll also find the officer. You're not all thumbs."

I raised my hands in desperation and said: "Oh God!"

I was surrounded from all sides and I was even the guilty party now. Rahim sprang up like a wounded animal: "Where's it? Where's that dress?"

I screamed: "Stop it Rahim. What do you want with my dress?"

I loved my dress so much. I had hung it on a nail behind the curtain and covered it with an old chador to protect it from getting dirty.

He reached the bedroom with a few long steps. I could not catch up with him. He pulled the curtain to one side and took the dress. He tried to rip it apart at the neck with both hands, but was not strong enough. He started tearing it with his teeth like an animal. Then, he ripped it in two with his hands and threw it into the yard from the window, saying: "Here goes your Crêpe de Chine dress. You can also dream about me becoming an officer."

I had had enough of him. I was appalled by him. I stared into his eyes as I walked up to him one step at at ime, and added articulately: "I repent to have married you. Go away and don't mention my name again. Go to your Kokab honey. These are the kind of women you deserve. Why don't you marry her! May I be damned if I object."

I could not tell if my face looked as repulsive in his eyes as his did in mine? As repugnant and detestable? He yelled: "I'll go marry her; I'll marry her just out of spite."

-To hell with it!

He had reached the middle of the parlour when he turned around and said: "Taking a wife needs money. Where've you put the money?" He looked for it in the niche. It wasn't there. He yelled: "I said where've you put the money?"

-It's the end of the month. What money? You turned it all into rice and stew and dishes of fruits and shoved it into the stomachs of your dignified relatives.

-Good for me. It serves you right. Where is it? Where's the God damned thing?

He wanted the key to my trunk; the same one I always kept locked according to his own instructions ever since his mother had come to stay with us and kept the key under the carpet or took it with me every time I left the house.

He lifted the carpet and took the key. He opened the trunk. He took what little money there was in it. He took a look around the room and took the

Cashmere shawl too. I screamed: Where're you taking that?" "Wherever I feel like it." He stepped forward: "Take those off."

-What?

-The bangles

-I won't. Shame on you.

-I said take them off.

He had lost his mind. I could not believe I was awake. He grabbed my hand violently and pulled the bangles off. The same bangles my sister had given me at the wedding ceremony. The skin on my hand was grazed. I said: "Hold on. I'll take them off myself."

He let go of my hand: "Take them off. Take them off nicely."

I took them off and threw them at him: "Take them and get lost."

-By God, let your father get lost.

I lost my mind this time. I ran towards him: "Shut up. Don't you mention my father's name. Wash your mouth out. You're not fit to pair up my father's shoes. Don't you say my father's name in this God forsaken house, you unscrupulous, immoral man."

-Your father's the unscrupulous one. If your God damned father had any morals, his fifteen-year old daughter wouldn't be taking the hinges off my shop door all that time. That same father with dog blood in him who…

I screamed: "You're the one with dog blood in you, howling after every bitch. You're the one barking at your own mother because Kokab left."

He slapped me so hard that I did not feel anything at first. I staggered and leaned on the wall. I never expected this one. Perhaps, deep down in my heart, I still hoped that he would regret everything. But, I came down to earth with the blow. My wings were clipped. This slap was a wakeup call for me. I could see the realities now.

The pain of the slap was less disturbing than the one in my broken heart.

I looked at him in shock for a bit. I had one hand on the wall, and the other on my face. I said: "You have every right. I am to blame. I deserved this slap. I should never have married you. But, I won't stay in this house a moment longer."

His mother appeared at the door looking worried. She was holding my son who was looking at us with a lump in his throat. His chin was quivering and he was ready to burst into tears. He was so scared. Rahim said: "Go on. Let me see where you can go?"

I said: "You just watch me."

In a surprisingly soft voice, his mother said: "Mahboub jan, come off your high horse now."

Rahim said: "Let her go. Let me see how."

I rushed into the bedroom. I took out my old suitcase and threw in a few of my clothes. I put on the necklace my father had given me and my mother's ring. I took the ashrafi gold coin he had given me for the birth of my son. Rahim said: "Give me that."

His mother said: "Leave it Rahim."

-I gave it to her and now I want it back.

I threw the coin at him; he picked it up straight away and put it in his pocket with the bangles. I went to the door and pulled my son out of my mother-in-law's arms. I picked up the suitcase, put on my chador, and left the room wobbling to the sides under the weight of the suitcase and my son. I put on my shoes. One of Rahim's shoes was in my way, with its back pressed down. I kicked it with disgust. I had become like him. The shoe flew into the yard and landed by the pond. I had to leave as soon as possible. I had to leave before I turned into a second version of this mother and son; before I drowned completely. I had failed to make a man out of Rahim. Instead, I was becoming like him.

I had reached the middle of the stairs when he rushed out of the room and ran after me barefooted. As he noticed that the weight of my load slowed down my descent, he jumped into the middle of the courtyard from the middle of the stairs and ran towards the step of the corridor leading to the front door. He sat there with crossed arms and blocked my way. His mother said: "Mahboubeh jan, why don't you stop this; you let go."

Rahim said: "Don't interfere."

I reached him. I stood in front of him and looked at that frantic face, at that useless brute. In my eyes, he was now a scoundrel of a thug. I said: "Get up, let me pass."

He did not answer. He stared at me, grinning blatantly.

I said: "Move away, I want to leave."

-You want to leave? As simple as that? You've packed my house and you want to leave?

I took a look at the suitcase and slammed it on the floor: "Get out of my way now, I want to leave."

-Alright, this is only half of it. But you still have the important half!

I looked at him, puzzled: "The important half?"

He got up calmly, took my son out of my arms and slowly placed him down next to the wall. Then, he went to one side and pointed to the door: "You may go now, go on, good riddance to bad rubbish…"

My heart missed a beat. My son was crying. I stood there, stiff as a board. My chador slipped off my head. If I hadn't been holding on to it, it would have fallen on the ground. I went towards the wall and leaned on it for a while. I was staring into thin air, dumbstruck, but I could not see a thing. Then, slowly I walked away from the wall and went towards the parlour, dragging my feet on the floor with my chador hanging behind me. I was his captive. My son had chained me to this life indeed and all this bedlam had only torn the veil of modesty between us. I could hear his voice from behind me, telling his mother: "Naneh, open your ears and listen carefully. She no longer has the right to take this child out of this house. Almas even has to take his bath with you. Understand? I trust him into your hands. *Ya Ali*[196], I'm off now. And he left.

I wanted to wake up and be in my father's house. To be in the same time-frame as when Ata al-Dowleh's son had come to ask for my hand; the same day as when Mansour had wanted me, or any other person for that matter;

anyone who was like me. I was a stranger in this house, an outsider. I did not understand their principles and needs. I was unfamiliar with their culture. I had made a grave mistake.

Rahim did not come home for the next three months. He left his mother in my life, to watch me like a merciless prison warden with a heart of stone, to be my son's watchdog, and continuously say: "My son is homeless now… Pray that he may have enough of Kokab soon and return to his home and life. Don't worry. He won't marry her. He's not a simpleton. He'll take her as a concubine for a time, and the dust will settle."

I did not pay any attention. Whether Rahim was dead or alive was all the same to me. My own life and death was also all the same to me. I would be better off dead. But, what would happen to my son in that case? What kind of a person would he grow up to be? Another Rahim? A second version of his father? I felt desperate, but had no one to come to my rescue.

I would stay up late into the night and do my embroidery. I could not sleep. At dawn, I would look at the blue sky with a heavy heart; how grey it seemed to me. I was listless. I could not get out of bed. It was as if I had spent the night shifting a mountain. I was sad that another day had dawned and I had to get out of bed; that I had to see my mother-in-law's face again, the sight of whom was an expiation of sins. If only Nezhat was here and could tell me what to do. She would teach me what to say to my mother-in-law. But no. She did not have my father's permission. She had her husband to consider. Would I ever see her again? I asked myself what shall I do in this house? Lonely, tired, dejected, away from my parents, and even without a husband. Had I left my father's house to live with an old woman who enjoyed tormenting me? I would go out of my mind with remorse. Dayeh came and brought my allowance: "Mahboubeh jan, what's the matter? You're not well?" "Dayeh jan, don't say anything to anyone! I've had words with Rahim."

I needed someone to talk to; someone to console me, to comfort me and wipe away the tears that ran down my face as soon as I opened my mouth. I needed someone to look at my quivering chin with sadness and sigh out of grief and regret. That is what dayeh was there for. Shaking her head in sorrow, she said: "Leave this place behind and come back to your father's house…"

-What about my son? He needs a father.

-What do you want to do then?

-I'll wait. He'll come a cropper. He'll come to his senses. I'll bite the bullet and endure the pain. All couples have fights.

-Don't be so submissive. You can do too much of a good thing you know! Don't be so ethical with an unethical person Mahboubeh. This woman's eyes are evil. I'm only telling you.

I did not tell dayeh that Rahim had been gone for three months. I did not say he had beaten me. I did not say he had enslaved me. I only said we had argued and pleaded with her not to tell my father, and to keep it a secret from my mother.

Spring would not pass. This damned season would not end. Its every single night and day brought back painful memories. Its every passing moment was filled with torment and sorrow. When will spring end? When will the sweet scent of honeysuckle leave me alone? A scent which triggered memories that had now become so bitter. I dreamt that I was standing outside Rahim's shop, infatuated and besotted. He smiled at me kindly and lovingly; I felt a warm rain drizzling on my face. Rain! But, the shop had a roof! No, this was not rain. I was crying. It was the warmth of my tears. Only my tears could burn so.

Summer came. It was night time. I was sitting in a corner of the room; the same room I would enviously call the parlour. I had lit the oil lamp and turned it up to see better while embroidering. Almas was sleeping by my side. His grandmother came up the stairs and asked: "Don't you want to sleep?"

-No. Are you taking the child tonight or will you let him stay with me?

I would not utter my child's name. The name Almas made my flesh crawl. To me, he was just my son.

She said: "He's asleep now; let him stay", and left.

I covered him up. I was humming with a kind of mysticism which gradually took over me. Sorrow did not go away, but settled in my heart like the dregs of wine. It was always present, ready to rise again and consume me like a fire. The sound of a key echoed in the lock. The front door opened and shut. Footsteps were heard. My heart sank, not from love, but disgust; from hatred. It was Rahim - jovial and cheerful, as if nothing had happened. He climbed the stairs and stood in the doorway. He was wearing new clothes and a new pair of shoes and, to my great amazement, I noticed that he had not lowered the back of his shoes. He said: "Salam."

I said: "Salam."

He placed one foot on the doorsill and bent down to open his shoelaces. Calmly, I said: "Rahim!" He looked up and smiled. Repulsed, I turned away from him and, as I was doing my embroidery with my head down, I asked: "Where've you been all this time? Wherever you were, you can go back there."

He said: "Fine." He laced up his shoes again and left

This time, he was away for six months. My son was nearly three years old when he returned, and Kokab was never mentioned again. I knew he had renounced her as a concubine.

I knew he had had enough of her too.

It was night time again when he returned. His mother was awake. My son was awake and looking at his father's face. Unabashed, he told his mother: "Don't you want to go and sleep?" His mother got up. Rahim said: "Take away this hawkbell too".

He was talking about our son. We were left alone. My heart was full of hatred. He came and sat by my side: "Mahboub jan, you're still pretty you know!"

I was silent.

-I renounced her as a concubine. Happy now?

I was amazed by his simplicity and stupidity. He did not know that nothing would ever make a betrayed woman happy. Nothing but revenge. Nothing, except if she succeeded in running him into the ground.

If she remains silent, if she is tolerant, if she feigns ignorance, it is only due to deliberations much stronger than taking revenge, the most significant of which is the presence of a child or children dependent on their mother and her existence. They are in need of her support. And yet, a betrayed woman is a dangerous, extinct volcano which, if it could erupt, it would burn everything in its way. She might even turn to ashes in her own fire. A fire which stems from the heart and engulfs the entire being.

He came closer to me and murmured in my ear: "I am losing my heart O lovers, O God."

I was shaking with horror, with the knowledge that he had been in the arms of a filthy woman, that he had imagined me to be so naïve that he tried to use a charm on me once again with which he had already deceived me. I was repelled by him. I was repelled by this verse, repelled by the skies and the earth. I pushed away his extended hand towards me: "Leave me alone Rahim. Don't touch me."

He raised his voice at me: "Are you going to throw a tantrum again? You wanted me, and now I'm back!"

He was far too foolish to see my deep-seated wound. How I longed to tell him I no longer wanted him. That the Rahim I wanted was dead. I wanted that young man who was pure and honest. He was captivated by my love. He was innocent and sincere. He was simple-hearted; he was like me. I do not want this person I see instead, this wolf, this hyena, this scavenger who sits here in front of me and laughs so blatantly. I will never want him. I have had enough. I am disgusted. But, I did not have the courage. I did not have the power. I did not have the strength to be beaten up. I shunned commotion. And so, like a lamb to the slaughter, I went into the next room with him, silent and docile.

No one saw my laughter again. My biggest happiness – if there ever was one – was displayed with a bitter smile. My son was always playing in the alleyway, covered in dust from head to toe, with a few other children looking just like him. I could not cope with him and his grandmother both. I had lost the game. The pride and joy of his grandmother was that her grandchild was a playmate of agha Seyed Sadegh's son, the grocer who had a fairly large house next to ours in the alley. They would send their help to our door first thing in the early morning: "Tell Almas to come and play with our Agha Morteza."

I would say: "No, he can't go. Is my son the child's dayeh? Is he a *laleh*[197] for Morteza's entertainment. Don't let him go."

She always rolled her eyes at me: Yeah?! What nonsense! You think you're God's gift to mankind. His agha's said he can go. Rahim himself gave permission. The guy's a grocer in the bazaar. He's not such a lowlife you know. He's holding the everflow ewer. Who do you suppose we are? Why shouldn't he go? It'll give me some time to get on with my work."

-Khanoum, I'll take care of him myself.

-I wouldn't feel so bad if you would.

And my son would go happily and, even worse, return rejoicing with a pocket full of sweets and candy. My mother-in-law would ask him: "Let me see what they've given you?"

It made me spiteful. I would go and buy large amounts of sweets, place the various confiture and nibbles that dayeh had brought over from my father's house on a dish and put everything in the middle of the room. They would eat it after lunch, or in the afternoon; but their thirst never seemed quenched. It was as if nothing gave them as much pleasure as that handful of sweets. I was worried for the future of my son.

Dayeh came: "What's new dayeh jan?"

-News of health and wellbeing love. Nezhat finally delivered twins; two girls as lovely as bouquets of flowers. Dear sweet Khojasteh khanoum plays the piano beautifully now. You have to see it. Manouchehr's turned out to be a really sweet boy, a thousand Masha'Allah. Your agha jan says don't you put your feet on the ground, put them on my eyes instead. Such a small child, and yet he seems to have lived for forty years. He's so polite, so adept..."

I missed them all. I longed to see them; to see Nezhat and her children; to hear Khojasteh play the piano; to see Manouchehr, whose happy laughter and the thrashing about of his arms and legs I could still picture in my mind in my uncle's gardens.

What else is new dayeh jan?

-Your cousin, Hamid khan, is addicted to opium. He spends all his time by the opium brazier day and night. He puts all his income in the bowl of his pipe and smokes it into thin air.

  She pulled herself forward a little: "By the way, did I tell you?"

-Tell me what?

-That Mansour agha has taken a wife?

-But I already knew that he took a wife a long time ago. You also told me he had a son.

She threw her head back with impatience: "No, I don't mean that wife. He took a second wife; a rival wife for Guity Ara's daughter. Her name's Ashraf al-Sadat. Her father was a respected man, a civil servant, but he's passed on."

My mouth was wide open in disbelief: "Really dayeh jan?

-Aha… It's been two or three months now. I forgot to tell you.

Amazed, I asked: "I didn't expect this from Mansour! What's his wife doing now?"

-Poor Mansour. He didn't want to marry again. Nimtaj khanoum forced him. She has told Mansour agha that you've to take a wife no matter what. Mansour has said for goodness' sake, I don't want a wife. She said no, you must take another wife, because I want to spend all my days in prayer, fasting, and worship. I can't be a proper wife to you – as you know the poor thing is pockmarked! She has put it like this to spare herself the humiliation. In the end, she rolled up her sleeves and found Ashraf khanoum for agha Mansour; a short, chubby girl with rosy cheeks. Nimtaj khanoum became *khamoum bozor*[198]*g* and Ashraf became *khamoum kouchik*[199]. Nobody paid any attention to Ashraf in the beginning. Nimtaj khanoum was the lady upstairs, and the lady downstairs. But, as her bad luck would have it, the girl became pregnant. Don't tell anyone, but the girl has turned out to be a real handful and difficult to deal with. They say she doesn't get along with khanoum bozorg. She has said how come Nimtaj khanoum has to be in charge of everything. I'm the pretty one, and she has to be the favourite?! Anyway, to cut a long story short, she's giving poor agha Mansour a hard time. He keeps telling her you well know that I came to an understanding with you beforehand; but she keeps saying I don't want to know. I'm a person in my own right, and Nimtaj is also a person in her own right; we are equals. She's made life a living hell for her husband. She's almost three months pregnant now. Mansour khan keeps telling Nimtaj it's your fault; you put me in these dire straits.

-So, what does Nimtaj say?

-Nothing. She doesn't utter a single word. She's such a lady. It's this very characteristic that has left Mansour agha with nothing to say. She opened up her heart to your khanoum jan only once, to tell her she blames herself for Mansour's situation, that she's the one who put him in this tight spot.

So, Mansour was no more fortunate than I after all. Oh, my poor cousin! It felt good. I was alleviated. I was not sure why all of this tasted like soft, sweet honey in my mouth.

It was the start of summer again. The sun shone on everything and brought out the smell of dry wood. The smell of wood mixed with the smell of painted doors and windows filled the air. Once again, Rahim smells of wood. Once again, the smell of rouge makes me sick. Once again, my mother-in-law is cooking ghormeh-sabzi. I hate that smell too. Once again, I'm tired. Once again, I'm poorly. Once again, the breakfast spread makes me sick. I go and stand by the window left open to appease the summer heat indoors. The bamboo mats are hanging from the windows. They smell of earth. I breathe a deep breath and go and vomit by the pond. I crave pome-granates. Rahim is laughing. My mother-in-law is saying congratulations. It is as if the sky has fallen on my head with all its weight. Oh, God forbid! See what happened? I am pregnant again!

I will not mention it to dayeh. I do not want to deepen my parents' pain. There is enough pain here to last me a lifetime. Rahim has become even more presumptuous. He knows only too well that I am at his mercy now, with both hands tied. Ah! What happened to my father's good prayer then? I have remained at the mercy of this demon with my hands tied. He turned more heinous with each passing day. He did not go to work in the mornings. He would not come home for lunch. His breath smelled of alcohol at nights. And I was afraid he might become addicted to opium in the end.

-Rahim, where were you at lunchtime?

-Where was I? I was at work, running around after this miserable job. It's not as if I've been to the happy gardens!

-You never stayed in the shop at lunchtime before!

-Have you forgotten? At what time did you come to see me back in those days then? Wasn't it at one o'clock in the afternoon? You stopped me from staying at work for lunch ever since you became my wife.

-So, why do you stay in bed until midday? Why won't you go to work earlier in the mornings, and come home for lunch?

-Come home to what? To watch you throw up or put up with your bad temper like a pain in a broken neck?

-But I'm pregnant. I don't feel good.

-We've also seen you when you're not pregnant… You're a bitter pill to swallow, even with a tonne of honey.

- You say that because you don't want me anymore, because you're bored with me.

-I'll slap you in the mouth! Stop pestering me so much. You've become my man in charge here!

I always cried when I was by myself. Mahboub, see what you have done to yourself? See what you have done? There is not an ounce of pity in Rahim's heart. He has no mercy, no manhood.

I was still in the first month of my pregnancy. I had packed my bath kit from the early morning. My mother-in-law asked: "Where to?"

-I'm going to the baths. Come on son. I'm also taking him.

-"No, it's not possible." She dragged the child away by the hand and picked him up: "Almas will go with me. His father's forbidden that you take him out."

Listless from the morning sickness, the difficulties of pregnancy, and all the mental pressures, I left the house in a slough of desperation. I was no longer ashamed of carrying my kit to the baths under my arm, of shopping, of walking through narrow lanes and arguing with people. I had become accustomed to it all. Little by little, I sank deeper and deeper in a marshland called married life. No matter how hard I tried, Rahim did not change. I wanted him to move on, to advance and become someone in his own right.

But, he had no aspirations. He made me suffer, and suffer I did. This was my married life. I carried on walking absorbed in my own thoughts. Despite my condition, I endured the closed, steamy atmosphere of the crowded baths. Then I returned to the dressing room and sat on the platform for a while. I dressed up and dried my hair with the white cotton bath kerchief. I felt nauseous again as I sat there. I could no longer help myself. I signalled at one of the rubbers who was passing by and wearing her chador over her waist-cloth. She realised I was not well and brought me a pan to be sick in.

Afterwards, she laughed and said: "Congratulations. Do you have morning sickness?"

I nodded. She laughed.

-This happy news deserves a round of sweets you know!

With a heavy heart, I said: "This isn't happiness for me. It's mournful."

- God forbid, why? Are you having problems with your husband?

Suddenly, I burst into tears. I had found someone to confide in at last. I did not have to be weary of her, because she was not my mother-in-law. I did not have to pretend to be happy and smile, because she was not my dayeh and because the news would not get back to my khanoum jan who would find out and suffer. There was no longer any need for reservations. Without even knowing me, this woman had put her finger on the cause of my torment and suffering so well! How well had she managed to make a judgement and sum everything up in just one sentence! She was someone I could confide in. I could open up my heart to her and be hopeful that there would be no riots the following morning. I could no longer hold back my tears.

-Does he give you a hard time?

I nodded.

-Does he beat you up?

-Yes

I was sobbing away. I - Basir ol-Molk's daughter - was crying like a child complaining to her mother about her playmate. I was crying and wiping my tears away with the corner of my kerchief to little avail, because mine were not teardrops, but a torrent.

-So why did you let yourself get pregnant?

-What could I do? It wasn't up to me! Do you have any idea how much heavy-lifting I'm doing? I fill a copper cauldron weighing nearly ten kilos with water and carry it up and down the kitchen stairs. I drink borage to make myself bleed. I jump down from heights. I've tried everything everyone's said. I've used every possible trick. I've taken anything I could get my hands on. But, it's no use. I don't know if eating opium will do the trick or not!

-What good will eating opium do? You'll just do away with yourself girl.

She looked around; then, in a low voice she said: "None of these things are any good. It won't work. Someone's got to flush it for you."

Seeing a ray of hope amid the darkness I lifted my head. I stopped crying and asked: "Who's got to flush it?"

-Do you really want to get shot of it?

-Yes, I really do. Do you know anyone?

-Yes, I know just the person.

I grabbed her hand in excitement: "Who is it?"

-What does it matter who it is. It's a woman who does this. She aborts ten babies every month.

-Let's go and see her right now.

She looked around fearfully: "Not now woman. I've to talk to her first. But, she has an appetite for money.

-Alright, I'll pay her what she's asking for. Your share of the sweet money's also safe with me.

She said: "Oh, Don't talk like this! I just want you to be safe. A thread of your hair's worth more than crores of money.

I laughed. She had only known me for an hour and she was already sacrificing crores of money for a thread of my hair. I asked: "When will you talk to her?"

-I'll go find her one day soon. If she accepts, the next time you come to the baths, we'll go see her together.

-Oh no, that would be too late. I'm already a month gone. I beg you, can't you go find her tomorrow?

-But, I'm stuck here; I've customers.

I put three tomans in her hand. She stared at the money in amazement. I said: "I'll pay for all your customers. I'll give you a day's pay. Go make an appointment with her for the day after tomorrow to get it over and done with."

She softened. Still, she said: "But, I can't do it this quickly! I'll go see her tomorrow afternoon and make a plan. What day is it today?"

-Sunday

-Can you come here Wednesday morning?

-Yes, I'll make it no matter what.

-Don't be late now! I'll wait here for you on Wednesday morning.

Somebody called her – come here Roghieh. She had customers. She said goodbye and left.

Wednesday was only three days away. I had to come up with an excuse to go to the baths again.

That faithful evening, I had dinner with Rahim, his mother and my son. I had worked up an appetite from the joy of my plan and tried to eat well. I wanted to be strong for the following day, to survive. Surprised, my mother-in-law watched me from the corner of her eye. Despite all my happiness, I was not without trepidations. I was scared. Come morning, I was going to put my life in the hands of a common woman I did not even know. I felt sorry for my son. It broke my heart to look at him and think of him as being left without a mother. I had a lump in my throat. I must have taken him into my arms and kissed him at least twenty times. I kissed his hands, his hair, and that round, chubby face with its dried up skin from playing in the dirt.

-Almas jan, don't you go playing in the dirt again…! Look how dried up your face and hands are. God forbid, you'll get a scald head. Almas jan, don't you play with the pond water anymore! Don't wash your hands and face in it love; the pond water's dirty, it's slimy. God forbid, you might get a pink eye.

It was as if I was leaving my last will and testament to him.

Sarcastically, my mother-in-law carried on: "Yeah love, I'll buy you a bucket of *Shahi water*[200] every day, so you can wash your butt with it after you've been to the latrine!"

She expected me to blow my top like a cracker, but I was far too happy with the thought of the cunning plot I had for her and her son to get upset. Besides, what she had said was really funny. I laughed heartily. I had become her mirror image. My son was still awake and playing when I turned to Rahim and said: "Rahim jan, I feel sleepy. Will you come to bed?"

He was busy with his calligraphy. Without paying attention, he said: "You go ahead."

-Without you?

He looked up, stared into my languishing eyes, and said: "I thought I made you sick!"

His heinous smile displayed his teeth. I also made an effort to smile: "Well, that's craving for you. You dislike something one day, and you want it the next."

My mother-in-law shook her head with disgust, picked up the child aggressively, and as she was leaving the room, she said: "For goodness' sake, it's obscene!! This woman knows no shame."

I packed my kit for the baths in a bundle. I took an extra set of clothes, plus some pieces of fabric, an extra chador, and all the money we had in the house – around sixty or seventy tomans. Dayeh had just come with my allowance and the rest was from my savings. Rahim had stopped giving me any house money for a long time now. He would even pay a visit to my chest every now and then and take my money. Otherwise, I would have had a lot more than that. I hid the money in my bundle, put on my chador and started to leave. As usual, my mother-in-law blocked my way: "Where to?"

As per Rahim's orders and after that infamous argument, I was answer able to her every time I wanted to leave the house.

-I'm going to the baths.

Surprised, she bit her hand: "Eh, how come? You were there only three days ago!"

I laughed frivolously, and answered blatantly: "You must ask Rahim as to the how and why. It's not my fault, is it!"

She was taken aback and moved away: "You've become really barefaced Mahboubeh."

I leaped out of the door like a bird out of a cage.

-Did you talk to her? Come on, let's go.

-Hang on; I've a customer. I've to take care of her first.

I was in a hurry. I said: "Leave it. I'll pay you for it."

-No, I can't. She's one of the wealthy. If I don't go, she'll take another rubber. I'll just give her a rub down and come back quickly. That's all.

I sat there and waited. I was happy to be getting rid of his baby. I had covered my face, but my entire body was shaking. I was afraid someone might turn up and recognise me. The bath workers came and went while giving me funny looks. Roghieh came at last. She was wearing an old, patched up cotton dress and had wrapped her damp chador around her. She said: "Let's go quickly. It's late."

-Let's take a coach.

We drove through all the back alleys to approach the downtown areas with rows of deprived housing densely packed together. Most of the inhabitants were poorly dressed and spoke with a particular accent. Some of the young men had turned down their heels, held their arms at a slight angle from their bodies, and walked with their feet apart. Their knees were bent as if stepping on springs as they walked. Some others had thrown their jackets over their shoulders and wrapped their handkerchiefs around their hands. As we got closer to southern Tehran, people's behaviour and habits changed. Everything seemed bizarre to me, and yet I went with great joy.

Roghieh ordered the coach to stop at the top of a lane. My body was frozen. We got off. I was short of breath and shaking. I took a deep breath. Roghieh asked: "Are you scared? We can go back if you've changed your mind."

She herself looked scared too. I said: "No, no! Go ahead. ou go in first."

I remember a blue, wooden door. Roghieh took hold of the knob and knocked. She yelled: "Galin khanoum!"

A woman answered with a common accent: "C'mon in. Door's open."

We went down a step and entered a brick courtyard. It was a small, modest house. A roofed porch was situated in front of us, supported by two gypsum pillars painted in blue. Two doors could be seen on the porch, each one leading to a different room. There was a small pond by the wall near the kitchen, barely larger than a washtub. A young woman, around thirty, wearing a kerchief and a blue, long-sleeved, flowered dress with an overall clean, pleasant appearance brought her head out and gestured to us. I started to go into the room facing me, but she said: "Not in there."

She pointed to a dark and dirty room in the courtyard next to the kitchen, the size of a small storage room. We walked into the room. Its four walls reeked of opium. Galin khanoum kept coming and going whilst talking aloud about her daily chores to an old woman who was either in the yard or in the basement, I could not tell. She was telling her to watch out for the boiling rice and place the mat over the pot once the rice had absorbed all the water, to keep the steam in and let it cook. I felt uneasy. I felt like a square peg in a round hole in the home of strangers. At last, she came into the room and told me with a laugh: "Well, *whoever eats musk melon must face the shivering[201].*"

She had a gold tooth. I was shaken. I thought she must not be dealing with proper women here. She also stared at me and told Roghieh: "Phooey, she's one of those proper ones!" Then, she turned to me and asked: "Are ya hitched?"

-Yes

-Lemme tell ya, I've no time for your hubby's fireworks! He ain't gonna make noise and gimme grief, is he?

Roghieh cut her short: "Her husband has left her and taken a four teen-year old wife. You can be sure nothing will happen."

-How much dough have you got?

I asked: "How much do you want?"

-Well, I ain't takin' no less than thirty or forty tomans.

Roghieh sighed in amazement. I said: "Alright, I accept."

As she saw my worried eyes, she said: "Alright then? Lie down darling. Don't worry, there's no pain. If you're scared, take a little opium the size of a lentil and you won't notice nothin'."

I had learned caution from my mother's midwife, who had also delivered my own son. I gave her the clean cuts of fabric I had brought with me and lay down in the corner of the room on a large wax-soaked sheet covered by a cloth, as she indicated. The paraphernalia and her readiness indicated that she was not a green woman and was experienced in these matters. She left the room and returned with a bowl of water. She placed something in the palm of my hand and said: "Take it."

I asked: "What's this?"

-It's opium darling. Take it for the pain.

I took the opium without hesitation. She sat down coolly and began chatting with Roghieh, while asking me repeatedly: "You sleepy yet?"

I was worried about home. It was almost noon. Little by little, I felt sleepy. I saw her holding a chicken feather, and asked her listlessly: "What's this?"

She held it up sarcastically and, imitating me, she said: "Huh! What's this? It's not a bogeyman; it's a chicken feather."

The pain I felt made me moan. Her hand stopped moving: "What is it missy? I ain't done nothin' yet!"

I could feel the pain, but I was too listless to yell. I kept telling myself it will be over soon. It will be over soon. Roghieh also kept watching and going oh no, oh no.

Galin khanoum said: "Well it hasn't been glued there, it's part of the flesh!

Don't lift up your back. I said park it! Don't lift up your back."

The pain was more than I could bear. I mewed like a cow.

I heard Galin khanoum say: "Alright, it's over now. There was no need for such a hissy fit!"

The feather in her hand was drenched in blood. I fell asleep.

Someone was calling me: "Get up, get up. Don't you want to go home?"

Seemingly, Roghieh and Galin khanoum had had lunch, smoked their hookah and drank tea. I got up all groggy.

-Can I get you something to eat?

-No, I want to go home. What' the time?

-It's two hours gone past midday. If I'd let you, you'd be sleeping like a log until night time.

With a stretched, weak voice I said: "Oooh… It's late."

I felt wrapped up like a baby as I sat up. I lost a large clot of blood as soon as I moved. I was happy that I had been wrapped up. Painstakingly, I took out the money bag I had hung around my neck when I was in the coach and gave Galin khanoum thirty tomans. As she noticed the rest of the money, she brushed what I had given her to one side, and said: "No dear; this ain't enough."

-But you said thirty to forty tomans.

-And you've got to give that exact thirty tomans? I've wasted an entire day on you. It's a long time from the morning till now! Other women come here, get their work done and go home straight away. You're too pampered.

I was too listless and too happy to argue. I asked: "So, are you sure that it's done now?"

-Oi, ta very much. You're lucky you were only a month gone. It was nothin', just a blood clot. You ain't seen some of the things I done!

She took another ten tomans from me and asked: "Do you want a coach?"

-Yes

She put on her chador and I walked to the top of the lane with her and Roghieh's help. She called out to a coach for me. With every motion of the coach I lost more blood. By the time we were close to our local baths I was nearly fainting. Roghieh was overcome by fear. Quietly, I put fifteen tomans in the palm of her hand. She said: "Khanoum jan, I'll get off here." She paused, then asked: "Are you alright?"

-Don't worry. I'm just fine. Go in peace.

She got off. My generosity surprised and delighted her. She had no idea how much I valued the help she had given me. As she walked into the baths, she turned around and glanced at me hesitantly one last time.

I paid the coachman and asked him to drive me home. I had no more strength left. The onset of pain in my abdomen was gradually escalating.

-Stop right here.

The coach stopped. I remained where I was. I was unable to get up and get off. The coachman turned around: "Why won't you get off?"

-I can't. I'm not well.

I stretched out my right hand to hold on to the front of the seat and get off. But, hard as I tried to move, I could not even drag myself forward from where I sat. The hood of the coach was down. I was holding on to my bundle. I cannot say whether the coachman was scared or just felt sorry for me. In a dash, he got up, jumped off the coach, and asked: "Where's your house?"

I pointed to the house: "It's this door here."

He took me by the waist from over my chador and lifted me up like a rag doll. He turned around, put me down behind the door and knocked once. Then, he jumped back on his seat and drove away at a gallop. I heard my mother-in-law's voice who was saying: "She's here! She's here!" Then Rahim must be home.

My knees trembled and bent under my weight from the loss of blood and the fear of seeing Rahim. As I leaned on the door, I slid down and sat on the ground. My bundle fell from my hand. I felt faint. The door opened and my mother-in-law stuck her head out. At first, she looked into the alley bewilderedly. When she could not see anyone, she looked to the right and then to the left. As soon as she saw me, she hit herself on the head: "Come Rahim, hurry!"

Rahim appeared at the door and looked at me.

-What's happened? Why's she on the ground?

-I think she's fainted. Take her into the room.

Rahim placed one hand under my knees and the other under my head and lifted me up like a feather. At the same time, he said: "Her bath kit naneh, bring in her bath kit."

My mother-in-law grabbed my bundle and closed the front door. She ran into the room ahead of us. When Rahim reached the room holding me in his arms, she had already spread the mattress on the floor of our bedroom and covered it with a sheet. Rahim looked at my sweaty forehead as he held me in his arms and said: "What happened Mahboubeh jan? Did you faint in the baths?"

My mother-in-law said: "Put her down. Can't you see she hasn't been to the baths!"

Rahim turned to her angrily and asked: "How can you tell?"

 -From her dry hair; from these clothes she was also wearing this morning; that she doesn't smell of having taken a bath…

Slowly, Rahim put me on the mattress. Even so, a gripping pain wrapped around my abdomen and I lost more blood from the movement.

His mother took the chador off my head. To cope with the heat, I was wearing a long, white dress with pink patterns and a frilled skirt reaching down to my ankles. Rahim's mother told him: "Lift her up so I can pull out the sheet from under her." As Rahim lifted me up, his mother breathed a sigh and said: "Look Rahim, she's bleeding!"

Rahim kneeled down by my mattress and stared at the red blood covering my skirt and the sheet; then, he looked at me in horror. My eyes were half-open. It was as if I was wrapped up in fog as I heard their distant voices. He said: "Mahboub jan, what's happened? Did you fall down? But, but… Why?"

His mother lifted my skirt up with shaky hands; she froze in that position and said angrily: "The sneaky girl! Fallen down? No my dear, she hasn't fallen down. She's gone and flushed her baby."

Rahim was stunned. He stared at his mother with a gaping mouth. He gulped a few times, and then asked: "What? What did you say?"

-Nothing, she's gone and aborted her baby.

In the blink of an eye, the vein on Rahim's neck swelled up. The look in his eyes changed. He lifted his hand to slap me in the face: "You sly afrit! You two-timing witch!"

His mother grabbed his hand in mid-air: "What're you doing? Do you want to kill her? She's already dying from the bleeding. Go get a hakim."

It was towards the end of October, but the weather was still warm. Even so, I felt cold. I was shaking. They closed the doors and pulled a quilt over me. I went to sleep; I woke up. It was night time. There were comings and goings around me. I was in pain. Someone was holding my hand. I had pain in my head, pain in my abdomen. But, it was no longer a severe pain. I lost more blood with every move. They fed me something, changed the rags and wiped the sweat off my forehead. Morning came. I moaned: "Close the curtains." I wanted to be in darkness. I could no longer tell the difference be- tween day and night. But the pain gradually subsided. I no longer felt cold, I no longer whimpered. I woke up. There was a lovely sunshine. I was hungry. My mother-in-law brought me some *kaachi*[202]. She looked very pale and had lost some weight. Her eyes were bloodshot from lack of sleep. I was able to sit up and lay back on the cushions. Weakly, I asked: "What day is it?"

-Saturday

-I slept all this time?

-You're lucky to be alive. God only knows how many hakims came to visit you. Poor Rahim. He's been in a pickle. Neither one of us has slept a wink in four nights. Only the grace of God kept you alive.

I leaned back on the cushion peacefully and smiled with happiness.

Rahim came. When he found out I was better, he did not set foot in my room. I was happy and recovering very quickly. My son came to me during the day and I played with him cheerfully. Rahim came home in the evenings, sat in the parlour and ate his dinner with his mother. He also slept in the parlour. His mother brought my dinner to me. I was truly happy and on my way to recovery. A month passed. I began to walk again. But, dayeh had not come to visit yet. Gradually, I began to worry. Rahim walked in through the door. I could tell from his eyes that he was ready to blow his top like a volcano. He looked into my eyes without any chitchat: "I need money."

-Dayeh hasn't come yet this month. I have no money.

-I said I need money. What did you do with the money?

-I spent it.

-You spent it on murder? You went and aborted my baby? Who did you give all your money to? Tell me who did this?

I knew things were going to escalate. I turned away with impatience and sat on the window sill.

-I put all the money I had under the tulip lamp. Go take it.

Without a word, he lifted the tulip lamp, took the money, put the lamp back in its place and left. I was like a headless chicken. I looked back in self-condemnation day in day out. Not a day went by when I did not ask myself: "What have you done to yourself Mahboubeh?"

Gradually, I was beginning to worry. Dayeh was very late in coming. What did this mean? A thousand things went through my mind. Is khanoum jan sick? Has something happened to my agha jan? Rahim would ask: "This dayeh hasn't come yet?"

-No, I don't know why; I'm worried.

He would laugh sarcastically: "Don't worry. Nothing's happened. She's taken the money and done a runner."

Our bond was even weaker now. Rahim had turned into a beau. He put on a hat and wore a suit and waistcoat. He had also grown a moustache.

He put oil on his hair and combed it sideways. In my eyes, he looked ridiculous. He would move back and forth in front of the mirror a thousand times. A month had passed, but we were still not on good terms with one another. I was surprised. How come he never brought up the subject of what had happened? How come he did not kick up a fuss? He was busy with himself. He admired himself in the mirror, and he was obviously fishing for compliments from me too in some way. But now, the sight of this ridiculous, common, shallow man sickened me. A man with no acumen. He had no accomplishments and his looks, if any, were no longer manifest to me. Now, to me, a real man was someone with decorum and dignity; someone who was intelligent and erudite, like my uncle, my father, Mansour, like Ata al-Dowleh's son that I had foolishly turned down. ***Oh, how I repent***. Now, I wished for a decent, upright man; an honest man; someone who looked after the weak and supported them. A man to sooth away the pains, someone to lean on. Appearances and looks no longer fooled me. I wanted a true human being, the salt of the earth. Rahim could not understand how and why he no longer appealed to me. He did not even care; and, likewise, his existence was of no importance to me.

I woke up one morning, happy to have succeeded in my plan. I put on a nice dress and some makeup. I put kohl on my eyes and blush on my cheeks. I had dilly dallied long enough for Rahim to leave the house. As soon as my mother-in-law saw me, she said: "You're happy as a clam today! What's up?"

-Nothing, I'm just happy.

-How come?

-Just like that.

-Have you got a trick up your sleeve again?

Someone was at the door. Dayeh came. Although she tried to put on a smile and a brave face, my heart sank as soon I saw her. Uncontrollably, I ran down the stairs barefooted and showered her with nonstop questions.

-Where have you been dayeh jan? What's happened? Don't lie to me. I can tell from your eyes. Has anything happened to my agha jan? khanoum jan? What then? I know something has happened. Tell me quickly.

Dayeh said: "Damn the devil. Hold your tongue girl. No, nothing's hap pened to your agha jan or khanoum jan. Everything's all right. Won't you give me some tea?"

She sat down and drank her tea. I had butterflies in my stomach. She put my money, which was a month late, in front of me with both hands. I was worried.

-You must forgive me for being late. We were preoccupied.

I said: "Dayeh, my stomach's in a knot. You'll be the death of me! Tell me what's happened?"

She dropped her head and began playing with the flower patterns of the carpet: "What can I say Mahboub jan. You'll get upset… But, but, Ashraf khanoum…"

-Ashraf khanoum? Mansour's wife? What's happened? Tell me!

-She died in childbirth.

She dried her tears with a corner of her headscarf. My mother-in-law and I were staring at her. On impulse, I wiped the lipstick off my lips: "She died in childbirth? What do you mean?"

-She was seven months pregnant. She went into early labour because she had put on too much weight. May she rest in peace, she just ate and slept. She was also short. She looked just like a roof roller towards the end. Her hands and feet were swollen like a bolster. Her flesh turned white if you pressed it down. You had to wait for it to get back to its normal shape again. None of her shoes fitted. Towards the end, she'd wear a pair of Mansour agha's shoes. No matter how often she was told to eat less, to stop indulging herself and go for walks so she'd have an easy birth, it was in one ear and out the other. About six or seven weeks ago, she went into labour unexpect- edly. She started bleeding at seven months gone. She was in pain for three days and three nights. Mansour khan brought in all the hakims and medi- cine in town. He left no stone unturned to bring them to her bedside. Poor khanoum bozorg. I mean Nimtaj khanoum. Despite all her domestics and comings and goings, she rolled up her sleeves to serve her rival. But, it was of no use. Her hour came on the third day.

-What about her baby? Did the baby die too?

-No. He's a chubby, rosy-cheeked little sweetie. God moves in mysterious ways. A premature, seven month old boy in perfect health. Khanoum bozorg has hired a dayeh to breastfeed him. She's taken the baby into her own care. She says it'll be like I have two sons now.

- What's Mansour doing? Is he very upset?

-Well yes, he's upset; but, just between us, not as much as he should be. Khanoum bozorg seems to be more upset than him. She pays more attention to her havou's son than she does her own. She won't put the baby down. We've all been by her side all this time. Either I'd go and your khanoum jan would look after Manouchehr, or she'd go and I'd stay home with Manouchehr. Nezhat and Khojasteh were by khanoum bozorg's side day and night.

That morning's joy left my heart and evaporated into thin air like a cloud in the sunshine. My heart ached for the bad fortune of a woman I had never met; for the predicament Mansour was in; for the poise and ladylike manners of Nimtaj. It ached from the plays of fate and this unfortunate destiny. I was surprised at my own thick skin and how I had managed to survive the abortion under those filthy conditions.

Rahim returned late at night. My son was sleeping in his grandmother's room on the other side of the courtyard. We were having dinner when his mother said: "Dayeh khanoum was here today." She was like a spy reporting back to Rahim. He said: "Well, well, congratulations; money has arrived then."

-Leave me alone Rahim. I really don't feel like it.

-When do you feel like it then?

His mother said sarcastically: "You were so chirpy this morning. But, when dayeh jan came with the news of all the deaths in town, you had a mood swing."

Rahim turned to me curiously: "Deaths? The news of whose death?"

Suddenly, I sensed that he might not mind hearing the news of my father's death. He knew in that case I would come into a nice share of the inheritance. I said: "Ashraf. Mansour's wife." And tears started rolling down my face.

Stressing on every word, he said: "Ooh! Oops! I was wondering what had happened! The… second… wife… of your… cousin… has died in childbirth. You never even knew her. What're you pining for? Hundreds of women die in childbirth every year. Are you going to mourn them all?"

Reproachfully, I said: "Rahim, she was a young woman. Humans need to have humanity after all[203]."

He replied sarcastically: "Really? Is that so? So how come there was no need for humanity when you tore out your own baby bit by bit?"

As his mother sat there, she turned her back on me and said: "Yes, goodness, you took the words right out of my mouth."

The volcano buried in Rahim's heart – which I imagined had subsided – erupted from beneath the ashes: "You go… you go and abort your own baby, my baby, without my consent and then you turn on the waterworks for Ashraf khanoum? Does this make you very humane? Shall I believe the neighbour's oath that he has not seen next door's rooster in his yard or shall I believe the tail of the rooster sticking out from underneath his cloak?"[204]

I said: "That was not a baby. It was just a blood clot. I got rid of it for a good reason."

-You had good reason? Such as what pray say?

My mother-in-law said: "My dear, her reason is that she wants to look after herself. She wants to put on makeup first thing every morning and fuss over herself. You can slave away, and I can be her maid, so that she can become the lady of both upstairs and downstairs, to sit around and give orders that you can't look at this person, you can't talk to that person, don't marry Kokab. Don't you dare have a baby with another woman!! But, she'll get rid of your baby so she can be free, so that she can pick up her son and Ya Ali, run to her khanoum *joun*[205] at the slightest excuse."

I said: "Khanoum, watch your language. Why won't you let me hold you in respect?"

Rahim got up, red in the face: "Is she lying? Is she lying?"

The light from the lamp shined on his livid face, bloodshot eyes, and handlebar moustache. He was gritting his teeth. What a loathsome face. I no longer knew what it was about him that I had fallen in love with. I said: "For God's sake Rahim, stop it."

-You don't want my baby, eh? It's beneath you? Now I'm an ick? Remember when you were devouring me in the carpentry?

- I was a child then. Now I know what I've done.

His hand came into contact with my face like a whip. My mother-in-law did not intervene this time. With great pleasure, she just said: "You asked for it."

As I was holding my face with one hand, I turned to her and asked: "Khanoum do you pray every day?"

Sarcastically, she said: "No, you're the only one who prays."

I said: "You pray and yet you make trouble between husband and wife like this? How can you light this fire and then turn towards God for your prayers? Are you not afraid of the next world? What do you stand to gain from any of this? How's my misery gainful to you? Have I ever done you any wrong? Have I done anything to you apart from holding you in the highest respect? Fear God khanoum, because I will not forgive you."

She raised her voice and began wailing. I no longer cared that the neighbours would hear, or that they would be standing behind the front door or hiding on their rooftops to take a peek and eavesdrop. I no longer asked them to lower their voices or say that we will lose face in front of everyone. I had become just like them. Gritting his teeth together, Rahim said angrily: "What's the matter with you? Why're you raising your voice over your head?"

I said: "Don't do this to me Rahim. I'm not your captive. I had a termination, good for me. Do you know why? Because of you; because of your mother and her sarcastic words. I'm not interested. I don't want another child. Another child would only enslave me more to your torments and your mother's. *The knife has reached the bone*[206]. I want to head to no man's land… You've driven me crazy. For how much longer can I stay dignified? How much longer can I forgive? You'll see, I might just take my child one day and leave!"

He put his hands to his waist: "Take your child and leave? *You'll see your child the day you are able to see behind your ears[207]*. I'll give you so many babies you won't have time to scratch your head. You got rid of this one, but what'll you do with the rest? From now on, you're gonna give birth every year." He took my hand and dragged me to the bedroom.

-Stop it Rahim. I'm not well. I'm sick. Leave me alone.

His mother got up and left the room, slamming the door. Her ruse had worked. I pulled my hand out of Rahim's. He said: "Sick?! There's nothing the matter with you."

He pulled me up by the hair. The pain brought me to my feet and guided me towards the other room. He threw me on the floor. My body was still weak and painful from the loss of blood. Falling to the ground broke the last of my resistance. I was at the end of my tether. Was this hateful bosom the same one I had longed for one day? ***Oh, Dear God, how I repent!***

The lack of my monthly flow brought me the good news that I was not pregnant. Rahim and his mother were as angry as wounded tigers. Rahim asked: "You're not pregnant?"

-No

-Happy?

Fearing him, I lied: "No."

-The night's young. No worries. We have another thirty nights until next month." And the next month came and went, and the bleeding brought me the good news of freedom again.

A month, two months, three months, six months, and another year passed. My son was five and I was still not pregnant. I felt safe now. I no longer prayed to God for Rahim to break his leg and not come home at nightfall. Rahim gave the order: "Go see a hakim."

So I went, but only out of fear. He gave me a bunch of herbs and useless medicines; nothing but snake oil. His mother accompanied me. She had come to make sure that I would see the hakim. She bought my prescription and kept watch over me until I finished taking them every night. She sat opposite me and stared until I had swallowed everything. I was compelled to take them and pray that they would not be effective. I prayed that they

would be useless which, as luck would have it, they were. The chicken feather had done its job. My internal organs had fused together. I would thank
God a thousand times a day, every day. Rahim and his mother were disappointed and angry.

Dayeh came. With hurt feelings, I said: "Dayeh jan, you're late again. My
eyes have been glued to the door."

-You've no idea what good news I have love!

-What is it? Tell me.

-It's Khojasteh's wedding.

I jumped for joy. The weight I had been carrying on my shoulders over
the past six years was lifted. Khojasteh would no longer lose out because of
my foolish love.

-Who? When? How?

-Oh! Hold your tongue for a minute girl and let me explain.

I hugged dayeh and gave her a big kiss.

-Whoa, you're choking me Mahboubeh! Believe it or not, I was the cause
of Khojasteh's wedding.

-You? How come?

She sat down, and like a mother who wanted to tell her child a fairy
tale, she made slurping noises with her mouth, and said: "Let me start at
the beginning, when I got so sick I could no longer stay on my feet. I was
coughing a lot. The cough was killing me. No matter how much your khanoum jan tried to cure me with all sorts of medicines, it didn't work. In the
end, my Khojasteh jan – that dear girl – said: "Khanoum jan, this won't do.
My dayeh jan's in a bad way. I'll take her to the hospital myself." She took
my hand; we got up, groomed ourselves and went to some hospital - I don't
rightly know where it was. There was a doctor there love, such a gentleman,
so breathtakingly handsome; he was a sight for sore eyes. Khojasteh stood
there, speechless. He had just returned from Europe. The first time he examined me, Khojasteh was in the waiting room. He gave me my medicine
and told me you'll get well soon mother. Go in good health. But, as soon as

he set eyes on Khojasteh, who had lifted her picheh – you know how Khojasteh's no good with her hijab – he told me: "Khanoum, sit down and let me examine you one more time, just to make sure…"

Dayeh and I kept laughing. She continued: "Then, I can't remember what it was he said that Khojasteh asked him a question in French. I think she must have asked about my health. They talked for a while in this foreign language and, to cut a long story short, Mr Doctor fell head over heels for her. He said to return the following week, and we said as you wish."

I asked: "Well, what next?"

-Nothing. We went again the following week. Again he said to go back the week after. We went back again. In the end, I told Khojasteh: "You know what love? I don't want to go anymore. You go by yourself. I'm feeling fine now, except for this thermometer that the doctor keeps stuffing in my mouth for no good reason at all; I've ulcers all over my mouth because of it." The last time we were there, the doctor asked Khojasteh out of the blue: "Will you allow me to visit your father in private?" And Khojasteh said: "I have to ask my father." On the way back, I said: "Khojasteh jan, I think you're stuck on him too!" She said: "Yes dayeh jan. He was like an angel from heaven when I first set eyes on him! But, if my agha jan says no, I'll obey. I don't want to break his heart again, like…" Dayeh bit her tongue.

-Say it dayeh jan. Like who? Like me? She's right. I won't get upset. The truth is not upsetting.

-Yes love. She said: "One such suffering's enough for an entire tribe." Anyway, doctor came and they talked. Your father seems rejuvenated with the joy of this son-in-law. The boy has won everyone's heart in the family. At first, he wanted to have a small ceremony, take his wife by the hand and take her to their home. He said he doesn't stand on formalities. Your agha jan said as you wish, but then I'll have to envy two lost weddings! So, his mother came to Tehran from their hometown. She's the elder of the family. They say she's the one who has sent all the young people in the family abroad to study. They all hold her in very high esteem. She's a lionhearted woman. No one says a word over her head. No one does anything without consulting her. What a grand lady! Tall and thin, with hair white as cotton wool. She braids her hair in two parts, wears a white, voile kerchief, and dresses in sedate, dignified clothes. She came and sat. She observed all the customs and exchanged compliments and greetings. She's a man in her own right. She came alone and talked to your father manfully. She said: "Alright now, Mustafa may not want a big wedding, but why should your daughter suffer! She's young and has her own dreams. How many times does a girl become a bride? I have my dreams too. There has to be a wedding with all due ceremonials." Your agha jan told the doctor: "I envy you such a mentor". Their wedding is in two months' time, on the eve of *Hazrat Faatemeh's*[208] (AS) birthday. You should see all the comings and goings! Then, she paused and said hesitantly: "Why don't you come too Mahboub jan."

I asked: "Has khanoum jan said that I should come?"

She pondered a little, and muttered: "No. But they won't throw you out if you do come!"

-No dayeh jan. Leave it be. Don't reopen old wounds.

I had bought a small night cap for my son. He liked it so much he wore it the whole time. It had red, green and blue geometric patterns on it. Every time it fell on the floor, he'd bring it to me: "Blow on it naneh. It's dusty."

-I'll blow on it if you say khanoum jan.

-Alright, khanoum jan. Blow on it now.

And my mother-in-law would roll her eyes.

> *Auntie took out a small night cap from the boxwood chest and showed it to Soudabeh.*
>
> *"This is the one. He wore it on his head. He looked like a doll to me with that round, chubby face."*

Dayeh had told me the dowry was being sent the week before the wedding, and that the khancheh would be brought on the eve of the wedding. I dressed up my son and put on my chador to leave the house. I wanted to stand and watch the bringing of the khancheh from a distance with my son. I wished for my son to see the splendor and grandor of his grandfather's household. I wanted to take part in the celebrations of Khojasteh's wedding in some way. My mother-in-law blocked my way: "Where're you going at sundown?"

-They're carrying the khancheh for Khojasteh. We're going to watch.

-If they wished for your highness to be present, they'd have invited you. No dear, you can't go. Rahim has said you don't have permission to take the boy out.

-Alright, I'll go by myself.

-What've you cooked up this time? Go if you want to go. But, you'll have to answer to Rahim yourself.

It was not worth it. It was not worth the hassle. I did not have the strength to get beaten up again. I was at the end of my tether and had lost a lot of weight. My clothes hung loose on me. Enough was enough. It was not worth the trouble. Again and again, I kept repeating to myself you brought this on yourself Mahboubeh. It was your own mistake. Even hard stones came to speak words and told you not to do it. And you said I want to do it, I'll do it. Now it serves you right. Take this now. I wanted to return to my room; but, my poor, innocent son who had been looking forward to going out began to cry.

My mother-in-law said: "Go play outside love. Do you want to go to Seyed Sadegh's place?" My son went outside and I, exhausted and disgusted, returned towards my two rooms.

It was towards the end of winter. My son was entering his seventh year. A light snow had covered everything when I woke up one morning. My son and I had crawled up to our necks under the korsi after breakfast. My son had snuggled up to me with his small body and had dosed off. Rahim was done on the roof and was now shovelling the snow in the yard. Despite my son's insistence, I had not given him permission to join his father outside. Rahim walked into the room, rubbing his hands together from the cold and crawled under the quilt at the top of the korsi. His cheeks and nose had turned red from the cold. He turned to my son and said jokingly: "Oh, Almas khan, what a cold weather it is!"

I told my son: "See, it's good that you didn't go out into the yard! You'd catch a cold otherwise."

Rahim said laughing: "Yes my dear, let your father catch a cold instead. Why should you?"

I laughed and kissed my son on the head, and he snuggled up to me. As Rahim was looking in my eyes, he told our son jokingly: "Almas jan, do you want us to make a little brother or sister for you quickly?"

I laughed and said: "Have some shame Rahim."

He rose to his feet: "It's too bad I've got to go." He was in such a good mood! He went to the adjoining room, leaving the connecting door open between the two. I was surprised. He did not even bother to go to work on a good day; so, where was he going on this snowy day? I asked: "Where to?"

In a tempting voice, he said: "Somewhere nice." He took his coat off the nail and the key to my chest from underneath the carpet.

-What do you want Rahim?

-Money

-There's no money left. It's the end of the month. I've kept this for house money and expenditures.

-Well, expenditures have to be expended!

How quickly he was able to forget that warm, pleasant feeling of family life of a moment ago. I asked: "Are you going drinking again?"

-I want to go and do as I please again. Was there anything else?" He combed his hair and said: "I'm off. Ta very much."

My son was asleep. I got up. It had been nearly a fortnight since I had been to the baths last. My mother-in-law kept better count than me. The cold put me off a bit, but it could not be helped. I couldn't not take a bath all winter. The sun came out from behind the clouds and spread its pleasant rays on the snow in the courtyard and on the korsi inside the room from behind the window. I pushed the door curtains to one side to let it warm the room. My son was asleep under the korsi. I took my bath kit and went to him in the parlour. He was still asleep. As I opened the door, the sound woke him up and he began to cry: "I want to come with you, I want to come too."

I kneeled down beside him: "Where do you want to come sweetheart? I'm going to the baths."

As much as he hated being rubbed down and have his hair washed, he still got up and stood on the korsi quilt. His large eyes were full of tears. Rahim's eyes! He kept sniffing. His little white chin prompted me to kiss him. Again he said: "I want to come."

-Do you want me to rub down your arms and wash your hair?

He nodded, then gathered his lips together and said: "Yes."

I laughed out loud: "You little monkey. If you stay, I'll give you something nice."

-What?

I knew he liked roasted wheat and hemp nuts; but we did not have in the house that day. I lied: "Roasted wheat and hemp nuts."

He jumped up and down joyfully and said: "Give it to me, give it to me."

-I'll tell khanoum to bring it for you right now.

I called his grandmother. She said: "Come, let's go Almas jan. I want to give you roasted wheat and hemp nuts. Your mother will be back in no time. Come back quickly Mahboubeh! Quickly, quickly…"

I ran and brought the white jacket I had knitted myself and put it on him. I said: "Khanoum, it's cold. Don't let him play outside."

-You go and stop worrying. Almas jan will stay with me.

As I left the house, my son was climbing over the small mound of snow which had been accumulated in a corner of the yard. The winter sun shining on his little night cap brought out its bright colours. My mother-in-law was carrying a tray of uncooked rice up from the kitchen, dragging her feet on the ground. She called out: "Almas jan, naneh, let's go into the room and clean this rice." I was returning home from the baths. The sun was out. That day's snow was the last of the season. I was moseying along and feeling relaxed. The sun warmed up my body; I had also bought some roasted wheat and hemp nuts for my son.

As I turned the corner into our lane, I was shocked to see the crowd that had gathered there. Idle people come out into the streets even in the winter. And in such large numbers too! What a crowd! Yet, this was too large a crowd to be neighbours cracking pumpkin seeds together and gossiping. What were the men doing here? And so many of them? I was a hundred feet away from them when I heard a cry. Something seemed to have happened to our neighbours. The woman next door was screaming. But no. I am wrong. She was standing there, outside our front door, looking at me. She was not even worried about her hijab. We stared at one another. I had lifted my picheh and she was wearing a chador. It was as if a ray of light connected our eyes. My eyes were filled with questions, and her eyes were submerged in unbearable agony. The owner of these eyes was distressed, she was tormented. Then, she broke the connection and turned away from me with a painful expression. Someone said: "His mother's here."

My heart sank. What does this mean? Were they talking about me? What was it? What had happened? I ran. Our front door was open. I pushed the crowd to one side. They were all locals. A few people were standing in the corridor leading to the courtyard. One of the boys who often played with Almas outside was also there. His face looked red from getting beaten up and crying. There was screaming. It was my mother-in-law's voice. I sat down in a panic and grabbed the little boy's skinny shoulders, asking: "What's happened? What's happened? Tell me!"

He placed his hand over his head to protect himself from a probable slap and began howling at the top of his voice. I was beside myself. A couple of local women were standing in the middle of the courtyard, facing the corridor. I stood up and stepped into the yard. With her head uncovered, my mother-in-law was pulling out her dishevelled red[209] and white hair and beating her chest. As soon as she saw me, she yelled: "Oh-oh…! You came! Come and see what has befallen you!" She was hitting herself on her thighs and rocking back and forth: "Come and see how my back has been bent in two."

I looked around the courtyard. On a plank of wood, under a white sheet, there lay a small shape. I could not tell what had happened. What is that small shape? I did not want to know. The later I found out, the better. But a voice in my head kept saying: "It's Rahim. It's Rahim!" And my gaze was transfixed on that white sheet right from where I stood, unable to move. My eyes were like two scorching flames, wanting to rip the sheet apart, but were too petrified. There was someone there. Rahim was there. But, Rahim was at the shop! Rahim was not so small! My mother-in-law screamed and beat her chest: *"Ooh, my Ali-Asghar… Ooh, my Ali-Asghar…"*[210]

No, I must not believe this. How come the sun is so dark? Why is this place so unfamiliar? Is this me standing here? Are these people watching me? It's not possible that this has happened to me. To the others maybe, but not to me. Ali-Asghar was a child! Ooh, so this is Almas? Lying here, underneath that white sheet? My bundle fell from my hand. I ran. Someone tried to grab my arm. The chador slipped off my head. I reached that white sheet and bent down to pull it back. I did not have the strength.I was glaring at its whiteness, but did not want to see. The later, the better. If I don't see it, I won't have to know. Once I see it, it is all over. I pulled back the sheet and I saw. His round, chubby face, those long lashes and white skin, all soaked in water. But, he had not taken a bath. Why was he wet then? His eyes were shut. The eyes of his father. Suddenly, I saw it. For the first time, I saw how much he resembled Nezhat, with those full lips and chubby cheeks. It was as if Nezhat was sleeping there. Oh… and I knew that from then on, every time I saw Nezhat I would remember him. That is, of course, if I ever saw Nezhat again; and I said aloud: "If I see Nezhat again, if I ever see Nezhat."

Intertwining voices behind me were saying: "She's gone mad; the poor thing has cracked up." And I yelled: "If I ever see Nezhat."

I tried to get up. What's the meaning of this? What's the matter with my back? I can't stand up. My knees remained bent. I pulled myself towards the wall. There seemed to be no more sun. I muttered: "Oh mother, oh father."

There was no one.

"Oh dayeh jan, oh dayeh jan, won't you help me?"

I whispered to myself. The piercing sound of my mother-in-law's screams tormented me. I whispered to myself. There were no tears.

Someone said caringly: "Come sit here."

I obeyed like a lamb. There was a stool or something. I was surrounded by four or five men and women. Women with tearful eyes and men with solemn faces. Of course, why didn't I think of it sooner? My poor, common mother-in-law wouldn't know. Because Rahim was not there, because we did not have a man in the house, she's just sitting there weeping. I held up my head. I was pulling myself up. I was pleading, breathing with an open mouth; I said panting: "For God's sake… Get a doctor someone… The man of the house isn't here."

Why did they keep looking at each other? Why did they keep their heads down? Why won't they get a move on?

-Someone get a doctor quick!

Someone said softly: "It's no more use."

The word 'no more' flashed in my mind and, suddenly, I came to myself. What does 'no more' mean? 'No more' means it's over? Almas is dead…?

As I began to speak, I was surprised by the sound of my own voice and the fact that my mouth was so dry. I kept swallowing the non-existent saliva to help me speak; but it was not possible. My lower lip split. The corners of my lips stuck together. It was as if a ball had been jammed down my throat. A low, croaky, hoarse voice left my throat as I asked: "What happened?"

-He fell in the pond.

What's this? There must be a mistake. Our pond isn't deep. His grandmother was here!

-Pond? Which pond?

-Seyed Sadegh the grocer's pond.

-He's dead?

Silence.

I screamed: "Is he dead?"

This is how easily I lost him. He slipped out of my hands like a fish. Everyone else's children are in good health. They're all holding their mother's hands. They'll all go home now, happy that this has not happened to their son. Only to mine. They'll say you see love, I told you not to lean over the pond! And I am all alone in the middle of this courtyard… I will never bear another child again.

I bent in two like a melting candle. Someone held me: "Go get her man. She's fainted."

I could not grasp what was happening. Bereavement and grief cannot be described. They had already taken me indoors when Rahim arrived. He came up the stairs. His eyes were bloodshot. I detested my own languor. Why were they spending so much time looking after me? Why won't they let me go into the yard? I said: "Rahim, bring him in here. It's cold outside." I stretched out my hand while pleading.

Rahim leaned back on the pier of the wall with bloodshot eyes and stared at me in silence.

The house was submerged in stillness. There was a ceasefire. My mother-in-law was on one side of the courtyard, and I on the other. Rahim could not bear any of it. He would leave the house. I wanted him by my side, so he could rub my frail shoulders as I rested my head on his. I wished I could say Rahim, the grief is killing me, save me. I wished he would say, don't do this Mahboub jan, don't do this to yourself. I wished he would stay up all night, like me, and stare at the ceiling; I wanted to see his tears fall on the bolster from the corner of his eyes. But, Rahim was not there. He was not my refuge. It was as if I was suspended in midair.

Dayeh came. I heard her talking to my mother-in-law. A fortnight had passed. I saw her come up the stairs in tears and take me in her arms without a word. I said: "Oh dayeh, dayeh, dayeh" and broke out in tears.

Dayeh left at sundown, but returned quickly.

-Why did you come back dayeh jan?

-I'll stay with you. I'll stay with you for a few days.

-What did khanoum jan say?

-What can she say? She's weeping.

-What about my agha jan?

-He's sitting alone in the room with his rosary beads and is not talking to anyone. He's pale as death.

She stayed by my side that night. Rahim slept in the next room. I was crying, murmuring and confiding in her: "Dayeh jan, the back of his hand was chapped and burning from the dust; he was in pain. Dayeh jan, when he used swear words, I'd slap him in his little mouth… Dayeh jan, he would get scared and cry when Rahim and I argued… Dayeh jan, I had no roasted wheat and hemp nuts to give him."

Dayeh was crying: "Stop it Mahboub, you're killing yourself. A child has to be disciplined. All parents hit their children. So, no one has to discipline their child for fear that he might fall in the pond one day?"

Grief had crippled me; it was driving me crazy. My chin was quivering all the time. I spent my days crying. As soon as I wanted to eat something, I remembered him. Where is he now? Is he hungry? Is he alone? Is he scared of the darkness? Oh, dayeh jan… Dayeh would say: "Rahim khan, take her out; take her to a pilgrimage."

And Rahim shook his head gloomily, to indicate that it was hopeless.

I could not bear the sight of my mother-in-law. Rahim would not talk to her either. I had told her a hundred times not to let this child roam the streets. The sound of her voice in the yard made my hair stand on end. It was the voice of *Azrael*[211].

I did not want to walk through the lane, to see the house of Seyed Sadegh the grocer; my son's slaughter place. I would not look to the corner of the yard. It was as if he was still lying there, underneath that white sheet. I bare-ly slept a wink at night. And what a sleep it was when I did! I would have given thanks for a hundred nights of sleeplessness. I did not want to sleep. I was afraid of going to sleep. I dreamt that he was in the room; I woke up; that he was sitting under the korsi and snuggling up to me; I woke up; that he was running after me in tears; I bolted awake and jumped up startled. Even my dreams of him were laced with pain and sorrow. Because I knew it was a lie. I knew I was dreaming; and in my painful, light nightly sleep, a woman called out to someone from afar… very far. I listened from a very far distance.

My Ali-Asghar… My Ali-Asghar…

Three months came to pass and the waves of pain and grief subsided gradually. Life appeared mundane and unruffled on the surface, but my burn-ing grief and sorrow had deposited in its depths, only to resurface with the slightest stirr to darken my soul. This is a pain which cannot be expressed, and I prayed to God that no one will ever find out what kind of pain it is.

Rahim was freed of it sooner than I. I was amazed to see him pick up my wooden comb one morning to put his hair and moustache in shape, turning left and right to see himself in the looking glass over the fireplace. He had such stamina!

I would not let him near me. How could I? How could I be happy over here, with my child over there…. No, I could not. I could not help it. A few more months went by. I was intoxicated by grief and not in a mood for arguments. When did Nowruz come? Where did time fly to? When was spring over that I did not even notice?

One night, after dinner, Rahim and I were sitting in the room. I was embroidering. I had nothing else to do. Rahim was sitting across the room from me. As if waking up from a deep, long sleep, I raised my head and looked at him. Not in passing, but in great detail, as if he had just returned from a long trip and I was weighing him up. His hair was oiled and combed to one side, happy and carefree. He had stretched out one leg, and folded his right leg in a right angle, resting his right hand on it as he smoked. He had taken up smoking lately. An ashtray was next to his right hand, on the carpet. He had alcohol on his breath. He would not give in to working, as usual. He got up and brought over his wooden box which held his calligraphy set and placed it next to him. He plunged the reed pen in the inkpot full of ink and *ligheh*[212] and began writing. I asked: What are you writing Rahim?"

He turned the piece of paper around towards me: "I am losing my heart O lovers, O God."

I cringed.

-How you love this verse! You've already written one!

I pointed to the niche. He laughed and said: "I feel like writing it again once every few years." He finished writing it and left it on the niche to dry.

The sun was already up when I woke up the following morning. I had no incentive to get up, no hope. It was almost noontime when I finally got up and went into the parlour. The calligraphy was no longer in the niche. Rahim had taken it with him.

It was near the end of the summer. Dayeh came. We were having tea in the room. Old wounds always opened up as soon as I set eyes on her and I burst into tears. Dayeh said: "Stop it love. Why do you torment yourself? When are you going to stop?"

-But dayeh jan, it's not only this pain. I can't even have children anymore.

Unwittingly, dayeh said: "So much the better. Thank God for that, with this womaniser of a husband that …"

-What?

-Nothing. I didn't say anything.

-Tell me dayeh. I know you know something.

-How should I know? I just said something out of the blue.

I gave her a piercing look and said firmly: "Tell me dayeh."

-What do you want me to say? I swear to God, there's nothing to tell. Firouz's wife, dadeh khanoum, has walked past his shop a couple of times. She was saying she'd seen things."

-Such as?

-I really don't know. Her words are not worth much. This is all she's said to me indirectly.

-What was she doing outside his shop?

-Well, she'd taken a message to your aunt's place. They'd kept her for lunch. She was returning after lunch when, on the way back, she'd gone past Rahim agha's shop.

-It's quite a long way from Rahim agha's shop to auntie Keshvar's place.

-Like I said, her words aren't worth much. She's lying.

-No, she's not lying. She's probably gone to see what's happening because she's so nosey… But, she's not lying…

-But for goodness' sake, don't say anything to Rahim agha now…! He'll think it's my fault.

-I'm not a child dayeh jan!

I already had my suspicions, but was unwilling to believe it. I pretended not to know. It was all the same to me. Nevertheless, I had guessed when he stopped coming home at lunchtimes, when he wore a suit, from the way he combed his hair, from his calligraphy, I am losing my heart O lovers, O God...

I ate my lunch. Rahim was not home. I pretended to be asleep. My mother-in-law was also napping in her room. Quietly, I picked up my chador and my shoes and tiptoed to the corridor. I put on my chador and picheh, wore my shoes, and left the house. It was only half past noon. I hurried through a tree-lined street and a few lanes and back alleys. Rahim's shop had two doors. The main door opened onto the main street. But it was closed. I turned into the side lane and then into the back lane which was parallel to the main road. A small door opened into that back lane from the shop. The small door was open. I could hear the sound of the saw. There was nothing happening there. I walked to the end of the lane and walked back again. Still nothing was happening. Slowly, I walked back and forth a few times. If there had been anyone out there, they would have surely become suspicious. But, there was not a soul to be seen. Everyone was having a nap. It was the third or fourth time that I was walking back and forth when a very short girl turned into the lane from the main street. I was standing a long way away at the end of the lane. Even so, I bent down and pretended to be wiping the dust off the bottom of my chador. When I stood up again, I saw her turning into the back lane at the end of which Rahim's shop door was. She had lifted her picheh. Very slowly, I walked closer with a palpitating heart. I could no longer hear the sound of the saw. I peeked quietly. The girl had a fat, chubby figure. She looked like a pumpkin underneath that old, worn out chador she was wearing. I could not see her face from far away. But I thought I heard her laugh. She looked around to make sure there was no one there. I sidestepped. When I looked again, she was gone. It took me a couple of minutes to pull myself together. My head was boiling at its very centre, not from the pain of losing a love, but because I felt crushed. This lowlife of a man was like a spider spinning a web again to catch another fly. The death of my son had dealt the last blow to our love. It had split our hearts apart with one blow, like a sharp, cutting dagger. And now, his shameless behaviour was rubbing salt into the wound.

The girl left the shop and began walking towards the end of the lane. I pulled myself to one side and quickly went into the main street. I had just arrived there when she walked past me. She was panting. Was it was from excitement or overweight? I don't know.

She was pulling down her picheh. Just for a moment, I had a glimpse of her chubby profile, which was pink and fat like a rising dough. A wide nose looked as if it had been punched and sunken into her face, with the tip reaching her lips without exaggeration. It made Kokab look good... All I can remember is this ugly, grotesque profile and that short, fat figure which swayed down the lane and disappeared like a roof roller. Unwittingly, I began walking in her shadow. A couple of lanes further up, she turned right again and disappeared from sight through the low, wooden door of a small house at the bottom of the dead-end. Feeling lost, I stood in the middle of the lane and looked around. I was about to turn back when a woman opened the door of the only house on my left and was taken aback by seeing me standing there, looking lost: "Was there something you wanted khanoum? Whose house are you looking for?"

I came to myself and walked towards her. I was thankful for the picheh which was hiding my face. It was as if someone was putting words into my mouth: "Khanoum, I wanted to ask for the hand of the daughter of this house in marriage for my brother. But first, I wanted to make some enquiries to see what sort of people they are. Do you know them?"

My body was trembling underneath the chador. The woman shot a quick glance at the house, and said sarcastically: "Really...! But they don't have a daughter. They can't have children!"

-So, who's that short chubby girl?

-The one with a squint in her eye? She's the daughter of Khavar khanoum's sister-in-law. The daughter of her husband's brother. She often roams around here.

I felt alleviated. You are such an incompetent oaf Rahim. This is just what you deserve. I asked: "What's her name?"

-Her name's Ma'soumeh.

-What does her uncle do?

-Her uncle's a policeman.

-What kind of a girl is she? Is she gifted or skilled in any way? Can she read and write or anything?

She laughed: "Gifted?" Then, she lowered her voice and said: "Please don't say I said anything! They'll flimflam you khanoum. They're not a good match for you. The girl has her head in the clouds. She's uncontrollable and unruly. Her uncle's wife is distraught by her, the poor woman; but, if she says anything to the girl, her husband will beat her black and blue. The whole community here is plagued by them. Even so… She's still alright in comparison. You should see the girl's brothers. Her *Dash*[213] Akbar is well-known around here."

-Why? What're they like?

-He's such a hooligan. He lives in *Abmangal*. They're animals. God forbid should they have an argument with anyone. One of them works at the soap works. The other one does something different every day. One day, He's a kneader. Another day, he's at the sheep-head cookery place. Sometimes he works at the green grocer's. He's such a troublemaker; he can't keep down a job. He's one of those rebels. Their mother knits loofahs and makes *sefi-dab*[214]. They're notorious people; no good for you."

I asked: "Did you say their uncle is a constable?"

-Yes. He's a clever swindler. He's a hustler. He even cheats family, friends and neighbours…

I was flabbergasted. Where on earth had Rahim found this one from?

The woman said: "Please come in and have some sherbet; you won't be bound by the ties of hospitality[215]!"

-Thank you so much. I must leave. I have far to go.

-Khanoum jan, for goodness' sake, this is just between us…! I only told you to please God. Your brother would be too good to get burnt by their fire. You won't tell them anything, will you? It'll cause a lot of trouble for us."

-Of course not khanoum. I'm not a child. Everything you said will stay just between us.

Slowly, I began walking back home. The later I arrived, the better. I was surprised to see that I was not all that upset. In fact, I was not upset at all. I was indifferent. I felt distanced from everything. These events did not concern me. It caused me no pain. My heart had turned to stone. Happiness and sorrow belonged to people who had souls, who were alive, who had purpose and hope in life. I had suffered so much; I had tasted the bitterness of disrespect and my soul had been burdened to such an extent that I felt numb. I had lost my sensitivity. I only felt the reckless abandon of someone with no nous and hindsight, no feelings. What blow could be stronger than the death of my son to awaken the feelings of pain and grief in me again? Indeed, there was so much sorrow and heartache accumulated within me that nothing could either abate or escalate it. I had forgotten what life without pain and grief felt like. The autumnal sun shined on the leaves of the sycamore trees, scattering its light and shade on the ground and walls. The narrow canal of water was murmuring away at my feet, like a little boy murmuring at his mother. I felt someone walking in my shadow and calling me softly, as softly as a whisper. Was it Almas? In the water? I was imagining things. I was dreaming with my eyes wide open. I carried on with my unhurried walk.

The quiet street was gradually getting busy. Everything and everyone could be found in it. But, my Almas was not there. A cool breeze was blowing from the Alborz Mountains, bringing wind of autumn. How I longed to sit in that autumnal sun by the water canal underneath the sycamores and stare at the sky and the trees until my eyes were reposed, until my feet were rested; until grief and sorrow let go of me; until the world ended. Indeed, there was a peacefulness in this quiet street, in the flow of the water, and in the light and shade of the sycamore leaves glimmering in the sun, which gave me solace and reminded me of a life without cares, filled with abandon. It took me back to the days of leaning back on a cushion next to an open window, of dosing off in the warmth of a sun streaming into the room and shining on my back. I slowed my pace to keep this feeling alive for as long as I could before getting home.

I walked into the house and stepped into the courtyard from the corridor. As always, I tried not to look to the lefthand side of the yard, to the corner where, a few months ago, my son had lied underneath a white sheet alongside the small pile of shovelled snow. I did not have to try too hard. I caught sight of my mother-in-law's hateful figure on the opposite side of the corridor. She stood there with her hands on her hips.

-Where've you been?

-Out

I held my head up and tried to walk past her. She asked: "I said where have you been?"

-It's none of your business khanoum. Am I a prisoner here?

-Your husband has given orders that anyone coming into this house or leaving it has to have my permission. Don't I have to know what's going on around here! Doesn't my poor son have the right to know what's happening in his own house?

Sarcastically, I said: "His own house? Since when has he become a home owner? You've been wrongly informed. This is my house khanoum. You have a very short memory."

She was taken aback, but did not give in: "I'm not interested. Tell me where you've been?"

In a biting tone I said: "If you had spent half this time that you spend watching my comings and goings watching your grandchild he'd be alive now."

Imitating me, she said: "And if you'd really gone to the baths instead of aborting your baby you wouldn't be barren now."

She had hit the target from the centre of which the flames of rage burst out, and I yelled: "Don't worry. Your new bride will give birth for you." And, as I saw her gaping at me, I added: "Do you want to know where I've been? I've been to choose a bride. I've been to arrange a marriage. Congratulations. I've been to ask for Ma'soumeh khanoum's hand for Rahim. Indeed, your son has made an excellent choice. It's a match made in heaven. It's true when they say *water finds the pit and the blind find the blind*[216]. Your son has found the right girl at last. You're much of a muchness. Her uncle is a bent copper, her brothers are soap workers and hooligans, and her mother sews bath loofahs. How's that? You approve? Birds of a feather flock together..."

At first, she did not understand what I was saying. She stared at me, and said: "You're telling tales. My poor son is slaving away from dawn to dusk…

I cut her off: "I saw it myself, with my own two eyes. He had pulled the girl inside the shop…"

Her penny dropped for sure. It even seemed to make her happy. She laughed: "Oh yeah…! So, what's bothering you is that someone's been flirting around with Rahim inside his shop? It's not his first time, is it? So, these girls should stay put in their homes! What can my poor child do? Is it his fault? He's young, not a hundred years old! They won't leave him alone, from the rich and wealthy to – as you say – the niece of a bent copper… But it's no trouble for him! There's enough to go round!" All her words were sardonic, more biting than the sting of a viper.

-No, it's no trouble at all. He should go and marry her. The best patch is off the same cloth. You either deserve that barefaced, obstinate Kokab, or this girl who can't even write her own name and your son gives her calligraphies of Hafez and Sa'di's poems. It's not his fault. These are the habits he's picked up along the way. Incidentally, I pray that he takes this girl as a wife so that you get your just deserve. Then, you'll appreciate me and count your blessings. Your son has no idea what a proper, respectable girl with backbone is! He's been freeloading and roaming around for so long now, he's become accustomed to it and picked up bad habits. He needs someone to grab him by the neck and make him pay the house money; and maybe then, he'll hit rock bottom and turn over a new leaf. I'm tired of all this. I've come to terms with everything you've said and done. But, all lay load on a willing horse. You took me for a ride. My dayeh jan was right to say you can do too much of a good thing.

-Your dayeh jan talks too much. What's my son's fault? The girl must have been after him. Didn't you do the same thing? What shenanigans! What's my son done to you? Have I ever done any wrong to you? Anyone would think he's poked you with a red hot rod! You didn't have to marry him. Still, he hasn't done anything wrong now. Maybe he wants to take a wife. My child wants to have a successor. You're barren. Supposing he does take a wife. What's it got to do with you? You'll still have your bread and butter and a husband to look after you. Other people take two, three wives, and not a peep's ever heard out of their homes. You're the only one who kicks up a fuss as soon as you hear the voice of a woman from seven neighbourhoods away. It's just you! If my relative comes over, you say she's Rahim's bit on the side. If you see a woman on the street, you say Rahim wants to marry her. Everyone has to watch their step so madam doesn't get upset. You know what? Even if Rahim doesn't want a wife, I'll find one for him and make him marry her no matter what.

In this latest battle which was raging, I was the one losing my footing again and being dragged in mud. I was losing myself and turning into the people I lived with. Rahim's mother would not desert the battleground. She was an omnipotent warrior who delighted in belligerence. I turned my back on her. Disputing with her was pointless. As I was going up the stairs to my room, I said: "Look who I'm talking to!"

Rahim came home in the early evening. His mother jumped out in front of him as he stepped inside and dragged him to her room. Ten, fifteen, thirty minutes went by before I heard his footsteps crossing the courtyard and saw him climbing the the stairs with a long face. I was sitting by the samovar. I said: "Salam."

-Drop dead! Where the hell have you been this afternoon?

-Your mother reported back?

-I said where the hell have you been?

Calmly, I said: "Nowhere. I was bored, so I went for a stroll. I came to the shop. Ma'soumeh khanoum was there. So, I thought it was best not to bother you."

For a moment, he stood there gaping. He could not believe that I was so well informed. His mother walked into the room with the same hostile attitude and sat in a corner, ready to start a fight. Rahim took advantage of the situation and pulled himself together: "So, that's how it is! You've been on my tracks?"

-I would've found out eventually, when you brought your bride into this house.

I turned to my mother-in-law and added sarcastically: "By the way, you know khanoum, Ma'soumeh khanoum has a squint. To her, Rahim agha's handsomeness is twofold."

Rahim came forward, kicked me, and said: "Don't make me crush you under my feet! So help me God, I'm home again!" And he went to take off his coat.

I had become accustomed to this kind of behaviour. Unmindful of the kick I had taken, I said: "I had noticed agha wouldn't go to the shop, and if he did, it was at two in the afternoon. I should've known he had a prior engagement!"

-So what if I do. If you can't take it that's too bad. Was there anything else?

-That's alright by me. But, perhaps her bent copper of an uncle and his soap making, hooligan of a brother might have objections.

I could clearly see the fear in his eyes. He came forward and said: "See if you can get me into trouble! If you mention their names one more time, I'll slap you so hard in the mouth your teeth will end up in your stomach!"

His mother barged in: "And she's also found her tongue lately. My house! My shop! The house is mine! I'm the owner of the shop. Rahim's nothing."

Rahim turned to me: "Yeah? You said that?"

I turned to his mother and asked: "Did I say anything about the shop?"

-No, you just talked about Rahim taking a wife!

Rahim was quiet. He was pacing up and down in the room. After a while, he asked: "But, who's told you that I want to take a wife?"

-Who told me? Your mother keeps telling me I'm barren!

I burst out into tears. I added sobbing: "She says Rahim wants a successor. I saw the girl flirting with you at the shop with my own two eyes."

His mother said: "Oho… How tender-hearted! Madam was born with a silver spoon in her mouth! A cat may look at a king!"

Rahim turned to his mother and said: "Get up and go to your own room. You're the one who lights all these fires!" His mother left grumbling. Rahim sat on the edge of the window and took his head in both hands. After a while, in a soft voice, as if speaking to himself, he said: "Not a day goes by when I come into this hellhole without having to argue. Not once did we go to sleep in peace. For goodness' sake Mahboubeh, why won't you let us live our lives?"

-Me? You're the one chasing a different person every day. You pretend to be working at the shop so you can mess around. At least tell me what's wrong with me? Am I blind? Deaf? Lame? You write your calligraphy for this girl who looks like an owl.

-Says who? Hang me if I have! You saw for yourself. As you said, she looks like an owl. She comes to the shop and flirts with me. I swear to God, I'm afraid of her brothers. I've been drinking with them a couple of times. Once, the girl brought a message from his brothers to the shop. That's all. Now, she won't leave me alone. She comes to the shop with a different excuse every time. If you don't want me to stay there for lunch, fine, I won't. Let me see if you've got any more excuses? Why would I let go of you with all your beauty and accomplishments, the daughter of Basir ol-Molk, and marry the daughter of a loofah and sefidab maker? Where did you leave your brains? God help me if I go to the shop at lunchtime ever again. I'm sorry! I repent! There, are you happy now?

I was not able to tell him that I had seen it all. That I saw him take her hand and pull her into the shop. I still wanted to have a life. Now that he was meeting me halfway, now that he had repented, it would be best if I met him halfway too.

He came and sat by my side: "Will you pour me some tea now?" I poured the tea and placed it in front of him. I was heartbroken. My hand was shaking. He took my hand and kissed it: "See what you're doing to yourself? You break my heart too every time I see you so sad, so dejected. You must think of me too. I'm not made of stone. I have lost my son, and now I'm losing my wife."

I burst out into tears again at the thought of my son: "Your mother says she wants to take a wife for you. She says I want my son to have a successor. She says…"

-My mother talks rubbish. If I ever want a child again, I want it with you; I don't want the child of any cheap woman. You're the one I want Mahboub jan. I want your child. Don't you know that by now? So, God hasn't destined for me to have children with you. You can't fight God. Should I marry and make you suffer? No Mahboubeh. I'm not that immoral. We'll stay together. We'll share our bread together. We'll stay together for as long as we live. And when I die, you'll be rid of me. You'll be free. Just come to my grave and pray for me every now and then.

I threw myself into his arms tearfully: "God forbid Rahim, don't talk like this. I hope to die before you, even if it's just a day earlier. If you want another wife, that's alright by me. Go get married." I remembered the magnanimity of Nimtaj khanoum, Mansour's wife, and felt passionate. I said: "You know what? I'll roll up my sleeves and find a wife for you myself. Not one of these trashy women; but, the daughter of a respectable person. I'll find a good wife for you."

-Give me a break Mahboubeh. What do I want with another wife? I'm having enough trouble looking after the one I havd. You and my mother are like chalk and cheese. I'm at the end of my tether. Just imagine adding a rival to all of this. Let's not talk about this anymore. Pour me another tea; this one has gone cold.

The pressures weighing down on my soul were lifted. I felt light. Once again, I caught sight of his kind look. Once again, his playful smile awakened feelings in my flesh I believed had died. I was a captive of my flesh. I was young, very young. I was still only twenty-one or two, even though I had put the experiences of half a century of pain and grief behind me. I thought to have died with the death of my son. To my surprise, I was a corpse which was still breathing, walking, eating, sleeping and waking up. I was not sure how much longer for? And this was painful. It never crossed my mind that I may long for my husband's arms again, but I did.

It was already past midnight. We were awake, lying side by side. Unlike all the other nights, when he fell asleep as soon as he came to bed, he was holding my hand and taking a smoke with his free hand. How I enjoyed this peace and quiet. We were both staring at the ceiling. All I could see was the glow in his eyes and at the tip of his cigarette.

As he was staring at the ceiling, his voice echoed in the room like the sound of a breeze: "I thought you didn't love me anymore." Just as softly, I said: "You're the one who doesn't love me anymore."

He smiled and pressed my hand. I could feel his breathing next to my neck. My tears began to flow with love and contentment. How could the owner of a face such as this one be bad? I was wrong. I was the bad one. I only thought of myself. What had I done to make him believe I no longer loved him? It was as if he could read my thoughts. He said: "When you aborted the baby, I thought you disliked me. I was always afraid. I was afraid you might pretend to be going to the baths and not come back anymore."

I said: "Rahim…!" And I could not hold back my tears.

He put out the cigarette in the ashtray next to him and turned towards me. He lifted himself up to rest his head on his left hand. He was leaning down over my face in the dark and looking at me closely. He wiped off my tears with the fingers of his right hand and, as if talking to a little girl, he said: "Hey, hey, are you crying? Shame on you girl!"

I was sobbing and enjoying his consoling tone, but my crying intensified. It was as if the barrage blocking my tears had broken down. The harvest of grief in my heart, for I had no one to talk to, was now melting away in my tears and pouring out. His caresses were scraping away at the clot covering the old wounds of my heart and healing them tenderly. If I died at that very moment, if God took my life that very night, I would have no grievances. Was there any room for grievances? What more did I want? God had no dues to me. I said: "Don't let me suffer anymore Rahim. I don't have the strength anymore. I have no one but you now. Stand by me. Hear me out."

He joked: "What's all this talk then? The daughter of Basir ol-Molk has no one? If you've no one, then what should everyone else say? Don't repeat this anywhere else! People will laugh at you. Everything the affluent Mahboubeh khanoum has is this Rahim with just the shirt on his back?"

An elating feeling rushed into my heart from all his modesty and the fact that he had at last confessed to his subservience for my sake; that he had admitted to my supremacy. I felt sorry for him. I loathed myself. I was ashamed of how I had treated him. I placed my fingers on his lips, and said: "Stop it Rahim. Don't say these things. You're everything to me. You're worth more than all the treasures of this world to me. I would live on a simple straw mat with you. I'm your wife. You're my master. Let those who want to laugh have a good laugh. If they don't like it, so be it. There's no separate you and me. Whatever I have is yours. I'm the one who wanted you. If you're ever in harm's way, I will simply die. Whoever you are, I'm proud of you. I'm the one who wanted you, and I'll stand by you. I have no regrets."

-Do you really mean it Mahboub?

-Try me Rahim. Try me.

-Don't do this Mahboub jan. Don't do this to yourself. I don't have the heart to see your tears.

How could I have forgotten his warm kisses? He smelled of cigarettes. He looked at me as if he had not seen me for years. He said: "You've lost weight Mahboub. You look different. Your cheeks are not chubby anymore. Your face is slim. Your eyes are larger. Your look is not playful."

-Am I ugly?

-No Mahboub jan. You've become a woman, a lady.

Before going to work the next morning, he called his mother and talked to her in a loud voice, so I could easily hear him in the room: "Naneh, Mahboub is free to come and go as she pleases. I don't want to hear that you've stopped her anymore!"

Those were the days! The days when the pain of my son's death and the ecstasy of the revival of my love for my husband made me dizzy and drunk; bitter sweet days and mystical nights.

Rahim never spent another lunch-time at the shop. He was home before sunset. He no longer had alcohol on his breath; he did not flatten the back of his shoes. His suit was clean and tidy. Dayeh would come and bring my money. I put it in the niche; Rahim would not touch it, as if it would burn his fingers like fire; as if it was a snake biting his hands. His mother looked at him sideways, bit her lips and shook her head regretfully. When he was away during the day, she mumbled to herself: "She's cast a spell on him", or "she's happy now; he's by her side day and night."

It was as if I no longer heard her. It was no longer of any importance to me. What did I have to fear when Rahim no longer paid any attention to her mumblings? Does one get entangled with the roaring wind? Did one get caught in a thunderous storm? No, one must wait; one must close the windows and take refuge in the arms of a loved one; take refuge in Rahim's arms.

Dayeh came. I went to Lalehzar with her to see an Armenian lady who had made my sisters' wedding dresses. I asked her to make a taffeta dress for me; a tightfitting, blue taffeta dress with a white turndown collar and small mother of pearl buttons. When I was trying it out, in that sweet Armenian accent she said: "If only all my customers were like you – the dress fits you perfectly. Your husband must really appreciate you."

I laughed out loud after such a long time. It made dayeh jan happy. I bought a pair of high heel shoes, a bottle of perfume, hair clips and earrings, lipstick and rouge, and all of it for the evenings when Rahim came home. If God has compassion for anyone, if there is a heaven on earth, and if bliss can be defined, it is nothing but the love of a husband and wife under the same roof; nothing but the anticipation and expectation of a woman who counts the hours eagerly for her husband's return; it is nothing but the haste of a man going home to a woman whom he knows is waiting with anticipation by a simmering samovar and a set dinner spread. A woman with a sweet smile and caressing hands.

The first month of autumn went by and October arrived. Rahim brought money in the evenings and put it in the niche; he brought fruits; he never came home empty-handed. I knew he was gradually getting on in years. He was nearing thirty. He had fallen off his high horse, which had mellowed and ripened him. He was tamed. Although we were at the start of the second month of autumn, the weather was not that cold yet. The red and yellow sycamore leaves warmed and rejoiced the heart in the autumn sunshine. Or maybe it was my heart which had been rejuvenated, which was calm and hopeful.

One night, Rahim came home tired, sat down and had some tea: "Well, well, Mahboub jan. You look so pretty tonight."

-I wasn't pretty before?

-You're prettier.

He kissed me and sat in a corner. But, he seemed preoccupied. I asked: "Shall I bring dinner Rahim jan?"

He hemmed and hawed.

I asked: "Aren't you hungry?"

-I'm not, to be honest. You eat.

-I won't eat if you don't. Why aren't you hungry? Has something happened?

-No, nothing's happened. I'm just feeling sorry for myself.

My heart missed a beat: "What's wrong? For God's sake Rahim, tell me what's happened? Why do you beat around the bush?"

I felt weak in the knees. I could not take any more bad news. He paused for a moment, and then muttered: "Well, there's this creditable carpenter, one of those who gets big jobs making the doors and windows of big houses and offices. He also makes chairs and tables. He even says he has made the doors and windows of the palaces of Reza Shah's sons – be it on his head if he's not telling the truth. Well, now, this guy has seen my work and approved of it. He came to me a few days ago and said whatever job I get, I want to give you a third of the work. But, the client mustn't know about it, because they know me and give me the job for my reputation and skills. If they find out I've given it to you, they'll take back their order. Are you interested or not?"

I said excitedly: "You should've said yes. You should've said I'll do it. What're you waiting for?"

-Well yes, I want to accept. If I get a few jobs like this one, I'll get to know the clients, and people will get to know me by word of mouth. Then, I can get jobs for myself. But the thing is, he says I also need to make an investment. The point is that I've no capital. I'll need wood. I'll need equipment. It's not that simple. I can't do it empty-handed!

-How much do you need to invest?

He thought for a moment and said: "However much is needed, I haven't a penny to my name."

-Well, we must think of something. Borrow from someone Rahim.

He lowered his head in shame, and said: "I asked him to lend me some money to buy the equipment and start work. I said I'll return it to him once I got paid. The poor man said he'll do it; except, he wants a collateral of some sort."

I started thinking. What could be done? Suddenly, I had an idea: "Well, there's something you can do Rahim. We can use the shop as collateral."

-No, we can't. The shop's no good. It's too small. It's not worth that much. He won't accept.

I was surprised. Still, I said: "Alright then, we'll use the house. How about that, is it enough?"

He gave it some thought and, as he was drawing lines with his finger on the carpet, he said: "I think it's good. But, he has to accept. Otherwise, we have to use both places as collateral."

-Why don't you propose the house first, see what he says. If you make the arrangements, I have no objections to pawning the house.

He lifted his head, but would not look into my eyes. He stared at the ceiling, and said: "No, I don't want to drag you to the registry office with us, and here and there with a lot of men to argue with. And for what? Just to pawn the house?

-Wherever we go, we'll be together. I won't be alone!

-No, it's not right. If you want to pawn the house... I say...

-Well, what do you say?

-How shall I put it? I think... it's best if you... put the house in my name first. Then, I can use it as collateral.

My heart shook. I was happy that he wasn't looking at me, because I was staring at him stunned. I could smell betrayal. He had not been able to convince me with his tall tale right from the start. Deep down, I had my doubts. But, I did not want to believe it. I did not want our good relationship to crumble again. I said: "What difference does it make Rahim jan? There's no difference between us! We'll just pop into the registry together, or we'll ask the registrar to come to our house for the signature."

He said: "I can't bring the old man all the way here to pawn a property. And I don't want my wife to come to the registry office. As you said, there's no difference between us. We'll go tomorrow and you'll put the house in my name. I'll do the rest."

I said: "Where's the rush? Why tomorrow? I need some time to think…"

As he was trying to hide his anger, he said: "Think about what? The guy's in a rush. If I take too long, he can find a hundred more people like me who would be only too willing to take him up on his offer. He won't sit around and wait for you to make up your mind. Anyway, what's there to think about? Don't you trust me?"

-I do Rahim jan. It's not a question of trust; but…

Gradually, he raised his voice: "What is it then? You don't want to put the house in my name? Are you afraid I'll take it away from you? Does it bother you?"

I fell to pieces. I closed up my heart on him once again. There was a vindictive look in his eyes all over again. I said coldly: "But I'm still a bit lost. I'm not too sure what's happening yet?!

-Is it because you're lost, or is it because you don't trust me? I knew you didn't love me!

-What're you saying Rahim? What has this got to do with love?

-What is love then? I've changed my ways. I've been doing as you said for a whole month now. I've played to your every tune. You said don't go to work, I said fine. Come home early, I said fine. You said you wanted to come and go as you pleased, I said go. And you're still saying you want to know what's happening? What's happening is that you can't find it in your heart to put the house in my name.

Astonished, I asked: "So that's why you've been as good as gold this whole month; because you wanted me to put the house in your name?"

-You make me mad! Do you think I want to cheat you?

I objected: "Rahim!"

-There's no need to say Rahim Rahim. Will you put the house in my name or not?

And, as he saw my silence, he said: "What do you want to do with this house anyway? You have no children, and I pay for your expenses… So, what difference does it make that the house is in my name or yours? Do you want to take it with you to the next life? Do you want your brother and sisters to have it and enjoy it after you, and that's that?"

I said calmly: "I see… So that's what this is all about. So, this tall tale of carpentry, and the houses of the rich, the offices, the palaces of Reza Shah's sons, and the partnership and collateral were all excuses? You were simply showing me the gate to greener pastures? So, you decided to bite the bullet for a month and stopped drinking and womanising to pull the wool over my eyes? Now that I've lost my son, you want me to put the house in your name so no one else can have it? You want to take away everything I have in this world and feather your own nest? No my dear, sweet dreams."

This was my wake up call. My eyes suddenly opened wide and the fog lifted. I could not believe such foolishness on my part. How come I did not understand it earlier? The mask had been lifted and the same monstrous, vicious face was exposed again. As he was beating his fist on the khersak carpet of my dowry, he yelled: "You have to put this house in my name. Do you understand?"

I answered defiantly: "I will do no such thing."

-We'll see about that. If you don't put this house in my name, you'll be the only one to blame for whatever happens to you.

-Why should I put the house in your name? I guess it's because you want to bring Ma'soumeh khanoum here!

-Of course I will. Why shouldn't I? I'll bring her here in spite of you. I'll bring her here to have ten children so that you can die of jealousy you barren woman.

-And then, I suppose I'll hang around and watch?

-No, you'll go to your agha jan's; the same one who threw you out.

The muscles in his neck were bulging out in anger. His hateful black vein was more visible than ever. He imitated me: "*Stand by me Rahim jan… I have no one but you.*"

I said: "That's enough Rahim. You've gone mad again!"

-It's your goddam father who's mad.

-Shut your mouth. Don't you dare utter my father's name!

-You want me to shut up?

His hand came down on my face as fast as lightening, followed by kicks and punches to my head. It was as if he was making up for the past month. Then, tired and angry, he let go of me and sat on the window sill. I was humiliated and tired of life. He asked: "Will you put the house in my name or not?"

-No, no, no. When you marry that Ma'soumeh khanoum, she'll give you a house.

-No, she won't give me a house. She'll become the lady of this house and you'll be her children's servant. I'm not the barren one, you are. I want a son. I want an heir. My mother's right. I want a successor.

I got up. His mother had come into the room and was watching with great pleasure. The ceasefire had been broken again. I turned towards Rahim and laughed angrily: "Not only are you so respectable, so scholarly, but the only thing left is for you to own property for your successors? You're afraid you won't have anyone in line to your throne? That's why you want a crown prince! Now, just imagine yourself breeding a few morons. It's best that you should be barren when you can't feed them. There'll be four less knife-pulling soap makers in the world. Four less marauders robbing people blind. It's better that the children of a father like you and a mother like squinty Ma'soumeh don't exist; children who have to squirm around in dust and filth, get bald from ringworms and catch trachoma. And God only knows where they'll end up eventually."

Instantly, he leaped up and hit me in the mouth again with such force that I felt faint. He yelled: "Didn't I tell you to keep your trap shut? Do you suppose you're so gorgeous? Have you seen yourself in the mirror lately? You're like tuberculosis germs, like death warmed up… I'm telling you, you'll either put this house in my name, or I'll stretch out your corpse right here in this spot." I put the back of my hand on my lips. When I took it away, it was wet with blood. His mother tried to speak in a well-wishing tone of voice: "Come on woman. Leave it be. Let go. Why do you make him so angry that he has to hit you like this? You know how wired your husband is! You know you'll do it in the end; so, why not do it sooner and save yourself a lot of heartache."

-You'll see the house the day you can see the back of your ears.

Rahim yelled: "You won't give it to me? I'll show you. I'll strip you bare and make you sit at home and starve until you come to your senses."

With abrupt, brisk movements, he stormed into the next room and took all the money from the niche. He opened my chest and grabbed the rest of the money and my diamond ring. He kept grumbling to himself: "That dragon; she gives in neither to kindness and straight forward talking nor to shouting and yelling. You'll love it when I've sorted you out!"

His mother said: "Didn't I tell you? Didn't I tell you she's got a sharp tongue? Didn't I tell you not to pamper her so much, that you won't be able to stop her again? There you go; she's now got a tongue this long[217] and this sharp...!"

She hit her left elbow with her right hand in order to show the length of my tongue. I said: "No khanoum jan, I always had a tongue right from the very beginning; everybody has one. No one's mute. It's just that some people try to keep it under control. They act like ladies. Barefacedness is not a hard act to follow! Keeping your composure is difficult. Not everyone can do it. But, you're unreceptive to such things. You thought I was a born loser because I obeyed you right from the start!? It's my own fault. As you make your bed, so you must lie in it. As you sow, so shall you reap. You made me regret my decision in that very first year; it's been a dog's life. I knew I had backed the wrong horse, that I was barking up the wrong tree. I let everyone go and held on to your son..."

She cut me off: "No dear, if you'd found someone better than my son, you wouldn't have let go. You probably deserved my son..."

Without paying any attention to us, Rahim rushed back from the other room and said: "Where's the bib necklace?"

I stepped back in fear. I had put on the necklace for him that night. It was a keepsake from my father. I put my hand on it: "I won't give it to you."

-The hell you won't.

He grabbed my arm and twisted it behind my back. He was no longer a human being. He had truly turned into a wild animal; like a pig, a wolf. He was a strange animal that evoked loathing more than terror. With a pull of his right hand, he tore the necklace from my neck. He turned to his mother and stressed: "God help you, and God help her if she sets foot outside of this house from now on." He ran to the front door and locked it. He came back and told me: "Do all your thinking until tomorrow morning. You might come to your senses. I want this house and I'll take it any which way I can. It will be much better if you give it to me of your own accord."

He went to his mother's room and they both spent the night there. I sat up by the oil lamp until the middle of the night. I could not sleep. My face, my mouth, my hands, my whole body ached. Even the back of my neck burned and ached from the pull of the necklace. Yet, the real pain was in my heart. Where was the Rahim I used to see in the shop? When did he go? Why did he go? Was I to blame, or was it his fault? Why didn't I let him stay with Kokab? What would Kokab have done if she had been in my shoes? Was she not more suitable for him? Did she not understand this man better than I did?

I was weary and appalled. There were no more tears. I sat there like a statue. I did not even have any thoughts in my head. I was gazing at the flower patterns of the carpet. Whom shall I complain to? Whom shall I complain about? I had leaped before looking. It was too late now. This was the point of no return. I did not know what to do. I only knew that I was at the end of my tether. Enough is enough. Love had served me out. My heart was on fire and torn to pieces. My spirit had died. I was just beginning to understand the meaning of life. I understood that you could not joke around with life; that life is not a game; it is not an obsession. The abyss I had plummeted into, the inferno into which I had tumbled head on, had ripened me. I realised that the hand of fate was not a mother's caressing hand on my hair. The face of life was not the kind, smiling face of my father looking at me. That this celestial dome was not the play thing I had imagined; a play thing which could be seized by force and cast aside with the tip of your toe when it no longer served your purpose. Reality was what I was facing there and then, and it was far too bitter to put into words. Little by little, I had grasped the implications of my father's words and perceived the naked truth in the light of day at last.

I cannot recall when I fell asleep or when I woke up. The oil lamp was still burning. The night was still pitch black. I turned out the lamp and put my head back on the carpet where I was and fell into a scattered, nightmarish sleep. Hasten O day. How patient and persevering you are, O night.

Will you never end? How much longer must I be confined to this darkness? When will this murkiness abandon me? O pain, O grief, let go of me or take my life. Dear God, set me free. Not bit by bit, but all at once. Save me from myself.

I woke up. The sky had turned grey, but it was still dark everywhere. What a night I had put behind me! I sat up where I had been lying down and leaned against the wall hugging my knees. I was staring into the court-yard, at the corner of the wall, at Almas' place. I heaved a sigh. I could see that he was coming up the stairs, sitting by my side, asking for roasted wheat and hemp nut, that he cried with fear when his father and I argued, that he was free at last

The door opened and my mother-in-law came into the room bringing the samovar. When did it get light? When did the day dawn?

I just sat there, quiet and motionless. Her eye caught me with surprise. She stood still for a moment, holding the samovar: "Ey! You were here all night?"

I did not answer. She came over quickly, set up the spread and placed the samovar in its usual place. She sat down by my side and, with a cunning tone of voice glazed over with sympathy, she said: "Dear oh dear, look at what he's done to you! Don't go making him this angry! He'll lame you in the end. He behaves just like his late father. He's snappy. Why don't you put the house in his name and get it over and done with. God only knows, I want the both of you to be happy.

Rahim arrived, dragging his heels: "Naneh, don't go telling her stories. Her head's full of lead. She's thickskulled. Move to one side, let me see. I can speak to her in her own language." He stood over my head, legs apart and hands on his hips. He said: "Will you put this house in my name or not?"

I did not answer.

-I'm talking to you. She just sits there like a black radish, staring into thin air. I asked will you put the house in my name or not?

I looked up. My lip was burning. It felt swollen. I said: "No."

He kicked my foot: "Oh, what a saucy thing you are! Just look at her, all turned away from life. You expiate your sins just by looking at her." He turned to his mother: "Naneh, I'm going now. By the time I get back, you've to roll up these carpets. I want to sell them. I need the money."

As he was leaving, his mother asked: "You won't have breakfast?"

-Feed this one to make her madder.

I knew my bib necklace, ring and money were in his pocket. He had already reached the middle of the stairs, but turned around and went into our bedroom. He picked up the tulip lamps from the niche and told his mother as he was leaving: "I'll take these too. I need money." As if someone had asked him for an explanation.

I remained where I was, quiet, without a word. His mother said: "Are you satisfied now? He'll go and sell everything and spend half of it on living it up tonight."

I shrugged my shoulders. She sat down to have breakfast. I got up and went into the other room and slammed the door. I could not even tolerate her any longer, let alone sit next to her and have breakfast with her. My face hurt. I stood in front of the small mirror in the niche. I was shocked by my own sight. The right side of my face was entirely black and blue from his slapping of the night before. My right eye was half closed and the corner of my lips, where he had battered me with the back of his hand, was swollen and purple. It scared me. I was amazed to be still alive. I was surprised at how I had survived his kicking and punching. My right ear still ached from the force of his slap. His mother raised her voice in anger: "The samovar is boiling. Breakfast is ready. Take it or leave it."

I heard her leaving the room and going down the stairs. An idea sparked in my head. I made my decision. Hurriedly, I took my suitcase and threw in some of my clothes and bits and pieces. I took my boxwood chest and squeezed it into the suitcase with all its contents. I put on my chador and rushed down the stairs. My mother-in-law blocked my way like a wounded tiger and stood there with her hands on her hips: "Well, well, well, having a nice day? And where's madam off to?"

-I want to leave. I've had enough.

-To go where? You think you can up and leave just like that…? Doesn't this house have an owner? Didn't you hear what your husband said last night?

-What husband? I don't have a husband anymore!

Her eyes opened wide: "Is that a fact? This is news to me!"

I opened my mouth and everything I had bottled up inside of me for years and waiting on the tip of my tongue, poured out: "That slob of a coward's not my husband. I'm ashamed to call him a man, to call him a husband."

She laughed: "Are you complaining about his manhood?

-No, I'm complaining about his manliness, his low qualities, and lack of ambition; of stepping over the weak and having no honour. You don't understand what I'm saying; neither does he. He hasn't learned these things. Who was he supposed to learn from? Who was supposed to teach him magnanimity and generosity? To know what honour is? What decency is! He kicks me when I'm down, but is afraid of Ma'soumeh's knife-pulling brothers. He puts his power on display in front of a woman; but, when it comes to men, he hides behind his mummy's skirt. He becomes the meek one. He goes quiet like a lamb. Only his moustache and suit show that he's a man, and that's that.

I no longer called my mother-in-law the formal 'You'. I no longer called her khanoum, because she was no lady. She did not deserve the title. She was an ignorant scoundrel. I no longer wanted to close my eyes on reality. I no longer had to pretend that my son's grandmother was a respectable woman to keep his good name. I no longer had a son. Or simply, it was because I too had become very much like them. I had learned from them. I could speak their language now. I had forgotten what was good and what was bad. I had forgotten about healthy relationships and respectable behaviour.

She sat on the edge of the corridor step and said: "You've packed up my son's life and you're leaving?"

-What life? Your son had a life? When he married me, there was just him, the shirt on his back and his breeches. He has a life now?

Very coolly, she said: "You'll leave the suitcase and then you can go.

I said: "Very well."

I turned around calmly and went up the stairs. She was relieved. She got up and went about her business while grumbling. I went into the room where I had once spent my wedding night. I was amazed at my own calmness. I closed the door. I had just come to my senses. Mahboubeh, what is it that you want to take from this house? Can you bear to wear these clothes again? To put on these shoes again? To wear these same hair clips in your hair? What do you want to do with all these things which are only reminders of life with a layabout beast? Why would you want these symbols of a lost youth, lost hopes, wounded pride and hurt feelings? Destroy them all. Destroy everything.

I took the scissors, opened up the suitcase and cut all my clothes to pieces one by one and threw them on the floor. The scissors would not cut my shoes. I picked up a shaving razor blade and slashed the front of the shoes. I cut my hand. But, I did not seem to feel anything. I had lost my mind. I pulled out the beddings into the middle of the room, still in their wrapper, but did not open the knot. Instead, I cut the wrap open in a number of places with the blade. I pulled out the mattresses and quilts. Then, I went for the satin quilts with the blade and scissors. The mattresses were next. I cut them open with such pleasure, as if they were Rahim's jugular; as if they were my mother-in-law's tongue; as if they were my own chest, my sleeping fortune. I rumbled to myself quietly: "You sun of a gun, as if I would leave these behind for you! You just wait for it! Dream on!"

With that same razor, I went for the carpets next. I bent down and pulled the razor blade over the khersak carpets with all the force in my hand, loving every minute of it. The thought of Rahim's reaction, his shock, anger and hopelessness made me feel happy. I wore the smile of revenge on my lips; on my bruised, swollen lips and on my battered face.

I picked up the samovar. It was still hot. I poured all the water over the beddings and rugs. The charcoals in its flue fell on the torn beddings. I picked up my black taffeta chador from Yazd[218] and folded it. I knew my mother-in-law was madly in love with this chador. I used it to pick up the charcoals one by one, so I would not burn my hand, and threw each one on one of the rugs. Fumes rose from the rugs in each burning spot. Holes were made in the black chador from the heat of the charcoal. I stood up and watched. My eye caught the boxwood chest. Should I smash that too? I wanted to burn it; to bury my past with it. But my heart was telling me Almas' night cap is in there; the keepsake of that delightful spring; it has the memories of your rebellions in it; the longings of your youth are hidden in it. Keep it as a mirror projecting the lessons you have learned. I wanted to open it and take Almas' night cap from it; but I panicked. I was fearful this might be that same Pandora's Box the story of which my father had told me before. I was afraid that if I opened it, its spell would conquer my being; that I might feel weak and stay, only to become a captive of abomination and never be able to free myself of pain and grief. I do not know what came over me. I just grabbed the chest, put my chador back on again and went down the stairs carrying this very boxwood chest that you see. As soon as I made it to the middle of the yard, my mother-in-law appeared again as if the devil herself, and sat on the edge of the corridor step.

-You're at it again girl! You're so pigheaded! The beating you took last night would've put an elephant to sleep. Are you looking for more?

I said: "Get out of my way, let me through."

-No way!

-I have left the suitcase in the room. Let me go now.

-What's this one under your arm then?

-This one's mine. It's none of your business.

-Everything in this house belongs to my son and is my business.

I said: "Thank God your son has left nothing that can be mine or his. I said get out of my way."

In her screeching voice, she shrieked: "You don't give up, do you? You pigheaded woman. Even if I let you through, do you have the courage to leave this house with that repulsive face of yours? You're an eyesore to everyone. Do you think…"

I cut her off and asked calmly: "So you won't move?"

-No.

I bent down slowly and put the chest in a corner of the yard. I took off my chador, folded it in two and placed it on the chest. Then, I turned towards her. I stretched out my left hand and grabbed her hair from over her kerchief, while raving: "Didn't I tell you to move?" I pulled her hair with all my might in such a way that she got off the step and yelled: "May you be crippled", and tried to defend herself by scratching me. I grabbed her hand with my right hand and bit it so hard I felt my teeth were going to pierce her flesh and come together on the other side. It was so delightful. She screamed so hard that seven houses down the road must have heard her without a doubt. Then, I let go of her flesh, not out of fear, but because I wanted to. My teeth marks remained on her wrist in two neat rows. As she was rubbing them with her other hand, both of us recognised the superiority of my power simultaneously. She had a small, tiny figure, like a thirteen-year old. I was amazed at how afraid I had been of this tiny figure and had listened to her for so many years. I do not know why I had not done this earlier! She began screaming and cursing. I said: "Shut up. Shut up…" I could not stand her screams. Her voice banged against my head like a hammer. Again, I said: "Will you shut up or not?"

I put one hand firmly on her mouth and grabbed the back of her neck with the other. Her eyes popped out from fear. I dragged her towards the left wall of the courtyard in that position, the same place where my son's body had once lain, and jammed her back into the wall. I wished she would understand that I wanted her to sit on the edge of the brickworks without me telling her. But, as she did not, l kicked her in the shin with my foot. Both her feet flew forward. She slipped through my fingers like a fish. First, her back hit the edge of the brickworks and then she hit the ground. She moaned: "Aah, my bones broke. Uh-oh, my back hit the wall. I'm wounded all over. You're killing me. I hope to God that you die" and she burst into tears.

She was howling and sobbing at the top of her lungs while beating her chest and swearing. I squatted in front of her. I waved my finger at her, like a teacher warning a disobedient student: "Didn't I tell you to shut your mouth? Didn't I tell you not to make another sound? Did I or didn't I?" And I put my hand over her mouth again. I was excited by my own power and enjoying it. She was still crying, but didn't let out a sound this time.

-Don't cry. I said you can't even cry. Not a peep.

I grabbed the knot of her kerchief under her chin and pulled her head towards my own bruised, swollen face; in a calm, bloodcurdling voice, I said: "You just open your ears and listen carefully to what I'm going to say. I'm going out of this door." I turned around and pointed towards the corridor and the front door with my left hand. "You'll sit right here until that crook ed, scumbag son of yours comes home. Even if you just try and make any noise! If you start yelling when I leave, even if I hear your voice from the end of the alley, I'll come back for you. I'll strangle you and throw your body into the pond, so everyone will think you've drowned. Understand?"

She nodded with a terrified look in her eyes. Fear had made her speechless. She had sensed that I was not joking. She could see that I had lost my head and was probably capable of such an act. But, I was no less scared myself. Suddenly, I knew I could easily do such a thing with great pleasure. It was not a threat to scare her. I truly believed in what I was saying, and did not find it difficult to take action. I knew I would strangle her instantly if I heard another peep out of her, another sound, just one more tear.

I sat there quietly for a moment and stared at her, waiting for a move or another cry. I hoped to God that she would remain quiet and not provide me with any excuses. God granted me my wish this time. The old woman was scared. She sat quietly; she was rigid. I got up calmly and kicked her in the thigh. Rahim was such a good teacher. A master of torture and persecution; and I had turned out to be such a talented student. Did Rahim also enjoy beating me up this much?! I said: "I spent all these years being courteous to you and respecting you. You didn't deserve it. I didn't know you were better at understanding foul language and profanities. This serves you just right."

Calmly, I put on my chador and tucked the chest under my arm. I did not turn back to look at the yard, to look at the house. I did not look at my son's empty place. I knew his place. It was at the graveyard. I could go to him later. There was no need for a goodbye glance. I opened the door, walked out, slammed it shut behind me, and I was free. I was no longer his captive. My father's prayers had been answered. The season was the same in which I had married.

It was autumn.

CHAPTER THREE

I walked through the streets, like the dead risen from the grave. I was exhausted. There was brouhaha in my head. The street was filled with the sound of horses galloping, coach wheels turning, noisy street peddlers, carts, crowds, and an occasional passing car. I had a headache. Where could I go? Where? My father had said you are no longer my daughter for as long as you are married to this man. Do not come to this house. Where could I go? To my sisters' homes? Looking like this? Should I go and shame them in front of their husbands? Should I go to auntie Keshvar's house and thrill my mother's foe? That would be like sleeping with the enemy! Should I go to my uncle's place? To my uncle's wife? And feel like a penny waiting for change? Where could I go? I'll go to Mirza Hassan Khan's place. To Esmat khanoum; my mother's rival. Come what may. I knew her house was a couple of lanes further down the road from my auntie's. I knew he was a tar and violin instructor. I knew he was well-known in the area. I went towards my auntie's place, slowly, on foot. Why rush? No one was waiting for me in this world. I walked past auntie's tree-lined garden and watched the golden splendour of tree tops under the autumnal sun with great envy. I counted two lanes and turned left. The wall of my aunt's garden on the right seemed to stretch to eternity. I asked for the address and found his house. It had a wooden door with a knocker shaped like a lion's head. I stood in front of the door. What was I doing here? I am causing so much embarrassment! I have to go back. But where to? I had burned all my bridges. I had nowhere to return to. I had no other choices. Sorrow raged in my heart and rose up to my throat. I hesitated for a moment and felt the coolness of the autumn air. I looked around aimlessly and, before I could change my mind, my hand took hold of the lion's head and knocked once as if not obeying my brain.

The door opened straight away. A young adolescent boy stood in the doorway. He was wearing a suit and a Pahlavi hat[219]. I guessed it must be Hadi, Esmat khanoum's son. I could tell he was about to go out. I had firmly covered my face. I said: "Salam." I sounded so soft and sad that I even surprised myself. This was not the same voice as the one from this morning.

-Salam from me. Can I help you?

-I want to speak to Esmat khanoum.

-And your honourable name is?!

-I… I… am the daughter of Mr Basir ol-Molk. Please tell Esmat khanoum it's Mahboubeh.

Embarrassed, he opened the door and said: "I'm sorry. I didn't recognise you. Please come in. Make yourself at home." He stood to one side. The courtyard was clean and bright. I stepped inside. He closed the door behind me, and said: "I'll go get my mother straight away."

He took a few steps and disappeared into the building through a door on the left. I looked around the courtyard. It was as if I had suddenly reached the peace and quiet of an abbey from the mayhems of a battleground As if I had walked through the coppersmith's bazaar and entered the seclusion of a library. What silence! What peace! What serenity! It was as if the house itself, the building, the stones, bricks, and windows had serenity; as if they had dignity, calmness, and tranquillity.

It was a small, clean traditional courtyard paved with bricks. Like all other yards, it had a small, circular pond in the middle. On the left, a leafy grapevine stood up with the help of a trellis on the edge of the wall. In a corner of the garden, a few chrysanthemum bushes captivated the heart – unlike my own house, where Rahim never even once planted a thing in its flowerbed. I asked him a hundred times, to no avail. He had no taste. He was a stranger to beauty and elegance.

In front of me, at the end of a porch measuring one metre in width and separated from the garden with a step, three green doors with square windows decorated with plain, white door curtains on the inside drew the look. The curtains had been tied in the middle with belts, looking like two head to head triangles. The sun shone on the doors and windows through the grapevine leaves, and its bright, glittering light − as if polished - danced on them in harmony with the movement of the foliage. Everything was washed and clean. The house was so peaceful that if Esmat khanoum had come any later I would have fallen asleep on my feet. But she came followed by Hadi. Esmat khanoum had never seen me till that day. She had not seen any of us; none of us, except for my father. And we had not seen her. I felt anxious, not knowing what she looked like. But, as soon as I set eyes on her face, I felt relaxed. She was tall and thin. She seemed much older than my mother to me. Whether it was old age, or the hardships of life, I do not know. She wore a timid smile on her thin lips, and had a small, slender nose. Her dark hair showed from underneath her scarf, over her not so large eyes. She lifted her thin eyebrows and opened her eyes wider than one normally would. Was it out of worry, or were they questioning eyes? Her face was white and freckled. The skin under her eyes was wrinkled. All in all, she had a timid, unassuming face; an ordinary face; the face of a person who was eager to serve her benefactor; not for her own personal gain, but simply for his pleasure. She was one of those individuals who felt compassion and looked after everyone. One of those people you cannot help but like. She was the first one to say hello as soon as she saw me: "Salam Mahboubeh khanoum. Why are you standing there? Please come in. Welcome." She opened the middle door on the porch which led to a small, but sparkling clean sitting room decorated with a half set of upholstered sofas and inexpensive carpets. You could see that the room was used to a lesser extent than the rest of the house. "You'll have to excuse us Mahboubeh khanoum. Please come in. Have you had breakfast? Hadi love, run and bring something to eat."

I lied: "Yes khanoum, thank you very much. No Hadi khan. Don't go to any trouble." I felt faint from hunger.

She said: "Well, why don't you have a cup of chai with us too. It's not much." She smiled at me with such kindness that I had to bite my lip to stop myself from bursting into tears.

She left the door open. I sat there, on a couch by the window. She pulled the curtain to one side to let in more sunlight. The light shined on my left side. How I loved it. It was like a warm hand caressing me and offering warmth to my cold, tired body.

Some time elapsed with the comings and goings. Hadi came, carrying a fairly large, round copper tray, followed by his mother who pushed an any-where table in front of me as she walked in. I said: "Please don't go to any trouble."

-Not at all! It's no trouble at all. We haven't done anything at all that's worthy of you.

Hadi placed the tray on the table. There was tea, sugar and sugar cubes, bread, butter, and morello cherry jam. As if Esmat khanoum had been a trained psychologist, she said: "I'll just pop into the kitchen for a couple of minutes while you're eating. I'll be back right away."

She left with Hadi. They stood and whispered in the yard for a few minutes. Apparently, she sent Hadi – who had changed his mind about going out– to do some shopping, and then she went into the kitchen.

As soon as Esmat khanoum disappeared from sight, I sat in the sun like a fat, greedy cat. I let go of the corners of my chador and ate with an appetite I had worked up while watching the garden, its flowers, and the warm autumn sun.

Esmat khanoum came and took away the breakfast tray. Their calmness amazed me. I had forgotten the ordinary routines of life. She returned and sat next to me. I had firmly covered my face again and she was looking at me in surprise. She was visibly asking herself why I hid my face from her too. I knew she had a thousand questions on the tip of her tongue. What was I doing there? Where was my husband? Surely, she had her doubts. She had guessed something, but was too polite to ask. She knew her limits well. She asked with composure: "How's agha? Why didn't he join us?"

I lost my train of thought. I was bewildered. Confused, I asked: "Sorry? What did you say?"

-Your husband. I asked how your husband is.

I said: "I don't have a husband anymore." My eyes welled up with tears. I lowered my head so she wouldn't see them.

Her own eyes nearly popped out of her head. Her mouth agape, she asked in astonishment: "Oh dear, why? What's happened? Are you separated? Are you not on speaking terms?"

Still holding my head down, I said: "It's worse than that."

-Why? What's he done?

I dropped my chador and turned my battered, swollen face towards her. She hit the back of her left hand with her right one, and said: "Ooh, I'll be damned. I'll send Hadi for a doctor right now."

-No Esmat khanoum. For goodness' sake, don't do that. There's no need for a doctor. It'll get better by itself. It's not as if it's the first time.

-It's not the first time? He's hit you before? Dear God, that cruel man. Look what he's done!

-It doesn't matter. I'm used to this sort of thing. Let Hadi khan get on with his school work and studies.

-Today is a holiday. It's Mab'as. Hadi was going somewhere else. It was nothing important.

So, it was Eid today. I had even lost count of celebrations and deaths. I asked: "So, it's a holiday today? Hassan khan is also home?"

-My brother has gone out. But, he'll be back for lunch. I hope he comes back sooner, so I can see what we can do! Is it very painful?

-My face? No. The pain is in here.

And I pointed to my heart as tears streamed down my face again. I could no longer stop them. They fell and I could not cope with it. Without wanting to pretend to be the wronged party, without having a lump in my throat, without even wanting to cry, tears streamed and streamed and streamed. I did not want to cry in front of this woman. I did not want to appear desperate. I was ashamed of displaying my hopelessness and misery. I was worried that I might lose her respect with these tears. And yet, it was out of my hands. I, who was proud as a peacock, I, who was sure as fate, I was now the object of pity here and there. If only my tears would dry up. If only I had been struck by lightning and not come here. What a heavy price to pay for what the eye saw and the heart desired. Now you can sit here, in this house, in this woman's house, your mother's rival who has no idea what's what, so she can gape at you in astonishment; so her son can put his hands together in the yard self-consciously and peep at you with regret and pity; so Hassan khan can come and think of something to do for you. As you sow, so shall you reap. Cry and let them watch you. But no, Esmat khanoum was shedding more tears than I was. She could not stop. I said: "See what a nuisance I've made of myself on Eid! I've also ruined your day. I had no idea it was Eid today. I'll take my leave now; I won't bother you any longer."

She said: "No please, don't worry. Make yourself at home. I won't let you leave! I swear to God I'll get upset if you talk like this. It's not as if your father hasn't done enough for us… And should I let his daughter, who is a guest in our home for a day, leave in this state?"

Tears streamed down my face again. Why wouldn't it leave me alone? Why did it erupt despite my wishes? And yet, I felt so comfortable regardless of everything. I was so calm. I wanted to put my head on her shoulders and confide in her, as if she was my patience stone[220], a shoulder to cry on. This woman was so friendly; a stranger to me, and yet so close. I said: "Did you know I was the one who fell in love with him." She knew. "Did you know I married him despite all the objections?" She knew. Her own brother had taken Rahim to buy his suit. "Did you know I had a son?" She knew. My father had told her. "Did you know my son drowned in a pond?" She knew. "Do you know how it broke my heart?" She knew. Her tears told me that she knew, that she understood; because she, too, had a son.

She served lunch after the midday call to prayers. No matter how much I insisted that she should wait for Hassan khan's return, she did not accept. I looked hungry to her. I felt weak. I had not eaten anything since the night before. She said: "Breakfast was nothing much."

I had to eat. I had to build up my stamina. We ate lunch with Hadi and his mother in that same sitting room, on a floor spread. Hadi kept peeking at my face without a word. Let him watch. It was all water under the bridge. Upon Esmat khanoum's insistence, I lied down on the couch by the window after lunch again and had tea in the sunlight. I felt comfortable; I was calm and peaceful. With legs stretched out and my head resting on the back of the couch, I enjoyed the autumn sun. I no longer feared Rahim's arrival. I no longer gritted my teeth together because of his mother. All these things were so far away from me now. They belonged in the past. I finally fell asleep.

It was around three o'clock in the afternoon when I was woken up by the soft stroke of Esmat khanoum's hand on my forehead. I opened my eyes and tried to remember where I was. The sun had moved on over my body and my corner was shaded now. Is it Rahim? Is it his mother? No, oh yes, how wonderful, this is Esmat khanoum who is saying in her soft, motherly voice: "Mahboubeh jan, sweetheart, wake up. Hassan khan wants to talk to you."

Although he had salt and pepper hair, Hassan khan was younger than I had imagined. He was of medium height, with a relatively large nose. His lips were fat, and the top half of his body leaned slightly forward. It was not very clear whether he had a small hump, or if he was really leaning forward. He had a deep, fatherly voice. My chador had fallen around my shoulders when he walked in. Before I could move, he said hello to me. I got on my feet. Before I could sit down again, he said: "Khanoum, what has this man done to you? How could he do this? How did he have the heart? And with a respectable lady such as yourself?"

I said to myself don't you dare cry! I tried very hard to hold back the tears. Even so, my eyes were wet. He asked: "What do you intend to do now? Would you like me to mediate?

-No, I want a divorce.

He was not surprised, nor did he object.

-Does your father know?

-No. I came here first. I was confused. I didn't know what I was doing. But now, I'll take my leave. I'll go to my father's house."

-No khanoum, that's not for the best. It's not good for your mother to see you like this. Let me send for your father to come here and see you first; then he can decide for himself!

Esmat khanoum said: "Dadash is right. If your mother sees you looking like this after all these years, God forbid, she'll die of grief. We have to send for your agha jan."

I could not believe that a concubine could empathise with her main rival like this. My experiences of the past six or seven years had hardened me. I had this impression that all the people in the world were aggressive savages, only looking after their own needs. One by one, the principles of humanity came back to me and took their rightful place in my mind. Hassan khan said: "Hadi, can you run quickly to Mr Basir ol-Molk's house?"

All saddled up, Hadi said: "Why not dear uncle; of course I can."

Even Hadi felt sorry for me and wanted to do something nice. His mother clutched her face lightly, and said: "Strike me dead! Hadi's never been to agha's house. Agha's forbidden that any of us ever go there. Khanoum might find out and become upset and troubled."

Hassan khan waved his hand impatiently: "I know what to do." He left the room and returned with a sealed envelope. He handed it to Hadi, and said: "You'll go to Mr Basir ol-Molk's house. You'll knock on the birouni door and say I want to talk to agha. You mustn't go in! You won't go in even if they insist. You'll say I don't have permission to enter. You'll just give the envelope to one of their people and you'll stress that it should be given to agha himself only. You'll say it's urgent."

I asked anxiously: "What have you written in the letter?"

In the same calm and reassuring voice, he said: "Don't worry my child; I haven't made a spectacle of things. I've only written please come here in order to discuss Mahboubeh khanoum's predicament in person, and I've signed my name. That's all."

I was perspiring with shame. I was cursing Rahim to myself. I looked up and told Hadi: "You'll forgive me Hadi khan. I've caused so much trouble for you. You'll get exhausted."

He smiled innocently and, with a childish kindness and nervousness, he said: "God no. I swear on my khanoum jan's life I won't get tired. I'll go now and come back straight away."

He was so naïve, so pure at the age of sixteen; the age of innocence; the age of optimism and obliviousness; the age of love and friendship; the age when you stumble through life and run aground, just like I did.

My heart began to race as Hadi left. I could no longer bear to sit still. I walked. I sat. I rubbed my hands together. My father was coming after all these years. I was going to see my father, if he came at all of course; if he wanted to see me at all.

Hassan khan and Esmat khanoum consoled me. My mouth had dried up.

My body was cold. Esmat khanoum gave me a glass of sherbet. She was not feeling any better herself. Hassan khan was sitting on the ledge of the porch, resting his elbow on his knee, running his fingers through his prayer beads and shaking his head regretfully. The sound of the door echoed. All three of use froze in our places. Hassan khan said: "You go into the room and let me prepare him for this."

I ran into the parlour and looked from behind the door curtain. Esmat khanoum opened the door. First, I saw my father come in followed by Hadi, whom my eyes could barely detect. I did not want my father to see me in that condition; an unfortunate, helpless woman afflicted by pain, instead of that pampered, vivacious, chirpy girl who walked with a graceful gait, her eyes glowing with pride. As soon as my father walked in, he called out: "Hassan khan."

But, there was no need for him to call. Hassan khan went to greet him. My father was busy talking to them. I could see his face from behind the window. The hair on his temples, just over his ears, was greying. His face was thinner and more seasoned. Streaks of white could be seen in his moustache. He was frail, and even more kind and gentle. Nevertheless, the look on his face was bitter and stern and, more importantly, troubled. The troubled look intensified with every passing moment spent whispering. His clothes were pressed and smart as usual. I could see the chain of his gold watch hanging over his waistcoat. Looking puzzled, he had put his left hand in the pocket of his waistcoat while holding his chin with his right hand and watching Hassan khan intensely with questioning eyes. At times, he glanced at Esmat khanoum who interrupted his brother. Then, there was a short pause. My father took a deep breath and asked a question. Hassan khan, whose face was turned away from me, pointed to his back and towards the parlour with his thumb. The sun was going down. My father took a couple of hasty steps towards the room and stopped. It seemed as if he was not much better off than me. He called: "Mahboubeh!" Tears welled up in my eyes. He took another step forward: "So why won't you come out?" He sounded gentle and sad.

I dropped my head, opened the door and leaned to the right, sideways. The left side of my face, the good side, was turned towards the yard. My head was hanging down and my hair was covering my face on both sides. I had clutched my fists tightly together to hold back the tears. Softly, I said: "Salam."

I was surprised to see that he heard me, and said: "Salam." He came closer and stood facing me. The battered side of my face was covered by my hair and turned towards the parlour. My father tried to look at my face. He wanted to see his daughter's face after so many years, and I was too scared to show it to him. My eyes were transfixed on the tip of his shiny black shoes. Calmly he said: "Have you run aground?"

I said: "Don't reproach me agha jan!" and my tears trickled onto the floor, in front of both our feet. In all my life, I had never seen such huge tear drops.

He said: "No, I'm not reproaching you. I'm glad you came. It's never too late to mend." His voice was shaky. He went quiet and took a deep breath. He got a hold of himself. Then, he said: "Look up, look at me."

I did not move.

-Are you upset with me?

I shook my head from side to side.

-Why won't you look at me then?

With a lump in my throat, I said: "I want to…" and then, I raised my head slowly.

My eyes were full of tears. At first, he did not react. His eyes just opened up wide in disbelief. He took a closer look at me, as if another person had been passed off to him as his own daughter. Hassan khan and his sister were looking at us with pity and sympathy. My father regained his composure immediately. He pulled his head back angrily as he ran his fingers through his hair, and said: "Oh…" Then, he went quiet. He took his hand off his head and looked at me. Then, as if he was speaking to himself, he said: "Look what he's done!" And, although he already knew the answer, he asked: "Who has done this to you!?"

-Rahim, agha jan, Rahim.

And I began to sob.

He began pacing up and down like a lion trapped in a cage. He walked to the left and to the right, and returned to my side.

-Your husband has done this to you? A man? With his own legal wife? With his own virtuous, defenseless wife? His own honour? Damn you man!

Calmly, Hassan khan said: "And apparently, it wasn't his first time either."

My father looked at me: "Is this true? And you still stayed? You put up with it? You lived with him?

-I kept thinking that I can change him agha jan.

-That you can change him? No my dear. He's incorrigible. Blood will tell. He's been battering you all this time and you have kept quiet? You didn't leave him? Look what he's done to you. What a strange animal! What's more, he's done this to a girl who turned her back on everything for this worthless being. To my daughter; a daughter no one had ever raised a voice at…" His voice broke up in his throat. For a passing moment, I saw the glitter of tears in his eyes. Instantly, he turned away from me and began to walk around. After a while, he continued: "So he's found himself a defenseless person? I'll teach him a good lesson, you mark my words. But why did you stay on girl? Why did you put up with it for so long, Mahboubeh? Why?"

He sounded calm, but reproachful. I said: "For my son, agha jan."

He did not utter a word, but went white as chalk. I regretted what I had said. He crossed his hands behind his back. A back which was now bent. He stared at the floor and remained silent. Esmat khanoum was crying without a sound. My father said: "I know; you have suffered a lot."

I said sobbing: "Agha jan, no one knows just how much, no one!"

He allowed for my crying to subside. He attempted to speak a few times, but his lips quivered and he was unable to say anything. Finally, the words came out: "Well, it's over now. Say no more. Don't concern yourself anymore; I'll fix everything. Don't you worry; welcome back. He's the one who has missed the boat by losing a woman like you. I don't understand how he couldn't appreciate a jewel like you. This, too, is his misfortune. These types of unfortunate people can't even appreciate what God has blessed them with."

Hassan khan said: "You're absolutely right agha. It's of no use to cast pearls before a swine."

We went in and sat down. Hadi brought the tea. My father said: "What do you plan to do now?"

-I want a divorce.

-That would be the right thing to do. Even so, give yourself time to think about it.

-I began thinking about it a year after my marriage, agha jan.

My father thought for a moment and said: "I can't take you home looking like this. Your poor mother will go to pieces."

Hassan khan said: "I agree."

My father turned to Hassan khan and said: "Will you allow Mahboubeh to stay here for a while? Long enough for the bruises on her face to mend? Then, I'll come for her myself and take her home."

Hassan khan and Esmat khanoum said in chorus: "Of course, please feel at home. She can stay here for as long as she wishes."

Just before leaving, my father took out a bunch of bank notes from his pocket and put them in my hand. He neither kissed me hello when he came in, nor did he kiss me goodbye when he left. I knew why! Because I was still Rahim's wife.

In the evenings, Esmat khanoum laid out her best bedding for me in the room to the right. She placed everything I needed in the room for me - comb, mirror and towel. Everything was new and clean. She even went to the bazaar one day and bought me a dress, undergarments, and a pair of socks. As much as I insisted, she would take no money from me. She would not let me do anything at all. She would say: "You are weak dear girl. I won't get tired by washing an extra dish; this is just a bite to eat; it's not as if I have killed the fatted calf. You must think of yourself."

She sat by my side at nights and, insisting that I lie down, we talked for a couple of hours and enjoyed each other's company. Every now and then, we all sat in the parlour with Hassan khan and talked about everything and anything under the sun. At times, Hassan khan softly played the tar for us. I would talk to Hadi about the Dar al-Fonoun. He was a talented, ambitious boy and enjoyed studying. My father had taken charge of his studies. He had promised to pay for him for as long as he wanted to study.

When I was alone with Esmat khanoum at night, I opened up my heart to her: "Esmat khanoum, I can't have children anymore. I want to look for a cure, I'm not sure if it'll work or not?"

-Why shouldn't it my dear. Insha'Allah it will. But don't make yourself suffer. Why do you want a child? You're still a child yourself. I'm telling you, a child's nothing but trouble. May God keep them safe for those who have them. But, if those who don't have them brood over it, then by God, they don't have their wits about them."

-Esmat khanoum, I'm not one of them. I don't brood over it. I'm past brooding. But I'm gutted. I'm butchered, barren, and all because of this wicked man.

Esmat khanoum would lean down, kiss me on the head and wipe away my tears. What drew me to this small, neat, shipshape building was its tranquillity, cleanliness and orderliness. And what attracted me to this kind woman, and her son and brother, was the serenity which reigned in their home. At first, I was surprised that no one dragged their feet in the courtyard first thing in the morning. I was amazed that no one grumbled or called each other at the top of their voice. Why won't the locals kick up a fuss around here every night and make their dead shudder in their graves? To begin with, I was cynical of everything and everyone. I had brought pessimism over with me from that confounded, cursed house. I interpreted every little move and every little word. I judged every gesture to be the host's bad intentions. If Esmat khanoum smiled at her son, I would think she was mocking me. If Hadi did not say hello to me straight away, I would think to myself that he wants me to leave their house sooner, to give them more space. If Hassan khan put his hand in his pocket in my presence and gave money to Esmat khanoum to send Hadi shopping for tea, sugar and tobacco, I imagined that he must want house money from me. But I calmed down gradually. I became accustomed to this normal life again. I was reacquainted with the old, respectable ways. I lost my acquired meanness and contemptibility. At last, I was able to drag myself out of the grime, to understand the meaning of life. I understood that when it was time for the man of the house to come home from work at night, a woman did not have to start shaking like a leaf from fear at sundown. Esmat khanoum's caresses and her son and brother's moderate ways not only cured my battered face and swollen lips, but they also healed my tired heart. I felt soothed. Some evenings, Hassan khan took permission and gently played the tar for us. Although I knew he liked his wine, never during my stay in that house did I see him touch a drop in my presence.

On the fourth day, which was a Sunday, my father came to see me. The swelling of my lips had subsided and my black and blue face had turned to a yellow colour. He said: "Nearly there! You look much better. I'll come and pick you up on Friday morning."

I said: "Agha jan, does khanoum jan know?"

-No, I haven't told anyone yet. I'll gradually prepare her the night before."

Esmat khanoum was not in the room. I looked down, and asked with embarrassment: "Will you tell her that I've been staying here during this time?

-There's no other way. What else can I say?

That must have been the first and last time that my father spoke of Esmat khanoum and her brother in our house in my mother's presence, and all because of me; because of my obstinacy and headstrongness; because of my slip-up.

I felt sorry for my mother till Friday morning. I kept waking up startled in the early morning hours, tossing and turning and wrestling with my own thoughts. My life flashed in front of my eyes like the silver screen and, when I was finally dripping with sweat and out of patience, I would sit up in my bed with a sudden move, hold my head between my hands and say: ***Oh, what have I done dear God? What have I done? I repent, I repent!***

My father returned on Friday morning. I was ready. I recognised his carriage from a distance. Firouz khan was sitting on the coachman's seat with the same bushy moustache and fuzzy hair. His hair had turned a little grey, as if it had been dusted with chalk. He was glancing at me with curiosity and sadness. The coach looked old too, like his coachman and owner. As if my father could read my mind, he said apologetically: "This coach is falling apart. I have to be thinking about buying a car."

Firouz khan said: "Salam, khanoum kouchik!"

These few words took me back to the sweet life of my past. Once again, I had a lump in my throat and, as I was getting on the coach, I said with great difficulty: "Salam Firouz khan; oh, how you've aged too!"

-Khanoum, the coach, the horses and I have all aged. We have to be sent to the tannery.

He was referring to my father and his decision to buy a car. My father said: "Perhaps the coach and the horses; but you have to stop eating and sleeping, and take the trouble to learn how to drive a car", and he laughed.

As the coachman was whipping the horses, he said laughingly from over his shoulder: "I'm past it agha. I only know how to whip horses."

-And I'll keep whipping you until you learn!

All three of us laughed. We were all three happy, each in their own way; each with their own thoughts and dreams.

Oh, that street again, that lane, the same little bazaar and… and that same damned carpentry, which was fortunately still boarded up. And then…, the garden wall and our house and… we had arrived.

My heart was in turmoil. I was beside myself. My father had said that my sisters were coming to lunch with their husbands and children, to see me. But, they had not arrived yet.

As soon as I walked in, it was as if a queen had arrived. My dayeh jan, dadeh khanoum, Haj Ali, and even the new maid my mother had hired, all came to greet me. But, where was my mother? Where was Manouchehr?

Dayeh jan, dadeh khanoum and the young maid passed me to one another and kissed me, but my eyes were fixed on the windows of the building. Absent-mindedly, I asked: "How're you Haj Ali?"

-Oh khanoum, I've grown old now; and my ears won't hear a thing anymore. I'm almost deaf.

As if he was not hard of hearing before! My father, who was happy and chirpy, or at least pretended to be, said: "Well, well, Haj Ali your Ghormeh Sabzi is burning. I can smell it from here."

Haj Ali laughed and limped away. My father snatched me away from the others and said: "That's enough. Where's khanoum bozorg?"

My dayeh jan said: "In the panjdari. She's been sitting there on a couch since this morning. She doesn't have the strength to lift a finger."

We started towards the building. My heart missed a beat as I looked up. At the top of the stairs, a little boy was hiding behind the pier of the wall and peeking curiously from there. He did not look anything like Almas. But he behaved just like him. I called out: "Manouchehr!"

He hid behind the wall. I ran up the stairwell every other step and took him in my arms. He was choked with tears. My father said: "Say hello to your sister son. This is Mahboub."

Manouchehr said: "Salam."

I was kissing him and taking in his scent. I had squatted in front of him to be his size. I was searching for my own son in him. As he was in my arms, he looked up at my father and said: "Nezhat's my sister. Khojasteh's my sister."

I gave him a little squeeze, and kissed him: "So am I, my dearest, so am I." I opened the door to the panjdari. My mother was sitting on the velvet couch. I stood by the door and said: "Salam khanoum jan."

She held out her arms and whimpered: "You came Mahboub? You came? I thought I would die and never see you again. I thought you'd never come, never come but to my grave."

Her eyes were bloodshot. The chador fell off my head, and I ran. I took refuge in her arms that smelled of mother, the smell of peace. It was the smell of my childhood. I kissed her face; I kissed her hands; the same hands which had pinched me one day, but not as hard as they should have. I placed my head on her bosom, so filled with my sorrow, and I felt calm at last.

Manouchehr was about to cry. He came to us. He was jealous that I was in our mother's arms, that she was kissing me so warmly and motherly. He burst out in tears and pushed himself between us, into my mother's arms, and sat on her lap. My mother wiped her tears and laughed: "You jealous little thing! You're a grown man now, shame on you." Manouchehr pointed at me and said: "But, she's older than me! How come she's not ashamed?" You could say that again!

My sisters arrived with their husbands and children. My parents had aged. My mother no longer had that freshness and sparkle. I do not know if it was just from the passing of time or the grief of my failure. My father behaved more demurely and wisely. Nezhat's husband was well-matured and more set in his ways. The children had grown up. Khojasteh had married. The new maid was jolly and agile. Perhaps, my presence was also strange and interesting in their eyes. It was as if I had come from a different world. As soon as I looked away, they sized me up with great interest; and, as soon as I looked back, they looked the othr way. Everyone was respectable and well dressed. I was amazed by their mellow manner of talking, free of all belligerence, free of all shouting and howling and shrieking. I compared Rahim to my sisters' husbands, and perspire with shame. Once, Khojasteh had asked me in this very same house what it was that I liked about him. And I had taken offense. Now, I was asking myself the same question, and I had no answer for it.

Nezhat had three bouncy, chubby kids who looked alike. It was as if they were from the same mould. She had delivered them almost one after the other. Her first born was a boy, and the other two were girls. Nezhat's husband was still head over heels for his wife's rounded up, chubby figure. But, Khojasteh had grown into quite a lady; tall, thin and sophisticated. She was very sociable and smartly dressed. Her conversation and conduct were harmonious and pleasant. Her piano playing was admirable, and her perfume was inebriating. She had a six-month old daughter who was as soft as a doll. My sisters kissed me with pity and sorrow. In their eyes, I had lost a lot of weight. I looked sick. I had to look after myself. I had to stop brooding. It was all over now. I was free at last. I kissed and kissed their children who stepped back shyly. Khojasteh's husband was a complete gentleman. His companionship soothed me. He was polite and respectful. He sat by my side with compassion, kindly taking my hand in his and giving me some appeasing, doctorly advice which nearly made me cry again. My family was gradually getting to know me all over again; and, little by little, I was finding my place with them once more. Nezhat took me to one side, and said: "Mahboub, you have to buy some decent clothes." In all this time, my father never mentioned my husband and our conjugal life.

The following morning, my father called my dayeh jan after breakfast: "Dayeh khanoum, you'll go find this chap and you'll tell him to be here on Monday afternoon, an hour before sunset." We all knew who this chap was.

An hour before sunset, my heart was racing again. I felt anxious; except, it was not out of love this time, but out of hatred and fear. Again, I could not breathe. Dear God, how much more of this do I have to take? How much longer do I have to feel this tightness in my chest? Until when did this throat of mine have to feel so dry? Until when? How much longer? I was so feeble and weak, so shaky and hollow inside that I felt if a wind blew, it would take me with it.

Close to sundown, my father sat in the panjdari. He did not tell me to join him. It was not prudent at any rate. I stood behind the door, just like the day he was coming to ask for my hand in marriage. On my father's orders, Firouz sat on the entrance steps of the andarouni. Haj Ali was standing next to the pond, hands joined together politely. Dadeh khanoum was coming and going when Dayeh khanoum's voice was heard saying: "Come this way."

She would not say please come in. The word 'please' was for dignified, respectable people only; for erudite people. It was for proper sons-in-law. But, it was also not nice to say come this way. It was uncouth. After all, he was still my husband.

I could hear his footsteps coming up the stairs; he said: "Ya Allah" and stepped into the panjdari.

Suddenly, all his gestures made me shudder; the way he took off his shoes, the way he said hello, put his hands together and stood there meekly, holding his head down. It was not just him, but also the fact that I had wanted him so much. Now, I could see him in a light I should have seen him six, seven years ago. The day he came to ask for my hand. That same day Khojasteh asked me is he the one you want?! A common, frivolous, illiterate man with no accomplishments; a ruffian who, although wearing a suit this time, his dirty shirt collar was still unbuttoned - not out of passion and fervour, but out of apathy and carelessness. His suit was wrinkled and his trousers were sagging at the knees. He was in disarray; his hair was a restless mess, as if it had not been combed in a long time. His beard had grown into stubble and his lips were dry and chapped. His face was depressed and grim. His sheer presence in this house was inappropriate and out of place, never mind being the son-in-law of this aged, mellow and venerable man who was sitting there so gracefully, observing him from head to toe. He seemed confused and a bit drunk. He paused for a while with his head down. Then, he raised his head and looked around him dumbfounded and agape, as if he was seeing the place for the first time; as if he could not believe that the daughter of this household could be his wife. It was as if he was dreaming.

Calmly and authoritatively, my father said: "Sit down."

He was going to kneel down on the floor, but my father pointed to a couch in the furthest corner of the room, and said: "Not there. Over here."

History repeated itself. They both behaved in the same manner they had done on the day he had come to ask for my hand. He obeyed and sat down. Silence fell; and then, my father said: "Thank you so much for everything you have done."

As he was playing with the rim of his hat with his head down, he answered: "By God, I haven't done anything wrong!"

Just as calmly, my father said: "What more did you want to do? Was my daughter a bad wife for you? Did she fail you in any way? What grievances did you have? "

I could sense my father's anger behind this calm façade. I could see the calm before the storm; a volcano ready to erupt and spew its flames. But, Rahim was a simpleton and a fool. He lacked the power of discrimination. He could not understand the situation. He was so crude, and my father's calm manners and questioning tone emboldened him. Unexpectedly, he turned about brave as a lion, as if wanting his dues: "Thanks very much to your daughter! You've no idea what she's done to my mother!"

In the same calm and demure manner, my father asked: "What has she done?"

-What's she done? What hasn't she done! She's set fire to my life. She's hit my mother. The poor old woman nearly collapsed with fear."

My father interrupted him: "She's set fire to your life? What life? What has she burnt? Tell me and I'll pay for the damages."

Rahim mumbled for a bit, then said: "Well, of course it was her own dowry. he rugs, the beddings, mattresses…"

My father said: "So much for that. Now, let's get back to your mother. How many times a month did she hit your mother?"

As if he was denouncing an unruly child, Rahim said: "Just on the day she left the house in a huff."

My father asked: "Just that one day? That's no good. I must punish her severely, and I will. Because, if I was in her shoes and had spent six or seven years suffering in silence and enduring such humiliation at the hands of this woman day in day out, I would have hit her seven days a week. My daughter has to be punished for this incompetence." He said that and grinned furiously.

Rahim raised his head and looked at him in surprise. He was just beginning to realise that my father was mocking him. I could see his face clearly from the gap in the door. His eyes were puffed up. He had not neglected his drink over these past couple of weeks for sure. He had spent the entire time in a drunken stupor. So, he had also suffered in his own way. But, I no longer felt sorry for him. I did not feel an ounce of pity. I enjoyed his suffering.

In an angry tone of voice, my father said: "Did you have no shame when you battered my daughter in this manner, you little man? And you still have the audacity to complain about your mother? After all, would a real man, a respectful man, a man with an epsilon of integrity and decency beat up his own wife, his own honour? A defenseless woman who has left her life behind to follow an idle rogue like you at that? You call this manliness? Did you have no shame when you took your wife's gold jewellery, took her money, took everything she had to go drinking, or to spend it on women worse than yourself in the *Qajar quarters*[221]." I froze behind the door. My eyes were wide open with astonishment, as were Rahim's eyes. Astounded, he said: "Me? Me? Who says I go to the Qajar quarters? Mahboubeh is lying."

-Shut your mouth. Don't you dare utter my daughter's name without ablution. So, she's lying, is she? She doesn't have a clue. I had sent someone on your tracks. I've been watching you all these years to see when you would come to your senses and feel remorse! To see when the knife will cut to the bone and my daughter will be fed up to the back teeth with you! To see how long it would take her to get tired of your drinking and filthy way of life! And you - you poor, miserable fool - you did not recognise the worth of this woman. You did not appreciate this angel that God sent you. Nobody will stand by such a hardman brute of a husband for as long as she did.

Rahim said: "How else should I have appreciated her? Should I have carried her on my head and shouted she's as sweet as halva, she's as sweet as halva?

He was beginning to get impertinent. My father picked it up sharply, and said: "Watch your mouth. There's no call for this kind of talk. You must divorce my daughter immediately. A triple *talaq*[222] without reconciliation. Do you understand?" Rahim turned white as a sheet. I knew him well. I knew his reactions so well when his interests were in danger, when he was angry, when he was afraid.

-Why should I divorce her? She's my wife. I love her. I won't divorce her.

-You love her? You've beaten her black and blue because you love her? What would have happened if she had died? Huh? I will teach you a good lesson in how a man must treat his wife. Not that my daughter will return to your house…! No. Just to make a man out of you. Just so you won't treat another poor soul who will fall into your hellish trap in the future like this, the way she did. Let this be a lesson to you.

Brazenly, he said: "So what? All husbands and wives quarrel and sulk every now and then! Instead of advising her to come back home, you're adding fuel to the fire? Mahboubeh wants me, I know that. And I want her. I'll never give her a divorce."

My father called out: "Mahboubeh, come in here." Holding my head high in my new Crêpe de Chine dress I had bought with dayeh jan, with coiffed hair, perfumed, wearing makeup, in high heels and proud and defiant, I walked into the room without my hijab. My desire to be stylish, pretty and faultless on this day was intentional. I wanted him to see me with insight one more time, for the last time. He was agape with admiration. He stared at me for a while.

He rose to his feet slowly and said: "Salam."

I did not answer. I was a lady meeting her servant. My only feelings for him were those of superiority and revenge. I hated the thought of him having ever touched me. I disliked him, myself, and my own body more than anything else. As much as I washed myself in the shower, threw away my old clothes, wore new ones, I was still not satisfied. He said: "Mahboub!"

-Shut up

I had learned from him. I had been a captive in his house, in his claws, for quite some time. I had been caged by him and his mother like a dove with a broken wing. I had put up with their profanities and remained silent because I had no protection, I was all by myself. We had now exchanged places.

Weary and helpless, he looked at my father, and then at me. He let go of himself on the couch: "Your agha jan wants you to get a divorce."

-It's not my agha jan, it's me.

-Why?

-You're so impudent! You still don't know why?

-But you wanted me!

-That was before. I don't anymore. I was a child. I didn't understand. If I did, I wouldn't have picked a bum like you.

All of a sudden, in a firm, cutting voice, he said: "I won't divorce you then. I'll make you stay until your hair turns the colour of your teeth."

My legs shook. I sat on a chair next to my father and looked at him. This is what I had feared. I knew he would say something like this; that he would use this weapon. I knew him well. He rose to his feet and laughed, the same playful, brazen laugh. My father said: "Wipe that grin off your face and shut your big mouth; sit down."

Rahim raised his voice. He was going wild again now that he had the winning card. He was bullying again. He wanted to intimidate my father in front of the domestics by shouting and screaming, shamelessly and dishonourably. He yelled: "We have nothing more to say. You're harassing me. I won't divorce my wife, so there. I love her and I won't divorce her. O Muslims, come to my rescue. Have you no sense of justice? This man wants to separate a man and his wife by force. He wants to separate the nail from the flesh."

The volcano erupted. The ocean turned stormy. My father's deep-seated anger blew up as he roared: "Lower your voice you sick bastard. Do you think you can scare me with your yelling? You amoral little swindler! Is this how you treated my daughter? Are you totally incapable of putting two coherent words together? What's the matter then? You think you can be intimidating here too? Do you suppose she's still going to put up with a rogue like you and keep a low profile to keep her honour? I spit on your God damn father's grave. The more humanely you're treated, the more we put up with you, the more impertinent you get? Do you suppose we can't raise our voices over our heads? Have you never come across a more foulmouthed person than yourself? Don't you believe for a moment that I'm worried about my honour! If I had honour, I would not have handed my daughter over to a cowardly bastard like you. I'm even more ignoble than you are if I don't get my daughter's divorce from you…"

I just sat there like a statue. The domestics were waiting around in consternation, ready to intervene in favour of their master. Dayeh jan and dadeh khanoum were clutching their faces in the middle of the courtyard. My mother stuck her head through the door in her black chador and objected: "Agha!! Agha!!"

For the first time in his life, I saw my father being sharp with her: "Leave and close the door khanoum." And my mother left and closed the door.

In a calm, but authoritative voice, my father said: "Open up your ears and listen carefully to what I have to say. It's in your own interest to sign the divorce papers. It's for your own good. If you sign, that's fine. If not, one…"

He began counting one by one with his fingers.

-If you don't pay my daughter's alimony to her in my presence every month and take a receipt while she's married to you, my daughter will not return to your house. The alimony must be concurrent with the woman's dignity and way of life. God and his Prophet have said this, and so does the law. My daughter has to have a maid, carpets, beddings and other means of life. You have to pay for her clothing, shoes and chador at least twice a year. You have to pay for the baths, medication, and living expenses. So much for that. Secondly, I must inform you that my daughter has put the house and the shop in my name. Therefore, you also have to buy her a house…"

Rahim interrupted him: "Where am I going to get the money from?"

-Exactly. This is the point. This is nothing yet. The main point still remains. You have to pay her dowr in full. As you know, it's a lot of money. You know that the dowr is like a debt and has to be paid on request. That is to say, a woman can request for her dowr to be paid at any time, either before the divorce or afterwards. Do you understand?

Rahim stretched out the palm of his hand: "*You can't pluck hair from the palm of a hand[223].*"

His hand seemed rough and disproportionate. Was I blind before? My father said: "But I will pluck it. I'll have the palm of this hand beaten until it grows hair. My daughter has also given her dowr away to me. You'll either pay it, or I'll throw you in the slammer until your Excellency's hair is also the colour of his teeth."

Rahim went quiet. He was no longer that chirpy nightingale, chattering away. My father continued: "But, if you agree to a divorce, I will firstly concede my right to the dowr. Secondly, I will put the shop in your name."

-But, what about the house?

-The house will get stuck in your throat. This little insolent chap is so arrogant!

-I also want the house. I can't very well live in the middle of nowhere, can I?

My father said: "This is your last chance to make up your mind. Only the shop. If you don't accept, I'll send for Ma'soumeh khanoum's bent copper of an uncle and her lout brothers. I will explain everything to them. I will also put my daughter's dowr and the shop in Ma'soumeh khanoum's name. My daughter will also give evidence in any court that you've been seducing this girl. You'll have to marry her, and your reins will then be in her hands and in the hands of her lout brothers. Please yourself."

Oh, how good I felt! I wanted to jump up and give my agha jan two great smacks. What they say is true, that you have to leave it to the experts.

Rahim was desperate. He was miserable, helpless and drained of blood; he would not have bled if you stabbed him. He asked: "When do I have to divorce her? Where do I have to go?"

-First thing tomorrow morning. You'll come here, to the door, and you'll go to the registry office with Firouz khan. I have given all the orders. You sign. Do you understand? It will be a triple divorce. Once you've signed the documents and it's all over, I'll concede the dowr and the shop to you the following day. I'll put the shop in your name in that same registry office.

-How do I know you'll keep your word afterwards?

-You'll know because I haven't bitten the hand that fed me the way you have.

I was truly enjoying my father's smoothness and sharp answers. Rahim asked: "Who'll pay the registry office?"

My father said: "I will" and he rose to his feet to leave the room.

This move meant that Rahim had to leave too. I also turned around to leave the room, when Rahim said: "Mahboub!"

My father turned around abruptly, and asked him aggressively: "What do you want with her?"

I wallowed in pride and joy that my father stood up for me and backed me up like this.

He said: "Please allow me to speak to her alone for two minutes. Won't you even let me say goodbye?"

My father hesitated. He looked at me. He was worried that I might give in to him again. He, too, knew that Rahim intended to deceive me again, to reach my heart again. He was afraid that his spell might bind me again. These two men, both Rahim and my father, imagined that my heart was still the same old, delicate thing; that it was still the heart of that young, inno-cent, complaisant girl who fell in the trap of a flowing hair lock or a crafty look. Men are truly simple beings. They are like children. I went towards Rahim and stood in front of him. In a cold, determined, firm and author-itative tone of voice, the voice of a stranger talking to another stranger, I said: "Tell me what it is that you want?"

As my father was leaving the room, he said: "I'll be nearby."

He was really addressing Rahim, just in case he intended to hurt me! Just in case he wanted to lift a finger on me. He went out and shut door. Ra-him raised his head and looked into my eyes. He smiled sadly. His hair was hanging on his forehead, and that dark vein on his neck was protruding. He gathered all his strength to give me a passionate look.

-You look so pretty Mahboub.

I answered coldly: "The time for this sort of talk is over."

He looked around in desperation: "You left without saying goodbye!"

I said: "But you had said your goodbyes properly to me the night before!" And added sarcastically: "By the way, how's your mother?"

-I sent her off to my cousin's.

-Oh really? You came to your senses six years too late!

-Come off your high horse Mahboub. Come back home.

I said: "No, I won't be cheated anymore. You'll see me again the day you see the back of your ears."

-You don't love me anymore Mahboub?

I remained quiet. I thought about his question. I searched my heart, and found the answer at last: "No. You didn't let me. Your personality overshadowed your looks."

I stood there in front of him. I was cold and forceful; he raised his head to look at me suppliantly: "I know I have done you wrong and I swear to God I'm repentant. But it wasn't all my fault you know. You're to blame too. You always did as I said. You always gave in. You gave me the impression that you love me so much, you want me so much that I didn't have to be afraid of losing you. Now, I know I was wrong. I'm remorseful Mahboubeh jan, I'm sorry."

I was sneering at him. I was enjoying my own feeling of supremacy and advantage.

-Huh… One cannot trust a wolf in sheep's clothing. As my father said, as soon as I come back, you'll turn your shop into a hangout for women worse than yourself."

- I slipped up. I promise it won't happen again. I ask for your forgiveness.

Let me kiss your hand. You were the one who spoiled me. I kept telling myself if a woman like Mahboubeh fell in love with me and spent her time hanging around me when I had no home and no shop, then now… now that…

-Now that what? Now that you own an extra pair of trousers[224]…?"

-You can say whatever you want. I thought I can always find another one like you; that I can have someone better than you. You were so meek. I thought you were a child, that you didn't understand anything. I'm telling you the truth. It was your own fault. You were the one who indulged me. I was young too. It's not as if I was a hundred years old. I swear to God, you owe me too. Please let me kiss your hand now.

I said: "You're right. I owe you too. And I owe you quite a bit. It's time to settle our accounts now. I've been meaning to pay back my debt to you for the past six, seven years."

I lifted my right hand and brought it down on his face with all my force, like lightening. The blow was so hard that his head turned to the right. His dishevelled hair twisted about and fell flickering back on his forehead. The palm of my own hand was hurting from the roughness of his stubble and the force of the blow. I could feel its stinging heat. He remained in that position for a moment. Then, he lowered his head, took my hand to his lips and kissed it softly. The back of my hand felt hot. Were these tears falling on my hand? Abruptly, I pulled it back. They were not tears. My hand was wet with the blood dripping from his nose. I wiped the back of my hand clean with a corner of my dress with hatred and disgust. He raised his head and said: "You've shed my blood Mahboub jan. Are you happy now? Are you satisfied?"

I felt satisfied, but not satisfied enough. The trace of my fingers could now be seen on a face which, if once upon a time a smidgeon of dust settled on it, I would have fallen apart with heartache and sorrow. Now, my eyes glared at a neck and a vein for which I would have gladly given up everything, just so I could kiss it once and die. Why fear death!? But now…?

I opened my mouth and said: "No. I'm not satisfied. I'd be much happier if I could rip open that cowardly vein of yours with a blade; only then would I be satisfied. I will be happy only when blood pours out of that artery in your neck. Once again, he grabbed my wrist firmly and pleaded: "This is the tiger I love Mahboubeh, this tiger; not that meek, clumsy lamb I had at home. Don't get divorced Mahboubeh jan. Don't get divorced. I will be lost without you."

With a laughter filled with rage and victory, I said: "So, I was a meek lamb in your eyes? If a woman tries to make a go of her life, she's a meek lamb?" I pulled my hand out of his and continued: "Leave me alone. Go to hell."

I could hear him whining behind me: "Mahboub, Mahboub jan, how can you?" And as I was closing the door behind me, he said: "You're so unfair."

All throughout my life, never again did I feel such burning love nor such stinging, bitter hatred towards another soul.

Two days later, I was divorced. Rahim had vacated my house and given the key to Firouz khan. I asked them to board it up until I decided what I wanted to do with it. I did not have the heart to see that house again.

My father was sitting in the panjdari. I went into the room after I had signed the register. Like the day of my wedding, his head was leaning on the back of the couch, with legs stretched out into the middle of the room. He was resting his wrists on the couch handles and his hands were hanging down. He was moving the fingers of his left hand along his rosary beads. I approached him and said: "It's over agha jan. I'm free."

I kneeled down beside the couch and kissed his right hand. He caressed my head lovingly. He stroked my hair for a while and then, he murmured gently: "You've become my own daughter again." And that was that. Never did I hear him or anyone else reproach me. My father had forbidden it.

"Where're you going Mahboub jan? Take me with you." "Mahboub jan, I want to sleep in your room tonight." "I want Mahboub jan to change my clothes."

Manouchehr stuck to me like a tick. He was not a separate entity from me. He had come to know me now. He had found his place in a corner of my heart. If I stood up, he would run and hold on to my legs. If I walked, he walked with me every step of the way. He had become my son. He had become my brother. He was my sweet life. I laughed and say jokingly: "Ma-nouchehr, are you glued to me again?"

I tickled him, and he laughed his heart out. If I sat down, he jumped on my head from behind. He kissed me and wet me with his spit. When I was deep in thought, he came to me and fiddled around with my hair and ears. I would say: "Leave me alone Manouchehr. I can't be bothered right now!"

He knew straight away that I was not joking; that I was serious. He would sit by my side quietly and look at me from the corner of his eyes, pressing his lips together, ready to cry. I would say: "Manouchehr jan, go and play. My headache will get better in a minute."

And he would say: "I have a headache too; I don't feel like playing."

He looked at me every second, and kept asking: "Are you better now abji? Are you better now abji?" until it made me laugh and open up my arms to him.

-You're so persistent child!

He would jump into my arms and giggle.

I had become his mother, his dayeh, his tutor. And, in return, his little being calmed me down.

Everyone came to see me. Auntie Keshvar nosily scrutinised me from head to toe. My uncle's wife had a victorious smile on her lips – yet sad at the same time – and her eyes were filled with reproach and regret. My mother's sister - whose son, the same short-legged chicken who had married a girl more short-legged than himself - was consumed with chagrin by Kho- jasteh's successful marriage and her own son's addiction to opium which had turned his face, lips, teeth, and my aunt's life dark, thus soothing my mother's aching heart.

They all came. All except Mansour. Mansour and his wife who was said to be six months pregnant. I was not complaining. I wasn't expecting it. He had every right. I had treated him badly. I had not even thought of him. Winter was upon us and wearing the hijab had already been banned. Our minds were too preoccupied by this unexpected event to worry about all the visiting and comings and goings. I had some suitors, more or less. They were all respectable men, but mostly set in their ways, divorced or widowers; or else, they had old, indifferent, cold, passionless wives and kids of all ages and sizes tagging along, without exception. Just the fact that they were asking for my hand was painful to me. I was fearful of my destiny and what lay ahead. My only consolation was the peace I had found again in my father's house and the eight-year old Manouchehr who was more capable of soothing my heart's wounds with the patting of his little hands than anyone else.

My mother and my dayeh jan did their utmost for me. My mother would not take a step without consulting me first. I visited Hassan khan every now and then. I would not tell my mother. Not that I wanted to hide it from her; I just did not want to disrespect her. Mother knew, but would not let on. She knew only too well how kind they had been to her daughter. She would ask: "Mahboub jan, where're you going?"

-There's something I have to do.

Manouchehr would jump up and down and say: "I want to come too. I want to come too." Mother knew what "There's something I have to do" meant, and she would say: "No my sweetheart, you can't go. It's no place for a child!" And she would turn to me: "Mahboub, take this jar of jam with you", "Mahboub, take this dish of baklava with you", "Mahboub, will you take some tea and sugarloaf with you?" Once, she even gave me a Cashmere shawl and said: "Take this with you."

It was as if we spoke in code: "Khanoum jan, no one expects anything from me."

-It's not a question of expectations. I want you to take this.

I returned from Hassan khan's place. When I got in, dayeh was laying the dinner spread. My mother was not in the room. Absentmindedly, she said: "Mansour khan's wife gave birth last night."

Jealousy jabbed at my heart like a thorn. A thorn of regret and sorrow: "Well, congratulations. What is it?"

-It's a girl. Agha Mansour is on cloud nine. When Nimtaj khanoum was told she had given birth to a girl, she's said this is what I wanted from God. Mansour agha also…

My mother, who had just walked in through the door, sensed how I felt and said: "Oh… so what if she's given birth. What're you going on about dayeh khanoum? It's not as if she has conquered the Khyber Pass[225]! A hundred people give birth every day; she's just one of them."

But, the scar of barrenness had opened up in my heart again. I knew I could never have what I wanted like Nimtaj, or any other woman. I could never again become a mother. God damn you Rahim.

A few days later, my mother said: "Mahboub jan, will you come with me to visit Nimtaj khanoum?"

-I don't want to come.

-Oh dear oh dear, whyever not? Your cousin's wife has given birth.

-Did Mansour come to visit his cousin that I should go and visit his wife? Did Nimtaj khanoum ask after me at all?

-Poor Nimtaj never leaves the house anyway. She's always apologising to everyone. She says her time is taken up by the house and minding the children. The poor thing has a sick heart too. Giving birth was dangerous to her health. She's lucky to be alive…

Dayeh cut her short: "Khanoum, these are all excuses. The problem lies somewhere else. She doesn't want anyone to see her face. For goodness' sake, it's not a face; it's as if the crows have used their beaks…"

Mother cut her short this time: "That's enough dayeh khanoum. Don't talk like this in front of me, I don't like it. She's such a wonderful woman. She has never even hurt a little ant."

I said: "Why don't you go, and I'll go to Nezhat's. Her husband's going out tonight and she's alone."

Dayeh and Manouchehr also went with my mother. Manouchehr was excited to see the baby; otherwise, he would never have left me alone. When they returned, I asked: "Well, what did the baby look like?" Cool as a cucumber, mother said: "It's not important. A baby is just a baby. A newborn doesn't look like much anyway," and she left the room.

Dayeh looked to make sure she was gone; then she said in a low voice: "It's a beautiful girl, like a bouquet of flowers; with pink, chubby cheeks and fair skin. Her eyes are as large as the bottom of tea estekans[226]. She's a joy to look at. Manouchehr wouldn't let go of her! He wanted to bring her home with him. He kissed her and hugged her until she started to cry. Your mother hit Manouchehr hard on the back of his hand."

I asked: "What did Nimtaj say?"

-Nothing. The poor thing pretended not to see. She kept saying he's just a child. Let him play with her. But it was obvious that her heart was in her mouth.

-What have they called her?

-Mansour agha wants to call her Nahid.

Nowruz came again; a Nowruz which was a real celebration for me, with the same past feelings of excitement. The same joy of baking sweets that I had forgotten; the same spring cleaning, the same shopping for new clothes and the same fireworks of seven years ago – just like before the time I managed to ruin my life and jump in the fire with both feet. Nezhat, her husband and her children, plus Khojasteh, her doctor husband and their daughter were all coming to our house for Chaharshanbeh Suri. My mother also invited my paternal aunt and uncle, together with their daughters, one of which had married and the other one who was engaged. Mansour, who was also invited, came with his two sons; Nimtaj khanoum's son and the belated Ashraf's son.

He was very formal and polite, even cold to some extent. He said hello to me and asked me how I was. It was as if he was still upset with me, still unhappy, same old same old. He, too, looked more mature and settled, like the rest of the family. He was very stylish and smartly dressed as usual, very polite and sociable. But, he was quieter, more serious and sedate. We made a lot of noise with the cousins, sisters, and the family kids. We jumped over the fire. I held Manouchehr in my arms and we jumped over the fire together. I took Khojasteh's daughter in my arms and jumped over the fire. I pulled the doctor's hand and made him jump over the fire. Nezhat's husband was worried that his suit might catch fire. Then, I jumped over the fire with each one of Mansour's sons. My long hair played around my face and shoulders. My face lit up and got red next to the fire. I was wearing a double pleated skirt and a warm sweater. I felt comfortable and free. Mansour was leaning back on the front wall of the building, looking very serious. The glow of the flames lit up his face too. He watched me, the children, his own sisters, and my sisters with total indifference. Occasionally, he exchanged a few words with my sisters' or his own sisters' husbands. He never even smiled once during this time.

I came away, tired and breathless. My uncle took my head in his hands and kissed it. I knew how much he loved me. He said: "My heart lights up when you laugh."

Nowruz that year was my sweetest New Year of all.

Nezhat said: "Our uncle's wife has invited everyone to the gardens in Shemiran for sizdah be dar, so that Nimtaj can also come."

Apathetically, I said: "I'm not coming. What's the point of going all the way to Shemiran from here?"

Nezhat laughed: "So, don't if you won't. There's no need to quarrel. Where should we go then?"

-Let's go to agha jan's gardens in Gholhak.

And we went to Gholhak. My dayeh jan had brought a tambourine. There was us, with Nezhat, Khojasteh, their husbands, and our female cousins who had forgone their father's gardens to be with me. Everyone wanted to be with me, and I wanted to be in their midst.

My eldest cousin said: "Mahboub, you're thinner and taller. You look lovely."

Nezhat joked around with my cousin as if I was not there, not sitting next to them, as if she was talking about an object: "At last, we know what lovely means! She doesn't even have the strength to breathe. If you put both your hands around her waist, your fingers will reach together. I say she should look more after herself and her diet, instead of buying so many clothes, perfumes, shoes and handbags. It's as if that chubby Mahboubeh of a few years ago is gone and this one's here in her place."

This was so true. That Mahboubeh was gone. She was dead.

We started with my sisters, cousins, and the children and went for a walk. We took off our shoes and dipped our feet in the water - a roaring, foaming water - which flowed into the gardens at one end, wholesome and cold, to leave it surging and swelling at the other. We climbed trees and rode on the donkey while Nezhat ran after us with that chubby figure of hers, puffing and panting. We rolled around with laughter. The men had all gone for a long walk and would not be back until noon. And I, at everyone's insistence and in front of all eyes, tied knots in the grass[227] - twice! The first time, laughing and wishing to be married, and the second time wishing for a child with a heavy heart.

In the afternoon, as soon as the lettuce and oxymel spread was laid, together with boiled broad beans, 'ash reshteh and tea, just when it was time for the men to start their game of backgammon and as dadeh khanoum was playing her tambourine and singing "Don't climb up the tree, your legs will get scratchy, your clothes will get mucky", Mansour's black Chevrolet drove up, and Mansour and his two sons arrived, with both of them walking at his sides like the two sons of Muslim Ibn-Aghil[228].

He came, exchanged greetings, and sat down. With his arrival, everyone – men and women – went quiet and sat still. He was not sullen or bad-tempered. But, as Nezhat put it, he was as stiff as a poker. Khojasteh grumbled in my ear and Nezhat's: "Where did he come from?"

Nezhat whispered: "He's come to show off his car to us," and giggled without making a sound.

Her plumb figure was shaking with laughter, prompting Khojasteh and I to laugh too. My mother gave us a sharp look and got up to put the lettuce and oxymel in front of Mansour. Mansour was sitting on the edge of the wooden bed, on the kilim. His legs were crossed and he was having a conversation with the doctor, Khojasteh's husband. I shied away from him, but he paid no attention to me. He seemed to be lost in his own misfortunes, just like I was. Mansour was truly a handsome man, well-dressed and cordial. He always observed the rule of thumb. He came across as a complete gentleman and an esquire. But, in my eyes, he was just another figure in a mural painting. I knew only too well that he was still upset with me, that he harboured a grudge against me. So, had he just come to show off his grandeur and opulence to me?

I rose to my feet. I called out to dayeh, took her to one side, and said: "Dayeh jan, is there any 'ash left for agha Mansour's driver? Give him some tea too."

I ruled over the household now that my mother was tired out and preferred to rest. She had gladly handed the running of the house over to me with ease of mind. Dayeh left. I stood there, looking at the garden, deep in thought. Manouchehr was running around my feet and playing tag with the other children. I was miles away. The same old thoughts had rushed to my head once again and my heart was melting away with the pain of past trials and the prospects of a grim future. No, it could not go on like this. I had to attend Namousse School, take the exam and study to become a teacher. I had to keep myself busy. I felt useless. I had to do something to stop myself from losing my mind. Yes, that was it. I wanted to become a teacher.

Manouchehr ran a circle around me again. He grabbed my skirt and peeked at his playmates, laughing and hiding behind me. Impatiently, I pulled my skirt out of his hands and said: "Manouchehr, go play some-where else. I don't feel like it," and I turned around.

It was just then that I caught a glimpse of a fleeting light for a brief moment; the light in Mansour's eyes, earnest and penetrating, gazing at me from head to toe. Only momentarily – and then he turned away. In that heartbeat, I told myself I had imagined it. Yet, my heart trembled, not out of love for Mansour, but from the fear of suddenly realising what had brought him to the gardens that day. Both Mansour and I felt apprehensive until it was time to go home at the end of the day. Until sundown, he sat stiff as a poker - as Nezhat put it - saying only an occasional word. He did not even smile. He was far too solemn for words. In order to make conversation with him, my mother asked politely: "How is Nahid jan?"

Mansour's face lit up instantly like the rising sun. A smile came to his lips, and he answered: "She's well, very well indeed. She's turning into a sweet child; she kisses your hand."

My mother said: "Kisses for her bright, moonlike[229] face."

Khojasteh picked up after my mother: "She's truly as beautiful as the bright moon. I have never seen such a beautiful baby."

And the thorn of sadness pierced my heart again. I was angry at Man-sour for no reason at all. I glanced at him, only to meet his cold, indifferent eyes. If my eyes could find the power, they would fire at him like a cannon ball. Mansour felt this only too well, and continued to look into my eyes with his cold, indifferent gaze.

Summer passed. Autumn went by and winter came. I would occasionally see Mansour during this time, at my uncle's house, at our house, at Nezhat's house, or at my cousins'. But I never saw that furtive look again, and I was grateful for it. Perhaps, it had just been my mistake. It is not right. These looks are not right. It is best that they do not exist. I felt nothing towards Mansour. I had enjoyed his admiring look, although short-lived. Like other women, I too enjoyed arousing a sense of admiration in others and listening to their compliments. But if a man should ever believe that this enjoyment is a sign of surrender, he is sadly mistaken. Love had enslaved me once and brought me to my knees. And then, it was as if a little door leading to my heart had shut down. Or perhaps, I had grown up, become wiser. Perhaps nature had run its course in my case, accomplished its task, and left me to my own devices. I longed to fall in love once again. In love with someone, maybe Mansour for instance, with the same ardour, the same enthusiasm, the same magnetism as before. If only I could be lovesick, incoherent and restless again. But, I knew that was no longer conceivable. It was over. As my father had said, I had run aground in the worst possible way.

***

It was pouring down with sleet. I got home in my overcoat and hat, clutching my umbrella. I went up the stairs, took off my coat and handed the umbrella to dayeh khanoum. My dayeh seemed uneasy. She was not her usual self. She wanted to say something, but could not bring herself round to doing it. Perhaps mother had forbidden it. The lights in the hallway were on. I asked: "Where's Manouchehr dayeh khanoum?" "He's in his room, doing his homework."

My mother appeared at that moment and, in a hushed voice, signalled to me with her hand: "Come here Mahboub. I want to talk to you."

-What is it khanoum jan?

-Mansour agha's been sitting here since this afternoon; he says I've come to talk to Mahboubeh. It's a private matter.

-To me?

-That's what he says.

-Where's he now?

-In the panjdari.

-Come in with me khanoum jan.

-No. Go by yourself, see what he wants with you. What do you want me to come for?

A little bird told my mother, dayeh jan and myself why he was there. There was laughter in my mother's eyes as she looked at dayeh.

-Salam

He was facing the window with his back to the door. He turned around slowly, rigid and formal, holding his hands behind him.

-It's my duty to say hello to you first.

-You've no idea how snowy it is outside!

-How can I not? I'm looking at it!

I smiled. I had said something silly. I was looking for something to break the ice. Silence was dangerous. It made him feel more intimate. He might find the courage to say something I did not want to hear. I went to the fireplace and warmed my hands. I could hear the crackling of wood. I asked: "Have you had anything to eat?" "Yes, I've been well taken care of."

I went towards the door and asked for some tea in a loud voice.

-Have another chai. It's not binding! I'm so cold. Tea is lovely in this weather.

He said: "Your wish is my command."

I looked into his eyes. They were cold and serious. And yet, his words were quite suggestive. I said hastily: "Why're you standing? Please sit down."

I put a chair next to the fireplace and sat down. As I watched him anxiously for an awkward moment, he also pulled up a chair to the other side of the fireplace and sat opposite me to my surprise. Dayeh served the tea. I was relieved. The more crowded the room was, the better I felt. I cannot play Leili and Majnoun anymore. I can no longer play these childish games. Dayeh also placed a small side table next to us and left. I knew she would be looking from the gap in the door. But, I forgot all about her right away as Mansour went straight to the point.

-Mahboubeh, I have come to talk to you. It's time now.

I was nervous. I wanted to get up. I put the estekan in its silver holder on the table, and said: "Well then, allow me to call my khanoum jan."

He leaned forward, took hold of my wrist and made me sit down; but he did not let go of my hand: "I said only with you."

My hand was resting on my knee, underneath his. It felt as if Nezhat was holding my hand, as if Khojasteh was holding it. But I saw him blush. He was not holding my hand tightly. He lowered his head, looked at our hands for a moment, and then pulled his away. Silence fell on the room. I no longer tried to break the stillness. He had said what he had come to say. He crossed his arms and legs and stared at the flames in the fireplace.

-Mahboubeh, I still want to marry you.

I shuddered. I envisaged the tormented face of a woman destroyed by smallpox, despite all her poise and noble birth. I saw that she had a baby girl; that she took care of her own son and that of her rival. I felt anger towards Mansour. I saw myself being lowered to Kokab's level. Mansour had not even asked me to marry him as such. His tone of voice was nearly authoritative, as if I was his given right; as if I had been hoping and waiting for such a proposal and counting the days for this moment. I said:

-But, I still don't want to marry you.

He got to his feet, went towards the window, and began watching the snow again. He remained silent for a while as he stood there with his hands in his pockets. Then, very calmly, like a father encouraging his child to jump over a brook, he said: "You will. You have to."

I was shocked. I said: "Mansour, you have a great lady for a wife. I haven't seen her for myself, but I've heard so much about her. She's kind, distinguished, educated and accomplished. I've heard so much about what a complete lady she is. She's looking after her rival's son, your son, so beautifully. And now, barely a year has passed since she gave birth and you've come to marry me?!"

He put his hand on his forehead, as if he was in pain, as if he was ashamed. He said: "Do you suppose I don't know these things? I've told Nimtaj a hundred times. She's been telling me you have to marry Mahboubeh from the day she heard you were divorced. She said if you won't ask for her hand, I'll do it myself. But I wouldn't give in. She was pregnant. I didn't want to torment her. Then, she was breastfeeding the baby. Moreover, her heart's not in such a good condition either. But, this is what she wants. She's making me. It was the same thing with Ashraf. Except, that time, I didn't want to get married. But this time, I do. I want you Mahboubeh."

He turned towards me. He approached me and placed his hand on the back of my chair. He leaned forward so far that I thought he was going to kiss me. At once, I thought to myself that if he did, I would either have to leave the room or slap him. But, he did not kiss me. He simply said: "Mahboubeh, I want you. I've always wanted you. ou have to marry me. You know very well that you do. Just tell me when?"

-Never

-Why?

-Because you have a wife, a good wife. And I've already been in love once. I lost my mind. I got married, and I lived to regret it. I can no longer love anyone Mansour. Not that I'm still thinking about that worthless man! Not at all! I'm simply no longer in that mood. I'm no longer in a receptive frame of mind. That sort of longing for anyone will never again nestle in my heart. I despise anything to do with love and marriage. Once bitten, twice shy. Perhaps, this too, was just my bad luck that I set eyes on Rahim the shop boy with only the shirt on his back, and it was love at first sight, that I let him get under my skin and followed him like a faithful dog. And yet, when I see you Mansour, a gentleman with such poise and grace, I feel as if you're my brother. Don't get upset now…! But I don't want you. So why should I make your wife suffer? I've had a taste of it myself. I know what it's like to love a man who spends his time with another woman! I know what it feels like! I've had a taste of that. I know only too well. I also know how much Nimtaj khanoum loves you. Why should I break her heart? By God, it's sinful.

Mansour sat down, and in an infinitely soft and kind voice, he said: "I know you're not in love with me, nor do I expect you to be. But, you started off on the wrong foot. You believed that married life's the same as blind love and that blind love will lead to eternal happiness. And when you found out that Rahim's not the idol you worshiped in your mind, you were appalled and disgusted by the whole thing, right? But it's not like that Mahboubeh.

Happiness runs away from blind love, the same way a jinn is afraid of *Bismillah*[230]. You made a mistake once; don't do it again. If you can find fault with me, turn me down. Otherwise, become my wife. Let love nestle in your heart little by little this time. I don't expect the same love from you that you had for Rahim. But, let me take care of you. Let me sooth your sorrows. Let me be your husband, and affection will follow. Love is like wine, Mahboubeh. You have to allow it to age for years until it finds its flavour and maturity to intoxicate you. Otherwise, if it is sweated out quickly like a high fever, it'll be over in no time at all. Give me time. Perhaps I can make you happy."

-You're right Mansour. I nearly perished with that high fever. I used to ask God why do you torment me like this? How have I sinned that you've set your wrath on me? That I should want Rahim, but Mansour has no place in my heart with all his virtues? Why…?

He interrupted me: "Don't blame God and his Prophet Mahboubeh. Why would God begrudge a fifteen, sixteen-year old girl? Be angry with her? This is the devil's doing. It's the forces of nature. It's the laws of survival that take hold of Basir ol-Molk's daughter, take her to a carpentry and make her fall madly in love with an amorous shop boy. I only understood this in later years. When you first married him - at the time when I was badly offended, when you had threaded on my pride and character - I kept telling myself look whom she's sold me out to! But, when I reflected on it, I told myself that Leili has to be seen through the eyes of Majnoun before he can be judged; that beauty is in the eye of the beholder. Damn this omnipotent nature! So, I went and married Nimtaj. My mother kept saying don't do it Mansour, don't do this to yourself. I said khanoum jan, I wanted Mahboubeh. Now that it wasn't meant to be, I'll marry just to make you happy. What difference does it make to you whom I marry? Whether she's a pretty or ugly? It was as if I did it in spite of everything and everyone, even myself. It's a long story. My mother said may God curse Mahboubeh. I said khanoum jan, curse her; curse her until your malediction takes an even stronger hold of me too. God cursed her that my life became so tragic. Now, keep on cursing her…!"

I said: "That's enough Mansour."

-No, this is just the beginning. Your life is ruined, isn't it? You say no matter how hard you try, you can't love again. Well, marry me then. Make me happy at least. It's no use crying over spilt milk. At least, let me benefit from your misfortune. I will marry you Mahboubeh, whether you like it or not. I made a mistake last time. I was young. I was foolish. played the hero. I shouldn't have given in when you said you didn't want me. I should've insisted on taking you to the registry office and marrying you no matter what. It would've been to both our advantages that way.

I would be lying if I said I did not enjoy the way he spoke and admired me. I stood up.

He said: "Where to?"

-I'll go get some more tea.

-Sit down. I've had enough tea tonight to last me a lifetime. What I want is for you to marry me. I'm amazed when I look at you. How you've changed over these past few years. Instead of bending your back, making you older and breaking you up, all that suffering has made you more beautiful. You've become more coquettish and you don't even know it. You've lost your puppy fat. You're slimmer and taller. Your look's more mature, and your face is more feminine and sweet. Your behaviour's more refined. It's no wonder that I wanted you to be my wife ever since I was a child.

I said: "What about Nimtaj khanoum?!"

-Well, that's a different story altogether. Unlike all newly-weds, we just sat down and talked on our wedding night. She said: "I've suffered too much. God only knows how much sarcasm I've had to take; that my younger sisters were married before me; that no one knocked on our door for me. All of this made me suffer. So, I prayed to my God silently. I asked him to grant me a reputable and respectable husband, even if just in name. I know I'm older than you are. I'm also pock faced. I have no expectations of you. Just be my husband. It's alright even if you don't spend the nights here with me. I'm happy. So long as they say what a wonderful husband Nimtaj has is enough for me. You're free from tonight to marry whomever you wish; a young, healthy wife. You must. You mustn't suffer for my sake. Just promise me one thing. Promise that you'll respect me, that you won't reproach me or allow others to humiliate me. That's all."

From that day onwards, I have never said a harsh word to her. She was the one who insisted that I should marry Ashraf. She would always say I know life for a handsome young man like you is difficult with someone like me. I explained the situation to Ashraf right from the start. We made our agreements. But then, she went back on her word after the first couple of months. She would say why should Nimtaj be khanoum bozorg, and me khanoum kouchik? Why do you go to her one night and come to me the next. Why won't you divorce her? And I said: "I'll divorce you, but I won't divorce Nimtaj. That woman's an angel." After you were divorced, Nimtaj said to me: "I know you're fond of Mahboubeh. Go and marry her." And I said: "Are you looking for trouble again?" She said: "No, there's a world of difference between her and Ashraf. She's from your own blood, she's of a good lineage, and she can't have…"

Mansour stopped himself short. Smiling, I completed his sentence for him: "And she can't have children, right? This is what she said? She didn't say if you marry a young girl, your wife will no longer be appealing to you once this one gets pregnant? Isn't this what she said?"

-Yes, this is what she said. She said someone like her won't strike me at the roots. She won't try to belittle my children in order to uphold her own. She said I would have to marry some day and that you're the best choice for me. She's right Mahboubeh. All you have to do is be respectful of Nimtaj. Let her be the lady of the house; let her heart be happy by being khanoum bozorg. You're the only owner of my heart. Discontented, I said: "You should've spoken to my agha jan first."

- So that you can make me feel humiliated and unsettled again, *like a stone resting on slippery ice*[231]? So that you can say you don't want me again? You were already headstrong and stubborn at fifteen. You were already rebellious. And yet, you ask me to speak to your agha jan at your age now? I won't listen to you anymore. You're the one I want Mahboubeh. All you have to do is accept Nimtaj. I'll do the rest.

-I haven't said yes yet that you're laying down the law!

-You will say yes. You have to say yes. Think hard about it.

I held my head high, like the day we spent time in my uncle's gardens, and I said angrily: "Are you reproaching me, casting my adolescent years in my teeth? My agha jan never reproached me, so what right do you have to do it? It makes you happy that I cannot have children? You don't really want me for myself. You just want me to compensate for Nimtaj's unsightliness; so that she can be the real thing, and I the substitute."

I knew only too well that I must not speak in those terms. I knew I was raising my voice over my head. I was shouting like Rahim's mother; making cynical remarks. But I was beside myself. I was edgy and irritable. And yet, it was not just anger making me roar in that way. It was not simply sorrow and grief. Although I did grieve over what I had done to myself, that I had mutilated myself, and that I could no longer have children. I was so weary of God punishing me. But, that was not all. I had learned my lesson well alongside Rahim the shop boy over the past six, seven years. I had been a conscientious student. I had learned the lessons of aggressiveness, belligerence and impudence by heart. I had lost my former calm, composure and abstinence and was easily outraged. Like my former husband, I had become void of positive moral characteristics. I had sunk to his level. I would close my eyes shut and open my mouth wide.

Mansour was looking into my eyes flabbergasted. He did not seem to expect this type of behaviour from me. I saw a flame of grief kindle in his eyes. I saw his chin, which resembled my own, quiver sorrowfully, in the same way my own chin quivered in anger. He stared at me, and then said calmly, very calmly: "If that's how you want to put it."

All of a sudden, I wanted him to ask me again. But, he didn't. He just said: "Think about it" and left.

My mother was happy. Father was happy. My uncle and his wife were happy. I did not know what to do. I searched my heart to find love for Mansour, but there was none there. There was not even any sign of kindness or attraction. Because there was no heart left at all; it was cold, so cold; made of stone. I told myself a hundred times a day that I will say no, I will not go through with it. What kind of joyless sin is this? Why should I break Nimtaj's heart when I do not even want him? Why should I make her suffer? But then, I saw my mother's eager eyes pleading silently, my father's keen eyes. Their begging, pleading silence left me no choice. I did not want to break their hearts again.

Every time there was talk of Mansour, my mother's eyes sparkled. My father smiled. I knew that agha jan had asked my mother not to talk about it to me. Not to pressurise me. My father knew better than to force me into an unwanted marriage. He was afraid of another failure. He was frightened of my fragile spirits. Yet, I knew only too well that I had to get married sooner or later. But to whom? Surely, my chances of remarrying were very slim. No young man would be willing to marry a sterile divorcée. All of this was not only because I had said yes to Rahim, but also because I went downtown with Roghieh, took out a part of me and threw it away. I killed my bird of good omen with a single feather. I knew only too well that such a passionate love would never burn inside me again, and I also hoped never to experience that heavy, bitter feeling of hatred either.

Now that I had achieved what I had languished for so amorously, and put behind me what I had turned away from disillusioned and frightened, I knew that my only chance of deliverance from this monotonous life, from the repetitiveness of waking up in the morning and going to sleep at night, from daytime idleness to midnight crying, from feeling null and void to praying for death to come to me, was a second marriage. Although I had grown into a cold, unfeeling woman, I still knew that Mansour was the only man I could bear to have in my life. I wanted to find peace. I was looking for a purpose to my life. I was glad to be appeasing the broken hearts of my parents and, with insight I could not envisage anyone better than Mansour for myself. This time, I wanted to choose intelligently and logically by consulting my parents. I was being asked to be khanoum kouchik for the remainder of my days. There was no other option. Whatever it was, it was better than loneliness. I had paid a very high price to gain this knowledge. I sent a message to Mansour: "I will become your wife."

He put three shares out of six of the Shemiran gardens in my name. But alas! No one mentioned a wedding reception. It was not possible to celebrate, for Nimtaj's sake. It would have set her heart ablaze. It would have been beyond tolerance for her. Thus, one night, my uncle and his wife, all brothers and sisters, cousins with their spouses and children, and my maternal and paternal aunts on their own, came to our house. Just like an ordinary get together. I was entertaining the guests together with dayeh. We sat together, talked and laughed. We had tea and sweets, and the mullah came and performed the ceremony. Once again, I was left wishing for a wedding reception.

Mansour took me to the Shemiran gardens, to his own place. The grand manor in the northern section of the gardens belonged to Nimtaj and her children. He took me to the southern section. There was a small, newly-built house with two to three rooms, at a distance of a hundred metres from the main building. The space in-between was taken up by a pond full of water, fruit trees and a few flowerbeds in front of the northern building, and one flowerbed outside the southern building. The southern building had been constructed for Ashraf khanoum. It became my home.

Nimtaj was not home. She had gone to a month long pilgrimage with the children. She had gone to the holy city of Mashhad. I knew why. She had left the house for us. I knew how restless her heart was on a night when Mansour's heart was so happy. My small house was not short of anything. My father had sent a dowry, and some things had also been provided by Mansour. There was a world of difference between this and my previous home. Mansour was kind. He was in love with me. His amorous behaviour reminded me of my own past. I felt kindness towards him. And although I felt sorry for him, I was still cold and indifferent. I tried to keep my feelings secret from him.

The satin bed linens had been spread on the spring bed with bronze legs and a bronze bed head. I was standing next to the window, watching Nimtaj's building. The main part of this household was that building over there. Mansour was sitting on the edge of the bed, watching me.

-You know Mahboubeh. It's not just your wild hair cascading around your shoulders that takes my breath away. It's not just your face that's so beautiful. You seem to be in a state of spiritual insobriety; your ways have become mystical.

I laughed and said: "You're never this amorous in a crowd. You're cold and grim. No one would believe these words of Mansour. Do you remember Chaharshanbeh Suri? You were so cold, serious, and ill-humoured that I wanted to ask you what was on your mind! Why are you so distant from the mundane and the ordinary world? What could be filling your mind so much as to make you so aloof and unaware of the joys of others!"

He said: "Really? Did you really want to know? As you jumped over the fire with your wild hair and your rosy cheeks, I was looking at you when you were so indifferent towards me. You were the embodiment of this verse to me:

With wild hair, besmiling and glowing and making merry
Clothe pulled apart, poetry on the lips and a cup to carry

And I knew that, deep inside, you wanted me; even though you may not have known it then."

I laughed coquettishly: "What nonsense! I was not even thinking about you that night."

-So why wouldn't you pay any attention to me then? Why did you make everyone jump over the fire except for me? How come Khojasteh and Nezhat were joking with me, but you ignored me? *If Leili did not long for my love, why did she only break my pot?*[232]

He smiled and spoke softly. His firm, masculine voice was mature and soothing at the same time.

I wanted to listen to him talk. I wanted him to read Hafez with his gentle, peaceful voice for me to listen to. If only the fire in the fireplace would never burn out. His kind, gentle words were a testimony to his rich cultural background. Thirsting for affection and tenderness, my shattered soul found solace in his sweet talking. His deep, caressing look soothed the wounds of my heart like an elixir. I knew I could depend on him. I knew he would support me. He was the kind of man who had respect for his wife.

He played the tar for me; just for me and for his own passion. The days passed, peaceful and unhurried, as if a runaway stream sloping downwards. The lights of Nimtaj's house were out for one month only.

The day Nimtaj returned from their pilgrimage to Mashhad with her own children and Ashraf's son, it was ten o'clock in the morning. I was sleeping next to Mansour, calm and relaxed. We were woken up by the noisy comings and goings and the children's lively cries. Mansour jumped up and saw the children from behind the window. They had arrived a day earlier than expected. He dressed up as fast as lightening, while continuously repeating: "Get dressed Mahboub. Hurry, khanoum's here. We've to go see her."

I jumped out of bed. I was going around in circles, opening and closing wardrobe doors, looking for something suitable to wear, to comb my hair and wash up. But Mansour's repetition of khanoum khanoum drove me insane. That he kept saying we have to go and see her upset me. I was not a fool. I was fully aware of my obligations. If only Mansour would stop giving orders and making me so nervous. Nevertheless, I kept smiling. I finally got round to wearing my shoes: "Fine Mansour jan, I'll be ready in a minute." And my blood boiled at the same time. I wanted to set fire to this life.

I did not put any makeup on. I did not want to go overboard. There was no need. Why would I want to show off, when my rival had already accepted her weak point? When she had already lost? Mansour started again: "Put up your hair Mahboub jan. Don't let it hang down like this."

I could not understand. If he really wanted me as much as he claimed, then why is he trying so hard to please Nimtaj? I opened my mouth and said: "Fine Mansour jan," and smiled at him. I was struggling with my hair when Nimtaj's maid brought a message that khanoum is coming over. She has gone to freshen up and will get here in a few minutes.

I had just managed to put my hair up when the door opened and a lady walked in, wearing a white, flower-patterned chador. I knew it was Nimtaj underneath, from the way she was covering her face. Only her very large, elongated eyes could be seen, although her eyelids had not been spared the ravages of smallpox.

-Salam

She sounded happy and cheerful. The pin I had put in my hair so hurriedly came undone and my hair flew open. Perhaps if Mansour had not insisted so much, I may have fastened it better, or used three or four hair pins instead of one.

I said: "Oh, I wanted to come to you."

Her gaze contemplated me from head to toe: "There is no difference. Anyway, you're newlywed. It was my duty to come and see you."

There was no sign of any jealousy or sarcasm in her words. The way she spoke even disarmed the enemy. I forgot about Mansour: "Please, come into the parlour. I must apologise, the fire's gone out!"

-No, no. I won't bother you. I'll come into the sitting room. It's more comfortable under the korsi.

-Please come in. You're welcome.

She was taller than me; almost the same height as Mansour. She sat under the korsi, which had also gone cold. I lit the fireplace. I could feel her gaze on by back, on my hair, all over me from head to toe. I said: "I'll be with you in a moment. Please excuse me."

My servant brought in the tea she had prepared. She also brought sweets and other nibbles, took a peek at us and left. The fire was now going well and warming up the room. Mansour had gone to see the children. He had put on that stiff, serious look again. I sat on the korsi quilt lopsided and paid her my compliments: "You're very welcome khanoum bozorg." And by using her 'khanoum bozorg' title, I displayed my acceptance of her superiority.

She looked at me in silence and said: "You are truly beautiful." Then, she took out a parcel from underneath her chador and handed it to me: "It's a present from Mashhad; a small gift for you from my journey."

It was nabat and a whole lot of saffron.

-Thank you for going to all this trouble.

Then, she placed a small box in the copper tray over the korsi: "I should've come much earlier to extend my congratulations. But I was travelling. This is a small gift for you. Please accept it."

I opened the box. It was a gold bib necklace, a bribe, a declaration of surrender. It was the offering of a weak ruler to the victorious sultan. I felt sorry for her. Quietly, I muttered: "There was no need. There was really no need."

Suddenly, the children's noise filled the house. The boys, her own son and belated Ashraf's son, were both clean and smart, both equal. She had not treated the boys any differently. I hesitated momentarily. I wondered who had the winning card here? Me or her? I asked her to send her maid to get Nahid. I kissed the boys. Despite their rowdiness, they were both very polite. They lady who was in charge of their upbringing was obviously very capable. Nahid was brought over and placed in my arms. I was swooning over her. I wanted her to be mine; to be my child. She did not cry in my arms. She just kept pulling herself towards the nibbles on the korsi and getting what she wanted. She was so sweet, so loveable, that she got everything she wanted from everyone. The boys were tired from their trip and left. Nahid fell asleep. I pulled the korsi quilt over her so she wouldn't catch cold. She was soft and delicate. I am not quite sure why, I suddenly felt like confiding in Nimtaj. I said: "You're so lucky."

She was taken aback: "I'm so lucky?"

-Yes, with these beautiful children that you have. Each one's like a bouquet of flowers.

Her eyes looked sad and she went quiet. Then, she took the chador off her head slowly and said: "Well, take a good look so you won't feel any regrets."

I was shaken. What had smallpox done to her! There was not an untouched place left in all her face and neck. Her hair was the worst. It could be counted one by one. The poor thing had tried to fortify it and make it grow back by using henna. Now I could understand why Mansour kept asking me to put my hair up. I felt ashamed. I felt like an unholy person. I was ashamed of my long, full head of hair. I was affected by her kind, strong character. I found her morality superior to mine. She was someone to be respected. It was at this moment that she found a place in my heart. It was hard to tell whether she had been pretty or ugly in rude health! Only her full lips had been spared by smallpox to a certain extent. She smiled a soft, sad smile and asked: "Am I still so lucky?"

Without thinking, I said: "I, too, am damaged. I can't have children," and my eyes filled with tears.

-I know.

She went quiet. Then, with her head down, she said softly: "I have come to ask a favour of you. Don't try to belittle me in Mansour's eyes, because I'm not his *sogoli*[233]; especially now that I've seen you. I'm a mother. Don't let it make you happy to make my children fatherless. Don't make us homeless. That's all I as of you."

As she pleaded at the height of ugliness and helplessness, I was charmed by her character and dignity. I said: "I would never do such a thing. I knew from the start that you have children. Even if agha wants to leave you short, I'll never let him. He'll have to throw me out first, before he does what he wants with you."

I was saying these things from the bottom of my heart. I was not pretending or being deceitful. I would not even allow myself to call my husband by his first name in front of her. I did not want her to sense the intimacy between him and me. I did not want her to suffer. She said: "Don't you ever think that I've asked Mansour to spend every other night at my place! It's enough for me to have a husband, to be under his wing. Now that God has given me these children, that my enemies can no longer gloat, I expect nothing more of him. All I ask is to be respected. Just to have his name and his protection for his children."

I said: "I won't let a single thing upset your children khanoum, not anyone's child. I had a son myself." And tears streamed down my face. I told myself: "Fiddlesticks, have you turned on the waterworks again? You just couldn't stop yourself again, could you? Again…" But, this old wound would not heal. It will never heal.

She became nervous, and said: "I'm sorry I've upset you first thing in the morning…"

-You didn't upset me. I did this to myself. I brought it onto myself. Not a day goes by when I don't say I repent.

She got up, kissed me on the head, and said warmly: "So many people want to be in your place. I'm one of them." Then, she put on her chador and left.

I sat by the korsi alone and stared out of the window. I was astonished by the games fate played on us. The three of us formed a droll, yet sad triangle. Although we had everything, we still had nothing. Nimtaj only wanted children and the name of a husband, to have a man's protection, and the rest was of no importance to her. Mansour wanted a young and beautiful wife to compensate for his wife's pocked face; and so help me God, I was the devil's advocate and the worst off of all three in this triangle; I had and did not have a husband. I had and did not have children. My presence in that house was required; and yet, to be there or not did not affect their lives in any way. We were two women complementing one another, with no choice but to tolerate the rival. We completed each other, but felt unhappy and dejected with each other's presence at the same time. This was my destiny, and the fate put to paper by my pen for Mansour and Nimtaj.

In our cosy corner in the little house at the end of the garden, we kept warm in the dead of winter and I, with the help of domestics and a gardener, did not have many chores left to do. In fact, I had nothing to do. A door opened into my living quarters from the north side. Ahead of the door, there was a porch filled with pots of bougainvillea and star thistle in the spring, and flowering jasmines in the summer. Inside the building, I had spread a rug on the small landing. Next to the entrance door, I had placed a carved wooden console with a fairly large bronze mirror hanging over it. I always had a large vase of flowers on this table. To the left, exactly opposite the mirror, a coat hanger made of walnut wood had been mounted on the wall. A door opened into my parlour just after the console and mirror. The rooms were filled with carpets and heavy upholstered sofas, and the walls were decorated with paintings chosen and bought by Mansour to his taste. The house had a mystic splendour, and yet I still felt sad. I roamed around in this building like a lost soul, and longed to exchange it all with a little boy. A boy wearing a colourful nightcap while playing by the pond.

Mansour loved drawing. He loved playing his tar. He loved books and had a little drink every now and then. On the left side of the building, there were two nesting rooms separated by a connecting door. Our bedroom window opened into the garden, and the east-facing living room behind it had a fireplace which was replaced by an oil heater in later years. This was my favourite room. It was fairly large. I had put a bench by the window and placed two furnished couches on both sides of the fireplace with a small coffee table in front of each one, decorated with tablecloths I had embroidered myself.

Even so, I always placed a korsi in front of the fireplace in the winter. It was a small, attractive korsi no one could easily ignore and walk past. Although Mansour's library was in Nimtaj's house, who was an avid reader herself, he had brought a number of his books to my place to read on the nights he was with me; he kept these on a bookshelf at the top end of the room, opposite the window; these were books which attracted the attention of any learned person. In the wintery nights of Shemiran, when the snow spread its white coat around us and still kept coming down flake by flake, when it was my turn – and it was my turn every other night – I brewed chai for him. I cooked his favourite meal with my own two hands in the small kitchen at the other end of the building facing the backyard; I placed the sweets I had made – and I was now a master baker thanks to idleness and solitude – in the middle of the large, round copper tray on the korsi; I wore beautiful clothes, put on my perfume, let my hair hang down to my waist, and wait for him to come. He would come and sit down. He was no longer solemn, no longer as stiff as if he had swallowed a cane. He softened up as soon as he walked in through the door, to become loving and passionate, and he called out: "Mahboub darling." And I would die of jealousy thinking is this how he calls Nimtaj too? In this same tone of voice? Did he call her "darling" too? He called her khanoum in my presence. But, he also called me khanoum in front of her. I managed to surprise myself with this uncalled for jealousy. I, who was not in love with Mansour, why was it that I wanted him so whole-heartedly to myself then? Why did I want him heart and soul? I wanted sole, unshared ownership, to the exclusion of all others; I wanted him to only pamper me and spoil me rotten. My female instincts had woken up in me. I wanted exclusivity like any other woman; I had become monopolistic, perhaps even more so than other women. I wanted to possess him.

He would sit and watch me; he ate his dinner, read, and then stared at me again as I walked and worked, sorted out the dishes and cleared up, laughed or got upset. He would say: "Don't you cut your hair short Mahboubeh! Let it hang on your shoulders." And every time he called me "Mahboub jan," it reminded me of Rahim and I was bitten by remorse. If I had not treated myself in that manner, if I had not made that wrong choice, I would not be khanoum kouchik right now, I would not be barren; I would be holding Mansour's baby in my arms. Although his children were like my own, but there was still a world of difference between the beauty of having my own children and looking after those of another woman.

Every time it was Nimtaj's turn, I kept telling myself you pushed him into her arms, and every time it was my turn, my heart filled with the joy of seeing him, having his companionship and taking possession of him. I told myself this is not out of love. It is from wanting to feel superior to Nimtaj. But, a voice inside my head screamed you have lost a priceless jewel. You have created a rival for yourself, and now you are being punished. And I surrendered to this punishment.

Mansour came and played the tar for me.

-Mansour jan, don't play it so loud. Nimtaj will hear and get upset.

He wanted to sit next to me: "Mansour jan, draw the curtains. Nimtaj will see us. It'll be painful for her to see."

When Mansour went to work during the day, the children came to me willingly. They were so sweet-spoken that I would give them all the nibbles I had in the house. Manouchehr also joined this carefree crowd during the summer. I enjoyed their racket and childish plays and watched them with envy. I could not help buying bags full of roasted wheat and hemp nuts, and all the children knew they had to come to me if they wanted any. Children are smart. They knew only too well that I adored them, and they loved me in return. Nimtaj was in charge of ordering the meals. She also hired and fired the help. Nimtaj educated the children.

When they came to see me, Nahid also toddled along behind them. The building belonging to Nimtaj was on two very large floors, and much grander than my house, because Nimtaj had children and I did not. I went to her side of the garden most of the time. Nimtaj seldom came to my building. Not out of malice, but because she was so busy. She only wore a scarf at home and did not hide her face from anyone. Nimtaj's maid, who had also brought her up and loved her very dearly, pulled a sour face every time she saw me. She was the only one in that house who was not happy with me. At times, I was the one who tutored the children. I played with Nahid who was teething and wanted to bite my hand. The children grew up, grownups aged, and the elderly like my father…

The electromagnetic phone rang. The children were falling over themselves to pick it up, but they could not reach it. It was my khanoum jan. My heart sank. I knew my agha jan was not well. I often went to visit him. But, on that particular day, my mother told me grimly that my father had asked for me. He had asked for his daughter. When we arrived in Mansour's black Chevrolet, everyone was already there. My father asked for his children one by one and talked to them. And one by one, they left his room with tearful eyes.

My father called for me and asked: "Mahboub isn't here?" I went in. Mansour was accompanying me. My father said: "You came my dear girl."

I kneeled beside his bed: "Yes agha jan. How are you feeling?"

-Very bad my dear girl, very bad.

My chin was quivering again. When would these tears let go of me? I did not know. I said: "Agha jan…"

He said: "Don't cry my dear. Death comes to us all."

-Oh no, I'm not cr…

Mansour sat on the side of my father's bed. His eyes were also bloodshot. He took my father's hand: "Salam amou jan."

-May you live long and grow old my son. I entrust Mahboub into your hands. I feel reassured that you'll look after her. Do you know how proud you made me when you married Mahboubeh?"

Mansour smiled faintly: "Don't talk like this amou jan."

-No, no. Don't be so modest. Listen Mahboubeh, I sold the house I had bought for you formerly, that you put in my name for the divorce. Did I do wrong?

I pictured my son under the white sheet, next to the wall. If only I could cut that piece out of that house and take it with me. Then, I would also keep it in this chest. I said: "No agha jan, you did right."

My father, who had full power of attorney from me, continued: "Instead, I bought you a plot of land in Gholhak, next to our own garden. Of course, I added a little bit of my own money to it. It's only four or five hundred square metres. But, it's still not bad. I wanted to know if you're happy with this arrangement?"

-I've always been happy with you agha jan.

-Mahboub, don't let Manouchehr be sad. I've also told your sisters. Manouchehr has to study. He must go wherever it's necessary. Don't hold back on spending; from his own share of money course. He must go to the best schools. I'm putting him in your charge; first you, then your mother. He might want to go abroad, and your mother might not consent out of motherly love. But, you must back him up. He has the right to do anything that's right for him. Anything that allows him to progress and advance. You're responsible for him. You're my successor in this matter. Do you understand?

I understood that I had to look upon Manouchehr as my own son. A son that no longer existed. But, I could not hold back the tears long enough to breathe, never mind speak. Mansour said: "Amou jan, do you trust me too? I promise on behalf of Mahboubeh and myself. Rest assured." My father said: "May you grow old my son. My mind is at ease." He went quiet, and then he made his will. He explained what he had left to me and Manouchehr one by one, although he had officially registered everything beforehand. Then he said: "Mahboub jan, I know you often go to see Esmat khanoum. But, I want to emphasise again that you always pay her a visit. Don't hesitate to help her and her son. They have no one."

-Of course I will agha jan. I would not have left them alone, even if you hadn't told me.

He laughed, stroked my head and said: "You're still a firebrand. Go now. I want to sleep."

My tears would not let go of me.

-Get up girl. What's this all about? I'm still here!

I got up. The scenes of Hafez poetry evenings, the night of Manouchehr's birth, my wedding day, Hassan khan's house, the day Rahim came to our house for the divorce and my father's yelling, all flashed in front of my eyes. Above all, I remembered Rahim's swearing. The profanities he used to call me and my father; the swearwords he called this respectable, harmless man. Suddenly, I wished he was there so I could cut open his jugular. I leaned over. My hand was still in my father's hand. I asked: "Agha jan…?" A lump blocked my throat again. I took a deep breath and said: "Agha jan… have you… forgiven me?"

I wish I had gone mute and not asked. Tears filled his eyes. He squeezed my hand firmly, shame-faced as I was, then brought it up and kissed it.

Life had once again found its routine. It was spring, autumn, winter, and summer once again. I was crazy. I wanted a child and could not have one. Why did I always have to wish for the impossible? I was looking for treatment. I began with home remedies first. I did everything anyone recommended – from illiterate female servants, to old wives, and sorcery – all to no avail. I already knew right from the start. I knew better than anyone what I had done to myself. I was afraid to go to trained physicians. I knew their diagnosis before going. Nevertheless, I told Mansour that I wanted to seek serious treatment. He laughed and said: "It's wonderful Mahboub jan."

But, he did not seem very enthusiastic. I sensed an indifference in him. He just said that for my sake. He already had children. Nothing was missing in his life. I knew this only too well, and it made my blood boil. Nimtaj knew that I was seeking treatment, and it filled her eyes with worry. I asked Khojasteh's husband for help. He introduced me to a number of his specialist colleagues. I went and sat in their waiting rooms with great anxiety. The smell of medicines filled my nose and gave me hope. My heart was in my throat and raced the same way it did that day I was happily going down town for a termination. The physicians were kind and polite. Initially, they all smiled, they were all optimistic. They said there is hope for a young lady like yourself. But, after a while, when I had been examined, when I had used their medications without results, the smiles were wiped off their faces. They became grave and serious. They shook their heads grimly from side to side and chewed their words. I stared at their mouths, as if to drag out a positive answer. I was like a condemned person awaiting the judge's last words. The call for pardon, or the order of execution. They understood how I felt, so they turned away to avoid looking into my eyes, and they would softly say that I must not lose hope, that God is great and merciful, that everything is possible if it is his will. And I moved on to the next doctor, another long period of treatment, and the same answer.

Eventually, I fell apart and washed my hands of everything. I had become ill, sensitive and vulnerable. I was quick-tempered, but only towards Mansour. I held back in the presence of others. I respected Nimtaj. I refrained from showing my feelings and only cried next to Mansour at nights. I made life bitter to taste for him and then became increasingly worried that he might take refuge in Nimtaj's arms. At last, I turned to Nezhat: "Nezhat, I'm dying of grief."

She looked at me sadly: "Don't do it Mahboub. Don't do this to yourself."

I raised my voice: "What can I do? I can't help it. I'm jealous of Nimtaj. I want Mansour to suffer; I don't want him to be happy. I want Mansour all to myself; to live just with me…"

Nezhat interrupted me and, in a reproachful yet advising tone of voice, she said: "Mahboubeh, don't get upset, but you've become bad-tempered and aggressive. You're looking for trouble. It's as if you can't have peace and quiet. You've become like your mother-in-law. Like Rahim's mother… Agha jan and khanoum jan did not bring us up this way. You're not ex-pected to behave in this manner. You've become unreasonable and difficult. You're looking for an excuse to blame other people for your own mistakes. You want to bully the weak. You're even jealous of that poor Nimtaj, who probably suffers every time she sees you, your looks, your hair! You only have yourself to blame for this calamity. You have to take the blame. As you make your bed, so you must lie in it."

She was right. She was saying the exact same thing I had already told myself a hundred times. Wistfully, I asked: "What should I do then Nezhat? Tell me what to do?"

-Take a trip. Leave Tehran for a month or two. Get away from your life here. Go to Mashhad. Go to Imam Reza's shrine (AS) and tie a wishing ribbon there. Your wish might come true. Go take the weight off your bones. In this way, you'll appreciate Mansour more, and he'll appreciate you!

I smiled bitterly: "I don't think he cares much whether I'm here or not!"

Nezhat rolled her eyes at me.

Surprised, Mansour said: "Two months…?"

-Yes Mansour. I have to go away for two months. I have to calm down.

He looked at me with a kind smile: "You? Calm down? I don't believe it. I've never seen anyone with a more fiery temper than you. There's no calmness to be found for you." He laughed and continued: "And this is what enkindles your love in me."

We left with my dayeh jan. She was the only one who could feel my pain and share it. She was the only one who had seen my son. We took up residence in a clean, tidy house belonging to one of my mother's distant relatives. I visited the shrine every day. I sat and stared at the mausoleum for hours, as if my heart had found a link to it; as if I would rid myself of all my pain and find peace just by looking at it. I spent the first month asking Imam Reza for a cure day and night.

-Just a boy. Just one.

Begging for the same thing every day, reciting the same thing over and over again to have my wish granted. Every morning, I would say:

-Dayeh jan, I dreamed of a dove last night.

-Bless you child. You'll have a baby.

-Dayeh jan, I dreamed of a swimming pool filled with clear, blue water.

-It's a good omen. You'll be cured child. Water is light.

-Daye jan, I dreamed of a man with a glowing face. He gave me a mirror.

-Well, well, there you go, you've got your cure from Imam Reza.

And then, my eyes gradually opened up to the realities. I accepted the truth bit by bit, at a slow pace, as if someone was calming me down with philosophical logic; as if someone was comforting me with scholarly advice and giving me solace. Yet, I was afraid that this feeling of calmness might be temporary. That upon my return to Tehran and by distancing myself from Imam Reza, the fire burning inside me would spark and burst at once, like a bubble resting over water. I was afraid that the flames inside me would flare up again, burn me and turn my life upside down. I did not trust myself. My own hot blood frightened me. I recited my *zekre*[234] day and night over the second month: "Oh Imam Reza, calm down my heart. This one wish isn't impossible at least! This shouldn't be a problem! Turn my crazy heart cold. Turn cold this fire burning inside my heart, or turn me cold by death."

I no longer cried. I no longer pleaded. I had reached a mystic surrender and resignation. I had accepted my infirmity with great desperation and I was looking forward to seeing Mansour on my return. I arrived in Tehran, and Shemiran. Everyone came to greet me - the boys, who were jofully waiting for their presents and rejoicing; Nahid, who was becoming prettier every day, and Nimtaj who was smiling timidly and saying they had really missed me. Mansour was not home. He arrived when we were already sitting down at the dinner table in Nimtaj's building. He walked in, cold and serious as usual; as if he had forgotten that I had been on a trip. First, he said hello to Nimtaj. He answered the children's hello, and then turned to me as I sat there serious and composed like him, and said: "Welcome back. Did you have a nice time?" I am not sure why I recalled the night of Chaharshanbeh Suri, and this verse:

"If Leili did not long for my love, why did she only break my pot?"

I answered just as officially: "May you always be happy, it was alright." In the light of the ceiling lamp, I saw traces of grey in his hair which was gradually receding on his forehead. He was sturdier, with a little more weight on him. The children were all happy and healthy. Ashraf's son was restless as usual. He was being naughty, kicking his brother's leg under the table and pulling the ribbon off Nahid's hair, making them both shout. Everyone looked fresher, healthier, and a little plumber than before, even Nim taj; as if my absence had been a blessing in disguise for them. A little smile appeared on the corner of my lips. Mansour glanced at me, and I saw the look of surprise in his eyes, just for a fleeting moment. Then, the same cold, serious look took over again, displaying a distant, higher-up head of household. But, I was confident that a fire raged under this cold, rigid face, which would blaze like wildfire as soon as he entered my room, turning this seemingly cold, aloof man soft, eager, and amorous. When I said goodnight and returned to my own building, Mansour was so submerged in reading the newspaper that he did not even answer me. I reclined peacefully on the couch in my room. I was wearing a long, striped blue and pink dress. My hair was loose around my shoulders, and I was wearing the gold ashrafi necklace that Mansour had given me. I loved this necklace, not because it was valuable, but because it was a present from Mansour.

He walked into the room unhurriedly and gently, closing the door behind him. His eyes were fixed on me, as if he was appreciating a china doll. He seemed overwhelmed by my presence. I held out my hand. He came towards me and opened his arms, docile and willing. He simply said: "For as long as I live, you must never again go anywhere without me." I laughed.

The light was on. He was sitting on the carpet floor cushion I had swapped with the winter korsi, playing the tar and sipping his drink. I said: "Mansour, Nahid will turn into a pretty girl." He took a sip of his drink and said in a carefree manner: "Yes, she'll look like her mother who would've been a pretty woman if she'd not caught smallpox. Nahid has taken after her mother."

I said: "Aha", and felt the green-eyed monster of jealousy take over and gobble me up. He was a tad tipsy and chattering away: "The poor thing wasn't always ugly. Smallpox destroyed her face. She's covered in it up to her shoulders." The rest of her body was untouched then. She had a shapely, pretty figure then. She must have. She was tall and thin, with fair skin, and walked with a strut. She walked and behaved like a princess, and anyone who saw her from behind was intrigued to see the face on this beautiful figure. So, that's how it is! He would not talk about her body. She is pretty then; she is beautiful. I said: "But, she seems to have put on weight."

Indifferently, and perhaps with disinterest, he said: "Because she's pregnant again." The sudden blow came down on my head. Envy and anger surged inside me. All that praying and worshipping, all that mystic calmness went up in smoke. My female instincts raged inside me again. The need to take possession; the desire to come first; the unwillingness to share the man of my life with someone else; expecting the heart in his chest to beat just for me. A simple desire I had been denied from the very first day.

I had eaten the forbidden fruit and been banned from paradise. What could I expect? Why did I lie to myself? Why was I reluctant to accept that Mansour had her by his side too? I was like a woman who had caught her husband red-handed for the first time, but I tried to keep my calm. I did not want to deceive myself any longer.

-How far gone is she?

-She's in her third month.

So, all that time I was going from doctor to doctor, blowing their doors off their hinges, Mansour was laughing with her behind my back. All those days and nights I spent in Mashhad pleading on God's doorstep, Nimtaj had morning sickness and was making sheep's eyes at Mansour. They were playing around with me. It boggled the mind. I said: "Congratulations. My voice had become coarse from malaise and jealousy. Mansour either did not understand or pretended not to. I got up to leave the room. Mansour said: "Mahboub, come and sit by next bo me."

-I have a headache Mansour. I want to go to bed.

He looked at me amorously, and said reproachfully: "Tonight, when I'm here?" He knew I felt angry and was very well aware of the reason why. I was even more stunned than him by this jealousy. Were these simply my womanly traits, or was I subtly getting attached to Mansour? Had I indiscernibly become interested in him? Yes, I was falling in love again. But, discreetly and softly-softly this time. The wine was maturing. That is why I was jealous again. No wonder I sat every night waiting to see him, and woke up every morning thinking of him. It was not habit, but tenderness. A tenderness I did not even want to admit to. I was afraid. I was afraid of falling in love, unaware that I already had. My body was still young and battling with my weary soul. I was afraid of my own body, because I could see that it was victorious over me. Love warmed my heart and ushered me into the midst of life's joys and delights, despite the longing I had felt to leave the world and go into seclusion. Except, it was happening slowly and measured this time. Had my prayers been partly answered?

I turned towards the door. Mansour pleaded: "Don't turn your back on me Mahboubeh." I said: "One night won't make a thousand nights **Rahim jan**" and bit my tongue straight away. He looked stiff, as if electrocuted, and stared at me; and I stared at him. He slammed the tar on the floor. I told myself it must be broken. He came towards me and took hold of my shoulders: "Look at me. Take a good look. I am Mansour, I am not Rahim. I am not the one you want, but the one you are trapped with. The one you run away from."

He let go of my shoulders and began pacing up and down. He placed one hand on the door frame, and pressed his forehead with the other. He imitated me: "Mansour jan, turn out the light. Don't play the tar, draw the curtains. Don't do that, don't laugh, just die. Nimtaj will hear… These are all excuses Mahboubeh. These are all excuses. You don't want me, I know. But, what can I do to make you want me half as much as I want you? This, I don't know. I will give everything I have to make you love me. I have been envious of your Rahim jan from the day you turned me down, until this very moment. I, with all my razzle-dazzle as you put it, wanted to be in his place. Tell me Mahboubeh, tell me what to do to make you want me? Jealousy is eating me up like leprosy."

He was furious. His voice trembled. But he did not yell. He did not swear. He did not hit me. He was sedate even during arguments. But, I was not so calm. I was angry too. I had lost my temper and was still a savage from my days of living in Rahim's house. Time was needed to calm me down. I said: "I made a mistake Mansour. That name just popped out of my mouth. I lived with him for seven years. Not happily. But I called his name every day, because I had to. I had become accustomed to it. And now, I said it not out of affection, but out of habit. You're feeling jealous? What can I say then? Am I not a human being? Don't I have a heart? Am I made of stone? Do you ever consider my feelings at all? Your wife is pregnant. While I was going from doctor to doctor, you were busy with her at the other end. I see and I keep quiet. I'm not complaining; not that she's an unpleasant woman. This is my own problem. I can't help it. It's out of my hands. I suffer. How much longer can I carry on like this? I can't see you by her side, in her room. Take a look at what I am Mansour! Dust in the wind. hat do I have? I love your children. I love Manouchehr. But I have nothing of my own. o one depends on me. It doesn't matter whether I'm dead or alive. I keep asking myself every day, what are you doing here Mahboubeh? What are you doing in the middle of this family, like a bone stuck in a wound? I tell myself you're some sort of pastime. You've definitely been given the right name. You're that Jasmine of the Night, simply to delight in. But then, I hear your footsteps again and my heart trembles. I wait for you again. My heart takes solace in seeing the tar you play at night, in seeing your books, your hat, your cane, your shirt on the bed. I try to keep myself happy and satisfied with that half of you which belongs to me. I was madly in love with Rahim once; but now, I hate him, I hate myself, and I hate this world. I'll never forgive myself for this poor choice I made. And yet, I don't know, perhaps the name Rahim symbolises love for me, perhaps it represents tenderness. Perhaps when I call you Rahim jan, it means you're the one I love, that I have nothing and no one, except for you. I'm not like Nimtaj. You're everything to me. I depend on you and I want you wholeheartedly. I can't lie; those passionate feelings will never come to life in me again. I wish they would. But it won't happen. Nevertheless, if waking up with the joy of seeing you and dreaming of you at night is not love, then what is? What does love mean? Why are you being so partial? If burning up with jealousy and denying it, if being tormented so that you can be content, so that you can be happy is not love, then what is? If you raise your voice at me in anger and I still wish to be in your arms at that very moment is not love, then what is? Give me time. Understand my pain. I wish I could love you the way I loved Rahim in that one year; blindly and carelessly, so instinctively, so… so wildly and without restraint. But, that was not love; it was infatuation, a whim. Mansour, it was an infatuation which struck like lightening and burned up."

Mansour was looking at me puzzled, and I looked back confused. It was only in that moment that what I had said and done sank in. It was only then that the significance of seven years of suffering came to light in my mind; quietly, like someone talking in her sleep, I said: "Yes Mansour, I'm only just realising it was simply an infatuation." Slowly, Mansour went and sat on the couch. He had calmed down. He was resting his elbows on his knees, and his head on the palm of his hands. He was dressed in a shirt, trousers and a waistcoat. He was an upright man of good character. I loved him very much. Sadly and softly, he said: "But that's how I love you – madly. God damn you Mahboubeh, see what you've done to yourself and to me? Do you think I'm happy without you? Or even with you? Do you think I'm happy with this way of life…?" He made a move towards the other building with his right hand and continued: "I tell myself a hundred times a day if only Mahboubeh would get pregnant. If only these children were hers. At night, I close my eyes and search for you in Nimtaj. Do you suppose it's easy for me, with a claim to intellectuality, to have two wives? To welcome guests with one wife, and go out to attend get-togethers and eat out with the other? To have different children by dif ferent women. You did all of this to me; you're to blame. You destroyed my life too Mahboubeh. Why do I still want you with that hot temper of yours? It's as if you possess snake charms. I see that you get along well with Nimtaj. You're a lady. I only wish Nimtaj was contrary. I would divorce her and be done with it. But, she's so submissive, what can I do? She's so harmless. I don't live with her out of love, but out of pity. She doesn't expect love from me either. I, too, suffer. Tolerating a woman you're not attracted to but only feel pity for is no less distressing. So, don't you torment me even more; don't make me even more miserable than I already am."

He went quiet. He rose to his feet and began pacing up and down the room. He was totally unaware of his surroundings. His foot hit the tar, which made a sound. He did not even bend down to pick up his instrument. He was submerged in his thoughts, as if not knowing where to begin. At last, he turned around to face me, and continued: "Do you remember when you told me so heartlessly that you didn't want me? That you had preferred a carpenter's shop boy to me? Do you have any idea what you did to me? No. You were only thinking of yourself.the only important things were you and your expectations. I wished I had control over you then, but I wasn't sure why I felt like that? Was it to crush you under my feet, or to take you in my arms? Did you know that I got on my horse that day and rode until the afternoon? That I surprised myself when my face was wet with tears? Did you know that I didn't want to go back home? I went to Shah Abdol Azim and stayed there for two days. I wanted to be in a place where I could go unrecognised; where nobody would question me; a place where my pain, the pain of my hurt pride, the pain of your ruthless love, would gradually subside. Did you know that I spent a couple of months in the Shemiran gardens that autumn?

During the day, I would visit my mother, pretending to be carefree in order to be spared her questions and curiosity; in order not to see my father's sad, puzzled look. And I returned to Shemiran at night. I would come all this way to sit down and play the tar. Nimtaj's father from next door, who had seen the midnight oil burning at our place, came to visit me. We would sit and talk. Or, I would go to their place. He was a man of letters. He never asked what pained me. What sorrows I hid in my heart. But, he talked to me of spirituality, weaving philosophy into the fabric of life. He would say:

These bitter days shall pass too
Sweet days shall come anew

I would laugh and say: "Yes they shall, but only with a bleeding heart they shall."

Gradually, I took solace in his conversation and regained control of myself. Then, he talked to me of irremediable misfortunes. He wanted to sooth my pain. He wanted to let me know tactfully that my pain was not real; that this was real pain. The real pain of a daughter as beautiful as the shining sun catching smallpox at the age of twelve and making her parents wish for their own death, and her death too, a hundred times a day. This was pain. The rest is ingratitude. Nimtaj would not hide her face from me. She never even dreamt that I might ask her to be my wife. She came and went, and looked at me with pity. She felt sorry for me and my pain, of which she knew nothing. And one day, I don't know what came over me when I asked her father for her hand. Perhaps I thought to myself my life is over now, at least let me make someone else happy. Perhaps, I wanted to take revenge on you, on myself. I was at loggerheads with the earth and the heavens above. I closed my eyes and made my decision. Neither my father's disapproval, nor my mother's crying and cursing made a difference. After all, the same blood as yours runs in my veins too. But I was worse off than you. You've no idea how many times a night I'd wake up, lying next to Nimtaj, and suffer jealously at the thought of you asleep next to that carpenter bloke! God damn you Mahboubeh. Why do you make me say these things? Are you trying to crush me?"

He let go of himself on the couch and stared at the floor. I kneeled beside him to look into his eyes. He did not look up. I asked: "Are you not talking to me Mansour?" He did not answer. I burst into tears and said: "I opened up my heart to you to feel lighter. Let me talk to you Mansour jan, let me open up my heart to you every now and then. Otherwise, I'll just die of grief." I sobbed: "Won't you look at me?"

-No, I don't want to see your tears.

As tears rolled down my face, I smiled and said: "What about now? Now that I'm smiling?"

He smiled at me: "Didn't I say you have snake charms!"

I dreamt that I was running. I was running in our old alley, up to the passageway. I was and was not wearing a chador. I had and did not have tears in my eyes. Somebody was looking at me, yet there was nobody there. I reached Rahim's shop, breathless. It was dusk. A gentle breeze was blowing. It seemed to be springtime. I could smell the flowers. The scent of Jasmine of the Night. Rahim was standing in the shadows. He had his back to me. I told myself thank God for that. See, this was all a dream! I have not married Rahim yet. I am only just going to marry him. Everything that had happened was just a nightmare, a horrendous nightmare. Rahim is standing there, gullible and innocent. Unaware of everything and anything. Quietly, as quietly as a sigh, I pleaded: "Rahim…" and my voice carried on like a breath, a deep breath from the chest.

Slowly, he turned around and came towards me. It was not Rahim, it was Mansour. He came forward and stretched out his hand to me, asking eagerly: "You came Kokab? Come."

I woke up to face reality. I saw everything as it was, I accepted it as it was. I accepted Mansour. I accepted my own situation. I accepted Nimtaj khanoum's pregnancy. I accepted that in reality, I was Kokab; that I was slowly giving my heart to Mansour and becoming dependent on him; that I was a prisoner of fate; that I had met my destiny and a more complete, better life was not plausible for me.

Nimtaj's maid came and, although she knew that I knew, she too, gave me the news of Nimtaj's pregnancy malignantly. I gave her money for the good news. A reward for bringing me the news of my rival's good fortune. I made 'ash reshteh for Nimtaj. I made her kachi, and other food cravings. I sat and waited until Nimtaj gave birth to another boy. Nahid became the apple of Mansour's eye.

We sold our family home and, two or three years later, Manouchehr left for Europe. We bought a house for my mother in one of the newer uptown areas. She moved there with dayeh, who was an old woman now. Mansour's eldest son also left following Manouchehr's departure. He went to England. Ashraf khanoum's son had her mother's nature. He was rebellious. He never finished his studies. He squandered all of his own and his mother's money. He always was, and still is, a cause for concern. Mansour suffered because of him, and the boy simply did not care. He could see that his father was worried about his future, and never lifted a finger to help himself. Then, Nimtaj's heart condition worsened. She got worse every day. As she got more poorly, the children gathered more around me. They were fledglings wanting to take refuge under my wings. Nimtaj khanoum asked for me and entrusted her children into my hands. She said: "Look out for Nahid, Mahboubeh khanoum, look after her. The other three are boys, they're men. *They can pull their own kilim out of the water[235]*. Nahid's young. She'll be marrying in a few years' time. And without a mother..."

I said: "Nimtaj khanoum, don't talk like this! There's nothing wrong with you!"

-No, there's no room for honeyed words. Listen to me. I only have one hand still out of the grave, for Nahid's sake... Be a mother to her when it's time for her to marry.

I said: "To tell you the truth, I'd like Nahid to marry Manouchehr. I don't know if you approve or not?"

Manouchehr was doing well in his studies in Europe. He was young. He looked handsome in the photographs. He was well-off. I knew that Nimtaj was inclined towards this marriage, although Nahid was no less than Manouchehr. She was pretty, smart, educated, and fluent in French. She was a good painter, and an athlete. Mansour had captured all his ideals in her. Besides having all this talent, most significantly yet, she was a thoughtful, kind and understanding girl. She spoke and acted with deliberation. She displayed a special kindness towards me, without upsetting her mother.

Nimtaj was thinking. I asked: "Do you approve khanoum?" "Only if she wants it herself; if she wants it herself." Then, she took my hand and pleaded: "Not by force Mahboubeh jan. Not by force. Guide her, but never force her to do anything. I ask this of you, because I know Mansour wants whatever you want. Your wish is his command. I'm afraid that he might, God forbid, force Nahid to marry Manouchehr for your sake; because Mansour loves you very much. He doesn't want you to get upset."

I laughed and said: "First of all, Nahid won't put up with such things. She's not the kind of girl to tolerate such treatment. Our daughters have put those days of submissiveness and docility behind in this day and age. Secondly, Mansour doesn't love either one of us. As far as I know, Mansour only loves one woman in the whole wide world; he worships only one woman, and that's Nahid. Rest assured." She smiled and calmed down. Once again, I became the executrix.

There was me and Mansour. There was me, the children, and that big house. I still longed for my own child. But now, I had Mansour wholly and entirely to myself. I no longer had to share him with anyone else. The children would not let go of me after their mother's death. They seemed afraid of losing me too. When Nahid came home from school, when Nahid came home from socialising, when she had a suitor, she would run and find me first. She talked to me. She followed me from one room into the next, wherever I went. When she got tired, she would scream: "Oh, that's enough. Please sit down. I want to say two serious words to you. I'm tired of running around after you." And I would say: "So, were you joking till now?" And I gladly dropped everything and sat down. I never found undeserved fault with her suitors. I gave my opinion. I pointed out the good things, and the bad. Then, I would say: "Go to your father now and decide together."

She could not imagine the riot in my heart, and how it subsided when she turned them down.

When Manouchehr returned from his journey, we all went to see him. The whole family was invited to my mother's house that evening. Nahid was nearly twenty years of age now. She was wearing a beige ensemble. She had a light makeup on and her hair was flowing around her shoulders. Every time I looked at her, I was grateful for the smallpox which had destroyed her mother's face. I knew only too well that if Nimtaj had not caught smallpox, I would not have stood a chance. I loved looking at Nahid's face. This is what Manouchehr's wife should be like. Manouchehr took me to one side: "Who's that girl sister?"

-Well, it's Nahid.

-Really?! The same spoiled, pasty looking girl?

-Don't be absurd. She was spoiled, but never pasty looking. Her suitors are taking our front door off its hinges.

-Ask her to marry me then, before the savvier people snatch her up.

The day the dowr was being set, I became the bride's mother. The dowr has to be this much. The wedding has to be so and so. Manouchehr's share of the Gholhak gardens has to be put in her name. Half-joking, half-serious, Nezhat said: "Eh?!!! Abji, are you on the bride's side or the groom's?" And she laughed half-heartedly. Nahid whispered in my ear: "I don't believe a dowr will bring happiness."

Neither did I, but I had a responsibility. I turned to Nezhat and said: "I'm on both sides abji. If Nahid was my own daughter, I'd give her away for free with both hands to a young man like Manouchehr. A girl like Nahid is too respectable for us to haggle over her dowr. But, I have a moral obligation towards her. The responsibility lies with me. No matter what I do, I still keep telling myself that her mother might have done a better job if she was here. Maybe her mother's not satisfied yet. Maybe I'm leaving her short. Now, if you don't want Manouchehr to put his own land in her name, I'll put my own Gholhak land in her name."

Everyone went quiet. Mansour was smiling at me. Nahid was sitting next to me, and God only knows how I longed for her to be mine and Mansour's daughter. God only knows how I regretted the past.

Nahid married and left. Now, I was left with Mansour and his youngest son. Mansour was by my side. He was my rock and support. He would tell me: "Mahboubeh, have you been to see Hassan Khan? Where's Hadi? What's he doing?"

Hadi khan had become a director general.

Our good life lasted another seven years. I had a cozy little family. I was happy and content. I would gradually forget the past. But, nature did not allow me to have a carefree moment. Everything began with an "Oh". Mansour bolted awake, held his side, and said: "Oh!"

I panicked: "What is it?"

-It's nothing. I must have a cold.

But, it was not a cold. It was cancer. It was just manifesting itself. In my panic, I did not know where to turn. I was just beginning to appreciate his presence. I understood the value of his existence in my life. The more he lost weight and weakened, the more I wanted him. I pitched my tent outside all the hospitals and surgeries. But, it was pointless. I wanted to send him abroad for treatment, but they said it was futile. It was too late. I watched him in his bed, gaunt and worn-out, all skin and bones. He was pale and pasty and I still wanted him. I reminisced about the days gone by, the pleasant days spent in his company. I remembered his stolen look at sizdah bedar, and I wanted to scream. My sweet, peaceful life was slipping through my fingers like droplets and wasting away. I strived to hang on to him, but lacked the power to do so. I did not want to lose him. This was so unfair. I was oblivious to my days and nights; I had gone crazy. I knocked on every door, tried everything. Was this love? If not, then what was it? He would say: "Mahboubeh, don't go; stay and talk to me. Let your hair hang wild, like they drove me wild all my life. Wear new clothes and let me feast my eyes on you. Let me watch you to my heart's content; I want to have your reflection in my eyes when I go."

And I pleaded: "Mansour, don't talk like this! You're not going anywhere."

-I don't want to go, but it can't be helped. What can I do! It's out of my hands. I can't even believe it myself. I don't want to believe it.

Khojasteh's husband visited him regularly. He sat with him and talked about anything and everything. Mansour was still very sociable. He was still the same welcoming, learned conversationalist Mansour when he was not in pain. I vividly remember him saying one night, half-joking, half serious: "I seek absolution from you doctor. I've troubled you much." And he added, laughing lethargically: "I need your clemency to turn the fires of hell into a flower garden for me."

The doctor laughed sadly and said: "You belong in heaven agha. Paradise with all its angels is entirely at your disposal. I'm the one in need of help."

Mansour pointed at me and said: "I really don't know why I've to be kicked out of this paradise."

My sweetheart is with me, why ask for more
Her companionship is filled with riches galore

He had a fever. He was not well. He was in pain. He would drown in sweat. His hand rested in mine as he consoled me with philosophical words. I said: "Mansour, God only knows how much I regret everything. If only you had beaten me up and dragged me to the registry office by force and wed me on that day in the Shemiran gardens."

He smiled with great effort, and answered: "One has to be rather tasteless to beat you up."

My heart bled. Mansour paused, and then he continued: "I'm worried for my son Mahboubeh. What will happen to my last-born when I'm gone?"

He pulled at my heart strings, but I said: "What am I here for then? Don't I count? Have I not been like a mother to him? Have I not taken care of him until now? Have I not brought him up? Has he ever wanted for anything? Don't go thinking I've done this only for you! It is because I love him too. When he sits next to me, it's as if he's my own son. I go crazy if he's late for just an hour."

-I know Mahboubeh. But, you're still young. You have to remarry. I don't have any objections. Although, I feel jealous…

I cut him off. I went to get the Koran from the niche. I sat next to him and asked: "Do you believe in the Koran Mansour?"

-Why do you ask?

-I swear on the Koran that I'll never marry again after you; rest assured. And I swear on this Koran that I'll be a mother to your son, both for your sake and also for my own. Thank God that I didn't have any children. Tell me that you're content for your son to me mine. God has sent him to me to replace my own son.

He sighed sadly and closed his eyes. He was so weak now. He said: "God only knows how much I wanted to have this son with you; how much I wanted all of them to be by you."

I said: "This is my punishment. But, instead, I have stolen your children", and I laughed.

He laughed too: "God damn you Mahboubeh."

-He already has, he already has. What more can he do; is there any other way to damn me?

I leaned over and kissed his feverish forehead and lips.

They said to make a vow for his recovery. To sell something which was dearest to me and give the money to three deprived patients with my own two hands. I took out the gold ashrafi necklace he had given me as a present, to sell. Everyone said it is too good to sell. They said to have it priced and give away the equivalent amount in money. I said nothing is too good for him. I sold it and gave the money away as alms, but nothing could help him. No matter which way I turned, it was useless. His hand was in mine. He was looking into my eyes. He was calling my name when he slipped away. I was alone. I lost my safe haven in the blink of an eye. It was only then that I understood the meaning of loneliness, and I put my best foot forward not to let his young son experience the same feeling. I was a true mother to the last-born of a man who had rebuilt my life. His death set my heart on fire. *I was raw, I matured, I burned*[236]. Mansour was my everything. He was the one who gave me hope to start the day and to go to bed at night. I breathed and lived for him. My affection for him had subtly taken root in my heart and now, uprooting it and throwing it away would be the end of me.

Although Nahid and Manouchehr never left my side, although they never deserted me to live on my own, there will always be an empty place in my heart. His tar still hangs on a corner of the wall in my room and I look at it at nights. I look at it when I recall the past. I can see him holding it and playing it gently. He smiles and says God damn you Mahboubeh. His gaze is kind and soothing. His memory is comforting to me.

> *Auntie went quiet. Night had already fallen. The garden lamps scattered a hazy light in the cold of the winter fog. Neither one thought of turning on the lights. Neither one wanted a bright light. Auntie wiped off her tears. Soudabeh wiped off her tears too, and leaned down and kissed auntie's hand – this old, wrinkled hand, adorned by a delicate agate ring; this small hand which young men had once longed to kiss.*
>
> *Auntie said: "Once upon a time, I thought that one of my father's prayers had not come true – the one about me becoming a lesson to others. Tonight, I realised that I've been wrong. I've become a lesson to others Soudabeh. I've become a lesson to you who are so dear to my heart, so like myself. It's as if you are me. I want you to be very careful Soudabeh jan. I want you to know that a night of wine drinking is not worth the morning after."*
>
> *Auntie was quiet and submerged in her thoughts. Suddenly, she remembered the pain in her leg, and moaned: "This pain's killing me." Then, she looked up towards the heavens: "Dear Lord, enough is enough. Don't let it drag on for a hundred years. Dear Lord, give absolution and take me away."*

She locked her chest and hung the key around her neck.

The garden door opened and Manouchehr's car drove in. He was returning from skiing with his young son and daughter. Auntie rose to her feet and left the room with the help of her cane before the children had time to run in happily, only to be disappointed by seeing her tears, and before Manouchehr — whose last gray hairs gave more character to his kind, noble face - was depressed by her sister's pain, whom he looked upon as a mother.

Soudabeh said: "But, my case is different auntie. I'm not a fifteen-year old, nor is he…"

She ate her words. Auntie smiled at her with kindness as she stood there, and completed her sentence: "Yes, you're not a fifteen-year old, and he's not a carpenter's shop boy. But, your two worlds are also set apart in their own way. If that's the case, if two people are incompatible in any way - it does not matter in what way - this can ruin their lives. Bad fortune does not take only one shape Soudabeh! It has all sorts of shapes and forms."

Auntie started towards her room. Soudabeh was deep in thought. She was trying to make a decision, but it was no longer that simple. She desired the night of wine drinking, but was weary of the morning after. Perhaps, nature was taking its course and wining again? Was history repeating itself?

Soudabeh took in her fragile figure in amazement, as auntie walked away. She could barely imagine her as a graceful young woman with elegant clothes, with her thick hair cascading around her shoulders, an amorous heart and an appetite for tragedy. Nevertheless, she was now proud of being like her. She felt a deep love and admiration for this elderly woman, broken-hearted by the passage of time. As she walked away, Soudabeh wasn't to know that her auntie, with her wealth of experience, wouldn't see another winter.

**Esfahan – Spring of 1373 HS
(1994 AD)**

Endnotes

1   Old Title of Nobility in Iran

2   Ibid

3   A traditional Persian musical string instrument

4   In ancient Persian mythology, all beings possessed their own life 'glass bottles' which, if removed and broken, would cause their death.

5   Dear Girl (dokhtar=girl)

6   A verse from the Koran which is recited by heart and blown towards a beloved from a distance to ward off the evil eye.

7   Reza Khan was 'Sardar-e Sepah', or Minister of War, before over-throwing Ahmad Shah Qajar of the Qajar dynasty and establishing the Pahlavi dynasty to become Reza Shah.

8   May you live long

9   Residential houses in traditional Iranian architecture had inner living quarters (andarouni) reserved for the female inhabitants of the house and close male relatives (mahram), and outer living quarters (birouni) for other male guests.

10   An underground tunnel system of water management developed by the Persians.

11   Water was stored in underground reservoirs in houses called 'ab-an-bar' prior to canalisation.

12   A platform and faucet where water was retrieved at the foot of the reservoir .

13   Southern provinces of Iran by the Persian Gulf

14 Dayeh=Nanny, Khanoum=Lady (Miss or Mrs/placed before or after the first name of a woman or her profession as a sign of respect).

15 'Agha jan' is a term of endearment used to mean 'dear father' in Persian (jan=dear).

16 Nazanin=Nice, charming

17 A term of endearment for women similar to 'agha jan'.

18 A veil worn by women as hijab.

19 The lady of all ladies

20 Shahzadeh = Princess (shortened to shazdeh)

21 An old term for physician, usually lacking academic training and treating patients with herbs.

22 Storage room/dressing room where trunks of clothing were kept.

23 Rasht is a city in the northern province of Guilan-Iran famous for its rice paddies.

24 Kermanshah is the centre of the western province of Kermanshahan-Iran, famous for its solid cooking oil.

25 Five contiguous latticed door windows in the main parlour called by the same name, where *panj* means five and *dar* means door.

26 A low table covered with quilts under which a charcoal brasier burns in winter days.

27 Nezami Ganjavi – 12th century Persian poet

28 Mammy

29 A cosmetic for the eye similar to an eyeliner – kohl.

30 Dating back to ancient Iran, a *saghakhaneh* was built inside a wall - or it was a tank filled with water - with a tap and bowl for passersby. It was decorated with illuminations and also considered a holy place to light candles and make a wish.

31 Loose black trousers with feet worn by women, designed to cover the shape of a woman's legs.

32 White meshed veil covering the face

33 A rigid black meshed visor made from horse tail hair. It is placed on the forehead, knotted at the back of the head with two pieces of string, and can be pivoted up and down to cover the face (worn by women).

34 Rahim means kind and merciful.

35 A Persian proverb meaning "The axe goes to the wood where it borrowed its helve".

36 Naneh=Mother, mama, mummy, nana / also a term of endearment for calling young people.

37 Those who go for pilgrimage to the holy city of Mashhad in northern Iran are called Mashhadi as a title of honour.

38 Kouchak: Pronounced kouchik colloquially; written kouchak (Khanoum kouchik = Little Miss or Missy).

39 Mahboubeh=Sweetheart / Mahboub=Beloved, darling

40 Kid (goatskin)

41 Smaller symmetrical rooms on each side of the panjdari (goushvareh = earring)

42 More catholic than the pope

43 Traditionally, the bride makes her entrance by bringing tea for the guests.

44 Greetings, hello, peace be upon you

45 It is said after praising a person to ward off the evil eye.

46 A welcoming expression – a virtual move

47 Big/elder

48 To read between the lines – Hadith means story

49 Exaggerated compliments of the old Persian culture – a panegyric.

50 Persian saying meaning to nip it in the bud on the first night of marriage, for the husband to take control.

51 Pounder or pestle – referring to a swaddled baby here resembling a pestle

52 Persian proverb meaning 'It is no skin off my nose'

53 God willing

54 Halva: Traditional saffron sweet made for funerals. A traditional Persian sweet – you cannot sweeten your life just by saying halva / many words will not fill a bushel).

55 Sometimes, local shopkeepers would not take smaller amounts of money from their regular customers. 'We' is used instead of 'I' in slang.

56 The third assassinated Caliph of Islam, whose bloodied shirt was hung in the mosque to condemn those who opposed him.

57 First woman singer in Iran

58 Shāhed = Witness: The first three verses of the poem following the principal poem read in the Divan of Hafez, is called a witness to the principal poem.

59 Mahboubeh of the Night or Jasmine of the Night in English – a flower that smells at night only
60 The Prophet's immediate family and himself (Ali, Fatima, Hassan, Hossein)

61 Hafez is recognised as a seer whose Divan (book of poems) is used for divination by closing the eyes, making a wish and opening the Divan at a random page.

62 Sugarplums were served for the birth of a boy.

63 Rue is an aromatic plant, dried and burned (like incense) to ward off the evil eye.

64 Bereshtuk is a traditional Iranian sweet, with wheat flour, chickpea flour, cardamom, and sugar as its basic ingredients.

65 Gheymeh is an Iranian dish made with diced beef, chips, and split peas as its main ingredients.

66 Traditional Iranian bread cooked in a furnace over hot pebbles, measuring at least 70 cm in height.

67 Muslim call to prayers read from a minaret; also read in the ear of newborns.

68 Call to stand up for the formal prayers

69 The 12th Imam and Messiah of the Shia faith

70 Birthdays were written inside the cover of Korans prior to having birth certificates.

71 These musicians are called motreb rou hozi, motreb = musician /rou = on / hoze (i) = pond – literally meaning musicians who perform on a low wooden cover fixed on the pond in the middle of gardens, together with the dancers and singers.

72 A primary school in the olden days

73 A northern province of Iran by the Caspian Sea

74 Sister

75 A Persian saying used for someone who is choosy

76 Frensied madman by definition; a label given to the character in love with Leili in Nezami's book, due to his love for her; this is an eastern love story, similar to Romeo and Juliette, when a prince in love cannot marry

his beloved and takes to the desert like a madman, similar to the sun roaming freely in the desert.

77 Tabriz is the capital of Azerbaijan Province – Iran.

78 University/Polytechnic

79 Ghormeh Sabzi is a stew of mixed herbs, beef and beans eaten with rice.

80 Tah=Bottom / Dig=Pan – literally bottom of pan. The crusty rice that forms at the bottom of the pan when cooking rice, very popular in Iran.

81 Douq is a savoury, minty yoghurt drink taken with meals.

82 The old summer residence areas of northern Tehran, now incorporated into the city.

83 Meaning 'you already have the wife you desire'.

84 A glass for drinking tea, of Russian origin.

85 The old summer residence area of northern Tehran, now incorporated into the city.

86 It was customary for the older daughter to marry first.

87 A Persian saying (… what can the poor thing do, he cannot give more than just a green leaf – instead of a more expensive flower), as in 'widow's mite.'

88 Termeh is a delicate hand-woven fabric (brocade) – including gold and silver threads - originally from Yazd Province in Iran.

89 Believed to allure men and woman to one another.

90 A hand to mouth existence.

91 Better to face a danger once than always be afraid.

92   A white, patterned chador that is worn inside the house if necessary. Black chadors are for outdoors and more official engagements.

93   Persian rice dish made with morello cherry jam and meat balls.

94   Aubergine dish made with whey.

95   A pilgrim who has completed Hajj to Mecca is called Haji. You can perform Hajj only if you can afford it financially.

96   Shah Abdol Azim is an old, sacred cemetery near Tehran.

97   In order to slaughter a camel, its knees are first hit with a blade to cut the ligaments and make it kneel.

98   Leili is the name of the female character in the classic love poem 'Leili and Majnoun' by Persian poet Nezami Ganjavi

99   A second wife / a rival wife

100   A shorter version of door curtains are also hung behind the windows

101   Non-related male person

102   Families ate their meals on the floor, spread on a tablecloth.

103   Adas = lentil / polo = rice. Iranian rice dish cooked with lentils meat and raisins.

104   Persian proverb meaning to give the run around

105   Seyyed is an honorific title given to male descendants of saints.

106   It is like spitting in our own faces (returns in the face); to give yourself a bad name – spitting into the wind.

107   To hang out your dirty laundry

108   In the old days, the hair of a woman guilty of a sin would be cut short.

109 Tramp

110 Hozekhaneh is a large, cool basement room with a small pond and a fountain where families rested in the summer afternoons.

111 Ya Allah literally means 'Dear God'; also used as a warning by men before entering a room where there may be uncovered women.

112 In the vernacular architecture of Iran, Hashti is an entrance space with a vaulted roof. Hashtis were designed in different forms, such as square, rectangular, octagonal, and hexagonal. In larger houses, this was also used as a waiting area.

113 Baghali polo is a Persian rice dish made with dill weed and broad beans.

114 Atash=fire / gardan = spinner – literally fire spinner. A device for lighting coal.

115 A wooden single bed, similar to a bench, used in Persian gardens to sit on instead of garden chairs and tables.

116 Halim is a ground, nutritious dish made with meat and wheat.

117 An analogy to mean he is tall and good-looking; may God protect him.

118 Shirini khoran (literally eating sweets) follows the engagement ceremony, where traditional sweets and tea are served.

119 The ascend of Prophet Mohammad (PBUH), when he received the 1st revelation.

120 Zan=woman/wife, amou=paternal uncle (literally a paternal uncle's wife).

121 Beat one to frighten another.

122 You won't have to lift a finger.

123 With a different spelling from the 'agha' used for men in Persian, this is a term of respect used for women.

124 To foment trouble.

125 To harp on one string.

126 People used to sleep on the flat, terraced roof of their houses used as a cool area during the hot summer nights.

127 Changing room – traditionally, a large octagonal changing room in public baths with raised platforms all around.

128 A triangular scarf/large kerchief.

129 An orsi is a gridded lifting window, sometimes with coloured glass.

130 Halal = Permitted / Halal blood = killing of sinful people.

131 Dadash = Brother. Elder brothers are called dadash by their younger siblings.

132 Khan is used as a term of politeness meaning Mister.

133 Mahd-e Olia was the wife of Mohammad Shah Qajar of the Qajar Dynasty and the mother of Nasser el-Din Shah. Literaly, Mahd-e Olia means 'one who gives birth to the lords.'

134 Shovelling sand against the tide.

135 Take Opium to commit suicide.

136 Sa'di is a 12th century famous Persian poet and writer

137 'Ash is a pottage made with fresh herbs and legumes.

138 Wudu is the ritual washing of parts of the body for the daily prayers.

139 Labadeh is a robe men wore over their clothes in the old days.

140   Guiveh are cheap light cotton shoes.

141   Toman is the Iranian currency.

142   Khersak is a thick-piled, hand-woven, cheap Persian rug. In Persian, khersak means small bear.

143   Mardangui is a glass lamp cover to protect the candle from the wind.

144   Khancheh are large round wooden trays on which the bride's dowry was carried by servants, to display the expensive housewares and their grandness on the streets for everyone to see.

145   Mirror and candlestick holders are an essential part of the wedding ceremony spread, representing brightness and light.

146   Sofreh-ye aghd is the traditional Persian wedding ceremony spread.

147   Kasseh nabat is a bowl made of saffron rock sugar.

148   Yar Mobarakbad = Felicitations

149   Lalehzar is an old street in Tehran, still a shopping hub today.

150   Sermon = It is customary to ask the bride three times for her consent to be married before she answers 'Yes' on the third time.

151   Zir-lafzi is a present of gold or jewellery given to the bride by the groom before she says 'Yes' after the third time.

152   Noghle is a special sugar coated almond sweet.

153   Similar to nana, used instead of mum by the old working class.

154   Nuptials: On a girl's wedding night, in the old days, the women in the family (or servants) would wait behind the bedroom door of the young couple until dawn, for the virginity of the bride to be proved. They would then go home proud.

155   The moon is the symbol of beauty. This shows the contrast between

the dark, sooty carpentry and Mahboubeh's beauty.

156   Abehozi: A peddler who went around and cleaned ponds in houses.

157   Mirab: The distributor of water, who would channel drinking water through qanats into homes, which took turns at night to store it.

158   Gousht koubideh: Persian dish with is a mixture of gousht (meat) and legumes minced together.

159   Sabzi polo: Rice dish made with fresh herbs, especially for Nowruz, eaten with lamb or fish.

160   Charak is an old unit of weight for a quarter or 750 grs.

161   Seer is an old unit of weight equal to 75 grs.

162   Princesses had more freedom of action, a number of whom took advantage of such freedom.

163   Masnavi is a book of poems written by Jalal el-Din Mohammad Rumi, the Masnavi is an extensive book of rhyming couplets, a Sufi masterpiece of six volumes of 4000 verses each.

164   Raw eggs are supposed to provide strength.

165   Chopping chives for someone = paying attention to someone, bootlicking, flattering.

166   Nowruz: The Persian New Year and spring equinox on March 21st.

167   Sabzeh: Usually wheat or lentil sprouts, grown in an attractive dish especially for the New Year.

168   Haft Sin: The traditional spread for the Nowruz Persian New Year, meaning seven (Haft) 'S's, including seven edible symbols which start with 'S' in Persian. Some of these are sabzeh, sonbol (hyacinth), seer (garlic), sumac, serkeh (vinegar), samanu (made with wheat germ), senjed (oleaster fruit) and seeb (apples); also a mirror, candles, painted eggs – all symoblising various things such as light, earth, fire, water, fertility,

love, etc. The UN General Assembly recognised the International day of Nowruz in 2010. The year changes at a different hour every year and is called tahvil-e saal (The moment the year changes).

169   It is customary to look at someone you love who brings you good luck when the year changes.

170   Tahvil-e saal: The moment the year changes

171   Sizdah is number 13 in Persian. The Nowruz celebrations last 12 days, and the last day is celebrated by spending the entire day in nature and having a picnic.

172   'Ash reshteh: Pottage made with fresh herbs, legumes, and reshteh (wheat noodles)

173   Chaharshanbeh Suri: The last Wednesday eve of the year, when people celebrate with fireworks and jumping over bonfires.

174   'Ghashogzani' or going door to door by hitting a metal bowl with a spoon (ghashogh) to receive nuts and sweets (treat or trick).

175   Namousse=Honour / Namousse School for girls established in 1326 HS (1947 AD).

176   Ashrafi was the name of the gold coin of the time.

177   Ashrafi gold coins were kept in large earthenware jars buried in the ground by wealthy people in the olden days of the Qajar Dynasty, before banks came into existence.

178   Sixth night: Babies were named on the sixth night after their birth.

179   Rostam: A great national hero in Persian mythology who was the first baby in history to be born by a cut made in the side of his mother mother because he was so large (present-day caesarian section).

180   Enayatollah means a gift from God.

181   Kalleh Paacheh: A delicacy made with sheep's head and legs.

182   Buying ready cooked food from outside was not customary and well thought of by the priviledged classes.

183   Varamin: A city in present day Tehran Province.

184   Patakhti: Party given after the wedding, when family and friends bring presents for the bride and groom.

185   A Persian saying – making excuses for not doing something due to inability - not for lack of wanting (Faati is short for Faatemeh, a girl's name).

186   Meaning it has turned white through experience – I was not born yesterday.

187   Keshvar and Zivar are the names of two girls who pulled a doll until it was torn in two.

188   Sam Aleikom: Peace be upon you / Hello. Here, 'sam' is slang or short for 'salam'.

189   Guilan is a province by the Caspian Sea, where it was customary for family and friends to take care of the bereaved family for one week by cooking their meals.When someone has everything, but still complains instead of being grateful, he is cited this proverb to mean that they have nothing to worry about in life except death, which is best taken care of in Guilan; also, many people drowned in the Caspian in the seaside cities, so death came often and easily.

190   From behind the mountains: Unworldly, behind the mountains where there is no civilization and no one lives there, the back of beyond.

191   The "lower back" refers to sexual prowess.

192   Crooked by nature is never made straight by education – in the same way a walnut will not stay on a dome / an ape is an ape, a varlet's a varlet, though they be clad in silk or scarlet.

193   Go as far away from me as possible and never return - In the old days, as there were no correct methods of setting the time in the Arabian

Peninsula, special people had the task of throwing a spear as far as they could in the flat desert (with no mountain peaks to see where the sun was setting), to establish whether the sun was still located at the Zenith. If the spear landed in sunlight, it was still daylight; otherwise, it would be considered night time.

194   They were busy with themselves.

195   Not to be at liberty to act as you wish, otherwise you would.

196   Ya Ali: Imam Ali is the first Imam of the Shia faith. The term *Ya Ali* is used at the beginning of a job or when leaving the house, meaning you are asking Imam Ali for a helping hand.

197   A unich whose job is to babysit is called a laleh.

198   Bozorg=Big, eldest (first wife here)

199   Kouchak: Pronounced kouchik colloquially; written kouchak. It means small, younger (or second wife here).

200   Water was canalised in Tehran after WWII. Prior to this, fresh drinkable water from the qanats was sold in large, horse-drawn tanks on the streets; this was known as "Shahi water", or Royal water, for its freshness.

201   Eating sweet musk melon is known to make people feel cold. In other words, you have to pay a price for certain pleasures. A Persian proverb with the English equivalent of facing the music.

202   Kāchi is an Iranian dessert made with flour, sugar, rosewater, butter, oil, and saffron; suitable for weak persons.

203   "This is the milk of human kindness", *Shakespeare (Macbeth)*.

204   You cannot hide the obvious facts / cover something up.

205   Joun: Colloquial pronunciation of 'jan'.

206   At wit's end

207   When two Sundays meet

208   Hazrat Faatemeh: The Prophet's daughter

209   Red from the colour of henna.

210   Ali-Asghar was the baby of Imam Hossein and the youngest martyr of the Battle of Karbala 61 AH/ 680 AD, when Imam Hossein and all his supporters were martyred; his father lifted him in his arms to show the enemy that they were not going to fight, but he was killed in his father's arms by an arrow. The villain Shemr slew Imam Hossein. It is used as an analogy here.

211   Azrael: The Archangel of Death

212   Ligheh: Small pieces of silk or rayon fabric placed in the inkpot to soak up the excess ink.

213   Dash: Slang and short for 'dadash' or brother.

214   Sefidab: An Ancient mineral cosmetic used in Iran to exfoliate.

215   Terms of flattery used in Iran / It is not binding.

216   Cut from the same cloth / Two of a kind

217   To have a Big mouth

218   Yazd: A city in Iran

219   Pahlavi hat: Introduced by Reza Shah in 1927, as part of his modernisation plans for Iran and the introduction of European clothing.

220   In old tales of Persia, a stone in which you could confide. It would grow in size with the accumulating grief as time passed and burst in the end to free its owner of his grief.

221   A fort was built by Mohammad Ali Shah Qajar for his family just outside Tehran, which came to be known as the Qajar quarters. Towards the end of the Qajar Dynasty rule, a gate was built in southwestern Tehran

by the name of Qazvin Gate, leaving the fort outside the gate, to gradually become a safe haven for outlaws and prostitutes.

222   Talaq means divorce. If it is pronounced three times by the husband, it is irrevocable.

223   You can't get blood out of a stone.

224   To get rich enough and buy an extra pair of trousers and take a second wife.

225   This is a saying which refers to the site of Khyber in Arabia which was conquered in a difficult battle by Imam Ali who then took hold of its famous gate with one hand. Thus, achieving any difficult task is referred to as conquering the Khyber Pass.

226   Coke bottle glasses

227   Young girls tie knots in the grass on Sizdah be dar as a popular tradition, wishing "to be in my husband's house next Sizdah be dar, holding a baby."

228   The sons of Muslim Ibn-Aghil who always walked side by side with their father

229   This term is not used to describe a circular shape in Persian, but to denote a woman's beauty by comparing it to the moon – moon-faced.

230   Jinn afraid of Bismillah (In the name of God) = A Persian saying meaning like chalk and cheese.
231   To feel like a fool

232   Verse from *Leili and Majnoun*. When young ones went to the well to collect water in the old days, if too much room was taken up, they would remove a pot to make room for themselves. In doing so, some of the pots for carrying water broke.

233   Sogoli = Favourite (wife)

234 Zekre: There are different types of "zekre", asking for a wish by repeating it.

235 They can take care of themselves in difficult situations [a kilim weighs very heavy when washed and wet].

236 A verse by Molana Jala el-Din Rumi